# SQUID'S GRIEF

DK MOK

Contact: DK Mok, PO Box 184, Beverly Hills NSW 2209, Australia



www.dkmok.com

First Edition: March 2016

DK Mok

Squid's Grief/by DK Mok—1st ed.

p.cm.

Summary:

When car-hacker Squid rescues a cheerful amnesiac from the trunk of a stolen car, her decision to help him recover his memory sets her on a collision course with the enigmatic crime lords who rule Baltus City.



Cover design by Errick A. Nunnally

ISBN: 978-0-9944315-0-9 (paperback)

ISBN: 978-0-9944315-1-6 (ebook)

For my family,
and for all the people looking for a
squid-shaped place in the world.

# ONE

Squid prayed for red.

A million crucial decisions and damning mistakes had brought her to this point, where her continued existence depended on the mercy of chaos theory. She could still dig herself out, somehow. All she needed was a miracle.

The ball whirred across the wooden dividers, jumping from slot to slot on the roulette wheel. Squid gripped the side of the table, broadcasting mental spam to every god, spirit or demon willing to cut her a deal.

*Just make it red.*

The wheel turned, the wheel slowed, and the ball settled on thirty-one. Black.

Squid stared as the croupier raked the tarnished silver watch across the felt. It seemed to tumble in slow motion into his battered wooden box, like a star sliding over the event horizon.

It had been a birthday present.

"You can always make more cash, Squid," said the tousled croupier.

Squid gripped the table harder, concentrating on making time go backwards.

"Not anymore."

"Trying to go straight again?" said the croupier.

Squid knew better than to reply. She knew better than to gamble, too, or borrow money from people called Kneecaps, but the past few weeks, months, years seemed like a chain reaction of decisions made between a rock and a hard place. It was a hell of a mess, but she could still fix it without resorting to what had started it all in the first place.

"I heard there's a back room where you can bet organs," said Squid.

The croupier's smile hardened, like a snap-frozen butterfly.

"O-positive," said Squid. "And I've got all my own teeth."

The croupier's reply faded on his lips, his expression darkening as a pack of hard-eyed men slunk through the doors. A hushed mutter rippled through the room, the interlopers having the same effect as a half-mad wolf wandering into a room full of exceptionally bright geese.

Squid froze as the rangy leader sliced his glance through the shifting crowd.

Everyone knew Mal. Some said his name was short for Malaria, because he'd killed more people than a parasitic outbreak. Some said it was short for Malware, because he'd crippled more businesses than a digital pandemic. Squid personally thought it was short for Malcolm, but she knew better than to say this.

Mal's gaze stopped on Squid, and their eyes met across the smoky room.

She saw the start of recognition dawning on his face, like a nuclear ground zero, but she was already bolting out the back door. A terrible crash ripped through the den, raw fury sailing after her like a wave.

It wasn't that Mal didn't have a concept of going around things, but if it was easier to push an old lady over than to step around her, he would. If it was easier to walk through plate glass than to open a door, well, that was Mal.

Squid pounded through the narrow streets, the pavement awash with fizzing neon lights and broken glass.

Baltus City was a nation unto itself, a city-state where extremes were crammed into uncomfortable proximity. The obscenely wealthy, the devastatingly poor, towering skyscrapers and sleepy suburbia, all pressed together beneath the massive orbital highways that laced the city like Celtic knots of steel and concrete. And within the borders of the teeming state, all were equally ruled by the enigmatic crime lords of Baltus City.

It should have been the backdrop to an unextraordinary life marked by repetitive work, lazy weekends, small pleasures and mindless diversions. Instead, Squid had wedged herself into an existence where she was lucky to crawl into the next day. All she needed was one lucky break, and she could get herself out of this. But psychos like Mal weren't making things easier.

Squid didn't stop running for another fifteen blocks, and even then, it was only because her feet were suddenly kicking air. She'd ducked into a decaying rat-run of an alley, like countless others tangled in the city. The regular lurkers knew better than to mug Squid unless they wanted a used tissue and a handful of blank IOUs, but the guy holding her by the throat obviously hadn't gotten the memo.

He must have been seven foot, and although he wasn't wearing a trenchcoat, he looked like he was waiting for one in his size to come wandering down the alley. He had a broken nose, and one eye bulged noticeably larger than the other.

"I have a message from Ferret," he said.

Squid grappled desperately with the hand around her neck, but it was like plucking at the edges of a tectonic plate. A message from Ferret had every chance of involving a melon baller. If you were lucky.

"Three thousand dollars or fifteen cars," the man continued. "You have twenty-four hours to settle the debt, or Ferret starts counting interest in fingers."

Without waiting for a reply, he disappeared into the inner-city fog, leaving Squid gasping on the damp concrete, gagging on the stink of rubbish and unidentified sludge.

And there it was. A rock and a hard place.

Squid pressed her eyes shut, trying to make sense of the exhausted thoughts running through her head. She hadn't slept in thirty-five hours, or maybe it was fifty-three. She'd crashed through some kind of psychological barrier, and for a while, everything had looked like cream buns. She blamed this for the gambling idea.

Now she was beyond exhausted. She was an obituary waiting to happen. An obituary that needed three thousand dollars.

Or fifteen cars.

Squid remembered the first job she'd flipped for Ferret. She'd been fresh out of high school, on a fast track to nowhere. She'd never had many friends, and when her mother left town, it was just her and Baltus City. To Squid, a "support network" was what you erected around an unstable building.

People always said getting a job was a world of *no*s followed by one *yes*. And that *yes* had come from Ferret.

The first job had been easy. She'd picked an expensive car in an expensive suburb. It wasn't until later that she'd found the birthday cake in the trunk, with a jauntily iced picture of a girl in a wheelchair. And the glove box full of repossession notices.

After that, she swore she'd only steal cars from people abusing disabled parking spots. Then, only cars belonging to criminals. And finally, only cars belonging to criminals who were currently using their cars to commit crimes. However, this meant pickings were slim and you got on the wrong side of people like Mal.

Squid stared blearily down the alley, towards the glow of flashing signs and falling halos. On the main walk, she'd find a street crooked with cars, piled nose to bumper outside the cheap bars and unlicensed casinos. She could settle her debt within hours and have enough left for the rent.

It was already past midnight, with people going from drunk to drunker. Most of them shouldn't even be driving, and it might even be an act of responsibility to take away their cars. But Squid had been down that road of logic before, and she knew where it led.

Here.

Squid dragged her feet homeward. Things would look better tomorrow, after she'd had a shower and grabbed some sleep. Making decisions after your brain had ceased to function only led to regrets. Squid's hand went automatically to her bare wrist, and her chest ached a little.

She took a shortcut through the slums, where the homeless congregated beneath sheets of damp cardboard, like human sediment in the cracks of society. Unlike the nearby shanty town, with its fancy tin roofs and luxurious sheets of plastic, the slums were a desolate junkyard, cupping the wide black waters of Baltus Bay. Water views were usually coveted, but not in Baltus City.

Squid padded through the silent slums, trying not to disturb the muttering piles of newspapers. The burning bins had cooled to ash, and even the ranters and paranoids had retired for the night. There was never much starlight in Baltus City, just the city's own reflection drowning out the sky.

She crept past mounds of flaccid tyres and broken prams. This was a place of abandoned, forgotten things. Including people.

Squid almost didn't see it at first. Just a few kicks of light suggesting a shape in the shadows. But she could recognise a shape like that from six feet under.

It was shadow-sleek and gorgeous, all curves and dark glass. It was the kind of car that didn't need gills or spoilers—it had *engineering*. It was less a physical presence and more like the thought of a car, like a fantasy conjured up in the mind of a delirious, sleep-deprived car thief.

It was like a gift.

It was almost like a deity saying, "Sorry about the watch; I wasn't really paying attention. Here you go."

Certainly, the car sported a few dents. And certainly, there were two men arguing in hushed voices behind it. However, none of this seemed nearly as important as the fact that the men seemed to be trying to push the car—*her car*—over the concrete siding and into the murky depths of the bay.

Squid knew the difference between men in suits and "men in suits". The car was probably stolen. They'd probably just used it in a robbery and were gearing up for a night of kicking puppies. What she was about to do was perfectly justified, perfectly sane.

Part of Squid knew that there was no possible way this could end well. Some part of her was screaming something about sleep deprivation and bad decisions and painful repercussions. Unfortunately, the part of her mind that was at the controls had flown off the rails and crashed into a giant cream bun.

The car rolled towards the ledge, and Squid found herself rushing through the shadows. She knew this part. She was good at this part. Her fingers swept over the scrambler in her pocket, streaming a silent lullaby of code to the car. She barely waited for the blink of green.

*Drop, roll, click.*

She was in the car and elbow-deep in wires. She could hear the startled voices outside, see the fists banging on the glass, but they were minor distractions. The secondary security system had kicked in: the engine was neutralised, the mainframe seized in lockdown. Squid's fingers darted through the circuitry behind the steering column, threading and rerouting the cables into her scrambler. It was like making up a song by using the same old notes to create a whole new piece of music.

The car jolted, and the knot of wires fell from her grasp. Somehow, the car was rolling forward, the engine stone-dead. Squid shot a panicked glance through the rear window and saw angular silhouettes shifting against the glass. They were pushing the car into the bay—with her in it.

She hauled on the handbrake and the car shuddered, locked tyres grinding in the dirt. Her hands flew frantically through the innards of the dashboard, the bay looming closer in the windscreen.

She wasn't sure how things always got from bad to worse, how simple wants turned into wretched cycles. How trying to pay the rent turned into tumbling into the bay, tangled in the cables of a stolen car. If a zoologist ever wrote a paper on people like Squid, it would read:

*Natural Habitat: Between a rock and a hard place.*

The car tipped forward, and Squid slammed her fist on the ignition button, the engine roaring into full-throated life. Her foot stomped on the accelerator, and for a moment, the car hung on the ledge, staring into the cold black waters.

*Just make it red.*

The car suddenly reversed into a cloud of curses, boots kicking at the doors. Squid spun the steering wheel, streaking out of the slums in a hurricane of cardboard sheets and plastic bags. The gangly figures were soon lost in the swirling wake, the car sliding seamlessly into the pulsing city.

It handled like a whisper on a bullet, gliding through the slick streets. It was with immense reluctance that Squid pulled into a rubbish-strewn alley a few blocks from her apartment. Business was business, and for the next twenty-four hours, her business was survival.

She rummaged through the glove box, tapping a name on her phone. The meter flashed briefly onscreen:

*Seven seconds of credit remaining.*

"Drop-Off Twenty-Six," said Squid.

She punched the button to disconnect.

*Five seconds of credit remaining.*

The glove box was empty—probably cleaned out by the henchmen. Squid patted down the chair pockets and assorted compartments, digging out a smattering of coins. For some reason, there were always a few coins wedged in the upholstery, and she suspected the manufacturers put them there, although she couldn't fathom why.

She could have stripped the gadgets from the console, but she didn't want to be here when Ferret arrived. She quickly popped the trunk for a final check and found something worse than a cake piped with a smiling girl.

She stared blankly at it, and it stared back.

Squid slammed the trunk shut, her head spinning, the world spinning, the universe coming off its axis and splattering into a conga line of dancing flamingos.

*You have to be kidding.*

Squid took a deep breath and heaved up the lid again.

The trussed-up man looked to be in his early thirties, smartly dressed and decidedly dazed. He'd been roughed up a bit, with a few nicks on his face and neck, a spattering of blood on his shirt. A wide piece of duct tape covered his mouth, and he squinted at her with some expectation.

Squid closed the trunk calmly. She crouched on the ground, gripping her head. She had to get a job. A real job. Something in an office, with cubicles, and tea breaks, and communal biscuits you could take home for dinner.

She was so tired, she wanted to throw up, but decisions kept flying at her like bricks through a windshield.

Problem: There was a man in the trunk.

Solution: Pavlova.

Squid buried her face in her hands, trying to force her thoughts into some kind of coherence. It was like trying to catch snow on a griddle.

The obvious solution was to leave him there. Maybe he was dangerous. Maybe he'd report her to the police. She could just leave him to Ferret.

She stared at the silent trunk. Someone was actually having a worse night than she was.

She pulled the tape from the man's mouth and began sawing urgently through the rope with her pocketknife.

"Hi…" said the man uncertainly.

"Don't look at me. Don't talk to me."

He stared compliantly at the sky for a while before his gaze turned back to Squid.

"Did I offend you or— Ow!"

Squid yanked her knife through the last of the rope.

"You never saw me," she said.

The thrum of an approaching car rumbled through the air, and Squid's heart began to somersault.

"Get out!" hissed Squid, half-dragging the man from the trunk.

She gave him a solid shove, and he stumbled a few steps before petering to a halt.

"Shoo!" she said, waving her hands frantically.

He stared at Squid in mild curiosity.

"Don't say I didn't warn you," said Squid, and she started to run.

She was three blocks away before she realised there were footsteps pounding behind her. She staggered to a halt, peering back at her pedestrian tailgater. The man from the trunk stood about thirty feet away, watching her with an expression of vague interest. Squid took a few steps back, and after a pause, the man took a few steps forward.

The hairs on the back of Squid's neck stood on end, and she wondered if things were about to enter horror-movie territory. Although, considering her situation, it might be an improvement.

Squid took a few cautious steps towards him, and the stranger tucked his hands in his pockets, looking nonchalant. If he hadn't had a busted lip, he might have tried to whistle.

"Are you hurt?" she said.

He suddenly smiled, as though Squid had opened a welcoming door in a winter storm.

"I don't know," he said.

"If you need to make a phone call, there's a Twenty-Four-Whatever on the corner."

"Thanks."

He continued to stare at Squid with a cheerful and slightly expectant expression. He didn't reek of alcohol or recreational powders, which ruled out a buck's night gone bad, but Squid was starting to wonder if perhaps there'd been a good reason for him being tied up in a trunk.

"Well," she said, backing away slowly, "you're probably wanting to head home…"

Squid took that to be the end of the conversation, and she began jogging away down the street. Footsteps padded after her.

She felt an overwhelming urge to handcuff the man to a lamp post.

"Are you following me?" she said.

"I'm not sure I should answer that."

Squid wasn't sure if he was toying with her, but there was something in his eyes that reminded her of a small child adrift in a bustling shopping centre, pretending not to be lost.

"What's your name?" said Squid.

The man opened his mouth and seemed surprised when nothing came out.

"I'm not sure."

"You have amnesia?" said Squid, her tone more accusatory than she'd intended.

"I'm sure it'll come to me," he said quickly.

The man appeared well manicured, wearing a silk-blend shirt and tailored pants, but there was something slightly stray-dog about him. Squid knew better than to get involved in someone else's problems, especially when she had a riot of her own, but judgement had taken a shot between the eyes tonight.

"Are you hungry?" she said.

The man thought about this, as though she'd asked him to calculate the quantum mass of pi.

"I don't know," he said.

Squid sighed.

The Twenty-Four-Whatever was a brightly lit box of acrylic and linoleum, lined with food that had probably been 3-D printed from corn syrup and MSG. Squid pushed through the smudged doors, and after a beat, the man from the trunk followed her inside.

"Hey, Ed," said Squid with a smile.

The squat man behind the counter grimaced as Squid rummaged through her wallet.

"What can I get for sixty-five cents?" said Squid.

"Lost," said Ed.

"How about a sandwich?"

Ed sighed, as though Squid had just foisted the troubles of the world onto his shoulders.

"The one at the end," said Ed. "The one with sprouts."

Squid was pretty sure the sandwich hadn't had sprouts yesterday, but a sixty five-cent sandwich was still a sandwich. But only just.

Back on the empty street, Squid pushed the sandwich into the man's hands.

"You should eat it before it turns into a salad," she said.

He stared at the bristling bread, as though not entirely sure what to make of it.

"Thanks."

"You should probably go to the police. Just don't mention me. I'm leaving now."

Squid had never learned the art of extracting herself gracefully from a conversation, although she'd stopped pointing behind people and running away.

The man started to follow her.

"Stay," said Squid firmly, holding out her hands as though halting a tide. "I don't want to you follow me."

She walked away, and this time, the man remained stationary. As she rounded the corner at the end of the block, she glanced back and saw him standing on the sidewalk, staring at the soggy sandwich in his hands.

*

No one believed the truce would last.

For decades, the underbelly of Baltus City had been ruled by a single criminal empire—Pearce's empire. No one knew much about Pearce, except that crossing him meant hitting the morgue in a bag the size of a grapefruit.

Only one other operation had survived his juggernaut. Verona had cobbled together her territory in the shade of Pearce's massive machinery, edging her way quietly into unoccupied niches. Before anyone could join the dots, her isolated niches had flowed together to create an organism to rival Pearce's.

For years, their organisations had casually avoided one another, but skirmishes had become unavoidable. Like the incident last night.

Pearce and Verona. The twin spheres of power in Baltus City had finally overlapped, and things were about to get messy.

Verona's hands moved across the holographic display, waving away schedules and dragging fiscal reports to the fore. Sunlight streamed into the room through transparent solar panels, the tall windows framed by the hanging gardens outside.

In the heart of trendy Downtown North, Verona's head office was a message: Pearce was child soldiers on the front line. Verona was zero-emission, autonomous killer-drones. Who do you want to work for?

Behind the holographic screen, Verona's assistant—Clef—stood dourly clutching a sheet of electronic paper.

"Where's Mal?" said Verona.

"Probably on rampage."

Verona's gaze stopped on Clef, and he cleared his throat.

"Preparing for tomorrow's shipment."

"Any movement from Pearce?" said Verona.

Clef glanced at the updates scrolling across his page.

"Nothing confirmed. But Callan and Grout are missing."

Verona's expression grew grim as she marked two red dots on a growing list. Pearce's syndicate grew more unassailable every day, and soon, he'd move to rectify the problem that was Verona. The city wasn't big enough for both of them, and Verona was determined to be the last one standing.

# TWO

Prosperity Mansions was an apartment block the size of a neighbourhood. A neighbourhood with as many factions as post-Soviet Europe, and more weapons. No one ventured into Prosperity Mansions unless they had the misfortune of living there, or they had pressing business, or they were in desperate need of a killer tzatziki. One had to be very careful, however, if what they wanted was the killer tzatziki, and not the "killer tzatziki". In the Mansions, punctuation could kill you faster than a shiv.

Squid had moved into the worst part of town out of a combination of defiance and desperation. She told herself it had been to get away from the snide looks and patronising eyes, but in truth, she couldn't afford anywhere that wasn't regularly sprayed with bullets.

She navigated her way through the dim, ramshackle corridors that resembled laneways in a miniature post-apocalyptic city. Some doors hung open, revealing glimpses of drifting smoke rings and tables laid with velvet pouches. From other apartments wafted the mouth-watering aroma of butter chicken and fresh sago pudding.

Squid couldn't remember the last time she'd eaten, and she now regretted not taking a bite from the sandwich before giving it to the amnesiac. It would have been a gross breach of etiquette, but her crash-and-burn social skills were partly to blame for her current predicament, anyway.

She shoved open her apartment door and realised too late that there'd been a crack of light at her feet. A man lay on her couch, reading a stained copy of *Jane Eyre.*

"Hi," said the amnesiac, smiling brightly.

Squid realised now, in a moment of deranged lucidity, that her earlier prayer had been answered by one of those twisted gods who granted one wish, only to hurl you into an ironic hell.

"What are you doing here?" choked Squid.

"Reading," said the man. "You like *Jane Eyre*?"

"I use it to squash roaches."

The man delicately replaced the book on a teetering stack of odds and ends.

"How'd you find me?" said Squid.

"Saw it on your licence when you were turning your wallet inside out."

"How'd you get in?"

"Turns out I can pick locks."

The man pulled a bent bobby pin from his pocket.

"Do you want it?" he said. "It was in the sandwich."

"No," said Squid, with the kind of preternatural calm that precedes a tsunami. "I do not want it. I want you to leave. Now. Permanently."

The man looked around the cramped studio.

"I like it here."

"Arghh!" Squid's tenuous grip on sanity snapped, and the man watched with fascination as she scampered around him, trying to pry him from the couch using a broken broomstick.

She could have called on her neighbours for assistance, but asking for help at Prosperity Mansions was like borrowing money at the Fess. You'd end up missing your kidneys and feeling like you got off lightly.

Squid threw the broomstick away, starting a small avalanche of jars and broken appliances in one corner.

"Leave, or I'll…" she began.

"Call the police?" said the man.

Squid's eye twitched, and she punched an icon on her phone.

"Someone's broken into my apartment," she said. "Can you come over? He's still—"

The phone gave a reproachful beep.

*Zero credit remaining.*

It was seventeen minutes before someone knocked at the door. A woman in her early thirties sauntered in, dressed in a leather jacket and khaki pants, her gaze sweeping the room quickly. Tufts of chopped hair the colour of damp malt poked out from beneath a dark green newsboy cap.

"Casey," said Squid plaintively, pointing to the man on the couch.

Casey looked sceptically around the dingy studio.

"He broke in?" said Casey.

"And he won't leave," said Squid.

Casey regarded the man for a moment, and he gave her a brief wave.

"Stuff like this wouldn't happen if you got your act together," said Casey.

"You're saying I brought this amnesiac home invasion on myself?"

"Amnesiac?"

"It's a long story."

"It always is," said Casey. "Squid, the longer you live this life—"

"It's not a career. It's just… bits here and there, until I get a proper job. I mean, technically, you're a crooked cop for turning a blind eye."

"It's not a blind eye," said Casey. "It's a long blink. If you're still messing with this stuff when I stop blinking, don't think I won't put you away. You've only got 'til—"

"August eighteenth; I know," said Squid.

"Knowing and doing are two different things."

"Thank you, Zen master. Look, I said I would."

Casey turned to the man on the couch. "What's your story?"

"I don't know yet," said the man politely.

Casey dragged her gaze over him, as though committing every detail to memory.

"Don't give me a reason to come back here," she said.

"No, ma'am," he replied.

"Good to meet you."

Casey extended a gloved hand, and after a brief pause, the man shook it. Squid stared in disbelief.

"You're just leaving him here?" said Squid.

"I won't bail you out of a mess you've created."

Casey paused in the doorway.

"Hey, where's the watch I gave you?"

"At repairs," said Squid.

Of all the punches she'd rolled with tonight, the look in Casey's eyes as she left was the hardest to take. Squid closed her eyes, feeling the man's silent presence like a mosquito on the ceiling.

"Please, just go," said Squid.

"You really want me to leave?" he said quietly.

"Emphatically."

Squid opened her eyes to find the apartment empty, and she collapsed gratefully onto the couch. All she needed was a few hours' sleep. Just enough to take the edge off her zombie status and give her a chance at clearing fourteen cars before Ferret set up his scales for a pound of flesh.

She stretched out across the mismatched cushions, her eyes lingering on a small patch of fresh blood on the armrest.

She found him wandering a few corridors away, following the scent of baking waffles.

"Hey!" said Squid.

The man turned, his expression like that of a tragic hero at the end of a movie, waiting for a letter he knows will never come.

"Just tonight, okay?" said Squid.

*

Squid's apartment wasn't designed for two people. Or people, full stop. There were rumours that Prosperity Mansions had been built off blueprints for a prison that had been scrapped due to breaches in regulations for humane detainment.

"I'll take the couch," said the man.

"You take the floor. I get the couch," said Squid.

"Oh. I just assumed the bed was buried under all the junk."

"It's not junk."

"It's like a rat's nest, if rats could have OCD," said the man cheerfully.

"And I suppose you live in a fashionable downtown loft? You're probably just some homeless guy."

"In threads like this? They're probably couture."

He groped for a tag and started to pull off his shirt.

"Whoa! This is not a shirt-optional household," said Squid.

"This isn't a house."

He grudgingly slid his shirt back on and began to unzip his trousers.

"Hold it right there," said Squid. "Any kind of pants removal happens in the bathroom."

The man paused, looking around the studio.

"That's a door? I thought it was a piece of cardboard stuck to the wall."

He disappeared into the bathroom. There was a long silence, and when he emerged, he seemed oddly subdued.

"No tags," shrugged the man.

"Maybe you found them itchy."

"Maybe someone didn't want me to know where I shopped."

"I think rolling you into the bay would have fixed that."

The man's expression clouded over, reminding Squid that where other people had tact, she had a mouth.

"You don't remember anything?" she said.

"Just the light, and then you."

Squid had the nervous suspicion that perhaps the man had imprinted on her, like baby ducks following a glove puppet.

The man suddenly perked up.

"You should give me a name. So you don't have to keep thinking of me as 'that guy'."

Squid felt she was veering into weird territory there, but at this point, she was going to roll with it.

"How about Grief?" she said.

"That's a little harsh."

"I used to have a dog called Grief," said Squid, suddenly awkward. "Never mind; I'll think of something else."

"Wait. I like it," said Grief.

He sat on the couch, smiling faintly to himself, as though the world were reshaping around him.

"I wonder if I can sing," he said. "I wonder if I can dance."

Grief tried a few experimental dance moves.

"Don't do that," said Squid.

"I wonder if I can cook. Where's your kitchen?"

Squid pointed to a disembodied electric hotplate wedged under a pile of shoeboxes.

"What do you plug it into?"

"I use it to crack walnuts," said Squid.

The ceiling light suddenly flickered off with a sad buzzing noise, plunging the room into an oppressive darkness.

"Squid?" said the man uncertainly, as though unsure if this was a diversion while she ran away again.

An off-key melody tinkled through the darkness, and a feeble yellow glow began to pulse from a hand-cranked night light. Squid pushed it into Grief's chest.

"Be useful," she said.

Grief continued cranking the musical lamp, and illuminated stars moved unsteadily over the walls and ceiling.

"I think this is a toy," he said.

"It's a night-light-slash-humidifier, but if you crank it while there's water in it, you get an electric shock. There were a stack of them at the tip."

Grief stopped cranking, and the light began to fade.

"Why don't you use that?" he said, reaching for an ornate red-silk lantern.

"Don't touch that!" Squid dove towards him as though he were about to set a baby on fire. "Don't touch *anything*."

Squid tossed several patchwork cushions onto the floor and dug out a dusty camp blanket.

"You can stop cranking when you want to go to sleep," she said, flopping onto the couch.

The melody continued to tinkle for a while, then faded as the light dimmed.

"How long were you in there?" said Squid softly.

"It felt like a long time."

Squid wanted to say something reassuring, but she knew from experience that those sorts of promises were rarely true. She'd been telling herself for nearly six years that things would look better tomorrow, only to find that tomorrow made you yearn for yesterday.

*Maybe it'll be different this time*, thought Squid as she drifted into sleep. *Maybe things will look better tomorrow.*

# THREE

Casey peeled off her leather glove as she strode down the corridor of Metropolitan West Police Headquarters, dropping it into a crisp evidence bag.

"Visha," called Casey as she swung into the lab.

A middle-aged woman with deep brown skin poked her head around a door.

"Gale was looking for you," said Visha, taking the evidence bag from Casey.

"External fingerprints," said Casey. "Can you run it through the system?"

"Paperwork?"

"I owe you one!" said Casey, giving Visha a thumbs-up as she slipped back into the corridor. Hopefully, Chief Superintendent Gale had finally approved Casey's standing request for a search warrant for the Kabukuri Club, along with her requisition for a small armoured tank.

"Casey." A chipper, dark-eyed man fell into step beside her. "Staying out of trouble?"

"Trouble's my job, Riego."

"Being a cop is your job. Subtle difference."

Riego had the kind of voice that sounded as though he was talking slightly faster than his mouth could move, in an accent that was a melting pot of colloquial Spanish, New York cabbie, and Hong Kong action movies.

"You worry too much," said Casey.

"I worry about you, but I worry more about me. You're the type who, if your partner was tragically killed in the line of duty, you'd go crazy. You'd bust open the weapons locker and tank through downtown like Judgement Day."

"I don't like you *that* much."

"That's why I'm not married. You'd see all my cute kids wailing at the funeral and you'd go berserk. Forget Hurricane Tyson; you'd flatten the city halfway to the coast. I can't be responsible for that."

"Riego, you're really morbid sometimes."

Casey occupied a floating cubicle that seemed to have broken off the main island, drifted down the corridor and around several bends. It was wedged between the snack machine and the chemical storage closet, which Riego had observed was not a healthy combination.

While Casey told herself she liked the privacy, it did mean she tended to miss out on general announcements, newsworthy chatter and communal pastry trays.

"I just worry about you, is all I'm saying," said Riego. "Where'd you disappear to?"

"Just out."

"You shouldn't go chasing trouble. Enough's going to find you."

"So, you just leave your job at the door? Go home and you're just like everybody else?"

"We *are* just like everybody else. Forget that and you'll end up like Deus."

There was a deliberate knock on the wall, and Deus cleared his throat.

"Casey. Riego."

Deus was only a year or two older than Casey, but he'd managed to make Chief Inspector while she'd hit a wall at Sergeant. He looked like one of those police-officer figurines distributed by PR, with his slick brown hair, dark blue eyes and long, measured stride, which made walking next to him seem like a competitive sport. Something about him reminded Casey of the shining school prefects who secretly beat up kids behind the bike sheds.

Deus tossed a slim file to Casey.

"Chief says you're on the Werner case," he said.

"Did I get demoted on my coffee break?" said Casey.

"You don't drink coffee," said Deus.

"You didn't answer my question."

Deus shrugged. "You don't like it, take it to Gale."

He strode away like a tall ship sailing through flotsam.

"I tell you, it's like talking to a stuffed bird full of dynamite," said Riego. "One day, you're going to say 'Hello' and wonder where your arm went."

Casey was already flicking through the file—the whole one sheet of paper.

Tol Werner. Twenty-seven. Pulled from the bay with a gunshot wound to the chest. No employment history. No criminal record. Just an address at the Chival.

No one lived at the Chival unless they were a "businessperson" or "unemployed". It had Pearce written all over it, ready for a rubber stamp saying INSUFFICIENT EVIDENCE, CHARGES DROPPED or ACQUITTED.

Nobody expected Casey to catch anyone. She could use it to frame a felon of her choice, or she could poke around before declaring it cold.

Or she could solve the case.

"Should I be worried?" said Riego.

"You can always change partners."

"I made a promise to your mother," said Riego, making a sign of the cross.

"You never met my mother."

"You don't have to meet someone to make a promise."

"You're bizarre sometimes," said Casey, shrugging on her jacket. "I guess we start with next of kin."

*

Pearce's headquarters occupied a towering heritage building in the heart of Old Central. The interior was a seamless blend of Victorian hotel and military base. Luxurious and ominous—much like Pearce himself, or so people imagined.

Right now, Ducabre exuded enough *ominous* to power a gothic city. As Pearce's deputy, it fell to him to deal with screw-ups like this. He regarded the head of Security dispassionately, and she continued to stare coolly at a point just left of his head. She reminded him of a willow rod: straight, sharp and liable to leave welts.

"Rojin," said Ducabre. "You understand the seriousness of the situation."

"I followed your instructions," said Rojin.

"You followed half my instructions." *And back to front*, he added mentally.

"We have dealt with the Verona element," said Rojin.

"Verona is not the priority. Any progress with the hardware?"

"My staff are not equipped to determine what is and isn't relevant. Technology is more qualified—"

"Technology does not have clearance on this matter," said Ducabre sharply. "You understand that discretion is critical."

"We should just destroy all the drives."

"Would you burn a city to kill a man?"

"Yes."

Ducabre paused. His own answer would have been "It depends on the man". And possibly the city.

"Your orders stand," said Ducabre.

"Understood."

*

Squid woke to the sound of running water, and for a moment, she thought the pipes had burst again. When gritty liquid failed to spray the room, the events of the previous night hit her like a truck in reverse. It seemed ludicrous that she could accumulate so many regrets in such a short period of time. And one of them was having a shower in her bathroom.

She pounded on the flimsy door, and the taps squeaked off.

"I had to wash the blood off my clothes," called Grief. "Have you got a spare shirt?"

Thinking sourly of the wet cubicle, Squid realised why some parents evicted their kids at eighteen. She rummaged through a dented box.

"I've got an old jersey," she called.

"Can you pass it in here?"

The bathroom door opened a crack.

"*Now* you're shy?" grumbled Squid, pushing the jersey through the gap.

"I'm protecting your modesty."

There was a silence.

"Were you a… large teenager?" said Grief delicately.

"They only had extra-large jerseys. The whole grade looked like retro rappers. Some of the smaller students got blown away before graduation. Wind, not guns. Or so they said."

Grief emerged from the bathroom, plucking at the blue-and-white jersey.

"You look like a jock," said Squid. "No, you look like one of those old guys who hangs out at Cancun, pretending they're in high school."

"You don't have any other guy clothes around?"

"I barely have any girl clothes."

Squid shoved past Grief, then stopped abruptly, noticing that his stubble was gone. Her eyes narrowed.

"Did you use my razor?" said Squid.

"That was yours?"

"Why don't you use my toothbrush while you're at it!"

Grief paused.

"That was yours?"

Squid tried to swallow the spasm of wrath constricting her throat.

"Please," she said very calmly. "*Don't. Touch. Anything.*"

The floor was wet, and so was the towel. But there was no point in straightening the picture frames when the house was on fire. She should just be grateful she still had a body to shower.

Ferret wasn't a fan of creative violence. He didn't believe in making flamboyant threats unless he was very literally capable of carrying them out. Most of the time, he was very practical in ways that made Squid want to crawl into pockets of nonexistence. She had once seen him do something terrible to someone using a piece of string and a door.

Squid rubbed the pale tan mark around her wrist. She had maybe fifteen hours to salvage the situation, but she was running out of options.

"You know, I'm not that bad-looking," called Grief. "Do you think I've had work done?"

Squid declined to dignify that with a reply.

"What do you reckon? Twenty-six? Twenty-seven?" he said.

"If time started going backwards, then yes, eventually," said Squid, struggling back into her rumpled clothes.

"How old are you?"

"Twenty-three," said Squid, pulling on her sneakers. "Okay, Grief. Free ride's over."

It was an overcast morning, and the muggy air smelled of old cats. Squid stood on the sidewalk outside Prosperity Mansions, watching the cars speed past. You only had to worry if they had their windows down.

"Well, good luck and all that," she said.

"Thanks," said Grief, making no move to leave.

"You're not going to follow me, are you?"

"Do you want me to say 'no'?"

Squid felt like smacking Grief across the head with a chunk of déjà vu.

"Don't you want to go home?" said Squid. "Your family's probably worried."

"I don't remember having a family."

"That's because you have amnesia. You should at least go to the hospital. Make sure you're not contagious."

"I feel fine."

"That's what people say right before they explode and infect everyone within splatter distance."

"What if I stay outside of splatter distance?"

"This isn't a game," said Squid. "I'm in the kind of mess you don't get out of clean. I'm going to be committing crimes today. Not cool crimes involving helicopters and suitcases full of cash. Crimes like punching a kid for her lunch money."

"Is she a bratty kid?"

Squid stared.

"Just go," she said finally. "You have a life to go back to. You don't know what I'd give to have that."

"Let me help," said Grief. "You kind of… helped me out of a tight spot. How about I help you get through the day?"

"You're going to help me steal cars?"

"I guess I've got a streak of bad boy," said Grief with a wry smile.

*

The Werners lived in Sapphire Waters, a gated community near the eastern parklands. Spotless houses fronted onto an artificial lake, with artificial swans gliding under the watchful eye of closed-circuit cameras.

Casey had never liked these places. The more that people put up borders and fences, the more they started thinking that different laws applied to different people. Some people needed stricter laws. Some people needed special laws. Some people made their own laws.

The Werners themselves seemed slightly overwhelmed to be living in Sapphire Waters, and the contents of their spacious home looked as though they'd been transplanted from a far more modest dwelling and then wedged between the new furniture.

They were a middle-aged couple, with creased faces that looked slightly worried, even when they were smiling. They showed Casey and

Riego baby photos of Tol, a drawing of a robot he'd done in grade school, videos from his high school prom, as though they already knew his case was destined for the too-hard basket.

"He bought us this place four years ago," said Mr Werner. "He worked so hard. He just wanted us to…"

Mr Werner choked up, and Ms Werner took his hand.

"Who did he work for?" said Casey.

"The Pearce Group," said Ms Werner. "So many technology places wanted him after graduation, but Pearce had the best offer."

"He never hurt anybody," said Mr Werner. "He just loved making things. Gadgets, all the time."

"I made you a list of his friends from university," said Ms Werner.

"I made you cupcakes," said Mr Werner, his eyes welling up.

Casey took the ice cream container of brightly iced cakes, her own chest tight with the couple's grief. It was a breach of protocol, but she didn't have the heart to refuse them.

"Please," said Ms Werner, holding onto Casey's sleeve. "Please find out who did this."

Even Riego was silent as they strode to the squad car. Casey had seen a lot in her time. Things that made you want to raze a nation or claw your own heart out. Things you never thought you'd recover from, and you never did. Not quite.

It never got easier. Every stricken person left behind. Every unsolved case gathering dust. Every killer who walked free. Every tyrant who believed they stood above the law.

At some point, you broke, or gave up, or stopped caring. Or went crazy.

*Yes, Riego should be worried. But not as much as Pearce.*

*

They called it Chinatown, but in reality, the immigrants had long ago moved into comfortable suburbia. Nowadays, Chinatown was a mishmash of territories, where the Yakuza scuffled with the bikers, and the Triads fought off incursions by the Mafia. And everyone avoided the apparently benign but worryingly well-organised religious groups who handed out pamphlets on every corner.

"How about that one?" said Grief, pointing to a shiny red Mercedes. "Statistically speaking, it's waiting to be stolen."

"No," said Squid.

"How about that one?"

"That's a rickshaw."

"For someone about to get concrete shoes, you're awfully fussy."

"I have standards," said Squid. "Something your former identity obviously doesn't understand."

"For all you know, I was a philanthropist philosopher who saved orphaned children and financed fistula hospitals. And it sounds like your 'standards' might have gotten you into this mess."

The quotation marks hung in the air like rotten fish on a hook.

"My 'standards'?" said Squid archly.

"You make up all these rules, like it's okay to steal from people abusing disabled spots, but not from people who are double-parked. It's like you're trying to prove you're not a bad person when you know that you are."

At that moment, Squid decided that Grief was some kind of divine punishment. He was karma incarnate, sent to teach her the Christmas spirit or send her to the asylum.

"I'm a mostly good person in a difficult situation," said Squid. "For all you know, you could be a serial killer."

Something flashed across Grief's eyes, quickly replaced by sunny indifference.

"Maybe I was an astronomer," mused Grief. "Or a psychic. Hey, think of a number."

Squid decided that if Grief could really read her mind, he'd back away fifty feet and possibly cover his head. However, her attention quickly switched to a dented white van pulling up outside the Pwn

Shop.

"Paydirt," muttered Squid, ducking behind an overflowing trash can.

"What did this guy do?" said Grief.

"Not the driver, the shop. Rezna commissions stuff. She wants more VR gear, they get more VR gear."

Squid waited until the spiky-haired driver disappeared into the shop before she kicked into action. It was a basic hack, and they were tearing down the cobbled lane in fourteen seconds flat. Grief just managed to close the passenger-side door before a passing hydrant almost claimed it.

"I think there's more stuff in here than in your apartment," said Grief. "Is that a sceptre?"

The van was crammed with blank-faced tablets, gleaming espresso machines, golf clubs, passports, and jewellery boxes spilling their treasures across the floor.

Squid remembered the first van she'd taken, picking through the contents like a stork in the wake of a flash flood. All those pretty things with silent stories, speaking volumes about the kind of life she'd never lead. She'd ended up sitting on the rusted floor, surrounded by strands of pearls and scratched Rolexes, bawling her eyes out.

"I bet you have a rule about this," said Grief.

It was true; Squid had a lot of rules. They helped her navigate through a life that bore little resemblance to the one she'd expected. Deep down, she still dreamed of warm lazy days, of freshly baked cookies and molten afternoons. Her rules told her she wasn't too far gone, that she could still claw her way back. That she still deserved that life.

"Yes, there's a rule," said Squid.

*

A famous writer of noir once said that if things got slow, have a man with a gun burst into the room. Casey felt like being that man with the gun.

She drew a line through the last name on the list, the page now sloshing with question marks, arrows, and memos like "jackass". Most of Werner's former friends had refused to take her call, hanging up hurriedly, or quickly putting on an accent and pretending to be the cleaner. Casey had given one guy a snap lecture on offensive cultural stereotypes before he'd cut the line.

Some of them had just maintained a stubborn silence, grimly repeating that they knew nothing. Others, she hadn't been able to track down, including the girl who'd collaborated with Werner on his final project at uni. The worst, however, had been the people who denied knowing Werner at all. As though they'd already erased him from their memories.

It seemed abhorrent that someone could be written out of existence so easily. All the things they'd seen, all the people they'd touched, all the little moments that didn't really matter but at the same time were all that really mattered, just waved away with a gun or a wad of money.

Casey's train of thought was interrupted by a ping on her monitor.

*No match on the fingerprints. - V*

Casey deleted the message. She wasn't sure whether to feel relieved that Squid's squatter didn't have a criminal record, or concerned that he'd be harder to track down if something happened. And something would happen, of course.

"Casey!"

Riego came running down the hall, and the fact that he was moving faster than a casual saunter was news in itself.

"Deputy Commissioner Drake's addressing the station!" he said.

Casey went from seated to flat sprint in under two seconds. She didn't know if it was simple oversight that they forgot to tell her about these things, or if there was a reason she'd been shunted into a distant alcove.

The briefing hall was standing room only, packed with officers of every rank, from every department. Casey tried to make her entrance as unobtrusive as possible, but she still managed to attract a fair number of irritable glares.

Deputy Commissioner Drake stood on a low stage, looking as crisp as a publicity photo. She was talking about responsive strategies and rapid deployment protocols, in that clear, cadenced voice everyone knew so well. Drake had charisma—not like a cult leader or a rockstar frontman. She was like a familiar postcard, your favourite teacher, a bolt of lightning and a slap of fresh air, all rolled into a hard smile and eyes that had seen more than you ever would.

Drake was the main reason Casey had joined the Force. While other kids had Superman or Skywalker, Casey had Deputy Commissioner Drake. Although, back then, it was Sergeant Drake, or Commander Drake. Casey didn't read comic books. She read the paper, and every day shone with some heroic triumph or heartbreaking setback in the saga of the city. Another drug cartel exposed, another elephant-smuggling ring busted. And always Drake, smiling out from the page with reassuring confidence.

However, the longer Casey spent in the Force, the more she felt the shine wearing away. She came to see that even heroes had to compromise. But even so, standing in the crowded hall, listening to that voice talk about good and right and rule of law, she could still remember a time when she had *believed.*

The address drew to a stirring close, and Deputy Commissioner Drake smiled graciously at the vigorous applause. It was at this moment that the doors to the hall swung open, framing Deus in the light.

"Casey! There's a trolley of stolen goods out the front with a note addressed to you!" he called over the fading applause.

The applause turned to crushing silence.

Casey felt a hundred pairs of eyes swivel to her like laser pointers, and she was certain that the overhead spotlight had swung onto her. She excused herself quickly, resisting the urge to shoot Deus a look of death as she passed.

Riego caught up as Casey pushed through the front doors, striding into the summer heat. There turned out to be four shopping trolleys parked by the kerb, each one overloaded with an assortment of household goods.

"He didn't have to say stolen goods," snapped Casey. "He couldn't possibly tell that they were stolen."

Riego held up a loose card tied to the trolley handle, clearly labelled in black marker.

CASEY. STOLEN GOODS.

Casey yanked the card off its string, and it quickly turned into a crushed wad in her fist. Evidence be damned.

"Why wasn't he at the speech, anyway?" said Casey.

"It doesn't matter," said Riego. "It's not like nobody knows about your questionable friends. Why do you think you haven't been promoted?"

"I thought it was my sarcasm."

There was an unhappy pause, and Riego prodded at a squeaky toy frog that seemed to be coughing up white powder.

"Why are you friends with her?" said Riego.

It was a good question. And Casey had a lot of answers. Because Squid scuttled through the city like a manic crab, hearing and seeing things that Casey couldn't. Because Squid worked for Ferret, who worked for Pearce, and Casey might need that someday. Because Squid couldn't bring herself to hock these stolen goods, because she wanted to feel marginally less like a thief. And no matter how distorted the logic, it made Casey believe that there was some kind of hope for the kid.

Yeah, Casey had a lot of answers. But none of them seemed particularly good today.

"Come on, let's get these off the street," she said.

*

They left the van at Drop-Off Twenty-Three, racing away as soon as the signal was sent. Running lost its appeal after six blocks, and they hitched a ride to Briar Village on the back of a freight truck. Grief leaned out the side as they hurtled down the freeway, grinning like a dog with its head out the window. Squid was certain people got decapitated that way, but he didn't seem to hear her in the headwind.

Briar Village had been a prestige shopping locality before the giga-malls took over. Now it was a run-down shadow of its former glory, but a few of the old boutiques held on.

The Auger had been here for over thirty years, and although Squid had seen it countless times, she never tired of gazing at it. The shop was a two-storey spiral of glass and polished steel, glittering like a seashell of ice. Delicate silver chains and strings of freshwater pearls hung from filigree hooks along the walls. Trays of ornate gold circlets and diamond-encrusted bands shone from black velvet counters.

Squid surreptitiously circled the store several times, finally settling into a sunken doorway across the road.

"That's a pretty store," said Grief.

"I've never been inside," said Squid. "I mean, when it's intact."

Grief stared intensely at the Auger.

"I think I have."

"You recognise it?"

Squid hopped onto her knees, peering excitedly at the store, as though expecting a flock of bluebirds to burst from the doors, holding a banner saying MYSTERY SOLVED! Instead, a giddy young couple emerged, arms entwined, admiring their matching pendants. Squid sagged slightly and then turned to Grief.

"What do you remember?"

"I don't know. I just remember the spiral."

"Hey, maybe if you went to more landmarks around the city, they'd trigger your memories. Has anything else come back to you?"

"I take it we're casing the joint?" said Grief.

The change in subject was so abrupt that Squid almost felt the breeze from the verbal door slamming shut. However, it reminded her that the deadline was ticking closer. She had more important things to do.

"This place gets ram-raided nearly every week," said Squid.

"And we're hoping it gets ram-raided today, like now?"

"Yup."

"Why don't we just steal a car and raid it ourselves?"

Squid looked at Grief as though he'd gone insane. Well, more insane. It suddenly dawned on Grief.

"You want to steal the *getaway* car?" said Grief.

He looked at her as though *she* were insane, and there was a brief standoff involving expressions of mocking disbelief. Squid broke off first.

"If you don't like my plan, you can go home."

"That's a plan? No wonder your life turned out so well."

"You can't even remember your life. You're probably a number-cruncher in a cubicle factory."

"With a face like this?"

Grief flashed an infomercial smile. Squid was starting to seriously wonder if Grief did, in fact, require some kind of medication that he wasn't presently taking.

She ignored him for a while, staring stubbornly at the doors to the Auger. She tensed at the sound of every passing car, slumping again as the engines faded. Grief sat quietly beside her, content to be fascinated by his own hands or a loose thread on Squid's shirt. He stopped tugging at it after she swatted him away for the fourth time and threatened to club him with her shoe.

After some time, Grief cleared his throat, and Squid removed a shoe menacingly.

"I know this is your gig," he said, "but I don't think they're getting raided today."

Squid looked across at the sinking sun. Somehow, she'd squandered an entire day and stolen only one van. She could have hocked the goods and settled a good part of her debt, instead of just pocketing a dollar of phone credit, but that would have been one more step along a road she'd gone too far down already. Grief was right—her standards just complicated a bad situation, but they were all that stopped her from becoming something she didn't want to be.

Time was running out, like it always did.

"What's so special about August eighteenth?" said Grief.

Squid glanced at him, wondering for a moment if he did have a touch of psychic as well as psychotic.

"It's my birthday."

Casey believed in cycles, and choices, and turning points. In your first twelve years, the world formed you. In the next twelve, you formed yourself. And all the rest were when you formed the world. Squid's cycle was drawing to a close, her last chance to shape herself before she baked into her chosen form.

She only had one option left, one she'd been keeping up her sleeve for a day like this. A day she'd hoped would never come. And, of course, here it was.

"We'd better start walking," said Squid, dusting herself off. "It'll be dark by the time we get there."

# FOUR

The Chival was a tower of sumptuous apartments in the most prestigious part of town. It rose in waves of red granite and cream marble, designed by architects who'd probably had their eyes gouged out afterwards as a sign of appreciation.

The Chival was Pearce's territory, deep and sweet, and police were less welcome there than at Prosperity Mansions. It had taken Casey eighteen phone calls and a brief shoving match to gain access to Werner's apartment.

In the end, a search warrant had been granted, undoubtedly over several dead bodies, but it was admit-one only. Pearce's way of saying "Come, if you dare". Casey had left Riego a suitably dramatic note—she was sure he'd appreciate it. He'd give her an earful when she got back, but nothing a hot cup of tea and some almond shortbread couldn't fix.

*If* she got back.

No officer had ever been killed in the Chival. Not on record, anyway. A few had gone missing, but their files were sitting in cold storage now. Like Werner's would, unless she did something.

When Casey arrived at Werner's door, she couldn't see what all the resistance had been about. The apartment had been completely stripped—it was like a model home for the pathologically minimalist. No photos, no books, no clothes, no tech. They hadn't even left any linen. Every surface smelled like it had been scrubbed with bleach and possibly acid. They could have butchered a zoo in here and she wouldn't have known.

Casey flicked out her nano-surveillance scanner and the screen lit up like New Year's Eve. The apartment wasn't just bugged; it was practically its own reality show. Either the cleanup crew had run out of time or this was another message for her.

*We're watching you.*

It took her over three hours to collect all the speck cameras and listening devices, gouging them from crevices and scraping them out from under paintwork. She stuffed the evidence bag into her satchel, hoping it was enough to muffle any still streaming their feeds. And she was pretty sure some were. She tossed a scrambler in there for good measure, but she doubted standard-issue gear would work on Pearce's tech.

Casey drew a quick layout of the room, sketching out the coverage of the surveillance devices. If they'd been watching for something in particular, maybe the distribution of the bugs would give her a clue.

She paused, looking at her shaded page. The coverage was one hundred percent, even in the bathroom. She'd hate to be the one sifting through that footage.

Casey couldn't suppress a shiver as she swept her gaze slowly around the apartment. Werner must have known he was being watched. This was the Chival. Plus, he was a tech-head. Casey's eyes stopped on the linen closet, her gaze darting back to the sketch in her hands.

The closet door opened outwards, and if you stopped it at this angle, right here—

Casey drew a line on the coverage map.

You created a tiny pocket of space not covered by the cameras. It was barely an inch wide, in the gap between the hinge and the inside shelf. Casey leaned in and saw a thin crack where the wood met the wall, where you couldn't fit anything except perhaps a piece of paper.

Casey pulled a loop of wire from her pocket and dragged it gently down the crack. It caught briefly on something, and she coaxed the wire along, drawing out a scrap of something white.

It looked like a short length of sticky tape, and on one side was a rectangle of paper covered with a single line of random numbers. If it was a cry for help, it had come too late. If it was a voice from the grave, she was determined to answer.

Casey made her way back to the stairwell—she didn't trust elevators in a place like this. The thick red carpet muffled noises better than a padded cell, which was why she didn't hear the two heavies until they were almost on top of her.

The scruffy blond man, Casey recognised. Jace had been a petty thug a few years back, but he'd clearly moved up the food chain. She'd busted him once for break-and-enter, and she hoped he wouldn't hold it against her now.

The lean, intense woman, Casey didn't know, but she had the look of someone who'd started out waiting tables before discovering that slitting throats afforded faster career progression. She had a thin black braid that looked as though it could slice open your throat if she flicked it just right. More worrying was the gun at her side—a Reaver .22 with built-in silencer. It was the kind of gun favoured by bounty hunters and certain kinds of mercenaries.

Somehow, looking at the woman gave Casey the feeling she was staring down the barrel of a missile cannon on countdown. They could only be here for one of two reasons. They were curious to see which resourceful officer had managed to rip a warrant from the zombie fingers of bureaucracy. Or they'd decided this resourceful officer needed to be fertiliser in the terraced garden. Casey could only hope her paperwork contrail would deter them from doing anything right here, right now.

"Hello, officer," drawled Jace.

"I have a warrant," said Casey calmly. "And I was just leaving."

She deliberately addressed this to the woman, who watched in casual silence.

"I don't think you're going to," said Jace, cracking his knuckles.

Casey knew it'd be over the moment she reached for her gun. Riego had always been better at the whole negotiating gig. She'd once seen him talk a suicidal man off the roof of his apartment, and Riego had been half-asleep and drunk on cherry liqueur chocolates at the time.

"I'm not looking for trouble," said Casey. "So, unless you want a squad on your doorstep, I suggest we stay out of each other's way."

Jace took a step forward, leaning in towards Casey.

"No one would come looking for you," he said, his voice soft and unpleasant. "They never came looking for the others."

Casey's hand jerked—she couldn't help it—and it took her breath away how quickly the woman moved. It was like watching a film with the middle cut out: one moment, the opening credits were rolling, the next moment, there was a Reaver trained between her eyes.

"Go on, Rojin; they wouldn't even open a file for this one," said Jace.

Casey briefly wished she'd given Jace a good kick in the head back when she'd arrested him. But she didn't believe you could beat the bad out of people. A belting just made them meaner, made them hate you more, made them an even bigger problem when they got out. But sometimes, Casey wished the law had a longer arm and a bigger stick.

Rojin remained perfectly still, the gun locked on Casey.

"Leave," said Rojin.

It was hard to turn her back on a gun, but Casey refused to walk backwards all the way to the stairs.

"You're no safer out there," called Jace with a malevolent grin. "Just ask Werner."

*

So, it had come to this.

Squid had crashed through every contingency plan and found herself here. It felt slightly surreal, like that sensation of walking onstage with a thousand critical eyes raking scores across your skin. Or in that moment just after you dive, praying that there's water in the pool.

This life she'd made, this terrible, wasted mess of a life. It reminded her of a deformed vase she'd made in pottery once, half-baked and too late to reshape. No matter how hard she tried, the clay just crumbled in her fingers. She kept telling herself she could fix it, go straight, start over. But here she was, so far gone, she could hardly see the light.

The murky sky had darkened to what passed for night in Baltus City. Rows of suburban houses lined the tidy street, pools of shadow forming where the streetlights failed to reach. And all along the street were cars: nondescript, working-class cars.

"Is this the bit where we punch a kid for her lunch money?" said Grief.

"No," said Squid. "This is where we rob the whole damned school."

She crept forward, just making out her target through the hedges: a typical urban mansion, brick all the way to the kerb. Security shutters sealed every window, but even so, a strange odour wafted out.

Everyone knew about the Lab. From the dirt-cheap stuff that would bust open your veins to mango-flavoured crack with top notes of green tea—anything you could snort, lick, or jab into your arm, odds were they made it here. The police had raided it a few times, but every time they burst through the doors, all they found was a rosy-cheeked family eating their Sunday roast. And every time they left, the shutters came down, and the ventilation ducts resumed churning out their foggy exhaust.

This was Verona's territory, which was probably why the police had stopped coming here. And Pearce's crew knew better than to start something they couldn't finish. At least, most did.

Squid took a shallow breath. She was about to hit the piñata, hoping it wasn't full of napalm.

"Everyone on this street works for the Lab," said Squid.

Grief counted the cars on the street.

"You're going to try to steal thirteen cars?"

"No. I'm *going to* steal thirteen cars. And this is the part where you should go home."

Squid did the lopsided calculations in her head. One minute per car, and there was a drop-off seven minutes away. Twenty minutes to run back. She could make it, with only maybe—she counted quickly—losing three fingers as interest. As long as he didn't take any thumbs…

"You're doing the maths wrong," said Grief.

Squid stared at him.

"You were mouthing the words," he said. "It happens when you spend too much time alone. Your socialisation breaks down."

"And you remember this from where?" said Squid.

Grief shrugged.

"It'll take longer than twenty minutes to run back. If I tail you, I can drive you back, cutting it to just over three hours."

Squid looked down at her fingers.

"Can you even drive?"

"Let's find out," said Grief, grinning.

After a few false starts, it turned out that Grief could drive, although Squid would hardly call it driving.

"The accelerator is the pedal on the right," said Squid.

"Do you want to get done for speeding?" said Grief.

The car was still moving at a fair clip when Squid jumped out, already sprinting for the next target. Wedge, wire, jab and twist, her chimaera scrambler breathing its chloroform codes all the while. Another down, too many to go. Any minute now, someone would notice the sound of engines humming away. Any minute now, a shadow would lunge out and solve all of Squid's problems in the worst possible way.

Three more cars delivered with a kiss of burning rubber, and Squid's heart pounded in her throat. Two more and she'd be free. Two more and she could turn it all around, like a ship drawing away from the edge of a thundering waterfall.

"Squid?" said Grief. "You don't look so good—"

She didn't hear him as she jumped from the moving car, racing to the last target. Counting Grief's car, she only needed one more. Which was just as well, since the street was clear except for one last vehicle. It sat smack in front of the Lab, so close you could press the doorbell from the driver's seat.

The vehicle was smooth and lean, with the aura of expensive machinery. While the other cars had been working dogs, this one was a prize Doberman, trained to rip out a lung so that you could still use it. Someone loved this car.

Someone who worked at the Lab.

"Squid," said Grief. "Are you okay? Maybe we should leave it."

"Get back to your car," said Squid.

"When was the last time you ate? Look, I'll sell something or find something. We should just—"

The rest was a rush of white noise as Squid sprinted towards the car. She disabled all three alarms and the automatic recorder before sliding into the soft leather seat. Her vision sparked with strange lights, and the air tasted of lemons and roast banana. There was a good reason people didn't hang around the Lab too long.

Her hands slid over the panels and buttons. It had one of those damned engine-killers that took forever to disable. If you didn't have the right face, fingerprints and eyeballs, it'd run like a dream for two and a half minutes before locking you in and ripping you a new set of the above. There was also the standard-issue model which just shut down the engine, but knowing Verona's people, Squid wanted to err on the side of caution.

The console blinked on and Squid saw the clock. Seven minutes. She had seven minutes to get this baby to Ferret. He had a watch that told the time in three dozen countries, on five planets, and it didn't just measure time—it dissected it into tiny pieces and pinned it to a cork board.

Six minutes. She could still make it if she drove through traffic and pedestrians. She just needed to bypass one last trick on this damned thing to get the engine started—

She heard the noise. Just a faint *click*. Then everything went wrong. It happened so fast, and out of order, and partially upside down. The car door ripped open and arms hauled her roughly from the seat. There was the sensation of running, of flying, of hitting the ground with a shockwave of searing heat tearing across her back.

There was a roar like a five-headed dragon on a bad trip, and Squid turned to see her prize car bursting into a blinding fireball, unrolling into the sky.

It didn't just explode. It sent decapitating wedges of metal jetting through the air, trailing flames like falling rockets. The blast took the front of the Lab with it, gouging a burning scoop from the building, daubing it with flame.

Grief lay partially over her, shielding her from the brunt of the blast.

"Grief," coughed Squid.

He opened his eyes cautiously, as though surprised to be conscious.

"You're squashing me," said Squid.

He rose quickly, patting out the flames on his back.

"That's my jersey," she said.

Grief looked from Squid to the burning crater where the car had been.

"Um, sorry? Squid, you really—"

"You have to go," said Squid urgently, as angry noises emanated from the remains of the Lab.

She raced to Grief's car, throwing herself into the driver's seat. Grief started to open the passenger-side door and Squid pulled it shut again.

"There's a laneway around the corner; it'll take you clear to the main road," she said. "They'll be looking for me, not you."

"Shouldn't I come with you?"

"This isn't your mess, Grief. Go home."

Grief clung to the edge of the window.

"What about your jersey?"

"Just go!"

Squid planted a sooty hand on his face and shoved, making sure he was clear before hitting the accelerator. She knew she should have said

"Thank you". She should have said and done a lot of things differently in her life, but it was too late for that now. Time had run out, and all her regrets trailed behind her like an extravagant bridal procession.

The last thing Squid saw as she roared away was the smoking figure of Mal emerging from the burning Lab, his eyes locked on the retreating car.

*

Drop-Off Seventeen was a disused parking lot behind an abandoned industrial site. It was the kind of place where people had showdowns, or gang fights, or underworld executions. In hindsight, Squid should have picked a less foreboding drop-off, like the pebbled road beside Peony Gardens, but it hardly mattered now.

She screeched into the lot, burning debris still clinging to the roof of the car. The other vehicles were already gone—smoothly absorbed into the Pearce machinery. The first one was probably already a different colour, with a brand-new chassis number.

Squid staggered from the car, trying to smooth her singed clothes. Her elbows were grazed from where she'd hit the bitumen, and she'd ripped another hole in her jeans. She could imagine this as her ten-year reunion "where are they now" photo, wedged between the corporate recruitment billionaire and the reality-TV chef.

"Five minutes late and one car short."

Ferret's voice was smooth and clipped, coming from behind her, of course. He would run halfway around the block just to make his approach from behind. However, it was less a dramatic affectation and more a prudent one.

Squid tried not to shiver as she took in Ferret's silhouette. He wasn't an intimidating man to look at. He looked like the kind of gentleman who might have taken an early retirement, the sort who spent his afternoons in the local coffee shop, drinking tea over the international newspapers. But Squid knew Ferret, and she knew what he could do with a cup of tea and a newspaper.

"Do you know how much five minutes of my time is worth?" continued Ferret.

"Last car… exploded…" wheezed Squid.

Ferret's expression went beyond stony into a whole new mineral classification. Behind Squid, the wreck quietly sizzled and popped as the flames dripped happily over the paintwork.

"Two hours," said Ferret. "Three more cars. And the debt is clear."

He started walking away, and Squid felt her stomach trying to bring up her lunch. Fortunately, she hadn't had any. Unfortunately, words came up instead.

"I want out," said Squid.

The words burbled out, like water from the mouth of a drowning man. There was a terrible silence, and for a long moment, she thought they'd be her final words.

"I've been very accommodating, Squid," said Ferret, his voice calm. "You said you only wanted to do cars; I let you do only cars. You'd be late with deliveries, and I'd give you warnings."

Ferret's expression was like that of an extremely disappointed father taking a belt from the hook. Squid found herself hyperventilating, and her head felt like a helium balloon, barely tethered to her neck.

"I'm sorry," she said. "I made a choice. I made a promise."

"This isn't some nine-to-five. You don't just give your notice and walk away."

Squid stood miserably on the cracked bitumen, slumping like a beanbag doll missing half of its stuffing. She knew what happened to people who tried to leave. If you were lucky, you ended up with a dramatic story about how you got your wooden leg. If you weren't, well, no one talked about what happened then. Although it didn't stop people from making hand gestures and disturbing sound effects.

"I know," said Squid quietly.

Ferret watched wordlessly as she continued to slowly deflate, almost curling in on herself as she waited.

"I think you owe me one last job, don't you?" said Ferret.

Squid eyed Ferret with a mixture of apprehension and hope.

"Eleven PM tomorrow," said Ferret. "Be ready."

He strode away into the shadows, his grey coat fading easily into the mist. Squid's knees finally gave way, and she sat on the broken gravel, taking deep, shaking breaths.

One last job.

She knew what that meant.

*

No one was entirely sure whether Verona ever went home. Or if she had a home. Or if she even slept. Rumours abounded that she was actually a cyborg, or twins, or a hologram. One thing Verona had learned from Pearce was that rumours and uncertainty could keep you on the throne longer than guns and money. Although guns and money certainly helped.

"Verona!"

The voice burst over her intercom, and Clef sounded urgent and irritated. At the same moment, the doors to her office flung open, which would normally be an act of suicide on the part of the intruder.

Verona didn't look up from her floating schematic of a new water-condensation farm, the three-dimensional hologram turning slowly at the slightest touch of her fingers. Mal stood in the doorway, his eyes smouldering brighter than the edges of his leather duster.

"Squid," said Mal.

That one word carried enough subtext to fill a study guide.

Clef chased into the room with a scanner wand in his hand, his expression stormy.

"I'm sorry," said Clef. "Mal still hasn't gotten his head around the idea of protoc—"

"How about you get your head around my fist?" growled Mal.

The two of them glared at each other with open distaste. Clef dragged the surveillance scanner around Mal, waving it closely around his face a little more than necessary.

"Clear," said Clef reluctantly.

Mal snatched the scanner, circling it around Clef before the indicator blinked green.

Verona ignored the exchange. She had always mocked criminal masterminds who surrounded themselves with fools, until she'd realised that good help was really hard to find, particularly if you were a criminal mastermind.

"The Lab's been destroyed," said Mal.

"Extent?" said Verona.

"We can salvage maybe thirty percent of the equipment. None of the stock."

"Culprit?"

Here, Clef and Mal exchanged a glance.

"Squid was there, with an accomplice," said Mal.

"Low-level car thief, works for Pearce," said Clef.

"And the accomplice?" said Verona.

"Didn't get a good look. He got away pretty fast," said Mal.

Verona paused, the schematic hanging motionless. It would be a bold move by Pearce to attack her so openly. It would be the equivalent of throwing down the gauntlet, and she hadn't thought him prepared to do that just yet.

"It could be payback for the other night," said Clef.

"We fired a few shots, took a few cars," said Mal. "Big deal."

Apparently, Pearce thought it was.

"Tighten security on tomorrow's shipment," said Verona.

It would seem the gloves were off.

# FIVE

Squid drifted through the streets like an empty wrapper, her hopes and memories evaporating until all that remained were the dregs of her imminent future.

She knew that Pearce didn't let people go unless he was holding them over a cliff. She was terrified of Ferret, and Ferret was terrified of Pearce, so Squid didn't even have a word for how she felt about Pearce. They said he commanded demons and cyborgs and slave-girl ninjas, but they said a lot of things at the Fess, especially on Toxic Tuesdays. One rumour held that Pearce's Rottweiler was responsible for half the unsolved murders in Baltus City.

One last job meant going out with a bang, often literally. You could man up and face it, or you could run. And running would relegate her to dead-man-walking status and a particularly gruesome finish. Squid's choices had brought her here, and maybe it was time to take some responsibility.

Grief had been right, amnesiac savant that he was. Squid hid behind a shield of rules and pseudo-ethics to disguise the fact that she'd screwed up. Stealing from the wicked, striking against those who used cars for evil. Once, a long time ago, Squid had tried to convince Casey that she was almost like a vigilante. She'd honestly thought that Casey was going to hit her.

Well, the fantasy was over. Time to put her affairs in order and face the music. It seemed dramatically apt that strains of moody jazz drifted down the corridors of Prosperity Mansions. Squid felt like Eurydice, following the heartbreaking notes of Orpheus's lyre, knowing the idiot would come undone at the cusp of freedom.

She stepped into her darkened apartment, the saxophone reaching a poignant diminuendo. It took her a moment to realise that the music was coming from inside the room, and her eyes quickly traced the shadow draped over the couch, a hand-cranked radio on his chest.

The jazz abruptly gave way to an off-key tinkling from the night lamp as Grief sat up.

"You look awful," said Grief.

"What are you doing here?" said Squid flatly.

"You said go home."

"I meant *your* home!"

Grief was silent, and the tinkling music sounded almost tragic as he cranked it slowly. Squid sighed and tossed a packet of squashed jam rolls onto the floor.

"I didn't know they still broadcast anything on that," she said, glancing at the warped wooden radio.

Grief was already investigating the oozing rolls, like a marine biologist studying a particularly freakish creature flopping on the deck.

"Why do they smell like rancid pork?" He plucked a piece of lettuce from the wrapper. "Did you pull these from a Dumpster?"

"It was that or the rancid pork," said Squid. "If you're not hungry, I can eat a whole packet of jam rolls on my own."

Grief extracted a squashed sponge and settled on the couch, inspecting the glistening red jam.

"I wonder if I like jam rolls," he said. "I wonder if I'm diabetic."

Grief popped the entire roll into his mouth.

"You know how to treat diabetic shock, right?" he said.

"Maybe I'll let natural selection have a win."

"You know, I reckon you'd be more successful in life if you got on better with people."

"And I reckon you wouldn't have ended up in a trunk if you weren't so pushy."

Squid settled on the floor and busied herself with the rolls.

"You know, the couch is big enough for two people to sit on," said Grief.

"My personal space is the size of this apartment."

Squid polished off another three rolls before curling up on the floor, her blood sugar doing acrobatics. She stared at the pitted ceiling, the paint peeling around a row of old bullet holes.

"I can't pretend to like people," said Squid. "I tried once, and it gave me an ulcer."

"Stress doesn't cause ulcers. *Helicobacter pylori* does."

"How come you know all these things, but not your own name?"

"I know my name. Just not my old one."

Memories were funny like that. Squid could remember her old life, but she remembered it like someone else's dream. It played through her mind like a silent film, so distant she could almost believe it had never happened. But once in a while, a half-remembered emotion would hit her, so visceral it stole her breath away.

Omelettes at the kitchen table. A sea of closed faces. Voices that broke her heart a piece at a time. Sitting alone in the washed-out sunshine. A world that had no place for her.

Squid reached into a dusty pile of books and extracted a large, faded paperback. The cover was cracked, the corners blunted by continual browsing. God, it had been a desolate lifetime ago since she'd looked at this.

"How about we try to jog your memory?" said Squid.

Grief leaned over curiously. "*Courses and Careers*?"

"I'll read out job titles, and you tell me if anything sounds familiar."

"Maybe I didn't have a job," said Grief. "I was probably a gentleman of leisure, cruising through the Pacific on my luxury yacht."

"Then maybe you'll remember how many chefs you had, or how often you used a masseur."

Grief sat attentively while Squid leafed through the yellowed pages.

"Auctioneer. Farrier. Probation officer," began Squid.

"Is this in alphabetical order? Because I think you're missing some pages."

"Are you doing this or am I?"

Squid waited pointedly before continuing.

"Bus driver. Nanny. Typing clerk."

"How old is this book?"

"If you don't want to do this—" Squid started closing the volume.

"Wait, please. Go on."

Grief rested his chin on the arm of the couch, politely watching Squid. Grudgingly, she continued to read from the book, through careers that seemed a world away. Architects, astronauts, micro-biologists, geophysicists. A slideshow of the extraordinary and the mundane, a multitude of choices that lay before each child until they stepped into the hard, cold world. But there'd been no place for Squid, no nine-to-five, no Squid-shaped niche. The only Squid-shaped hole would be the one they buried her in.

"Anything?" said Squid.

"Maybe I was a shy florist by day and a flamboyant rock god by night," said Grief.

"I don't think 'rock god' was one of the careers."

Grief rolled over, turning thoughtful eyes to Squid.

"Why didn't you follow one of those careers?"

"I don't get along with people. I wish I did. I wish there was some tablet I could take, so I could walk into a crowd and say, 'Ah, people', instead of 'Argh! People!' Even now, you're creeping me out, radiating your peopleness."

"My peopleness?"

"You're doing it now."

Grief looked down at himself, as though expecting to see coiling tentacles.

"Anyway, it doesn't matter," said Squid. "You should concentrate on remembering who you are. Maybe the amnesiac thing seems cute now, but you can't go on like this."

Grief caught Squid's expression, and she turned away quickly.

"You want me to go," he said.

"It's not about what I want."

Squid stared at the floor, trying not to think about tomorrow. For once, tomorrow was not going to be a better day.

"How did you know the car was going to explode?" she said.

In all her years, Squid had never come across a security device that would incinerate the intruder and half the block.

"There were about thirty kilos of C-4 strapped under the car."

"A car bomb?"

"Well, it'd be a stupid way to transport it."

On the one hand, it wasn't surprising that someone would want to blow Mal up. But it was unthinkable that someone would dare to attack Verona's right hand, or right fist, in the heart of her turf. Unless something had changed dramatically in the balance of power.

"How did you know to look under the car?" said Squid.

Grief stood up, stretching his back.

"I don't know."

He pulled out the neatly folded blanket and started ineffectually fluffing a pillowcase that seemed to contain empty tissue boxes. He'd risked his life to save hers, as though it had been the most natural thing in the world. Surely, someone like him had a place he belonged. A place he was needed. Squid kicked a cushion onto the floor and curled up under her thin blanket.

"I guess the adventure continues tomorrow," said Grief with a grin, pouncing on the cushion like an ant discovering an undefended macaron.

*Yes*, thought Squid. *And then for the finale.*

*

The worst part was the uncertainty.

Ducabre watched the reports streaming in, queries raining like arrows from people wanting to know if things had *begun.* All across the city, people watched each other warily, waiting for the word.

And the word was *Wait.*

"There's a cop poking around the Werner case," said Jace, standing in front of the desk with his arms crossed.

"Is she a part of the Stain?" said Ducabre.

"Unclear," said Rojin. "Perhaps we should send a message either way."

"Like your message to Verona's man?" said Ducabre dryly.

They'd never trace it back to Rojin, of course. It'd just be some random hoodlum who'd taken it into his head to blow up a random car. But Ducabre knew Rojin had taken the other night personally.

"I don't know what you mean," said Rojin.

"We're not going to fight a war on two fronts," said Ducabre. "Especially when you can't even find one man."

Rojin's eyes flashed, and Ducabre held her gaze. One day, she might try her luck moving up that final rung. And after what had happened to Pearce's Rottweiler, Ducabre knew what she was capable of.

Everyone knew that Rojin was fast, but the crucial question was: was she faster than Ducabre?

Jace edged backwards slightly.

"Understood," said Rojin.

*

He surfaced from the darkness, and there was a moment of confusion, of pounding fear, as though he'd been falling and woken just before hitting the ground. His gaze swept around the windowless room, taking in the piles of junk, the soft lamplight and the sound of someone brushing their teeth in the next room.

The nightmare seeped away, and Grief sank back onto the floor.

He was safe.

He didn't know why he'd be otherwise, or what chased him in the darkness beyond sleep. All he knew was here, and now, and this. Amnesia wasn't as bad as he'd thought; that is, if he could remember what he'd thought it'd be like.

It wasn't like waking up or being born. It was like being created. Like Athena, springing full-grown from the forehead of Zeus. Grief briefly wondered whether gods immediately knew their purpose—god of the sun, god of love. Or whether they had to discover their calling, leaving behind a wake of awkward natural disasters and supernatural hijinks.

Grief had come into being, and the first thing he'd seen was a frightened girl who always looked on the verge of throwing up. He partially attributed this to the fact that she ate out of Dumpsters. Perhaps he was the god of hygienic food preparation.

Squid emerged from the bathroom, looking surprisingly calm and refreshed.

"Have you been wearing those for three days?" said Grief.

Squid's expression was like an icepick in the eye.

"Um, so, what are we doing today?" said Grief.

He expected her to launch into a tirade about how there was no "we", but instead, her expression smoothed into beatific purpose.

"I'm going to help you get your memory back," said Squid. "We're going to visit landmarks around the city, and hopefully something will jog your memory. Or someone will recognise you. Or we'll find a poster warning of an escapee from the asylum."

"I don't think they call them asylums anymore."

"Not the legal ones," said Squid ominously.

"So, we're doing that all day?"

"All day," said Squid with a bright smile.

"Don't you have things to do? Like get more cars for Ferret?"

"Not today."

Grief sniffed the empty jam wrapper, eyeing Squid with concern.

"Squid… Did something happen?"

Her gaze wavered for just a moment, as though struggling to keep a psychological gate closed against a herd of crazed buffalo.

"Aside from you?" said Squid, tightening her shoelaces.

"Did Ferret—"

"Let's go," said Squid. "No point in wasting daylight."

Something sad flashed across her eyes, and she blinked it away quickly. Grief pretended not to notice, pulling out a smile.

"Where did you want to start?" he said.

*

The morning was pale blue, mottled with sunshine. Squid could almost believe it was the first day of the rest of her life, if she didn't already know it'd be her last.

Part of her wanted to spend the day unconscious. But part of her held on to some strange, demented hope that Grief had been sent as one last chance to redeem herself. That this quest to restore his identity, this one good deed, would be enough to wipe out all the wrong she'd done, and balance the books before—

"I bet I was popular," said Grief as they strolled along the shopping strip. "No, I bet I thought I was popular, but everyone secretly hated me."

"They probably openly hated you, but you just didn't notice."

"I bet it's like one of those movies where in the first five minutes, I'm a real bastard, and then after the accident, I become this lovable, cuddly guy," continued Grief.

"Firstly, you still *are* a real bastard. Secondly, being tied up and pushed into the bay doesn't count as an *accident*."

"I can just picture it. Super-rich playboy with more money than God and less taste than a catfish. Wakes up with amnesia, shacks up with the homeless, eating out of Dumpsters and learning the meaning of hardship."

"This 'shacks up with the homeless' thing: are you talking about me?"

Grief was already chasing another colourful line of thought, like a child jumping after butterflies.

"Maybe I'm an escaped genetic experiment. With superhuman abilities. Hey, I'll race you to the post box!"

Grief sprinted away and Squid shuffled halfheartedly after him. If her life were a movie, it'd start off as a living-room drama, turn into a gritty tragedy partway through and hurtle towards the finale as a comedy, before coming to a shocking conclusion that'd leave the audience complaining to the classifications board.

"You were probably just some rich guy in the wrong place at the wrong time," said Squid. "At best, they were holding you for ransom. At worst, you got in over your head. Drugs. Debts. Giant octopus fighting."

"Is that people fighting giant octopuses, or giant octopuses fighting each other?"

"Once, it was a giant octopus fighting a giant pickle jar, but I think it was rigged."

Squid suddenly dipped into a narrow laneway, crouching behind a broken fence.

"Here's our ride," she said.

A nondescript bakery backed onto the laneway, and a battered white van sat tiredly in the driveway. Red letters had been hand-painted onto the vehicle door, declaring UNCONTAMINATED LUCKY BREAD!

"Are they bad bakers?" said Grief.

"We're not stealing the van," said Squid. "We're borrowing it."

Every Sunday, the Uncontaminated Lucky Bread bakers loaded up their unsold bread and took it to the tip. On occasion, Squid would helpfully rid them of their unwanted bread, saving them the trouble of having to drive all the way there themselves.

Squid shook her head—she was still trying to justify herself, still twisting the world to make her the misunderstood hero.

As they rattled away down the lane, a flour-dusted man came running from the bakery, shaking a fist resignedly after them.

"Couldn't you just ask them?" said Grief, glancing at the stale and slightly fuzzy baked goods.

"It's easy for you. But it's like a fish telling a drowning guy, 'Just breathe'."

"I think you underestimate yourself."

Squid kicked the van into gear as they shot onto the main road.

"Well, mutant playboy genius, let's find out where you came from."

*

They left the suburbs behind and hit the freeway, coasting over the city on ribbons of asphalt. Squid gave a running commentary as they threaded through a patchwork of neighbourhoods.

"This is the Luvidius district," she said, "where all the rich goths live in their mausoleum mansions. Those are the Arker compounds—they're trying to collect two of every animal in case the world ends. They get raided by customs all the time."

They stopped in a knothole of a neighbourhood, wedged between the Community Gardens and the Subnuclear Smelterworks. No one bought vegetables here except the occasional wild-eyed botanist.

"This was one of my favourite places," bubbled Squid, disappearing into a crooked shop that stood six feet wide and three storeys high. A sign announced MR BLOOM'S EMPORIUM, spelled out with bolts and mousetraps.

The store was crowded with swords, clocks, and cabinets of glass flowers, with dismantled revolvers overflowing onto silk brocade cushions.

"If you're looking for something, but you're not sure if it exists, this is the place to go," said Squid.

They sailed across the city again, to a deserted enclave once known as Little Afghanistan, then Little Somalia, before some wise guy nicknamed it Little Did They Know.

"I used to love spending the afternoon here," said Squid, slipping though the curtains of a ramshackle cinema.

The Art Haus was notorious for not checking patrons' tickets, even though they numbered in the single digits on a good day. Aside from being located in an area where shooting was the most popular pastime, be it drugs, hoops, or each other, the Art Haus showed only black-and-white movies. Occasionally backwards.

The proprietor, Habitha Lee, sat alone beside the projector most days, watching her favourite films over and over.

"Back when crime looked classy," sighed Squid. "Cat burglars in Chanel. But real crime is skinned knees and chipped teeth and showers once a week. And real people getting hurt."

"Why don't you get out?" asked Grief.

"Why can't you remember who you are?"

"Sorry if my former self didn't hang around the same places you do," said Grief defensively. "Maybe if we had cocktails at the yacht club, something would trigger my memory."

Squid suddenly sat up, her eyes gleaming.

"I've got just the place."

*

Infinity Mall was a shopping superhighway. It was bigger than Buckingham Palace and busier than Tokyo in peak hour. Inside, networks of glossy white conveyer belts glided past sparkling shopfronts. Step on, step off, for your shopping convenience.

It was a constant hive of activity, twenty-four hours a day, three-sixty-five days a year. Everyone went to Infinity Mall except the most contagious of the homeless and the most reclusive of the wealthy. They said if you stood at the entrance to Infinity Mall, you'd eventually bump into everyone you knew.

"This isn't exactly the yacht club," said Grief, blinking in the bright, apple-scented light.

"Everyone's been to Infinity Mall, even the people who swear they haven't," said Squid.

Signs flashed and holograms waved while interactive welcome-bots called customers by name.

"We have to be quick," said Squid, turning up her collar. "They've got facial recognition cameras, and for some reason, I'm on the blacklist."

"Maybe because you're a thief?"

"I steal cars from criminals. I don't shoplift designer clothes."

"Clearly," said Grief with a grin.

Squid scowled, darting past an ice confectionery stand and into the couture avenue. A distinctive chandelier of pale green stars glittered overhead.

"Does anything seem familiar?" said Squid hopefully.

Grief passed his gaze over the glitzy awnings and sleek attendants, finally shaking his head.

"I guess I shop on San Cruza Drive."

Squid had once tried taking a shortcut through San Cruza Drive. She'd ended up running for her life from a horde of guards with designer stun guns.

Grief continued to glance around with polite interest, like a tourist being shown some baffling object of intense cultural significance.

"Are you saying that you've never been—"

Squid was interrupted by booted footsteps pounding across the marble. Four security guards pushed through the crowd, their personal sirens chiming a loop of three ascending notes, which everyone recognised as meaning: *Security breach in progress, but please continue shopping. And have a nice day.*

Squid spotted another four coming from the food court, and these guys already had their electrified batons out.

"Time to go," she said.

She sprinted down the main walkway, Grief following close behind. Another team of guards joined the chase, barking into their collar-comms as Squid vaulted a display of giant donuts and skidded across a portable skating rink. Something flashed in the corner of her eye, and a nearby shopper screamed as a Taser barb struck him.

"They're shooting at us!" said Squid.

"Well, you just knocked out their team leader with a giant donut," said Grief.

"What?"

A bolas whirled past and entangled an elderly woman, who promptly began screaming curse words volatile enough to down a fighter jet.

"Security guards aren't allowed to carry those!" yelled Squid.

"Maybe you can write them a letter," said Grief.

The public speaker system took up the siren as Squid barrelled towards the exit. Behind her, tables crashed and shoppers shrieked and civil-damages lawyers handed out their business cards.

Squid and Grief shot through the doors, roaring from the parking lot as the automated gates wished them a good day.

*

It had been an interesting day. But every day had been interesting so far. There were things he knew, like how to breathe, or what the road rules were, or why good people did bad things. But everything else was a mystery. What he liked, what he felt, what he wanted. Everything prompted a new sensation. It was like rediscovering the world.

While Grief found the whole experience fascinating, it seemed to frustrate Squid. He was therefore a little worried when she pulled over with a triumphant expression.

"Well, we know this is familiar," she said.

Grief glanced out the window and felt his chest clench slightly. The glass spire rose from the squat brick shops, like an ethereal ornament fallen from the sky.

"It's a pretty shop," said Grief.

"You said you'd been here before."

Squid waited impatiently outside while Grief fiddled with his seatbelt.

"I can see it fine from here," he said.

"Maybe you bought something," said Squid. "Maybe you'll remember what it was."

Grief slid from the van reluctantly. There was something familiar about this place, but all he got was a jagged flash of feeling, tight and choking. Like touching a live wire in the dark.

Squid gazed at the Auger with open yearning, probably unaware that her hands were clenched into little fists, like a five-year-old on her birthday.

"You like shiny things, huh?" said Grief.

"Hey, you're probably the one who dropped a packet here."

Inside the Auger, Nathalie Dumonde stood behind the counter, elegant in black and cream. She had been here when the area was awash with money and chic, and she would be here when they tore it down for high-rise parking lots. The Auger had been a magnet for celebrities and artists once. Now it was a popular spot for young lovers wanting to express their devotion to one another by braving a store better known for its weekly ram-raids than its exquisite jewellery. But Nathalie Dumonde would keep reinforcing the glass and adding more steelwork. She would keep rebuilding.

The bell tinkled softly as Grief and Squid entered, afternoon light cascading down the spiral walls, painting sunsets on the white marble floor.

Dumonde's hand flew automatically to the alarm at the sight of Squid but stopped abruptly as she spotted Grief. She looked from one to the other in wary confusion.

"Hello," said Grief warmly.

Dumonde returned an unsteady smile.

"You're here… together?" she said, as though expecting Grief to suddenly notice the parasitic lamprey tailing him.

"Is that a problem?" said Grief, still smiling pleasantly.

"Not at all," said Dumonde, drawing her manicured hands back to the counter. "I'm pleased to see you back again."

Squid hopped excitedly, like a fangirl whose crush was looking in her general direction.

"You know him?" said Squid.

"Er…" Dumonde looked to Grief for direction.

Grief's heart pounded viciously, harder than when the Lab had spilled with angry gangland chemists baying for blood and fire extinguishers. He could end this so easily with a few clever words and an apologetic shrug. Squid would be disappointed, but surely she was used to that. Grief looked at Squid's expression, shining with such strange, desperate hope.

"About my last purchase," he said.

Dumonde looked vaguely panicked.

"You're not happy with it? I followed your—"

"I'm thinking of getting something like it again," said Grief. "But I'm not sure my friend would like it. Could you show her something similar?"

"Your specifications were very distinctive. I've made no others like it," said Dumonde. "But perhaps a similar style and size?"

She removed a large velvet box from the safe, lifting the lid carefully. Squid made a noise like she'd inhaled a small penguin.

It was an unremarkable silver band, carrying the largest diamond Grief had ever seen. Admittedly, it was the first diamond he could recall seeing, but he was pretty sure it was damned big. It was a steep, brilliant cut, sitting in its claw like a knob of blue fire.

"Is that for wearing or for crushing coconuts?" breathed Squid.

"I think my friend would prefer something more modest," said Grief. "But thank you. We'll keep browsing."

After it became obvious that Squid was just going to stand there gawping, Grief steered her gracefully out of the Auger.

"You bought that?" said Squid.

"Apparently."

Squid stopped in front of Grief.

"You cared enough about someone to buy them a ring you could sink the Titanic with. Don't you want to remember them?"

"They can't have been that special if they wanted something that tacky."

"Dumonde said it was custom-made, so you probably designed it yourself," Squid retorted. "I bet you proposed while sailing down the canals of Venice, and you paid the gondolier to sing some cheesy ballad."

"You sound like you'd have more fun living my life than I would."

There was a pause, each imagining a very different scene.

"I bet you had fun," said Squid.

There was something inexplicably sad in her eyes, and Grief felt a peculiar pang. He put on a lazy smile as he pulled open the van door.

"Sure I did. I probably proposed to a different girl in every city."

"Maybe that's how you ended up in a trunk."

Grief wound down the window as they clanked towards the highway, the afternoon breeze ruffling his hair.

"One more stop before we wind it up," said Squid.

"And then?"

She pretended to study the oncoming traffic.

"And then tomorrow is another day," said Squid.

# SIX

It had taken Casey three days to get hold of the preliminary autopsy report. Met West Command was still buzzing after the explosion at the Lab, and in the tide of rumours about rumblings of war, no one cared about some dead-end case about a criminal lackey.

"Did you see the stats this morning?" said Riego. "If that graph was for sales, we'd all own islands in the South Pacific."

Casey didn't have a problem with gang warfare per se. What Casey had a problem with was crossfire.

"It's going to get worse unless someone puts a stop to it," she said.

"You say it like someone can," said Riego. "There's no Superman going to swoop down and save the city."

"No, there's just us."

*If we did our jobs properly.*

Werner had been technically unemployed, but he'd rocked an expensive pad downtown. And no one had ever bothered to ask the right questions. The city was full of blind eyes and greased palms. Pearce and Verona ruled with impunity, turning the thin blue line into an imaginary one.

"You've got that look," said Riego. "Like you're thinking about putting on a costume and whacking people's heads together. The rumours about vigilante cops are bad enough without you turning poster girl."

"I was thinking more 'postal girl'."

"It's not funny, Casey. You think so much, your brain's going to overheat and do something crazy."

"Like try and crack the case?" Casey flicked through the coroner's report.

The slim file didn't tell her much more than she could have gathered from a basic visual. Bullet through the chest, internal trauma and broken bones consistent with hitting the water from a height. Casey's finger paused on a line. There had been particles of glass in the entry wound. As though he'd been shot through a window—a sniper, maybe. For some reason, they didn't want him to see it coming.

Casey jumped at the brisk knock on the wall.

"Detective," said Deus. "Your friend made a scene at the mall again."

"She's not my friend," Casey found herself saying. "She's an acquaintance."

She felt like a jerk as soon as she said it, but what she hated more was that Deus knew it.

"The footage is on loop in the cafeteria, just FYI," said Deus, his expression neutral as he left.

A pencil broke in Casey's hand, and Riego carefully removed it from her fist.

"It's not just in my head, is it?" said Casey. "He's deliberately going out of his way to make life hard for me."

"In my village, they used to hit guys like that with knobbly sticks until they left," said Riego.

"You grew up in Neo Salem."

"I'm just saying," said Riego, draining his hot chocolate. "Maybe he secretly likes you. Like how the school captain always has a crush on the psycho girl."

"Whoa, when did I go from being aloof outsider to psycho girl?"

"I'm getting a refill," said Riego suddenly, getting up.

Casey watched him disappear down the corridor, twirling the paper cup in his hand. Riego would joke about the grimmest of things, but he'd never say what was really on his mind. Casey's association with Squid looked bad. It looked bad for *him*. Riego's own career had stalled the day he got partnered with Casey, and he'd say that it suited him just fine—the higher up the ladder, the easier to fall. He'd saunter through the office with a cocky smile and a morsel of news for every ear, but he knew they didn't take him seriously. Not since they'd paired him with the wingnut.

Casey leafed through the report again. She could nose around some more, even make some educated accusations, but she'd never secure a conviction. Part of her wanted to drop the case, be a team player, get a nice cubicle near the coffee machine.

But part of her wanted to tear up the city, flipping it over like a giant rock to expose all the blind, crawling things that multiplied beneath. Maybe there was no justice, but there was her. And maybe that would have to be enough.

*

It was late afternoon by the time they left the metropolis, the freeway bursting out of the concrete forest. They zoomed through abandoned industrial parks, silent chimneys and rusted chains giving way to open fields and sloping hills. You couldn't grow anything out here except spinifex and salt weed, but from a distance, it looked like waves of gold.

"If you're not afraid to run the radioactive gauntlet, it's really peaceful out here," said Squid. "There's this one place I used to go to all the time. I think it's my favourite place in the whole—"

Grief suddenly pulled on the handbrake, and the van lurched to a stop on the deserted road.

"Okay," said Grief. "I feel like I'm watching a slide show at a funeral. What's the deal?"

Squid kept her eyes firmly ahead. "I was just trying to be nice."

"You keep talking in the past tense: 'I used to this', 'this was my that'. What happened last night?"

Squid's knuckles turned white, but when she spoke, her voice was calm.

"I have to do one last job for him. In Pearce terminology, that means I'm going to die tonight."

She spoke as though she were explaining a foreign menu. This means "honey-glazed". That means "salt-roasted". And that means "imminent death with a dash of Greek tragedy".

"You don't have to do the job. You could go to the police. You could disappear to Spain, or Egypt, or Colombia. You could run—"

"You don't run from Pearce," said Squid. "At least, not for long. Casey always said it'd catch up to me one day. It just happens to be today."

Strange analogies welled up in Grief's mind, involving frogs and cream and the importance of never giving up, but he doubted Squid would hear him. She skidded through life as it collapsed around her, unaware of anything beyond the demons that chased her towards the precipice.

Squid thought that today was the last day of her life, and she'd chosen to spend it with him. Most people would have gone on a hedonistic bender or a violent rampage, tracked down lost loves, gone skydiving, settled old scores or reconciled with family. She'd dragged him from one end of the city to the other, trying to send him home.

Grief eased the brake off gently.

"What did you want to show me?"

They drove in sombre silence the rest of the way, chugging along the dusty ochre road. While Grief's thoughts fluttered with dark wings and haunting voices, Squid's mind eased as the city faded behind them, like a mirage dreamed up by some travelling storyteller.

Out here, you could imagine a world without fences, without streets, without people. Out here, the only creatures were the beetles and the bees, and with their sesame-sized brains, they were hardly judging you, measuring you, discarding you. Edible or not edible was the extent of their assessment, and Squid could live with that.

Their destination rose into view two miles down the road, but Squid could feel its presence from half a world away. A great solitary tree stood on the peak of a slow-rising hill, adrift in a sea of yellow grass. Pale grey branches twisted outwards, deep green leaves fanning across the horizon like half a snowflake. It was like coming home.

The high-school counsellor had instructed Squid on "safe places". When things get too much, when you feel like hurling chairs through windows or crawling into air conditioning ducts, think about your safe place. A place where you don't feel those things, where you feel… right.

This was her safe place incarnate. A place where she could hide from the world and pretend that only she existed. Or that she didn't exist at all.

Squid stretched out beneath the undulating branches, the fragrant leaves breaking up the sunlight. Grief surveyed the landscape with thoughtful eyes before sprawling onto the grass a courteous distance away.

"I used to dream about driving away," said Squid. "Out of the city, beyond the farms and forests, to the edge of the world. And beyond that."

"And leave everything behind?"

"You have."

"It's a hiatus."

Squid closed her eyes, letting the stillness wash over her. It was like hanging in a perfect moment, when reality was so distant and so theoretical, you could almost shape it just by wishing.

"Don't you sometimes wish you'd just wake up and find your life was perfect?" said Squid.

"I think I already did."

Grief lay with his eyes closed, a long piece of yellow grass between his teeth. It was difficult to tell if he was being philosophical, or facetious, or medically imbalanced. However, he seemed content to be there, lying on the prickly grass, oblivious to the lizard crawling through his hair.

"Maybe you were a farmer," said Squid, "with hands like those."

"I'm sure they're golfing calluses."

The shadows gradually lengthened, and the whole field turned to blazing scarlet, giving the rolling hills an end-of-days look. Squid rose to her feet, plucking the grass from her clothes. She could wait for Pearce to find her, but she'd spent too much of her life waiting. Waiting for things to change. Waiting for things to get better. And all the while, things slid further and further from her control.

Time to step forward. Time to take control. Even if it was too little, too late, it was better to go out with a bang than a whimper.

"Time to wind up the tour," said Squid.

*

The van rattled into the slums just as the sun sank into the bay, colouring the rubbish-strewn wasteland in mythical shades of amber and gold. The slums were a place of fallen gods and lost souls, inhabited by the human equivalent of odd socks. These were the offbeat, the insane, and the unattractively diseased, scattered with people who claimed to be the deposed presidents of small, obsolete European nations. Fortunately, the hardcore criminals avoided the slums, being busy running the city.

Squid parked in a clear space fringed with empty barrels and began unloading the sacks of bread. Due to legal liability issues stemming from a case in which a man had choked to death on a poorly mixed chunk of baking soda, bakeries in Baltus City were reluctant to donate their leftover bread to charities. However, Squid saw no problem with dumping the bread in a place where the homeless might, at their own risk, eat it.

"Hey, Squid! Any ginger loaf this week?" boomed a broad-shouldered Asian man known as Lee Fifteen.

For a while, the slums had tried names like Tall Lee and Fat Lee, but unless you had them all lined up, it was difficult to tell which you were talking to. It had also led to some unpleasant conflicts, mostly involving the people who made up names like Fat Lee.

Squid tossed a loaf to Lee Fifteen and noticed that he was sporting a black eye and a limp. This wasn't unusual in the slums, but Lee Fifteen was a pretty genial guy, better known for defusing fights than getting into them.

"What happened to you?" said Squid.

"Couple of guys swung by yesterday, asking questions about a stolen car," said Lee Fifteen.

A shiver passed over Squid.

"Pearce's guys?"

Lee Fifteen shrugged. "Not the usual suspects. A blond thug and a woman with freaky eyes—like a dog who got kicked when it was a puppy, and it's holding a serious grudge. The rest looked like your typical walking fists."

"What did they want to know?"

"If anyone knew anything about the car. If they saw anything."

"Did anyone?"

"Don't think so."

Lee Fifteen winked as he started to walk away. "Thanks for the manna, Squid."

"Hey," called Squid. "Where's Kirsk?"

A loose crowd had gathered around the discarded bread. Kirsk was usually one of the first to get here.

"Uh, she's gone away for a bit," said Lee Fifteen.

He couldn't have spelled "evasive" any larger if he'd hired a skywriter, but people had their reasons. You had to respect that. Squid tossed him a bag of broken cookies.

"I saved her some gingerbread men. Just in case you see her."

Squid turned to see Grief working his way through a second apricot Danish.

"Hey! Those are for the homeless," she said.

"I think we count," said Grief.

Although Squid ate less than a bear in winter, she held onto the clear distinction between herself and the people who lived in the slums. She was still "normal". She kind of had a home, and sort of had a job, and mostly ate things that didn't make her sick. But even so, she couldn't help feeling that without Ferret, without Pearce, she'd be another shape huddled around a burning bin, muttering to herself about the good old days. Like Ebit, yakking like he's still on Wall Street. Or Kirsk, boasting about her days at Solomon University.

Grief offered her a dented cupcake, the chocolate icing flaking off.

"I scraped off the fuzzy bits," he said.

Squid sat down beside Grief, watching the locals disperse with their bakery booty.

"You're really going ahead with it?" said Grief.

"My mother took me to a soothsayer once, when I was little," said Squid. "She told me I'd die before I turned twenty-four."

"You don't believe that."

"I don't find it implausible."

Squid took a bite from the cupcake, watching the shoreline sink into twilight.

"That's the thing with soothsayers—no sugar coating," she continued. "Not like those psychics who only tell you the happy stuff, or the stuff that doesn't matter. My mother had a friend who was told by three different soothsayers that she'd die before she turned forty."

"What happened to her?"

"Don't know."

There was a dour pause.

"You really shouldn't tell stories like that unless you have an ending," said Grief. "I don't think I believed in psychics. I think I was more of a science man."

"A science man with expensive tastes."

"Nerds can have great hair."

Narrow columns of smoke rose as evening fires lit up around the slums, the aroma of toasting bread battling with the stink of the bay.

"I think I read a study once that said the best predictor of someone's lifespan was how long they thought they'd live for," said Grief.

"That sounds like a really badly controlled study."

Grief drew his foot along the cracked dirt.

"I think it means you have to want to live."

"Believe me," said Squid, rising to her feet, "that's not the problem."

They swung by the parking lot outside the Fess, siphoning an unlucky car to refill the van.

"If you ever need quick cash and don't mind a little blood on your hands, the Fess is the place," said Squid.

The Confessional was technically a bar, but you didn't come here for the cheap booze. It was partly a meeting place and partly a trading post for the shifting population of middle-tier criminals. Need henchmen in a hurry? Need to offload some nuclear material before it literally burns a hole in your pocket? The Fess is the place.

They returned the van with a full tank and a scribbled thank-you note. Squid liked to think it made a difference—that the effort to acknowledge, communicate, apologise, somehow humanised the act a little. But she'd been lying to herself for so long, it was hard to tell if it made a difference to anyone but herself.

The call came at eleven on the dot.

"Pier twelve. Hanley Wharf" was all Ferret said.

Squid stood beneath the street lamp, looking at the blank face of the phone.

"Time's up," she said, trying to smile, and not sure why.

"I'll come with you," said Grief.

She smiled wryly at his serious expression.

"The advantage of being a loner is that you don't get other people involved in your personal apocalypse."

"How heroic," said Grief, his tone dry enough to dehydrate a watermelon.

"You know, it's going to drive me crazy for eternity that I never found out who you were. Maybe if you stare into the distance, you'll have a flashback."

Squid looked at Grief expectantly, but all she saw were his eyes blinking back at her.

Somehow, she had been expecting a more dramatic goodbye. She didn't need him to be an obnoxiously wealthy tech tycoon, or the prince of some small but respectable nation, but something, anything, would have been enough.

"Thank you," said Grief. "For today."

And that was it.

"Do I get a goodbye hug?" said Grief as Squid jogged away.

"Go home, Grief," called Squid over her shoulder. "Go home."

*

It was crunching towards midnight and Casey had hit a dead end. She was hoping if she hit it hard enough, she'd punch through to the other side, but all she had was the mental equivalent of bruised fists.

It was graveyard shift at her end of the station. All the real work was happening in the operations wing and on the streets. Casey flicked through the tabs on her screen, her eyes blurry from reading and rereading the same information. Werner had already vanished from the Chival's tenant history, and his university records had been wiped clean. If Casey hadn't already printed hard copies, she'd swear the boy had never existed. Her colleagues snickered at her notepad and pen, but if anyone wanted to erase her notes, they had to get within punching distance first.

Information seemed to be a fuse that burned as quickly as it was laid, winding and looping around itself in this endless race against the darkness. You could make people disappear in this city before the bodies were even cold. Pearce and Verona had erased their own trails so long ago that no one even knew what they looked like.

Rumours birthed more rumours, and Pearce had been every nationality, every age, and had even changed gender a few times. It seemed impossible to catch something you couldn't see, something you didn't know, something that strode the city in myth and violence. Loose talk and speculation had become a swamp of misdirection, and

Pearce obviously liked it that way.

There were certainly more rumours than facts in the Werner case. Some said it was payback by Verona, who'd tried to recruit Werner before he joined Pearce. Others said he'd fallen victim to the secret vigilante group who were taking out the top talent one by one. And still others said Werner had seen something, heard something that he wasn't supposed to.

Casey flipped over the piece of tape from Werner's apartment, looking at the line of digits again. Too long for a phone number or a locker combination. Cryptic letters from a dead man.

"Working late, Casey?"

Deus leaned against the wall, the silent corridor stretching behind him. Casey was pretty sure he had no business in this section at this hour, which reinforced her "making life difficult" theory.

"Just following up some leads," said Casey.

It wasn't exactly lying. It was like telling people you were allergic to cats because you didn't want them putting their pet kitten on your head. It was situational management.

"Need any help?" said Deus.

His expression remained carefully neutral. This had the effect of making Casey more suspicious than if he'd oozed sarcasm.

"I'm good. Thanks."

Deus glanced over the half-sorted piles of papers and folders, as though visually grading them. For all Casey knew, he wrote tidiness reports for Gale. Casey kept her hand casually closed over Werner's scrap of paper.

"You won't find the killer by wading through paperwork," said Deus.

"How would you find the killer?"

Deus smiled, and it was like a flash of razor wire.

"Just let me know if you need any help," he said, giving a brief wave as he continued down the corridor.

# SEVEN

She expected there to be gunslinger music, like in a one-saloon town at high noon. Squid stood on the rise overlooking Hanley Wharf: a towering maze of shipping containers sprawling all the way to water's edge. Gigantic cranes stood motionless, blotting out the stars in mechanical silhouettes.

No ships came in after curfew, but cargo was still discreetly moved before inspections in the morning. Squid hoped this last job didn't involve anything infectious, or explosive, or both. She imagined there might be some Goliath of a henchman she'd have to fight, or a bomb she'd have to throw herself over. Or maybe Pearce had an old friend in need of a new heart. Or a vampire buddy in need of fresh blood.

As Squid made her way through the narrow maze, a distant path of starlight threading overhead, she started having second thoughts. And third, fourth and fifth thoughts. In fact, the whole "taking responsibility" thing was beginning to sound like the ravings of someone who'd had too much fungus on their cupcake.

Just as she was wondering what the weather in Colombia was like, an arm dragged her into the shadows, a hand clamped over her mouth. She caught the faint scent of basil and fresh earth.

"You're late," said Ferret, his voice low.

He released Squid and indicated that she should follow him quietly.

"Sorry," whispered Squid. "I got stuck behind a bus."

This was technically true. While throwing up behind a vintage double-decker on Fourth Street, Squid's sleeve had gotten caught on the quaint wrought-iron number plate. Aside from having to take an unwilling detour along the bus route, she'd eventually lost half her sleeve.

"Verona has a ship docking at pier seventeen in twenty-three minutes," said Ferret. "A twenty-foot container with the shipping mark *VBT* will be unloaded onto a truck with falsified cargo plates. Your job is to get that truck and the container to Drop-Off Forty-Seven. Whatever it takes."

It sounded pretty simple, which meant it was undoubtedly fatal. The fact that Pearce was trying to snatch a shipment from Verona was a particularly disturbing sign.

"What's in the container?"

"Just get it to the drop-off," said Ferret.

They paused behind a barricade of rusted red containers, and Squid choked as she glimpsed the pier through the forest of corrugated steel.

The pier crawled with Verona's sharply suited minions guiding the unlit ship to shore. There must have been at least a hundred personnel and twice as many guns. Ferret and his unseen crew must have already dealt with the perimeter guards, but this wasn't much help to Squid.

Her target, an unassuming white truck, sat in the loading zone at least three hundred feet away, behind a gauntlet of guards to rival the days of open gangland warfare. And in the middle of it all, making rapid signals to coordinate the activity, was a very familiar figure.

Mal.

The hairs on Squid's arms stood on end, like a deeply uncomfortable Mexican wave travelling across her skin. She wondered how far she'd get before they bothered to shoot her, or if Mal would let her get real close before doing the honours with a set of bare knuckles and a smile. Squid felt her stomach lurch.

The battered green shipping container was lowered onto the waiting tray, landing with a dull clang.

"On my mark," said Ferret.

"What? There's a mark?"

The truck's locking mechanism clamped onto the container, and an escort of glossy black cars prepared to form a convoy. Ferret glanced at his watch.

"Go."

Ferret's arm swung out of his coat, aiming across the crowded pier. Mal jerked back suddenly, and everything seemed to go into slow motion, the world falling silent except for Squid's hollow breathing. Mal's head snapped towards her, a streak of red across his cheek, his arm already raised. A line of bullet holes rushed across the container towards Squid, and then she was running.

Bullets flew across the pier as Verona's crew darted for cover, returning fire. Chips of concrete stung Squid's legs as she raced towards the truck, amazed at every second she remained alive. They said the army discouraged recruits from playing paintball, as it made them realise how easy it was to get shot. Not like in the movies, where you could dodge a bullet or outrun a machine gun.

She never heard the bullet coming, because at that moment, a figure barrelled into her, sending them both crashing into the side of a nearby car.

"Argh," bleated Squid, wondering if this was how it all ended.

"Let me guess: you have no idea why all these people are shooting at you," said Grief.

Squid ducked as another hail of bullets passed overhead.

"What are you doing here?" she said.

"You're not hard to find. I just followed the trail of angry people."

Grief held out a scrap of torn sleeve. After a pause, he dabbed at Squid's nose. She snatched the rag from him.

"Don't do that."

The windscreen shattered above them in a starburst of glass, and across the docking zone, the truck pulled away. Convoy or no convoy, the driver wasn't sticking around. Every split second was crucial, and Squid's feet took over as she sprinted towards the retreating container. The truck picked up speed as it headed for the road—once it hit the bitumen, she wouldn't stand a chance.

Everything greyed out around her: the spray of empty cartridges, figures yelling frantic instructions, the obligatory explosions as barrels spilled in the melee. The only thing that mattered was the truck.

Her entire life had amounted to less than a spatter on the sidewalk. She had created nothing. Excelled at nothing. Moved no one. In the end, *this* was all she was good at. But it was her curtain call, and she'd bloody well give them something to remember.

Squid leapt, arms outstretched. By some quirk of physics related to what happens if you shine a torch while on a train travelling at the speed of light in an alternate universe, Squid's hands closed on metal handles. She lost a shoe to the hungry road before she pulled her feet onto the edge of the tray, and she almost lost her head to a lunging lamppost.

As she edged her way forward, pressing herself into one corrugated groove after another, the truck swerved maniacally all over the road. The driver was either determined to swipe off his unwelcome passenger, or he was having an epileptic fit in the cabin.

She hoped it was the latter, although she felt a little guilty at this. It'd certainly solve the problem of how she was going to wrest control of the vehicle from an armed Verona henchman. The truck took a bend at breakneck speed, and Squid's fingers started to slide from the side of the container. Her fleeting thought, as one hand lost traction, was that she had to admire the way the guy was taking the corners.

This thought lasted precisely the length of time it took for the other hand to come free. Squid threw herself across the final gap and clung to the door of the cabin, fingers gripping the handle for dear life. She stared in the window and absorbed the scene like a snapshot.

The driver turned, his face a shock of bloodshot eyes, his pallor grey as a corpse. From the darkness beside him, a gun aimed at Squid. There was actually a heavyset man attached to the gun, but all Squid saw was the finger pulling the trigger.

A strange thing happened then. Just before Squid ducked, the window behind the heavyset man shattered inwards, and he seemed to just slurp out through the jagged gap, away into the night. She heard a heavy *bang* echo along the container, then an awful crunch, and a ragged scream fading along the road behind her.

Squid clung to the door, her heart pounding against the metal. She supposed this was why they called it "one last job". She pulled herself up in time to see a figure sliding in through the opposite window, landing in the newly vacated seat.

"Want me to clear a spot for you?" said Grief, smiling at Squid, but there was something odd about his smile, something cold and unfamiliar.

Squid glanced at the driver, who clung grimly to the wheel like a man praying for deliverance. The flash of a passing streetlight illuminated his profile.

"Bravo?" said Squid, squeezing into the cabin.

"Argh..." said Bravo weakly.

"Bravo McKay...?"

Squid was pretty excited to see the ex-racing legend in person, but this was vastly outweighed by the sheer terror of impending death. She could have asked him how he'd gotten into a mess like this, but she already knew the answer. People fell into trouble, and no one owned trouble like Pearce.

"How about we pull over, and you get out and tell them that I pushed you?" said Squid. "I could punch you in the face if it'd help?"

Squid actually wasn't sure if she could punch someone in the face, especially not someone like Bravo. The only person she'd ever punched was Mal, and that hadn't been in the face.

"I can't," said Bravo. His eyes seemed to float in pockets of shadow.

Another flash of lamplight, and Squid saw the tangle of wires. Red wires, black wires, urgent-looking yellow wires, streaming out from the console and wrapping around Bravo's wrists, crawling under his shirt.

"If I get out of this seat, my heart's going to explode," said Bravo.

Squid let out a slow breath, her eyes racing along the interwoven wires. This was way out of her league, but if she could somehow create a dummy loop by diverting the primary signal—

Before she could react, Grief grabbed a fistful of wires and yanked them clean from the guts of the truck. Bravo gave a hollow gasp, and sparks fizzled briefly through the cabin.

"That setup won't make your heart explode," said Grief. "I could show you a setup that'd make your heart explode, but pray I never do. So, are you going to jump or should we make this fun?"

Squid stared at Grief, and it was like looking at a stranger. Gone were the bright, friendly eyes, and in their place was the kind of expression you saw on posters under WANTED: DEAD OR ALIVE.

Bravo was obviously thinking the same thing as he pushed past Squid, groping for the cabin door. Squid slammed her foot on the brake, trying to hold onto the panicked man.

"Wait!" she said.

The truck squealed to a crawl and Bravo tumbled out the door, rolling away into the darkness.

"Argh…"

What Squid wanted to do was paste herself against the cabin door and scream, "What the hell is wrong with you?" to the person who looked like Grief. However, she had tried this tactic with various people on numerous occasions and found it to be generally unhelpful.

Squid slid into the driver's seat and stomped on the accelerator.

Nothing happened.

The truck continued to roll slowly forward, threatening to come to a complete halt. Squid's eyes flashed across the console, taking in the retinal camera and the dermal pads on the steering wheel.

Grief sagged a little in his seat.

"I feel funny," he said.

Squid didn't have time to explore the exact meaning of "funny". The damned ID recognition was missing half its guts, and they'd custom-jumped the engine for a single run. If she couldn't get this baby started, they'd be sitting ducks when the—

Grief turned around, somehow sensing the mob of lights before they crested the rise. The convoy was catching up.

Squid's hands were a blur. She hardly knew what she was doing, but she hoped her fingers did. She could hear the hum of engines approaching. Grief drew a pistol from his belt and hunched against the door, watching as the lights flowed down the freeway.

"Where'd you get that?" said Squid.

"The other guy didn't need it."

The truck suddenly jolted, and for a moment, Squid thought they'd been hit. Then a familiar purr rumbled up beneath her feet, and she could have cried for a hundred different reasons. She practically stood on the accelerator, the truck creaking forward as it strained under its mysterious cargo.

The lights of the Baltus Bay Bridge loomed ahead, like archways to another world. If she made it to the other side, she could lose them in the dilapidated runs of the East Quarter. But she wasn't going to make it across the bridge.

The truck was only hitting forty now, and the growl of a dozen cars jumping the tar was closing fast. Squid desperately wired and rewired the gears, scraping for a touch more power.

"I'm sorry for using your toothbrush," said Grief quietly.

"That's not important now."

They thundered over the grid and onto the bridge, arches of light sweeping overhead. The convoy roared off the freeway behind them, less than eight hundred feet away and gaining.

"We're not going to make it," said Squid.

There was an odd silence.

"No. But you will."

Grief flung open the passenger-side door and leaned out into the ripping air, one hand gripping the edge of the frame. He grinned like he was tacking into the wind on an azure day.

"Drive, Squid. Just drive."

And then he jumped.

"Grief!"

Squid almost swerved off the bridge, scraping jagged tears along the barrier before screeching back onto the road. She stared in the rearview mirror and saw a lone figure standing on the bridge, silhouetted in the headlights of the approaching convoy.

She heard gunshots. A scream of tyres and the crunch of metal. A cold, hollow feeling filled her chest, and she didn't look back after that.

*Just drive.*

A knot of suburbs flashed past, mailboxes flying as her pursuers tried to close the gap. They chased her through the industrial zone, and she lost a few to the uncovered pits and unstable walls.

A bullet took out her side mirror, and Squid had the disconcerting feeling that she was driving with blinkers on. In the strange delirium of her mind, it seemed like a metaphor or a message.

You couldn't look back, only forward. What lay behind you didn't matter, if it even existed. All that you were, all that you could have been, were just broken bits of mirror on the side of the road. What you were now was a ten-tonne truck screaming through the city with a payload the crime lords of Baltus wanted really, really badly.

*So, whatcha gonna do, Squid?*

*Just drive.*

*

Ferret watched the blinking dot moving farther and farther towards the edge of his screen. If he had to scroll to the next segment of the map, he was going to be very cross. He was certain that Squid was aware of this, which was possibly why the dot was moving faster than a fully loaded truck ought to be able.

Ferret shot another sniper as he strode to his car, wondering if he should wear a scarf reading BOSS MONSTER so random punks could level up before they tried their luck. Ferret pulled away from the firefight—his cleanup crew would tell him who won.

He had some retrenching to do.

*

The city was a howling blur.

Squid felt like an astronaut, launching into space with the sneaking suspicion that she was on the wrong ship. Her leg had locked into position, the entire truck rattling fit to come apart. Still, she kept her eyes ahead, as though all the host of Hell were on her back.

It was therefore slightly surreal when flames began to lap at the cabin doors. Squid risked a glance out the window, and a bullet punched through the frame inches from her face.

The truck was on fire.

They must have punched the fuel tank with a bloody kuzi shell, and she was lucky the whole rig hadn't exploded. The entire undercarriage blazed, and the steering was starting to go. You didn't have to know about engines to recognise the dying scream of a vehicle about to take everyone with it.

It took her a moment to realise that the odd metallic thudding was coming from the container. Or, rather, from on top of the container. For a strange, crazed moment, she thought it might be Grief, doing something equally strange and crazed. But then someone started shooting her a new sunroof, and Squid knew it was time to take a bow.

She thundered through the slums for the last time, the span of the bay glittering beneath a clear sky. She took the final corner like a Tokyo drifter, the skin coming off her fingers as she fought to hold the wheel in position. Unfortunately, you couldn't really drift a twenty-foot truck around a hairpin bend, and Squid felt the shaft snap loose, the cabin tilting in that horribly inexorable way.

She wasn't sure how many times the truck rolled, skidding across the ground in a moving inferno. The container smashed open, the doors twisting off and spilling its cargo through the slums.

Eyeballs.

Hundreds of thousands of bionic eyeballs rolled from the container like a wave of gumballs pouring from a candy machine.

*At least it isn't full of orphans destined for organ farms,* thought Squid woozily as the truck smashed through the concrete siding and into the black embrace of Baltus Bay.

*

He'd used up his cartridges on five tyres and a windscreen, but after the first car hit the pylon, he found himself with a few more rounds.

Grief had been hoping for a pile-up, although he'd expected to cause it by falling under the wheels of the first car. His instincts had different ideas.

It had been terrifying and exhilarating and disturbing. He'd watched himself take careful aim, diving for cover as the first few cars crashed into the concrete barriers. Torn suits spilled from the wrecks, bullets ricocheting around Grief like a thunderstorm of brass.

When a fresh mob of cars blazed onto the bridge, Grief's life flashed before his eyes, and it had been disappointingly short. Mostly, it consisted of being snapped at by Squid, and he wanted so much more. Not the snapping, but the living.

He wanted peach tea gelatos on a terrace overlooking the sea. He wanted to cruise along the boardwalk when it was so hot, your sandals melted. He wanted to curl up in bed with a mug of hot chocolate, listening to the rain pummel against the glass.

He wanted… He wanted…

He wanted memories, but he wanted to *make* them.

The gunfire intensified, but surprisingly, it wasn't directed at him. Grief stole a glance around the pylon and saw his assailants opening fire on the new arrivals. Pearce's crew had joined the party.

The bridge turned into an open rumble, a dramatic three-sixty of flapping coats and smoking cars, double-gun action and stunts that really shouldn't happen without a bluescreen.

Grief felt that this was his cue to leave, and he didn't realise he'd let his guard down until he turned and saw the blond man about to shoot him in the head.

It was a terrible moment.

For both of them.

The blond man froze—for just a fraction of a second but enough for Grief to wrench the gun away from him. In almost the same moment, the man produced another gun, but his whole arm shook.

A gasp gurgled all the way through the blond man, words strangling their way up his throat.

"You… I wasn't… I didn't…" said the man.

Grief knew he should shoot. It was clearly a standoff only one of them would survive, and Grief didn't want to die like this. He wasn't sure how, or when, or if he wanted to die at all, but this wouldn't make the top one hundred.

The problem was, Grief didn't know if he could kill a man. If he could look him in the eyes and pull the trigger.

A deafening explosion suddenly rocked the bridge, and Grief saw a flare of hellish light below. On the distant edge of the bay, the truck—Squid's truck—exploded into tendrils of flame. It rolled towards the edge—

*No.*

—leaving a trail of burning debris scattered along the banks, skidding forward with unstoppable momentum—

*Please.*

—it tore up the concrete like hands gouging out a fresh grave—

*Oh, God.*

—plunging into the bay with an almighty crash. Even from the bridge, Grief could see the foamy white tides rippling across the black waters, and the darkness swallowed up the flickering light.

Grief turned to the man with cold, malevolent eyes.

He had his answer.

*

It was officially the worst day of her life.

Squid squelched out of the bay, shivering, gagging, and smelling of dead pigeons. Luckily for Squid, she was fairly used to extracting herself from burning cars, sinking cars, cars filling with poisonous gases. Burning trucks full of eyeballs was a new one, but if the container had been full of nuclear warheads, it'd be a completely different story.

She was wondering how long it'd take Ferret to find her when a distant scream carried across the water. It was a horrible sound, full of terror and gut-wrenching anticipation. A figure fell from the bridge, like a tiny doll plummeting towards the hard, flat water.

They said it was like hitting concrete, falling from a height like that. She wanted to close her eyes before the figure hit the water, but she made herself watch, all the way down. In a way, you could pretend it wasn't real if you didn't see it happen. If you closed your eyes at the last moment, you could call it an obscure death.

But life wasn't like that. If you pretended death didn't happen, it kept on happening. If you blocked your ears and hummed, you wouldn't hear them when they came for you. So, you watched, and listened, and survived. Even if it meant you saw things that turned you inside out.

And now, it was her turn.

She heard him this time and wondered if it was a courtesy, although she hardly warranted it now.

"Ferret," said Squid.

It seemed that he stood in a shadow of his own creation, pooled around him like a fallen cloak. His expression was one of cold disappointment.

"That was nowhere near Drop-Off Forty-Seven."

Squid stared at the muddy ground. She knew how this story ended. She couldn't say it had been fun, but it had been hers. To the bitter end. Cheers.

"For what it's worth, I'm sorry I couldn't repay you," said Squid.

As last words went, they were pretty lousy. But if they carved it on her headstone, at least they'd know it was hers. Hot tears trailed down her face, but she told herself it was just allergies.

Ferret gave a short, hard sigh, his hands deep in his pockets.

"I can't promise no one will come after you," said Ferret. "I can't promise *I* won't come after you."

His words sank in slower than a feather through cold maltose.

"Huh?" said Squid.

"You wanted out. You're out."

Squid had just lost a truckload of eyes, and they were letting her walk. It wasn't just unexpected; it was damned near impossible. Admittedly, Verona had just been cheated of a crucial payload, which counted as a win for Pearce, but still…

Squid took a few tentative steps away, expecting an exit wound to bloom from her chest. She glanced over her shoulder, but Ferret was already gone.

"Enjoy your new life, Squid." His words hung in the humid air.

The world seemed eerily dreamlike, as though Squid had fallen through the looking glass and crashed through a dozen psychedelic worlds before landing here. Everything looked the same, but—

She was free.

Her elation was short-lived, as footsteps pounded in her direction. Most of the eyeballs had already been pocketed by the quick-fingered homeless—it was like throwing a leg of ham onto a nest of army ants. There wasn't enough left for Verona's team to worry about, and hopefully everyone thought Squid was dead. Especially Mal.

Squid ducked behind a crate of plastic rafflesias just to be safe. A man sprinted towards the edge of the bay, his arms coming together as he prepared to dive.

"Grief?"

He skidded to a stop, one hand reaching for his hip. His expression turned to breathless surprise.

"Squid?"

He moved towards her, and Squid took several steps back.

"You still have a gun?" she said.

"No, I…"

Grief looked down at himself, as though not entirely sure.

"No. Sorry, I don't know why I did that."

Grief looked at the mangled trail gouging into the bay, then back at Squid, a clump of seaweed still wrapped around her ankle.

"How did you…?"

"It's an occupational hazard," said Squid.

Grief continued to stare at Squid, and she suspected there was something clinging to her shirt that was seeing dry land for the first time.

"Are you okay?" said Grief.

Squid thought about this question for the first time in a long while. A breeze blew in from the outskirts of the city, carrying the faintest scent of open country.

"Let's go home," she said.

*

Holographic screens hovered around Verona like a fractured hall of mirrors, faces blinking on and off, replaced by charts and scrambled footage.

"Casualty report," said Verona.

"Capacity at Mercy, switching to Saint Aloise," said a pale face on one of the screens.

"Triage to Victory. They're closer and newly allied," said Verona. "Targus, regroup to Sirius. Clef, coordinate recovery. Sebel, I want a report on the cleanup at zero three hundred."

Verona flicked the screens to one-way streaming. The value of that experimental cargo could have funded her entire operation for six months and secured the loyalty of eighteen strategic officials.

She had realised long before that you could deal in drugs and petty crime, but you needed volume to get any kind of return. And you ended up killing most of your clientele, one way or the other.

However, you only needed one bionic eye, or one artificial lung, to recoup your costs a hundredfold. And your clientele survived much longer, and would need your services again and again. Crime didn't have to be about suffering. It could be about… opportunity.

Pearce had obviously come to a similar conclusion, but this hadn't been an opportunistic scuffle. This wasn't about turf. This was a declaration of open war.

Either Pearce was more confident than she'd given him credit for, or he was panicked about something. She'd like to think that something had forced his hand, that he was trying to distract her from something far more serious. But there was a good chance Pearce had weighed the odds and decided that they settled firmly in his favour.

A new face logged onscreen, a flashing red icon in the corner. Verona sighed, swiping her finger through the *Answer* corner.

"Mal, report," said Verona.

A streak of blood dragged down one cheek, and assorted cuts and bruises decorated his face. He looked like a kid who'd just buried another child in the sandpit and was now being told to come inside and practise the violin.

"Squid," said Mal.

Verona couldn't tell if he was swearing or trying to communicate something. She settled for a "please clarify" expression.

"She was part of the ambush," said Mal.

"The low-level car thief?"

"Her accomplice was there, too," growled Mal. "Took out six bloody cars and their cameras."

"Their cameras?"

"By the time the rear caught up, he was bunkered behind a pylon." Mal spat the word as though someone had erected those pylons just to piss him off.

"Assist Clef with the recovery. I want to see all the footage from the convoy."

Mal logged out, still scowling. Unless he was punching something into atoms, he had the attention span of a dead goldfish. However, Verona would have plenty of work for him soon.

If Pearce wanted a war, she'd give him a war. No one believed the truce would last, but Pearce had been the one to break it.

# EIGHT

Everything looked crisper, brighter, more in focus. Even the air smelled better—like fresh bread and nectarines. Squid looked up at the blank night sky, and she could almost see the stars.

"They just let you go?" said Grief. "They didn't strap anything to you that had a timer on it?"

"You sound almost disappointed that I didn't get whacked."

"Did you want me to check anyway?" Grief eyed Squid with a worried expression.

"Keep your eyes on the road, buddy. They didn't make me drink anything. They didn't implant anything. They didn't make any suspiciously morbid puns. Then again, I didn't get a gold watch with my name on it, but I can live with that."

"I think that would count as something with a timer on it."

The streets were silent in that null hour before dawn, when early risers had yet to wake, and night-lifers had crawled home to crash.

"I'm free," said Squid, taking a deep breath. "I'm alive. Everything feels so much lighter."

"It's the low blood sugar."

"I said I'm fine."

"You're not walking in a straight line."

"It's called evasive manoeuvring."

As much as Squid would have liked to believe that Grief was bursting with concern for her, he was chasing a line of questions that took them further from the ones Squid wanted to ask.

"That Dumpster looks pretty fresh. Should we grab breakfast?" said Grief.

Now, *that* was evasive manoeuvring.

"What happened back there?" said Squid. "In the truck."

"I guess I watched too many bad action movies." Grief tried to smile, but it wobbled off his face.

In Squid's opinion, action movies could teach you to talk trash, but they couldn't teach you to drag a ninety-kilo man through a broken window while clinging to the side of a speeding truck.

They stepped across the dim threshold of Prosperity Mansions.

"I'm sorry if I… upset you," said Grief. "Hey, don't you have a toy just like that?"

A scarred man strolled past with a plush brown octopus in his hands.

"Hey! Where'd you get that?" said Squid.

"Management's evicted another tenant. All the good stuff's already gone," said the man.

Squid snatched the octopus from him and sprinted up the stairwell, like someone running to the scene of an accident, several hours too late. She apprehended a few more stragglers on the way, recovering a broken clock, an old T-shirt, a deflated beach ball, and a small pot of deranged bamboo.

She was breathless by the time she reached the twenty-seventh floor, but the show was already over. Her door had been boarded shut, as though the landlord had felt it more important to keep her out than to get a new tenant. Squid kicked at the door for a while, yelling furious streams of abuse until she sank exhausted to her knees.

Grief sat down beside her, waiting for the tears to subside.

"I'll find a bag for your things," he said gently. "We'll find the rest of your stuff."

"It's allergies," hiccupped Squid. "I'm fine."

She told herself the pain would subside. They were just things. But through the long, dark nights, through the nightmarish days, they'd been so much more. They'd been her memories. Pieces of colour she could hold. Reminders of a life that wasn't buried in hopeless regrets.

Now her memories had been scattered to the winds, her identity already fading. It was important to remember, to understand what went wrong, to recognise what you'd done right. To cherish the good moments as well as the bad, because they made you who you were.

"Are you getting any of this?" said Squid, wondering why there were daisies floating from the ceiling.

Grief's expression was like that of a nurse gently guiding a senile patient back to bed.

"How about we get some breakfast, and then we'll just take things a step at a time?" said Grief, slowly leading Squid back out into the breaking dawn.

*

Over the years, Ducabre had risen through the ranks of Pearce's organisation with remarkable speed, which made him someone to be reckoned with. Ferret, on the other hand, was one of the longest-serving operators in the organisation, which said volumes about his survival skills.

The office crackled with subtle assessment and delicate challenge.

"That was a very expensive shipment," said Ducabre.

"I'm sure Verona will be very disappointed," said Ferret.

"As is Pearce."

Ferret wanted to casually ask "Where is Pearce, by the way?" but that would have been a step too far. There was a reason the floor of Ducabre's office was permanently covered in plastic sheets. Ferret remained sensibly silent.

"Have the parties responsible been appropriately disciplined?" said Ducabre.

"The driver no longer works for us," said Ferret.

"I trust that's a euphemism."

"I believe permanent termination wasn't necessary."

Ducabre's eyes were like lead shot, dull and dangerous.

"Do explain."

"I believe her skills will prove useful in the future."

If there were a record for the longest period of time without blinking, they'd both be on the scoreboard.

There was a sharp knock at the door.

"Watch yourself, Ferret," said Ducabre. "Pearce doesn't tolerate failure for long."

Ferret passed the head of Security on his way out. She didn't even look at him as she strode by, but she'd probably scanned him for weapons, height, weight and body-bag dimensions, nonetheless.

Ferret paused in the corridor and overheard a snatch of conversation through the closed doors. This was mostly due to the listening device he was pressing to the polished oak.

*"Jace is dead."* Rojin's voice. *"There was an unidentified combatant on the bridge—not one of Verona's. Not one of ours."*

*"Motive?"*

*"Unclear."* Rojin again. *"Jace was the only one who got a good look at him. He was wearing some kind of jersey with a name on it—"*

Ferret moved away as footsteps approached, and he gave the security camera a wink. He'd learned long ago that if you chose not to terminate someone, it occasionally created an unspoken debt that could be recovered in all kinds of ways.

You just needed patience.

*

She didn't know how long she slept. Squid had vague memories of a chocolate bar being pushed into her hand, and she might have eaten it. Or maybe she'd just dreamed that she'd eaten it.

She woke on a sheet of cardboard, her muscles stiff and aching. The narrow lane smelled of raw fish, but then again, that might have been her. Squid picked up the plush octopus lying beside her, looking into its black, bulging eyes.

"Look, it's a Squid holding an octopus!" said Grief.

Squid's expression turned into a series of horizontal lines. Grief beamed and continued to style his hair in the silver reflection of a chocolate wrapper.

"So, are we homeless now?" said Grief, proceeding to floss with the wrapper.

"No. We're… We're just going to find the rest of my stuff, and then we'll get a new place."

*A better place. A place with a kitchen and a window and a hot tub.* Squid pressed her lips into a wavering line. She got to her feet, and Grief tucked the piece of cardboard under his arm.

"You're taking that with you?" said Squid.

"Not that I don't have confidence in your housing plan, but it took me ages to find this."

It was a cloudy, muggy day, carrying the promise of summer storms. Squid had no idea how she was going to get her possessions back, having no money, no job, and nothing to trade except maybe Grief, although she hadn't told him about that part yet.

The first stop was Chinatown, with its bustling trade of ill-gotten goods. The alleys bristled with pawn shops, and they got their first hit after only fourteen stops.

"Squid," said the middle-aged woman behind the counter, her expression the equivalent of someone slapping a bat meaningfully in their palm.

"Why does everyone say your name like that?" whispered Grief.

"Hey, Fletch, how much for that?" said Squid, pointing to a palm-sized cushion with a badly embroidered jellyfish. Squid had sewn that in second grade, and no one had ever accurately guessed the picture.

"Seven bucks," said Fletch.

Squid couldn't imagine the cushion being worth that much unless there was eight dollars sewn inside. She searched for words that would somehow involve her getting the cushion without actually imparting any money.

Fletch crossed her arms with a slightly unpleasant smile.

"How about your friend gives me a massage and I'll let you have the cushion?" said Fletch.

Squid gaped when she realised Fletch was being serious.

"She wouldn't get much for seven bucks," muttered Grief. His smile faded at Squid's expression. "You're not serious."

Squid looked at the cushion. It was just a cushion. Just a cushion she'd made in second grade, that had survived with her through grade school, high school, a family implosion and six years of hell.

"You offered me a foot massage the other night," said Squid.

"Well that was you, and I thought you wanted one."

"I was trying to push your head away from the couch with my foot!"

Grief frowned. "Fine. I'll do it. But then you have to give me a massage."

Squid stared at the cushion through the foggy glass. Her first day of going straight, and she was already pimping out her homeless amnesiac. She let out a slow breath, and in her mind, the battered cushion went up in a plume of smoke.

"Never mind," she said. "We'll save it for the lantern."

The remainder of the afternoon passed in slightly awkward silence, and although they located a veritable community of Squid's former possessions, the lantern remained elusive.

"What's so special about the lantern?" said Grief as they left another unhappy hocker.

"It was a present," said Squid.

It was a memory, one of the best she had. It was her eighth birthday. Nothing spectacular, just a good day. But good days had been rare. She remembered them sitting around a lopsided birthday cake, the lantern burning brightly—brand-new and lacquer red. Her father was laughing, long before he'd left one night with a suitcase and his overcoat. Her mother was cutting the cake, a lifetime before she'd lost the house and moved away.

It was a lantern, luminous and red. It was the memory of happiness.

The memory of hope.

Squid pushed through one final door.

"Trey!" she said.

The man behind the counter looked vaguely like a slouching panther. Any more relaxed and he'd be horizontal.

"Squid, I'm so glad to see you." Trey gave a humourless grin. "You must be here to repay that cash you borrowed."

"You know, about that—"

An object under the glass suddenly caught her eye, and Squid rushed the counter so fast that Trey reached for his shotgun. Squid pressed herself to the cabinet like an affection-deprived puppy in a pet store.

Her watch. Her silver watch. Sitting amidst a dozen other scratched and dented pieces.

"How much for that?" said Squid.

"Two hundred dollars," said Trey.

"It's a twenty-dollar watch!"

"It's not about intrinsic value; it's about demand."

Squid suddenly wished she were a better poker player.

"That'd be a hell of a massage," said Grief under his breath.

Squid ignored him.

"I'll get the money. Just hold it for me. Please?"

"You know I can't," shrugged Trey. "Business is business, and you're hardly my best customer."

"Give me one day," said Squid. "Just one day."

"I've heard it before. Sorry."

The door jangled as they left, Squid's mind writhing with desperate schemes.

"How would you get two hundred bucks in one day, anyway?" said Grief.

Squid didn't reply, standing on the uneven cobbles with a blank expression. It'd be such a cliché to slide straight back into her old life—after all, what else was she good for? But she'd been given a second chance. And everything came at a cost.

It started to rain—heavy, soaking drops that smelled like rust. They stood in the downpour, two drenched figures side by side.

"You're right," said Squid. "It's just junk."

"I didn't—"

"Let's get out of the rain."

*

It seemed as though it rained for days. Or perhaps months. Even years. Squid wondered if she'd turned into one of those eighty-year-old women trapped in their memories, gazing into the mirror and seeing themselves at twenty-three.

Squid looked at Grief, who peered out from under the shop awning, searching for their next potential shelter.

"You haven't aged a day," murmured Squid.

Grief noticed her glazed expression.

"Hey, you still owe me a massage?" he said.

"But I didn't get the cushion!"

"So, *now* you're lucid."

Soon, a broom-wielding shopkeeper forced them to sprint across the street to another leaking stretch of canvas. Unfortunately, this store's preferred deterrent was a motion-triggered air horn, which also had the effect of discouraging customers, but this seemed to be collateral damage the shopkeeper was willing to suffer.

Squid and Grief ended up under a bench in Orchid Park, the rain drumming hard on the wooden slats. The orchids bloomed like mad in the humid weather, and the air hung heavy with their fragrance.

"You know," said Grief, "maybe you should ask Casey for help."

"Asking people for favours is how I got into this mess."

"No, avoiding people until things hit critical is how you got into this mess."

"What are you even still doing here?"

Grief's eyes swam with hurt, and at only three inches away, it filled the frame.

"I mean," said Squid quickly, "why don't you find a better place to hang out? I'm sure some bored rich person would take you in. You have 'amusing enigma' written all over you."

Grief's expression suddenly hardened, and Squid had the feeling she'd just said the wrong thing. Again. She watched the rain bouncing off crimson butterfly orchids, feeling as though she were lying in a coffin.

"We could always move in with your homeless buddies," said Grief.

"No."

The drumming of the rain became a steady throbbing in Squid's head. It was never going to stop raining. It was going to rain until the lakes overflowed and the seas spilled over and washed the world clean of sin.

"Squid? Are you cold?"

"No."

"You're shivering."

"It's from anger," sighed Squid.

"Is this like your allergies?"

Squid closed her eyes. Pride could be a terrible thing, but sometimes it was all you had.

"You have me," said Grief. "Sorry, you were doing that mouth thing—"

"Okay," said Squid. "We'll check in with Casey, but we're not asking for help. Maybe just borrowing a razor."

"Thanks," said Grief. "It stopped being designer stubble a while ago, and now it's just crazy-man beard."

An urgent beeping suddenly pierced the rain, and for a moment, Squid thought some anti-homeless drone had found them. After a few frantic moments and a couple of bruises, Squid realised it was her phone, and she gave it a quick shake to refresh the charge.

"Hello?" said Squid.

"Hey, Squid, still alive?" said Casey.

"Mostly."

"Need to see you. Got a moment?"

"Am I in trouble?"

"You tell me."

Squid swallowed. "Uh, usual place?"

"In an hour. Over."

Squid's mind picked carefully over the possibly incriminating things she'd done recently.

"Do you think it's about the eyeballs?" said Squid.

"You mean driving a burning truck full of stolen goods into the bay is illegal?"

It wasn't August eighteenth yet, but Squid's Get-Out-of-Jail-Free card was falling apart from overuse. Maybe Casey was calling it in.

Pearce had let her walk, but it didn't mean the law would. Maybe it was time to face the music.

*

The rain eased to a misty drizzle, and in the afternoon, it finally stopped. The sky was a wan eggshell blue, streaked with wispy clouds.

Casey was already waiting on the corner of Mills and DeSouza when Squid arrived, her homeless squatter in tow. Squid looked as though she'd been dredged from the bay and only partially resuscitated.

"Squid, I know I say this a lot, but you smell awful," said Casey.

"Well, you didn't have to see me. You could have just written a letter," said Squid.

"I dropped by your apartment."

Squid shifted uncomfortably. "Yeah, I'm kind of between places right now."

Casey glanced at Squid's scruffy companion.

"You still haven't found a good home for him?" said Casey, framing him in her phone. "Look, I can circulate a photo around

Missing Persons, see if—"

Casey bit back a gasp. She'd barely seen him move, but suddenly he was gripping her wrist, the lens of the phone aiming skyward. She reached automatically for her gun, and found his hand already there, clamped firmly over the safety.

"Thanks," said Grief. "But I'm happy with my own investigations."

They stood locked for a moment, and Casey saw the cold warning deep in his eyes.

"Grief…" squeaked Squid.

Her eyes were huge as she pried Grief away. She herded Casey several yards down the street, as though worried proximity might cause some kind of combustion.

"You want to tell me what that was about?" said Casey.

"It's been a rough few days," said Squid, her voice higher than normal. "He's harmless. Maybe a bit mental. Probably a rich eccentric. According to the Auger, he once bought a diamond the size of a Fuji apple. He probably has a thing about photos stealing his mojo. Ha-ha…"

Squid's eyes darted around as though expecting a planet to fall from the sky and flatten her.

"Squid, are you all right?"

She'd seen Squid in all kinds of states, mostly half-starved, hysterically panicked and delirious from sleep deprivation. She seemed to have taken a bite from all three today.

"I'm fine. I'm great."

Casey eyed her dubiously. "You seriously can't go on like this. You've got to get a real job and a real house. And real friends—not just people you find squatting in your apartment."

"You're my friend."

"Until August eighteenth."

Casey knew the importance of deadlines. She'd seen colleagues get too involved, too invested, dragged over the edge for people who kept making excuses instead of changes. But she wanted to believe that

Squid was different.

Years ago, Casey had nosed around the Kabukuri Club, wondering why the precinct hadn't acted on rumours of secret basements and trafficked children. She'd been ambushed about a block from the club, and found herself wedged in a crevice of an alley, trying to return fire while scar-pocked men in silk suits emptied their Tommy guns, turning the brickwork around her into sand. Out of nowhere, a bullet-riddled Charger had smoked past, managing to sideswipe every gunman before disappearing into the smog. Casey hadn't known Squid back then, but she came to recognise that handling, that frantic veering over the moral median strip.

She eyed Squid now, wondering which side of the road she was on today.

"I already quit the gig," said Squid. "I'm going straight now. Like I said I would."

Squid's expression was so eager, so sincere, that Casey could almost believe it.

"You didn't hear it from me," said Casey, "but there's a house on Marley Drive, number twenty-six. Murder-suicide last week, but it's been mostly cleaned. They haven't switched off the water yet."

Casey pulled out her wallet.

"I don't want your money," said Squid.

"Consider it a favour to the Centre for Disease Control. Get yourself some soap and a change of clothes."

Squid reluctantly tucked the money into a damp pocket.

"I heard you're on the Werner case," said Squid.

"Dead ends and brick walls," said Casey. "Don't suppose you know anything?"

Squid shook her head. "Not my department. But you should ask around the slums. They hear more than you think."

Squid squelched away down the street, followed by her companion.

"Hey!" called Casey. "You didn't have anything to do with that bionic eye shipment, did you?"

"Thanks, Casey!" yelled Squid as she disappeared around the corner.

Grief glanced over his shoulder at Casey and, after a pause, gave a smile and a wave before vanishing from view.

# NINE

Twenty-six Marley Drive. Smack bang in the middle of the Hartfield District. Picket fences and friendly neighbours for miles around.

As far as anyone could tell, the Charltons had been perfectly happy. Until Mrs Charlton got up one morning and shot her husband dead while he had his morning smoothie. From what investigators could gather, she then shot their two Pomeranians before turning the gun on herself.

"They seemed like such a nice couple" appeared seventy-three times in the police interview transcripts. There'd been some chatter at the Fess about it. Some people were convinced there was an underworld angle—maybe she was dealing to the local high school. Maybe he was selling classified intel on the side. Verona would have staged it to look like murder-suicide. Pearce would have killed the dogs to make a point. In the end, the general consensus was that it'd been a classic case of suburbia gone wrong.

Most of the blood was gone. You could imagine the couple had just stepped out if it wasn't for the searing smell of industrial bleach. A fringe of camellia trees obscured the house enough for Squid and Grief to open the windows, the scent of summer floating through the sombre house.

Squid chased away her morbid thoughts and wisps of guilt. She couldn't do anything for the dead, but she could still help the living. She could be a better person, lead a better life, and take this chance to be useful to the world. Or, at least, no longer a part of the problem.

It was the first hot shower she'd had in months, and when she finally emerged in a fresh shirt and jeans, she could almost believe that she belonged in that soft cream living room. Grief lay sprawled on the plush carpet.

"I've decided I like houses," he said, sprawling in a different direction. "I can sleep in whatever position I want and not cause an avalanche."

"There are beds, you know," said Squid.

Grief stared at the ceiling thoughtfully. "I've never slept in a bed."

"For all you know, your alter ego sleeps in an emperor-sized bed stuffed with quetzal feathers."

Squid settled tentatively on the buttery leather couch, her gaze drawn to the smiling family photo on the coffee table. She'd spent so long craving normality that she'd forgotten how dysfunctional it was. People weren't designed to get along. Greed, jealousy, fear, hatred. Humans had been smashing each other's heads open since they'd figured out opposable thumbs, and a hundred thousand years later, they'd just found different ways to do it.

"Squid, what would your perfect life be like?" said Grief.

Squid dragged her gaze from the photo.

"A world without people."

"I think that's how evil overlords start."

Squid hugged her knees to her chest. "You never really escape it, do you? People being people to other people. Whether it's in your home or on the streets, your partner or a perfect stranger. You can run, but it's never far enough."

Grief looked across at Squid.

"You only see the bad because you surround yourself with it. But there are people out there doing good, being kind, caring for each other. There are heroes, striving to make the world better. If you wanted that, you could find it. You could create it."

"You don't know that."

"But I believe it. And sometimes, that's just as important."

"You're crazy."

"But loveable."

Squid grumbled as she curled up on the couch, looking through the sunny yellow curtains to the peaceful street outside. She could imagine a life, maybe, of hot meals and soft beds. Of coming home, of feeling safe. A life, maybe, with people. But not too many.

She'd imagined that life before, a long time ago, and she could still feel every closing door like a kick in the face. But she wasn't eighteen anymore, full of helpless angst and desperate bravado. She knew where the other path led, and she wouldn't go back there. Ferret had given her a comma where there should have been a full stop. And from here on in, the story was hers to write.

*Tomorrow will be better*, thought Squid. *Because I'll* make it *better*.

*

Ferret cracked his knuckles, his fingers bending in places that normally shouldn't bend. In the darkened room, a blank screen hung in front of him, and he tapped his fingers across the softly lit keypad. A crosshair of light homed in on his left eye and, almost immediately, a blinking cursor slid across the screen.

*REBIRTH has entered the Sphere.*

An elegantly rendered poker spread materialised onscreen, above a black chat-strip. Canary-yellow text streamed upwards.

*SMUGGLING: You're going down tonight, rust kicka!*

Ferret smirked, his fingers gliding over the keys.

*REBIRTH: Always happy to take your shirt.*

A third player stepped in, Ferrari-red words scrolling into view.

*TECHNOLOGY: Less talk. More action.*

*NARCOTICS has entered the Sphere.*

*SMUGGLING: Game on, ozone sucka!*

Technology dealt. She always dealt, and if you had a problem with that, you found yourself another virtual table. The cards tonight were golden glass, clinking softly on the felt with the grace of a trillion lines of programming. Her whimsy one night had been cards with woodcut images from the Spanish Inquisition. That had been a very short game.

It was a loose ritual, of sorts. All four had crossed paths during their ascent through Pearce's syndicate, developing a certain understanding of one another. No one would ever countenance the word "alliance", but all four knew that a well-placed favour could sometimes save you when an arsenal of tanks could not.

Narcotics won the first hand, sending Smuggling into paroxysms of consonants. Technology took a sweet pot, and Ferret held his own, but Narcotics was on a hot streak tonight.

*SMUGGLING: I'm out. Bunsen's clearly hopped on something.*

*NARCOTICS: I resent that.*

*SMUGGLING: Resent this: <censored>.*

Ferret couldn't be sure if Smuggling had actually typed *<censored>*, or if Technology had introduced stricter language controls after some of their more heated games.

*NARCOTICS: I'll send you something for your temper. A pleasure, as always.*

*NARCOTICS has left the Sphere.*

The cards vaporised into helixes of blue smoke. If you loitered too long after the game, Technology started screening vintage hacker movies while giving an acerbic running commentary. Smuggling never stayed longer than the opening titles.

*SMUGGLING: Hey, Rebirth, heard about the eyeballs-up. Hope the D-Man didn't blow too hard.*

While they all used coded references, Smuggling took things to a whole new level of potentially awkward ambiguity. Ferret had met Smuggling in person and been mildly alarmed to discover that he spoke the same way. The only person even less coherent than Smuggling was Narcotics. However, while Smuggling had the equivalent of a broad psychological accent, Narcotics was just… peculiar.

*REBIRTH: Survived the heat. Something else is burning.*

There was a thoughtful silence, and Ferret wondered if he'd been too obscure.

*SMUGGLING: Staying away from the smoke. But I think it's the ship.*

*SMUGGLING has left the Sphere.*

Ferret felt the faintest chill crawl up his spine. It took a lot to get Smuggling worried, but he'd clearly sensed the wobble in Pearce's chain of command. Things like that were usually resolved quickly, with the weak links devoured by the rising stars. But Ferret couldn't help feeling that for some reason, the weak link was being hidden.

*REBIRTH: Thanks for the eye. Any word?*

This roughly translated to: *Thanks for checking that I came out of Ducabre's office vertically. Did you pick up any interesting news after I left?*

*TECHNOLOGY: Still no light in the circle.*

Ducabre had recently put his office on a private circuit—isolated from Technology's grid. From what Ferret could gather, an odd assortment of offices and storage units at Pearce HQ had gone onto the same private circuit, in a selective information blackout.

Ferret couldn't be sure if Technology was taking it personally. She'd been even more reticent than usual lately, but Ferret had put it down to the Werner incident.

*REBIRTH: Sorry to hear about the boy. I heard he was one of your brightest.*

*TECHNOLOGY: He was.*

Ferret had only met Werner once or twice, when the boy had been assigned to demonstrate the new nimbus jammers. He seemed like a nice kid—a little adrift in his own world, but one of those basically decent people who'd gone badly astray. There were a couple of those in the syndicate, and almost all of them ended up like Werner.

*REBIRTH: It's never easy.*

Ferret never enjoyed meting out consequences, even to those who deserved it. He was of the opinion that it diminished you a little each time, although there were many who believed the reverse. He knew how hard it would have been for Technology to make that call, even if Security took care of the details.

The words unscrolled in dark red.

*TECHNOLOGY: Out of my hands. In the Darc…*

Ferret reread the line. Technology hadn't made the call. Someone had gone over her head, which meant Werner's murder had just gone from housekeeping matter to conspiracy linchpin.

Ferret was no storm chaser, but he knew that if you found the fire before the fire found you, sometimes you could change its direction.

*

It wasn't a scream, but it sounded like it wanted to be.

Squid scrambled from the couch and crashed over the coffee table before she'd even woken up. In a moment of disorientation, she thought she was still caught in a dream, surrounded by squares of blue light framed in floating white gauze.

The darkened living room solidified around her: the polished shelves of souvenirs, the dusty computer desk, the man half-propped on the floor, gasping as though dragged barely alive from a terrifying nightmare.

"Grief?" said Squid.

His eyes turned towards her, but he stared at something else, someplace else. Squid's first instinct was to hide behind the couch, possibly several houses away. Instead, she eased slowly towards Grief, trying not to look at the expression in his eyes.

"It's okay," said Squid. "You're safe."

She reached out hesitantly and patted him awkwardly on the shoulder. To say that Squid wasn't very good at the whole comforting thing would have been a gross understatement verging on the criminally misleading. Grief continued to stare, unseeing, gripped in his night terrors. He struggled with every breath, as though drowning in the darkness.

"Did you want me to switch on the light?" said Squid, shifting to get up.

Grief suddenly wrapped his arms around her, so tight that Squid was convinced it was a wrestling move. He buried his face in her shoulder, and she could feel his whole body shaking.

"Help me…"

The words seemed to come from far away, as though surfacing after an arduous journey through fifty different kinds of hell.

Squid tried to pat Grief on the back, but her arms were pinned to her sides like toothpicks under electrical tape. She settled for repeating "it's okay" in what she hoped was a reassuring tone, and rocking gently back and forth in a way she'd always found calming.

Grief let out a whimper, the tension easing slowly from him until he slumped onto the tangle of blankets.

"Grief?"

Squid crawled out from his arms and cautiously pressed two fingers to his jugular. He shivered, like someone dragged from the water after too long under the ice, his pulse a broken metronome.

She covered him with all the blankets she could find, but still he shivered, his teeth chattering in his restless sleep. Squid eventually crawled under the blankets with him, wrapping an arm around his shoulder.

She didn't know what nightmares haunted Grief, but she understood fear and bravado. She knew what it was like to wake in a cold sweat, sobbing from the sheer futility of your own existence. But through the long dark days, Squid still had her identity, wretched though it was. Your past was an anchor that saw you through the storms and hurricanes of life, giving you a point of reference from which to build your future. She couldn't imagine what it'd be like to be alone and afraid, cut adrift from even your own history.

It hadn't occurred to her to ask where all that blood had come from, that first night. To find out if he was injured or afraid. She hadn't even offered him a Band-Aid. All she'd cared about was getting him off her hands.

Don't ask. Don't reach out. Don't get involved. Squid had spent her life hiding in her shell of isolation, hoping that the world would go away. But the world had a habit of finding you. You could either keep running or you could hug a disturbed amnesiac and hope things looked better in the morning.

Grief's shivering gradually subsided, his breathing growing deep and slow. Squid fell asleep to thoughts of running, but this time, she was chasing the shadows.

*

The screen blinked with a flickerbook of faces, a parade of lost souls staring out at Casey.

Working the Missing Persons department was a lucky dip of stark extremes. For every kid found playing in a neighbour's yard, there were ten shallow graves by the highway. Casey couldn't handle the uncertainty, never knowing which ending you were going to get. With Homicide, the victim was already dead. You could move on. With Missing Persons, there was always hope, and with hope came heartbreak. And too many years of heartbreak could kill you.

Casey skimmed the database, every face like a yearbook photo where the only question that mattered was "Where are they now?" But that wasn't Casey's problem today. Her problem was a man almost faster than Squid and a lot harder to read.

Casey had mocked up an ID Sketch of Squid's mysterious squatter. A trillion computations ran silently through the network, comparing her Sketch with every image in the police database. Criminal records, passports, airport scans, public surveillance. If Grief existed, he'd be here somewhere.

Technically, Casey needed permission to run one of these, but she felt it was one of those formalities that gave "bureaucratic red tape" a bad name. She ranked it somewhere between toilet passes and warrants in the chain of accountable policing.

There was nothing out of the ordinary about Grief, aside from the fact that Squid tolerated his presence. Crazy homeless men came in all kinds, but there was something about Grief that didn't sit right with Casey. Something about his eyes. Like they belonged in someone else's face.

A message beeped onscreen.

*Search completed. 0 matches.*

Casey scrolled through the log, looking for an error that wasn't there. Not even the president had a file this clean. Hell, not even Casey had a file this clean.

"Casey!"

Riego strolled down the corridor with a smile, and Casey quickly blanked her computer, stuffing the ID Sketch printout in her jacket.

"That doesn't look suspicious at all," said Riego cheerfully.

"Just killing time 'til you showed up. Are those cookies?"

Riego dutifully handed over a foil bag.

"All these secret projects, secret meetings," he said. "You're going to end up with a wall covered in photos of pentagrams and demonic sponge cakes."

"Hey, I wasn't the only one who thought the icing sugar looked like Satan. And you're the one who wouldn't eat it."

"Got to watch my blood-sugar," said Riego. "Looks bad if a cop dies from diabetes. So, where are we headed?"

"You don't have diabetes," said Casey. "And that's not why you didn't eat the cake. We're hitting the slums."

Riego didn't say it, but the thought was like a billboard. They were grasping at straws now, circling the drain. They needed a break, or Gale would slap them with a "Show Cause". And Casey was sabotaging her own career just fine.

All Casey had to do was stamp the file and walk away. But even though Werner was a hundred percent dead, his parents still held onto a kind of hope. Believing in things like justice and closure. Believing that Casey could give them that.

Maybe she was grasping at straws, but at least she'd have a fistful of straw. And a resourceful person could do a lot with a fistful of straw. Especially in Baltus City.

# TEN

Squid woke to sunlight streaming through lace curtains, the aroma of pancakes drifting from the kitchen. She lay for a while under the fluffy blankets, soaking in the sensation of clean sheets and soft carpet.

She found Grief in the kitchen, tending a frying pan loaded with pancakes.

"Wow, last night was hot," said Grief. "Hot like Fahrenheit, not hot like a shower scene. I think I lost three kilos. Do I look thinner?"

He presented his profile, flipping the pancakes with a deft toss of the pan.

"No," said Squid sleepily, pulling herself onto a kitchen stool. "What are you doing?"

"Being helpful. You should try it."

"Being helpful is how I ended up with you," grumbled Squid.

Grief grinned as he slid a pile of pancakes onto two plates.

"I can cook," he said triumphantly. "So, did you roll off the couch last night?"

Squid blinked blearily at Grief.

"So, you're okay?"

"Why wouldn't I be?" Grief drizzled honey over his slightly misshapen stack.

"It's just that… last night…"

Grief was suddenly very still, his expression blank.

"Never mind," said Squid. "Where'd you get pancakes from?"

"There were some long-life goods in the linen cupboard. Oh, I found this!"

Grief slapped several sheets of newspaper on the table.

"You 'found' today's employment section?" said Squid, eyeing the ragged tear along the edge.

"It was on the neighbour's lawn," said Grief. "Isn't this exciting? We're going to get jobs, and buy things, and maybe redecorate the house! Look, Financial Director!"

"I'm not qualified," said Squid.

"Administrative Assistant."

"I hate offices."

"Sales Assistant."

"I hate people."

"Cattery Attendant."

"Cats are allergic to me."

Grief looked at Squid dourly. "Is this how you ended up in a life of crime? Because that's just poor."

Squid was actually still stuck on the "redecorate the house" comment, which she found concerning for multiple reasons.

"How about Fun-ness Facilitator?" said Grief.

"Fun-ness is not a word."

"Well, it's a job. You've got to let go of all these hang-ups."

"They're not hang-ups. They're—"

"Standards," said Grief. "I remember."

Squid stared at her half-eaten pancakes. She knew she wasn't going to find the holy trinity of employment: a job she didn't hate, that paid enough, that wasn't illegal.

She had gotten derailed on that last point before, but now she knew it was the *first* two points you had to compromise on. Ninety-nine percent of people were grinding through the hours, wishing they were lounging on a beach instead, or spelunking, or hang-gliding around the world. Squid would be lucky to get a job. Any job. Standards might have kept her soul afloat in the darkness, but they might well sink it in the light.

She dragged her finger tentatively down the column.

"What does a 'Financial Benevolence Transference Officer' even do?" said Squid.

"You shake a bucket while dressed as a whale."

"How about a 'Novelty Nourishment Guidance Infotainer?"

"You convince people to buy junk food while dressed as that food."

"What's with all the dressing up as stuff?" said Squid irritably.

"You're looking in the Casual Work section."

Squid grumbled some more, her temples beginning to throb. She remembered these same choices, these same excuses, but from a life she'd lost long ago. Even now, she felt as though she'd wake at any moment and find herself lying in the rain, chewing on an empty wrapper. If she wanted to hold on to this life, this reality, something would have to change. *She* would have to change.

"Feels strange, doesn't it?" said Grief. "Starting over."

"Like falling into a parallel world. Or…"

"Dying and waking up somebody else."

They sat in silence for a moment, a warm breeze floating through the house.

"You know, we should find a job that'll help you get your memories back," said Squid, brightening up.

"I don't think 'Playboy Billionaire' is an occupation," said Grief, rocking back in his chair with a yawn.

It wasn't that Squid was desperate to see Grief go. He'd been handy, in the same way a human shield was handy. It was like having a big, exuberant jar-opener following you around, and although it came in useful once in a while, you got the feeling that it really should be living with other jar-openers.

Squid's gaze stopped on a small, nervous-looking ad, and her finger punched the page.

"Laboratory Test Subject," said Squid. "That's what we're going to do."

"That doesn't sound like a job so much as a war crime."

"It's perfect. No selling people stuff they don't need, or making them eat things that'll give them goitres, or being nice to people you'd rather push off the pier."

What Squid didn't mention was the added bonus of laboratory equipment. From Grief's earlier reaction, he wouldn't voluntarily submit to testing for blood type, genetic markers or undiagnosed mental disorders, but if Squid could discreetly figure out how to run complicated medical diagnostics—

"Are you trying to read my mind?" said Squid.

Grief studied her with casual scrutiny, as though not entirely convinced he didn't have psychic powers. He glanced back at the circled ad, looking dubious.

"Come on, you can pick the next one," said Squid.

"No matter what?"

Squid swallowed a huge chunk of misgiving.

"Sure."

With any luck, by the time the "next one" rolled around, Grief would be back on his private cruiser, sailing towards the Mediterranean.

"Okay," said Grief. "But if the lab test involves being crammed in an office full of people and cats, it's on you."

As far as Squid was concerned, it just might be worth it.

*

They called it Pearce's morgue.

The slums were a no-go zone for anyone with half a brain or a sense of hygiene. You ended up here if you had nowhere else to go. If the city itself had washed you to its shores. Bodies regularly turned up on the polluted banks, and the police had even given one of the more reliable residents a back-to-base phone to call them in.

Casey tried not to breathe too deeply as she stepped out of the car. Riego had already tied a kerchief around his face, bandit-style, claiming he had the cultural background to pull it off.

Squid spent far too much time there, and Casey suspected she was cosying up to the locals in preparation for the day she ended up there.

It wasn't that Casey didn't have faith in Squid and all her promises to turn things around. It's just that Squid was, well, Squid.

Casey had still been a constable the first time they'd met. An alarming amount of pure Upshot had turned up in the Met West visitor parking lot, still sealed in plastic dealer packs. The conspiracy theories were getting ugly by the time they reviewed the surveillance tapes, and what they found was a scrawny kid unloading forty pounds of powder from the trunk of a stolen car. Even stranger, however, was that after unloading the goods, the girl sat on the concrete and bawled for five minutes solid before driving away.

It'd been another four months before Casey met Squid in person, and their encounter had gone pretty much the same way. Five years later, Squid was still running on the same wheel, wondering why the light wasn't getting any closer.

"You've got that look," said Riego. "That 'oh, cruel world' look. You want me to do this?"

"I'm good," said Casey, shaking off her flashback. "I'll start from this side. We'll work our way in."

Casey started with the residents closest to the water's edge, although they tended to be the least coherent—their sense of smell among the faculties they'd lost.

Some of the residents remained stuck in the past, mostly their own, but there were a few Cleopatras and a couple of Caesars. Casey hoped they'd find each other in this bleak world within a world. Some residents were in a completely different dimension altogether: some of them nirvanas, in which they ruled almighty; others were trapped in nightmares that tore their sanity to shreds.

However, most of the slum-dwellers were people who'd just fallen through the cracks. Slipped on a rough patch and hit rock bottom before they could catch themselves, the world closing up behind them like they'd never existed.

"Nobody heard nothing," said Riego. "Quiet as a dead mouse in nuclear winter."

Casey eyed a scruffy middle-aged man who swaggered towards them with the kind of cocky confidence she recognised from her days on the beat.

"So, whose lot are you?" said the man.

"We're from Met West," said Casey. "I'm Detective Casey. This is Detective Riego. We're just asking a few questions."

"Right. Where were you when they burned down my box and tried to give Lee Fifteen a third eye?" said the man.

"Who's 'they'?" said Casey.

"That's *your* job, sunshine."

"I'm doing it, sweetheart," said Casey, flipping open her notepad.

"I can see why Squid spends so much time here," muttered Riego. "Gotta love the attitude."

The man's expression abruptly changed, like a door sliding warily open.

"You know Squid?" he said.

"Yeah," sighed Casey.

"You're the cop friend? The one who's going to clean up this city?"

Casey hesitated.

"I'm going to try."

The man looked Casey up and down, as though calculating the odds and opening the floor for bets.

"The name's Ebit," he said. "Used to be a broker back in the day. Made and lost and made a billion before my morning coffee. Same guy, but funny how no one'll give you a job if you smell like pee and look like crap."

"People are funny that way," said Casey.

"Some people," said Ebit, his eyes sharply probing again. "I'm guessing you want to talk to Kirsk. She's been laying low since her friend washed up."

"Her friend?" said Casey. "You don't mean Werner?"

"They went to uni together," said Ebit, weaving his way through crumbling mountains of garbage. "Everyone's pretty hush because

Squid means well but what she knows, Ferret knows. And you don't want Ferret knowing you exist."

Ebit knocked a rapid rhythm on a sheet of cardboard which seemed to be attached to a pile of broken crates. After a pause, the cardboard shifted, and a young woman with smudged spectacles peered out.

"You got it wrong," said the woman.

"Whatever," said Ebit. "Kirsk, you've got visitors."

The hovel was a nest of wires and burnt-out circuit boards. Cracked screens were hooked up to leaking generators, and salvaged machinery filled the tiny space.

Kirsk couldn't have been much older than Squid, but her face told a different story. Her cracked skin was dotted with sores, her teeth edged brown with decay. Her mousey hair was tied up with a striped sock, and her fingernails were bitten down to the pink. Light filtered dimly through the damp slats, but Casey could see the red around her eyes.

"You're Dianella Kirsk," said Casey. "The student Werner did his final project with."

"Maybe. Why?" said Kirsk.

"We're investigating Werner's death, and we're hoping you can help us," said Casey.

"Everyone knows who put him in the bay. But no one's going to do anything about it."

"I am," said Casey.

There was something so quietly steadfast, so immovable about those words, that Kirsk was momentarily taken aback. She stared down her hands, unthinkingly twisting a piece of cable into various configurations.

"He used to visit me," said Kirsk quietly. "Even after he got that hotshot job. Even after I ended up here. He'd sit there and talk about the latest bizarre headlines, or some stupid movie he'd just seen."

Kirsk stared at an upturned crate, her fingers twisting the cable tighter and tighter.

"Did Werner ever talk about work?" said Casey.

"He didn't have a death wish, no," said Kirsk. "He knew what he was getting into with Pearce. At least, he thought he did."

Everybody knew the deal: the house always won, and Pearce owned the house. But there'd always be someone cocky enough, foolish enough or desperate enough to think they could outsmart, outrun or outlive Pearce. Someone who thought they'd be the exception, right up until the trigger was pulled or the water closed in over their heads.

"What happened?" said Casey.

"This is off the record, right? Otherwise, I'll denounce it as the ravings of a crazy homeless woman."

Casey set down her notepad, and Riego drew a little cross over his heart.

"Werner was one of your freak-of-the-week prodigies," said Kirsk. "Programming, biomechanics, engineering. He could turn a sketch into a machine in less than a week. Once, we built an autonomous hover-drone with articulated arms and a little scooper, and made it chase irresponsible dog-walkers through the parks, down the streets, even into buildings, waving its little scoop and blaring, 'You forgot your poop!' We almost got expelled, but you can bet Pearce later made a killing converting the tech for military contracts. The biometric scans they use at clubs? Werner wrote the code for that when he was seventeen. Pearce turned it into citywide standard."

The picture should have been getting clearer, but if Werner was a golden goose, Pearce would have needed a pretty compelling reason to drop the axe. Unless it wasn't Pearce but Verona who'd taken out the boy wizard.

"Sounds like Werner was making a lot of money for Pearce," said Casey.

"Pearce didn't just get Werner; he got the whole back catalogue," said Kirsk. "Werner's been churning out ideas since he could hold a stylus. He used to carry a tablet everywhere he went, constantly streaming encrypted notes back to his hard drive. He didn't trust the nimbus."

Casey latched onto the clue. A drive containing all of Werner's ideas, embryonic and complete, including the project he was working on just before he died. Whoever had the drive had Werner, post-mortem.

"Any idea where he kept that?" said Casey.

"Refer to my comment about the death wish. Werner never talked about work. He never talked about Pearce. At the beginning, he was careful. Towards the end, he was full-blown paranoid."

Pearce did that to you. Casey had seen crims go from smart-mouthed hoodlums to twitching wrecks wearing belts of TNT in about the time it took to make a belt of TNT. You needed a certain kind of mind to survive Pearce's universe.

"Any idea what had Werner running scared?"

Kirsk's fingers were red from pulling at the cable, her eyes wet.

"He thought he was being watched, all the time, everywhere. He stopped seeing his parents; he stopped going out. He spent more and more time at the Iluvian. Six months ago, he said he couldn't come around anymore. Said it was for my own safety."

Casey and Riego exchanged a glance. The Iluvian was a gigantic club in the heart of the city. It dwarfed its nearest rival like Jupiter looming over Europa, and if the Chival hated cops, the Iluvian was a whole new realm of animosity. But what made the Iluvian special wasn't its fountains of fire or champagne spas; it was the fact that it remained unaligned. Neutral ground in a city carved up. And possibly the only place where Pearce's watchful eyes were blind.

"I should have done something," said Kirsk, her eyes burning with angry tears.

"There was probably nothing you could have done," said Casey.

"If you believed that sort of thing, you wouldn't be a cop."

Casey had no response to that. They'd been given a manual on platitudes once: what to say, what not to say, what to avoid on pain of legal prosecution. Casey had never gotten the hang of it, and Riego had used his to stabilise a shaky desk.

"So, how'd you end up here, anyway?" said Riego. "Coconut cookie?"

Riego proffered a paper bag. Casey was fairly certain this came under the "things not to do" section. Kirsk selected two pale yellow cookies.

"Just didn't work out," said Kirsk. "Me and society. With all the results-oriented research and programmer sweatshops. Doing pointless things for mindless people. Giving your soul to the man and waiting to die."

"My grandmother on my sister's father's side did the same thing," said Riego. "Just packed her basket one day and said, 'I've had it with you people!' and went to live by herself in a hut by the river five days' walk away."

"Um, yes," said Casey, who was fairly certain Riego's grandmother ran a private gallery on Mallorn Avenue.

"Here, I can wake up when I want. Work on what I want," said Kirsk. "Sure, it'll cost me thirty years of life expectancy, and free dental surgery would be nice, but the price of freedom. Right?"

Casey searched for words but only found the feeling that things should somehow be different. That people shouldn't have to make that kind of trade.

"It's wherever you find happiness," said Riego. "Thanks for your help, Kirsk."

"One more question," said Casey. "Do these numbers mean anything to you?"

Casey held out her notebook, a transcript of the numbers from Werner's slip of tape jotted on the page.

"Could be a combination. A password for a file," said Kirsk. "Werner wouldn't use numbers, though—a two-bit scrambler could crack that in a second."

"Well, let us know if you think of anything else," said Casey.

Back outside, she kept her gaze ahead as they crunched across the dirt, her hands deep in her pockets. The more she saw of those left behind, the more she felt the Werner-shaped gap in the world.

"I know what you're thinking," said Casey.

"I doubt that," said Riego.

"It's tenuous, it's low priority, it's an unwarranted use of resources."

"You're like those bull ants, where you pull off the body but the head won't let go. We used to use those instead of stitches."

"Riego…"

"I'm going home for a shower. I haven't smelled like this since I did the beat on Heartbreak Boulevard."

Casey dropped him off outside his apartment, and he gave a cursory wave as he disappeared up the stairs. For a guy who talked so much, he left an awful lot unsaid. He acted like he didn't care about his career, his reputation, but she saw the islands of silence in his endless chatter. Riego hung out with everybody, but he always seemed to go home alone.

Casey wasn't ready to drop the Werner case, but Riego didn't deserve to be dragged through the mud with her. It was time to change tactics.

*

It was rumoured that Mortimer University had been designed by a very angry, very depressed architect, whose design had been an act of vengeance against the world for his frustrated career as a jazz bagpiper.

All the university buildings were airless concrete vaults with small windows and uncomfortably low ceilings. Thick layers of peeling posters covered every exterior wall, giving the windswept campus a slightly post-apocalyptic feel.

"Maybe it'll be a questionnaire," said Squid. "Or one of those things where you eat different kinds of cake and say which one you liked best."

"I think you're getting 'lab testing' confused with 'focus groups'," said Grief. "Or possibly a birthday party."

"Does anything seem familiar?" said Squid, as they made their way through a howling wind tunnel, inverted umbrellas tumbling past.

"Should it?"

"Just thought you might have gone to university," shrugged Squid.

"I'm probably self-educated. Like those billionaires who worked their way up from mailroom lackey to CEO through sheer grit and chutzpah."

"And ruthless backstabbing."

Grief's expression froze for just a moment, but Squid was good at catching flickers. It was one of the ways you survived Ferret.

"Who needs subterfuge when you've got charm?" said Grief, tossing his head back with a suave smile.

"And that relates to you how?"

"You know, sometimes if you're nice to people, people are nice back."

"Interesting theory."

They arrived at the bleak Science Building, where students debated ethics on the withered front lawn. The sixth floor appeared to be an eerie time capsule of the seventies, with speckled orange linoleum and beige doors.

"Did I just get a foot taller?" said Grief, stooping to avoid a fluorescent light.

"Maybe it's part of the experiment," said Squid. "I hope there won't be interviews."

She could feel her palms growing sweaty, uncomfortable flashbacks bubbling to the surface. Questions, answers, talking. It seemed so unnecessarily complicated and arbitrary. Some people were rewarded for saying clever, pleasant things, and others were ostracised for being honest.

Squid could still remember the career counsellor's voice carrying through the faded yellow room.

*"What would you like to be when you grow up?"*

*"Alone."*

*Squid hadn't even realised she'd said it aloud until the class started laughing.*

Squid took a slow breath, cringing at the sharp odour of methylated spirits.

"It'll be fine," she said, mostly to herself. "I doubt they'll be fussy. And the university's always got odd jobs cleaning up chemical spills and disposing of mutant gerbils."

"Should I ask how you dispose of mutant gerbils?"

"Look, room six-fifteen," said Squid, knocking on the chipboard door.

A man in his twenties answered the door, dressed in a loose lab coat with an unreadable badge. It appeared to be a very dense disclaimer. Squid held up the circled ad hopefully, craning to see if there was any cake in the room. When the man spoke, his voice was flatter than week-old roadkill.

"Hello. My name is Adrian. We are currently testing an experimental analgesic, and we ecstatically welcome your contribution. You will be required to take this tablet, which may or may not be a placebo, and we will then apply dermal electric shocks while you rate your level of pain. Please sign here."

Grief plucked the pen from Squid's hand.

"What's the maximum voltage of the electric shocks?" said Grief.

"We can't disclose that," said Adrian.

"What's the duration of each application?" said Grief.

"We can't disclose that."

"And how much do we get paid?" said Grief, his tone flatter than Adrian's.

"There is no monetary compensation, but you do get a biscuit and a fun-sized orange juice."

Squid glanced at Grief and suddenly wished that Adrian hadn't used the word "fun" right now.

"You mean we came all this way for a biscuit?" said Grief, his voice ominously calm.

"And a fun-sized—"

"It's still a biscuit," said Squid quickly. "I've done worse things for money."

Grief's gaze snapped to Squid.

"I mean, not 'Zap. Argh!' You know, never mind. We don't have to do it."

Grief turned back to Adrian, a strange fire rising in his eyes. "This ad is in the employment section."

"Welcome to Baltus City," said Adrian.

It was true that Baltus City had no minimum wage. You could pay peanuts. Literally. It was supposed to foster entrepreneurial vigour and the capitalist spirit of self-improvement. Unfortunately, it also fostered petty crime and the kind of explosion that was about to obliterate Adrian.

"Okay, thanks anyway!" yelled Squid as she dragged Grief from the room, a feat reminiscent of someone pulling a bus with their teeth.

Grief stood in the corridor with his fists clenched, a dangerous look in his eyes.

"Well, that was educational," said Squid.

Adrian poked his head out the doorway, clearly having a poor sense of self-preservation.

"If you're looking for lucre, I need the labs down the hall cleaned for this afternoon's practical. Our usual staff came down with radiation poisoning."

Rooms six-eleven and six-twelve were student laboratories fitted with metal benches, gas taps, and shelves loaded with equipment. It was here that some students would become scientists, and others would become hospitalised. A large sign was pinned to the front of the room: DO NOT EAT WHAT YOU ARE DISSECTING.

However, this wasn't the most disturbing thing about the lab. Squid balked in the doorway, experiencing post-traumatic flashbacks.

"Did someone explode in here?" said Squid.

Grief clucked with disapproval as he strolled between the metal benches.

"Students," said Grief. "What do you expect?"

Sticky chunks detached slowly from the ceiling while bubbling sludge burped in the overflowing sinks. Grief snapped on a pair of latex gloves and began collecting trays of dismembered critters.

"I'm going to start over here," croaked Squid.

She shuffled discreetly to the supply closet, browsing quickly through its contents. Blood glucose strips, cholesterol swabs, drug detection kits. Squid wasn't sure how any of those would help except to confirm that Grief was a reasonably clean-living amnesiac. Her gaze paused on a pile of slim boxes labelled *Speedi Need DNA Tests: Think you're adopted? Not sure if the kid's yours? Need to clear your name, FAST? All you need are ten strands of hair.*

Squid glanced across the lab, where Grief was peeling a length of intestine from a bench. Hair shouldn't be too hard. It wasn't like trying to get a blood sample or asking him to close his eyes and open his mouth for a saliva swab. The results might not mean much, but if she could access some kind of database, it might start to narrow things down.

Squid sidled over to Grief, casually dabbing at the tables with a sunken sponge.

"Hey, I think you've got something in your hair," said Squid, reaching up.

Grief leaned back, eyeing her suspiciously. Squid reached farther forward, and Grief leaned farther away. She was tempted to see how far he could actually bend, but he squinted at her like a scientist watching a hungry beetle, trying to decide whether to squash the beetle or let it take a nip. Squid glanced at Grief's hand and decided it was poised in a squashing configuration.

"Since when are you the grooming type?" said Grief.

"What do you mean?" Squid tried to sound insulted.

"You've got something on your shirt."

Grief reached over and Squid took an instinctive step back.

"Hmmm," he said, like a detective in a drawing-room mystery.

"Fine. Walk around with innards in your hair."

Grief resumed scraping dried toad from the table, and Squid paced around, waiting for an opening. Grief put down the paint scraper.

"I feel like I'm in that story where the fox is being circled by the chicken—"

"I think it was the other way around—"

"How about you finish up in here, and I'll start on the lab next door?" said Grief, handing Squid a plunger.

"Wait, I—"

The door closed, and Squid looked around at the dripping trays and overflowing sinks.

So, this was work.

Squid returned the stained textbooks to the shelves, and a title caught her eye.

*Amnesia: Pathology, Etiology, Diagnosis and Treatment.*

*

Grief had never seen so many brains. Then again, he'd had a lot of firsts lately. First jam roll, first job, first gunfight—

*His eyes, like an animal about to die—*

Grief did a slow circuit of the lab, inspecting jars of spongy brains, their surfaces pinned with neatly labelled flags. Thinly sliced cross sections hung in blocks of acrylic, every sulcus and gyrus like a delicately folded landscape.

His gaze travelled the walls, taking in vivid posters of circulatory-system flow charts and smiling people with their organs visible. But there was something wrong with their faces, because people without their skin didn't smile—

*The firelight from the bay snuffed out, and he stepped towards the blond man. A step, that's all. He remembered the look on the man's face. Like a bolt of pure animal fear. He'd vaulted the barrier before Grief could reach him, and all he heard was the long, tumbling scream—*

Grief leaned against a bench, his eyes popping with stars.

*Eyes, he remembered eyes. All staring at him with such—*

Grief wiped the sweat from his face. It was probably the brains, dredging old horror movies from his subconscious. Perhaps he'd been a fan of thrillers, or slashers, or maybe he'd watched the news a lot.

This lab was a lot cleaner than the one next door, and it didn't take much to straighten it up. He felt bad for Squid wading through gizzards, but it was probably character building. Her years of living rough had left her pretty maladjusted, jittering with her own thoughts and flinching at the slightest movement. She needed a bit of mindless work, a bit of stability, a bit of care.

For some reason, taking care of Squid made Grief feel better. Sure, it reminded him slightly of those old men cradling rag dolls, crooning softly to black button eyes. But Squid clearly needed help, possibly clinically.

She seemed to run on a rattling engine of contradictory impulses, desperately craving to be a part of the world she seemed to loathe. Sometimes, she'd push him away so hard, he could feel it for days, but then she would crawl under the blankets with him or find strange reasons to touch his hair.

Grief wiped down a large laminated poster of the brain, various regions highlighted in different colours. The mind was a complicated, temperamental thing. Grief knew this better than anyone. It wasn't that he didn't want to remember, but he had so many reasons for loitering in his search. Firstly, he was having an interesting time, and the longer he lingered in this state, the more material he would have for his eventual bestselling book: *Rich Dude, Poor Dude.*

Secondly, he wasn't convinced that his former life would welcome him back. Someone had dumped him in a trunk after braining him pretty badly. He couldn't be sure there wasn't someone out there who'd be very interested to know that he was still alive.

Thirdly, and he held this aloft as a moral slam dunk, he was helping a socially disturbed former criminal get her life back on track. This was certainly altruism in all its glory and a clear sign that he was a decent, upstanding kind of guy.

However, it was hard to reconcile that thought with the frozen image of the man leaping from the bridge.

There was a loud *crack* of glass, and the cabinet door shattered under Grief's hand, the cleaning rag still clutched in his fist. He glanced guiltily over his shoulder and quickly swept up the pieces, breaking off the jagged remnants of the glass—

*Shards of glass, dragging through skin—*

Grief dropped the fragment, frantically pulling off his bloodied gloves. He backed into a table, staring at the grubby white latex on the floor. It must have just been the light, or a tinted reflection. Or his imagination.

He tossed the gloves into the bin. When he got home, he'd have to watch a serious marathon of fluffy romantic comedies.

It took him a moment to realise that the raised voices next door weren't also a figment of his imagination. Grief raced for the door, but by then, the unearthly shrieking had started.

*

Squid generally liked books. They were calm and nonintrusive, and if you didn't want them in your face, you could shove them under a couch. Magazines were more hit-and-miss, since the only centrefold bodies that didn't kneecap Squid's self-esteem were automotive and planetary.

The lab contained a whole section of books on amnesia and memory, and Squid found herself sitting on the floor, surrounded by half-open texts. Amnesia seemed to come in as many varieties as gelato.

*I'll have the traumatic retrograde, with a dash of hysterical posthypnotic anterograde, but hold the Korsakoff.*

There were types of amnesia where people couldn't remember any new information, but they could still sing their high school anthem. Then there was the type where people could remember things that had happened, but they couldn't remember things that they had to do in the future. Not to mention the kind of amnesia that wiped people blank, and they had to learn to eat and talk all over again.

There were so many things that could go wrong with someone's brain. Too much dope, not enough vitamin B, falling anvils. Squid had narrowed Grief's diagnosis to traumatic amnesia with features of retrograde, which roughly translated to: he was hit on the head and can't remember his past. Except he seemed to remember a lot of things he'd seen or heard: stories, movies, sayings. He could remember San Cruza Drive but not Infinity Mall. He knew what a Financial Benevolence Transference Officer was but not if he liked strawberries.

There were so many inconsistencies in his recall that Squid might as well declare it a new kind of amnesia altogether. Although if she called it Squid's Amnesia, it would probably end up in *Cephalopod Scientifica* under "Forgetful Calamari".

Her finger trailed down the page on psychological aspects of amnesia, and paused on a heading.

*Dissociative amnesia. The person retains general knowledge, but cannot recall information pertaining to their identity. In some cases, the person creates a new personality.*

*Cause: Psychological trauma.*

*Treatment: Therapy.*

Parts of it sounded remarkably like Grief's condition, but other parts sounded vaguely quacktastic. Squid was generally wary of anything involving multiple personalities, past lives or generic "therapy". The slums bubbled with every kind of disorder you could imagine, and from what she could gather, non-specific therapy was the term you used for something that sounded like a good idea at the time but made no sense later. Like carpeted bathrooms.

Squid swept her gaze over the scattered books—the texts mostly agreed that non-degenerative amnesia generally resolved itself within a few hours or days. However, Grief seemed to stubbornly remember no more today than he had the moment she'd opened the trunk.

She had the disconcerting feeling that the longer Grief existed, the less likely it was that his former identity would return. It'd be as though an entire person, with their thoughts and history, their affections and passions, would just fade into nothing.

Perhaps it was time for more drastic action.

The doors to the laboratory swung open, and Squid leapt to her feet, the books falling from her lap. Adrian stood in the doorway with a horrified expression, a crowd of students behind him.

"I was just going to finish now," said Squid, holding up her plunger.

A large frog clambered out of a slimy sink and burped out a smaller frog.

"We needed the lab *now*," said Adrian.

There was a strange urgency to his voice, and Squid noticed the grey plastic trays each student carried. Something furry and leathery and webbed lay beside the shining scalpels. And they were starting to stir.

"Adrian," said a girl with a brown plait. "I think the sedative's wearing off..."

Adrian waved aggressively at Squid. "You! Get out!"

"But we cleaned most—" began Squid.

Adrian rushed around the lab, herding the students into place.

"Set up! Set up!" he yelled.

"Oh, God, they're waking up!" cried one student.

The leathery creatures twitched awake, beady eyes blinking open. High-pitched squeaks filled the air, implements clattering to the ground as the bats launched into flight.

"Argh!" screamed Adrian. "Contamination! Contamination! Run for your lives!"

The room whirled with a panic of terrified bats and shrieking students, the rush of wings choking the room. Students took cover under the tables, commando-crawling towards the door as trays and scalpels went flying.

Squid struggled towards the windows, the room a blizzard of dark shapes. A passing claw slashed at her cheek, and another bat became briefly tangled in her hair. Squid shoved at a window, but it stopped at a crack. They called it suicide-proofing, but she knew a thing or two about windows like this.

"Incoming!" Squid hollered through the gap.

She swept up a metal stool and hurled it through the window, smashing the pane of glass into sunlight. The bats did one last circuit of the lab before streaming through the broken frame in a cloud of ear-shattering screeches.

The doors to the lab burst open once more, and Grief stood there with a scalpel in his hand, staring at the shell-shocked scene. Somewhere, a student whimpered.

"Well, my lab's done," said Grief.

*

The university clinic patched up the scratches and bites, the university counsellors consoled the tearful students, and the university legal department assured everyone that the bats didn't have contagious diseases of any kind.

Squid and Grief made a hasty exit after campus security arrived, and they began the long walk home.

"I'm sorry you cleaned all that for nothing," said Squid.

"It wasn't for nothing," said Grief, tucking some folded papers into his pocket.

Squid kicked a pebble along the ground, wishing it was a tin can. Or Adrian.

"See why I ended up in a life of crime?" said Squid.

"It was a bad day. It happens."

"But I only get bad days. I'm one long, bad day that never ends. Why are you smiling?"

"No reason," said Grief. "It's just that we're going home to a hot shower, clean blankets, more pancakes. It doesn't feel like a bad day."

Squid left the pebble alone, trudging along the side of the road.

"I know," she sighed. "New start. New attitude. It's just…"

*It would have been nice*, thought Squid. *To have something work out for once.*

"You have something in your hair," said Grief.

He reached over and Squid flinched but didn't pull away. He gently untangled a small bat from her hair, and the animal blinked drowsily before flapping unsteadily away.

"I think it's unfair for them to blame me for their dodgy laboratory protocols," said Squid. "Carrying around trays of poorly sedated bats is just asking for trouble. I'm sure there are regulations against that kind of thing. *Now* what are you smiling about?"

"You are so bad at this life thing."

"Yeah, well, I'm trying."

The sun sank slowly beneath the highways, creating a strange twilight while the afternoon light retreated below.

"I can't wait to pick the next job," said Grief. "What's that face?"

"Nothing. I just inhaled a bug."

Grief waited for Squid's pained expression to fade.

"Maybe it'll be fun," said Grief. "Maybe it'll be exciting."

*Maybe it won't end with people screaming at me*, thought Squid.

Grief stood at the edge of the bypass and stretched out his arms, as though breathing in the city. He exhaled slowly and smiled.

"Maybe we'll have a good day, Squid."

# ELEVEN

Casey slipped through the corridors of Met West, theories slotting around her brain like squares on a sliding puzzle.

Werner had known he was being watched. Whatever he'd gotten himself into, he'd seen it coming. And a guy like Werner would have kept some insurance, left some clues.

His hard drive was probably locked in Pearce's vaults. Anything at his apartment would have gone the same way. But if Werner had kept copies of something without Pearce's consent, if he'd somehow managed to smuggle data through the suffocating layers of security, there was only one place he could have hidden it.

Casey swung to a stop at the faded blue counter, slapping a glassy data wafer on the desk.

"Galston, how're you going?" said Casey, her voice overflowing with chummy pretty-please.

A man with a long red ponytail leaned his elbows on the counter.

"Tell me that's a pre-release copy of *Zombie-Assassin Samurai*," said Galston flatly.

"I need a warrant for the Iluvian. The application's level two, minimal intrusion. Homicide."

Casey slid the wafer towards Galston, whose gaze didn't even dip.

"Why don't I request one for Pearce HQ while I'm at it? Or maybe the starship *Enterprise*?"

"Sarcasm is only the sound of your heart shrivelling up."

"Give it up, Casey. We both know you could be chasing a mutant army and you still wouldn't get into the Iluvian."

Casey hated a lot of things about her job. The violent, gruesome things cut you up, but at least they were the fight. They were the things that kept you angry, kept you moving. But when good people gave up, when you saw them falling into jaded resignation, it made you wonder if you weren't just kidding yourself.

Believing you could make a difference was a leap of faith that, more often than not, ended in a long drop and a wide spatter.

"Don't be the red-tape guy, Galston," said Casey. "I can put this one away."

"Now you're pushing it. Everyone knows you've got nothing."

Casey's fingers tightened around the wafer. Now she was cranky.

"I'd do my job better if you did yours," said Casey. "What are you doing on graveyard, anyway? Where's Riley?"

Galston's expression didn't change.

"Her car got firebombed after she submitted your request for the Chival warrant."

Casey's stomach fell eighteen floors, a stab of white noise filling her ears. Every time the news hit, another cop down, you felt the thin blue line get a little thinner.

"Is she…" began Casey.

"Shrapnel and burns. And pieces of cat. Handed in her resignation this morning."

Riley had been a borderline believer, caught between intractable pragmatism and tattered hope. Casey had come in with a flamethrower about justice and duty, and Riley had believed her for a moment. And now she was a message.

Casey got it, loud and clear. Like a Scud missile in a schoolyard. Back down, walk away. Nice family you got there.

Pearce spread through the city like a virus, jumping from person to person. The fear grew, became endemic, became normal. You didn't cross Pearce. End of story.

But Casey was reading a different book, and she liked her ending better.

"Who's taking the case?" said Casey.

Galston stepped back, already returning to his endless cataloguing.

"Who do you think?"

*

She meant to knock, but she'd already swung open the door by the time her manners kicked in. Casey also hadn't meant to fling the door quite so hard, but she was in a hurry.

"—already in motion—"

Deus glanced up, his wrist comms casting a faint blue light across his features.

"I'll have to call you back," said Deus, calmly swiping the screen blank. He leaned back in his chair. "You certainly like to make an entrance."

"Sorry," said Casey. "I can come back later."

Her tone strongly suggested she didn't want to come back later. Deus gestured to a chair, which Casey politely ignored.

"How can I help you?" said Deus.

"You took the firebomber case."

"I did."

There was a pause oozing with brinksmanship. Deus could've done the decent thing and offered some details, but "friendly" wasn't the word that came to mind when people thought of Deus. The word was generally "Oh" followed by various four-letter combinations.

"Any leads?" said Casey.

"You should come to the briefing room more often. Sam Olsen was arrested last night. We found matching detonators in his apartment, and he confessed this morning. He's in lock-up now."

Casey kept her expression neutral while her mind staggered around screaming at how he'd managed to track down the culprit in less time than it took most cops to read the file. Deus wasn't smiling, but she could see the smug gratification in his eyes.

"You know, Casey, there's no shame in asking for help."

He sounded like he was trying to convince her that halitosis was the new black.

"And how could you help?"

Casey wanted to slap herself as soon as she'd said it, but Deus managed to put his cases to bed while she was still pulling all-nighters. It galled her to think that maybe he was just the better cop. Maybe there was a valid reason for the extra pips, and it wasn't just that he looked better in dress uniform.

"I have resources," said Deus. "Just let me know what you need, and I'm sure we can come to some kind of… arrangement."

Casey could almost hear sinister strains of violin music drifting through the office, the brass banker's lamp casting moody shadows. Something about Deus made her feel as though he were holding out a piece of cake with one hand while hefting a baton with the other. Half the station regarded him with caution, if not actual fear, yet his record was as spotless as his starched shirt.

Casey stared hard at the metaphorical piece of cake and metaphorically tightened her belt.

"I'm all right for now," she said.

Deus smiled faintly, as though sharing a private joke with an invisible companion.

"You know, Casey, being stubborn isn't always an asset."

Casey wasn't being the tough guy for the hell of it—she knew the trail was getting colder. The culprit was still out there, and whatever Werner had died for was still cloaked in lies and obfuscation. She didn't need the glory of solving it alone. If you wanted adulation, you were in the wrong profession. She wanted it solved; she wanted Pearce on his knees.

But Casey also knew about compromise, about the helping hand that became a hand on your shoulder. Deus wouldn't give her something for nothing, and favours had a way of turning into silence, into blind eyes, into a nod and a wink that ended horribly far from where it began. And she wasn't ready for that.

"Good luck with the Olsen trial," she said.

"If you change your mind…"

"I know where to find you."

The corridor seemed overly bright after Deus's atmospheric office, and Casey had to blink away the speckles as she strode towards the east wing. She could sift through the evidence again, but the trail wasn't just cold; it was decomposing. Everywhere she turned, people were acting as though Werner's case had already been closed.

City Surveillance had claimed that an electrical fault had wiped all bayside footage from the night of the murder. Ballistics had put her in a queue that stretched for months. And her request for a more detailed forensic report had been met with the kind of administrative silence that bordered on the hostile.

She needed a breakthrough, and the key was the Iluvian.

Casey almost barrelled into a figure as she rounded the corner, her shoulder knocking into a cluster of epaulettes. She scrambled into a mortified salute, her face burning.

"Deputy Commissioner Drake!" said Casey.

"As you were," said Drake, dusting herself off. "Detective Sergeant Casey, isn't it?"

Drake was one of those people who always knew who you were, whether you led the army or swept the floors. That's what people loved about Drake—she was that photogenic package of homely charm and kickass competence. She gave people confidence in a city that didn't deserve it.

"Yes, sir," said Casey, standing straighter than she had at graduation.

"I heard you're on the Werner case," said Drake, but Casey heard the unspoken "still".

If Casey had a spade, she'd have dug a hole and crawled inside. Drake would have heard the station chatter, and Casey knew what they said about her. It was written clearly enough on the walls of the unisex restrooms.

"Yes, sir."

"Red tape and brick walls, right?" said Drake with a wry smile.

"No, sir! Sort of, sir…"

No one liked a whinger. You didn't join the Force because it was easy. You found a way to make the impossible happen. You found a way to create justice in a world that didn't believe in it.

"I know these are just words, but don't be discouraged," said Drake. "People like you are the heart of the Force. People who believe. People who don't give up. You'll go through your career, you'll go through life, with people telling you it can't be done. Or that it's a waste of time. The most important thing is to hold onto the belief that it *can* be done. It *should* be done. That some things matter more than time or reputation or even your own life. You don't win every battle, but keep heart. By not going with the crowd, you create an eddy. And enough eddies can eventually turn the tide."

Casey's heart swelled to the sound of imaginary dawn bugles. Deputy Commissioner Drake had just given her a Speech. Most non-government organisations had to book months in advance, and donate large sums to charity, to get a speaker's visit from Drake. Casey had just gotten a personal address at three in the morning, down the hall from the lost property room.

"Yes, sir. Thank you, sir," said Casey.

Drake's parting smile was like a summer afternoon from childhood memory, and Casey gazed after her in quiet adoration. Drake paused, a curiously solemn expression in her eyes.

"One more thing, Casey. Sometimes, the company you keep is less important than what you're trying to do. Not everyone understands that."

"Yes, sir," said Casey, a little uncertainly.

Drake disappeared around a corner, her clipped, confident footsteps fading to silence. Casey continued down the deserted corridor, trying not to wonder why Deputy Commissioner Drake had been in the east wing of Met West at three in the morning.

*

Squid didn't have a problem with early starts. For most of her adult life, the blur of days and nights were distinguished only by varying levels of panic, and sleep was wherever you could get it.

But she'd left behind that life of indistinct twilights and cold, hungry dawns. And surely it was a sign of commitment to her new life that she remained in bed for as long as possible.

Unfortunately, Grief had different ideas, bursting into each morning with the excitement of a kid on Christmas day. Squid had seriously considered the feasibility of sedating him, but she was having trouble concocting a narcotic using flour and long-life milk. Which was how she came to be standing on the heritage drag of the central business district, slouching in the wan morning light.

"Behold!" cried Grief, thrusting his arms at an imposing sandstone building. "The city library!"

Squid didn't feel this deserved a response. She was familiar with the library—it was a good place to crash if you were running on empty. All you had to do was open a book and slump over the desk, and you could pass for an exhausted student. You just had to make sure you picked a sufficiently obscure text; otherwise, you'd end up being woken by an eager nerd wanting to study-buddy over images of explicit Grecian pottery.

"Why are we here?" mumbled Squid, still thinking about warm blankets and slowly crawling sunlight.

"We're getting a job!" said Grief, unfurling his arms like a model revealing an exceptionally sexy car.

"Idonwanwrklibry…" said Squid, noticing that even the ambitious suits hadn't filtered into the district yet.

"Resources!" said Grief. "Systematic search procedures to maximise our chances of joining the ranks of the consistently employed."

"Ngarh…"

Grief crossed his arms. "Now you're just making noises."

Squid followed Grief into the vaulted building, with book-lined walkways spiralling overhead. Baltus City Library had been converted from a former cathedral, in a move that the local scientists had crowed over. The Church had promptly donated ten thousand books on religious study, with the express understanding that not adding them to the collection would send the library management to Hell.

After a brisk inspection of the floor map, Grief homed in on the research stations, a row of sleek black screens tilting up from redwood desks. His hand paused over the screen, as though flipping a page in some mental manual, before his fingers darted over the glowing symbols.

"Job search," grinned Grief, punching a stylised orange icon.

Squid wasn't a fan of AI-assisted job matching. In high school, they'd been forced to complete a computerised interview which had interrogated them on their interests, skills and goals. The program was supposed to collate the information and inform you of your ideal occupation.

While her school mates' screens had pinged with everything from "veterinarian" to "dictator", Squid's screen had continued to show an hourglass icon long after the class had ended. She had snuck into the classroom early the next morning and found a single line of text on the screen.

*No match found.*

Over the next few days, Squid had crept into the room after school and tried the test again and again. She'd changed her answers until they barely resembled her at all, and finally got "Human Battery".

"Over a hundred thousand positions vacant," said Grief, scrolling through the search options. "We've got to find something, right?"

Squid sighed, taking the seat next to Grief.

"Exclude jobs that require formal qualifications," she said.

The timer spun in soothing yellow lights, and the number on the screen reduced to twenty thousand matches.

"Exclude jobs that require experience," said Squid.

Eight thousand positions remaining.

"Exclude jobs over three hours' commute away."

Two hundred.

"Exclude jobs that pay less than five dollars an hour."

Grief tapped in the criteria, and after a brief yellow swirl, the final result appeared.

*Zero matches.*

"Well," said Squid, getting to her feet. "Good luck with that."

"Hey." Grief grabbed the back of Squid's jacket and found himself holding an empty windbreaker.

He eventually found Squid on the third floor, scrunched in a corner, reading a pastel-coloured book titled *How to Get Along with People (At the Expense of Your Own Happiness).* Grief settled onto the beanbag beside her, the soft rustling of paper like an ocean of unspoken words.

"It's not like I'm not trying," said Squid.

"I know."

"If I had a dollar for every person who said 'no', I wouldn't have to work."

"So, if someone said 'yes' for a legitimate job, you'd take it?" said Grief.

Squid stared down at the book, her hands curled into unhappy fists.

"I suppose."

Grief cocked an eyebrow.

"I mean, yes," said Squid, her expression like the last soldier standing in a losing battle.

"Great!" said Grief, pulling a slip of paper from his pocket. "I have just the thing."

Squid tensed, eyeing the job docket warily.

"Waitstaff," read Grief. "No experience necessary. All applicants welcome. Immediate start for instant cash."

Squid's eyes were glued to the heading.

"That's the Iluvian," she said flatly.

"It's a club, right?"

"Not *a* club. *The* club. It's everything to everyone, and the closest you come to selling yourself without actually selling yourself. If they tell you to clean up a client's regurgitated mess, you have to clean up the client's regurgitated mess."

"It's called a job," said Grief.

"I don't think the Iluvian has that concept."

"A job is whatever puts food on the table. You'd rather be shot at than clean up someone's mess?"

"You'd rather scrape brains from the wall than face who you really are?" said Squid.

They glared at each other, barbs of tension waving like vine fronds searching for a hold. After a long pause, Grief scrunched up the job docket, slouching into the beanbag. They sat in silence, and Squid stared glumly at the retro-patterned book in her hands. On the cover was a drawing of a smiling mask, tears sliding from the eye holes.

Squid took her jacket from Grief's lap, slotting the book back into place.

"Maybe it's not as bad as they say," said Squid.

Grief bounced to his feet, his face lighting up.

"Maybe it'll be fun," said Grief.

Squid didn't reply, but her expression resembled the mask on the cover. The sky blazed blue as they left the library, heading for their next port in a storm.

*

The Iluvian wasn't just a club.

It was New York, Vegas, Dubai and ancient Rome all rolled into one gigantic throbbing heart at the centre of Baltus City. It occupied four towering city blocks interconnected with transparent walkways like a neon ant-farm. The first fifty floors were a mecca of bars and clubs for the common masses: colourful dance clubs, corporate bars, cheap swill holes and drunken meat-markets. The next twenty-eight floors were reserved for more exclusive clientele: fashionable bars, celebrity clubs, glamorous halls for glittering events. People would kill to get on the Iluvian A-list—another reason the Iluvian and law enforcement didn't see eye to eye.

The final twenty-two floors were private rooms: luxury suites for the Iluvian's special guests. Rented by the minute, at rates that would put a modest country into debt, most of the city's elite had rooms permanently reserved. The Iluvian was a haven for secret meetings, illicit affairs, and dangerous liaisons of all kinds.

Koh Namiel had built the Iluvian from the ground up and declared it neutral ground. There were rumours he'd made his fortune selling weapons to rogue nuclear powers before deciding that he preferred designing stylish karaoke bars.

He was the kind of man who didn't believe in mutually assured destruction. He believed in having a faster trigger and a deeper bunker. On his turf, you didn't cause trouble.

Even in broad daylight, the Iluvian lit up the sky like Babylon on fire. The lower levels blared with flamboyant holograms and pulsing spotlights, while the upper floors dripped with hypnotic cascades of flame. At the pinnacle of the building, artificial starlight drifted down the marble walls.

"I think I've been here before," said Grief, his gaze sweeping over the monolith.

"I bet you were a party junkie," said Squid. "Dancing on the tabletops, singing into a spoon."

"That sounds like fun," said Grief, trotting eagerly towards the ominous metal archway labelled STAFF ENTRANCE.

The double doors were triple-riveted and flanked by six guards who looked as though they might be there to keep people in as well as out.

"Grief," said Squid. "When we get in there, stay close and keep your mouth shut."

"Aren't you being a little—"

"You don't know the Iluvian, and I try not to. And you can take that from someone who hangs at the Fess."

Grief nodded reluctantly, standing quietly behind Squid as she held out the job docket.

"Two for the job," said Squid.

The guards swept the pair with a scanner wand before waving them through, the doors clanking firmly shut behind them. The corridor was the size of a railway tunnel and about as inviting. Archways loomed at regular intervals, like sphincters in a stone intestine, and at each one stood a scanning station.

A thin but steady stream of recruits jostled nervously down the hall, and Grief stuck close to Squid as they passed through each station. The Iluvian seemed to have every type of scanner invented, including some that were banned from use on humans. Weapons, recording devices, biological contaminants, radioactive material. If you had it on you, you'd better pray there was an afterlife.

Phones and wearable tech were surrendered early on, and towards the end of the process, you felt like you'd been violated in several dozen different ways.

"That was pretty intense," said Grief.

His tone was light, but Squid could see the hint of worry in his eyes. The last station was a bright white cubicle with a disconcerting number of lasers, cameras and leather straps. One by one, recruits entered the cubicle, placing their hands on a black screen, their heads held in a stationary rig while retinal, facial and fingerprint scans were conducted. You could change your fingers, your face, and sometimes even your DNA, but no one had yet found a way to beat the retinal scans.

If you were a private eye or a cop, this was where your journey ended. Squid almost expected a big red-and-green light to be fixed to the wall, dinging pleasantly if you were clear and giving a sharp *Eerhh!* if you were doomed. Unfortunately, there was only silence as each person passed through, the only indicator of your fate being the rapid descent of armed guards.

There was a sudden commotion ahead as a man in his early forties was dragged away by a cluster of guards in riot gear.

"Wait!" cried the man. "I used to be an officer, but I resigned years ago! Check the records! Check the records!"

He was dragged through an unmarked door, and there was a sharp noise, like a cross between a *zap* and a *blat*, followed by an emphatic silence.

"I bet they do that every hour to freak out the newbies," whispered Grief.

Squid did not find this reassuring as she was herded into the cubicle, her hands pressed onto the cool screen by mechanical grips. Her heart pounded erratically as the camera buzzed down to eye level, a bright white light filling her vision.

Squid was pretty sure she'd never done anything to annoy the Iluvian management. She avoided this whole area as a rule because she had her hands full surviving Mal, and Namiel was in a whole different stratosphere.

The rig suddenly released with a hiss, and the cubicle partition swung open to reveal two guards and a smartly uniformed Iluvian staff member.

"Please proceed to orientation," said the staff member.

"Is there an interview?" said Squid.

"That was the interview."

Squid walked towards the final doorway, glancing over her shoulder at the occupied cubicle. As the seconds dragged on, she started to wonder if she hadn't made a terrible mistake. She had no idea if Grief was on the Iluvian blacklist. For all she knew, Namiel had put Grief in the trunk and was patiently waiting for him to resurface. She took a few steps back towards the cubicle, and several guards moved from their positions along the walls.

Squid was starting to slip into panic mode when the partition swung open, and Grief jogged out.

"I feel like we should get some kind of certificate after that," said Grief, shaking himself down.

The guards continued to watch them as they passed into the orientation room.

"I think the reward is not getting blatted," said Squid.

The orientation room was clinically white and lit like an interrogation chamber. Huge plaques featured prominently on every wall, carrying the staff credos.

DISCRETION.

SERVICE.

NEVER RETALIATE.

For an unsuspecting recruit, if the ordeal up to this point hadn't triggered warning bells, the plaques spelled it out like a line of meathooks. The Iluvian wasn't the kind of place that had tea breaks and casual Fridays.

The recruits were herded into military rows, and a crisply dressed orientation leader inspected the intake. His fitted black T-shirt and trousers marked him as a mid-level staffer, and the dark red straps crossing over his chest and back denoted the rank of floor manager. A two-way radio hung at his hip, and he carried a glass of water in one hand.

"My name is Ash," said the orientation leader, his voice clear and brisk. "Your responsibilities at the Iluvian are very simple."

Ash pointed to a looming plaque.

"Discretion."

He paused, as though letting the word sink in.

"Service."

Another pause.

"*Never retaliate.*"

That last phrase was like a brand sizzling across every forehead. Some of the recruits glanced nervously at one another, while some stared firmly ahead. Ash stopped in front of a young man with cool eyes and, without warning, slapped him hard across the face.

"Hey!" snarled the man, his fist already pulling back.

"Never retaliate," said Ash.

There was a breathless silence, everyone waiting for the man's reaction. He lowered his fist slowly, eyes smouldering.

Ash continued along the line, pausing in front of a woman with dark hair. Before she could brace herself, the contents of the glass hit her in the face. She gasped through her dripping fringe, clenching her fists.

"Never retaliate," repeated Ash, sweeping his gaze over the pale faces.

"We get the point," muttered Grief.

Ash's gaze snapped to the vicinity of the voice, and he strode slowly along the line. He paused in front of Grief, and the corner of Squid's eye twitched madly. Flashbacks to the speeding truck jumped around her mind—the stranger in Grief's face, the savagery in his eyes. She prayed Ash wasn't going to do anything they'd all regret.

Ash seemed to reach the same conclusion and took one step farther down the line. Squid swallowed, trying to remain perfectly still as Ash studied her like someone trying to decide how many legs to pull off. He leaned forward, and Squid squinted her eyes half-shut, deciding that if he bit off her ear, she was bloody well going to retaliate.

She saw him pull his finger from his mouth, and felt a wet trail drag across her cheek. Squid was unable to suppress a rather loud "Ugh!" which she felt was hardly retaliation unless you were at a super posh high tea.

"Never retaliate," said Ash, stepping back to address the room. "The rules are simple. If you don't like them, there's the door."

All eyes turned towards the heavy green door, and every thought was "Yes, but what's *behind* the door?"

"The Iluvian offers immaculate service, from the ground floor to the penthouse," said Ash, clearly taking silence to be consent. "Do your job well, and you can retire from the tips. Breach the house rules, and…"

Ash paused ominously.

"Don't breach the house rules," he said with a faintly disturbing smile. "The Weeklies will help you with your uniforms. Welcome to the Iluvian."

The room broke into hushed chatter as soon as Ash left the room, and low-level staffers guided the recruits to flimsy changing stalls.

Squid let out a long breath, and saw Grief looking quietly stricken.

"I'm so sorry," said Grief. "I had no idea it'd be—"

"It's okay. Although, ugh!" Squid shivered. "He was really running out of ideas."

"I'm so sorry." Grief wiped at Squid's cheek with his sleeve.

"Argh, I'm fine." Squid pushed him away gently. "You forget I've been dealing with lowlifes and psychos for years. I've been spat on, slapped up, been thrown from moving vehicles, and set on fire. Sometimes in the same day. I've had my share of face-licking crazies who've wanted to make a set of cufflinks with my teeth."

Grief stared at her, one eye squinting in a strange way.

"Anyway, it's a job, right?" said Squid.

She tried to smile, but from Grief's reaction, she needed practice.

"This way, please," said a staffer, ushering Squid towards a stall.

The young staffer wore a black tank top, tight black hipster pants and black gloves, the reflective yellow stripes across her chest and back marking her as low-level waitstaff.

"I'm York," said the woman, handing Squid a folded uniform. "Give that a go."

Squid struggled into the fitted black clothes patterned with reflective yellow lines. They were designed so that even blind-drunk patrons in a pitch black club could spot the service. And the size. Squid slunk out of the change stall.

"Wow," said Grief. "Your expression reminds me of those kittens dressed up in frilly doll's clothing, plotting surly vengeance on the world."

Squid scowled and was suddenly caught between the impulses to stare and look away.

"I think your outfit's a size too small," she said.

Grief pointed defensively to York.

"You want tips, don't you?" said York, giving Grief a friendly punch on the arm.

Grief shrugged helplessly at Squid.

"Come on," said York, heading for a softly lit corridor. "We're on level three, so apologies in advance. You're a Daily until you've been here for a week. Unfortunately, the blow-ins get the punks and the drunks. Survive enough of that, and you get to look after the real clientele."

"Career progression, that's good, right?" said Grief.

"Did you miss the bit about 'survive enough of that'?" said Squid.

"It's not hard if you can grin and bear it," said York. "Just collect the glasses, wipe the tables, keep the floor clean. And—" She gave a wry smile. "Never retaliate."

They pushed through the swinging doors, and the blast of noise hit them like a wrecking ball. The air reverberated with a hollow, chromatic beat, like enormous jars of water being drummed with steel pipes. Complicated chords rippled over one another in a frenzy of electronic rhythms, while thousands of energetic bodies thrashed and swayed to the beat.

Level three was a massive series of interconnected halls, each one thundering with a different style of music. The targeted acoustics meant that walking from one hall to the next gave you the sensation of having passed through an aural forcefield, with noises from one hall confined to that area.

Grief nodded his head to the beat, his eyes shining in the pulsing lights.

"Seem familiar?" said Squid.

"What? No. Maybe after a few drinks." Grief grinned. "I'm kidding. Let's make some money."

He slapped his gloved hands together and disappeared into the throbbing crowd. Squid stood for a moment, feeling a strange, crushing wave of isolation. As though the whole world were dancing, and she couldn't hear the music.

"Hey!" called a burly teenager. "Ice."

Squid stared blankly at the teen, and he rattled his glass impatiently.

"Ice!" repeated the teen. "You deficient or something?"

Squid snorted a faint trail of steam and calmly took the glass from his hand.

"Right away," she said.

Things went downhill from there. Squid was used to being kicked and shoved and having drinks thrown at her, but she'd never been compelled to take it with a smile. In her old life, she could run away, plead or fight back when cornered. But here, in this new life, it was a part of the package.

Dignity: Zero. Money: One.

All the faces blurred into an indistinguishable collage of sneers and insults. Her head pounded from the music, and her feet were bruised from being constantly stomped on. Squid limped towards the bar and unloaded another tray of dirty glasses.

"Hey, Squid!" Grief squeezed over to her, and the bartender slid a fresh tray of drinks towards him. "How's it going?"

"Fine," said Squid, pushing the sticky hair from her eyes.

Grief looked suspiciously chipper, his hair still in remarkably good shape, and his uniform virtually unstained.

"I'm getting awesome tips," confided Grief. "This guy gave me twenty bucks just to drink a glass of water upside down."

"And I thought you were haemorrhaging cerebral fluid."

Squid offered Grief a napkin, and he wiped at his nose.

"How're you coping?" said Grief.

"I made three dollars, and I think one of them thought I was a beggar."

*And I smell like vomit, look like crap, and feel like driving a burning truck into the building.*

"I'm fine," said Squid, giving the smile thing another try.

Grief looked slightly worried. "Did you want to finish the shift early?"

"No, I'm, you know, I should get that."

Squid didn't even bother putting the sentence together, just leaving it behind like pieces of do-it-yourself furniture.

She trudged towards a scream of "Service!" wondering if Namiel actually had a time distortion device in the Iluvian to make the hours longer. A passing patron shoved Squid out of the way, and she crashed into a nearby table, sending its drinks all over a group of young men in designer clothes.

*Of course, it couldn't have been a church group in second-hand cardigans*, thought Squid as the men swore and blurted angry exclamations.

"I'm sorry," said Squid, quickly mopping up the spill. "I'll have the bar get you two rounds on the house."

"You're going to do more than that," snarled a man with violet hair, grabbing Squid's arm.

To Squid, the moment hung in that strange dimension reserved for critical decisions. Her instinct was to grab a fork and give the guy something more than spilled drinks to worry about. However, this was her job now. It was part of her promise to lead a better life. She'd made so many mistakes, hurt so many people, and gone down a dark road so far, she hadn't thought it possible to get back. And now, it was time for her to make good on those promises.

"What would you like me to do?" said Squid calmly.

"This is a three-hundred-dollar Kubi shirt," said the violet-haired man. "And you're—"

"Boys, is there a problem?" York swung over to the table with a winning smile, hands on her hips.

"York," said the violet-haired man. "Just training the help."

"Sorry, Squid's new and she's just all over the place." York deftly extracted Squid from the man's grasp. "Let me sort this out for you, Leigh. You know I'll always look after you."

York led Squid through the jostling crowd, back towards the bar.

"I'm sorry," said Squid miserably. "This is my first job."

Squid didn't count the lab, since that was mentally filed under "Disasters".

"It's okay," said York. "I'll give him and his mates a one-night pass to Suva on level fifty-two, and they'll be choking on their good luck."

"You can do that?" said Squid.

Suva had a door list in the single digits and cocktails that would blow your mind. Sometimes literally.

"I know people who know people," said York. "I plan on getting to Monthly status here, and networks keep you in the game. Six months, and I can put myself through med school."

Med school. Networks. Squid felt like a bowl of spilled dogfood next to York's soufflé. It occurred to Squid that York was actually younger than her, but somehow, she bubbled with such confidence, such ease, sweeping through life on a wave of sociable charm.

"You okay?" said York.

"Yeah. I'm sorry you had to clean up my mess."

"I believe in secular karma," shrugged York, giving Squid a warm smile. "Look, the bar's run out of vodka raspberries. How about you bring down a carton from the kitchen?"

And if it wasn't bad enough, York was also insidiously nice. As Squid stepped into the relative quiet of the staff corridor, she couldn't help looking at someone like York and thinking, *That should be me.*

*If I were the hero of my own story, I'd be cool and confident and nice*, thought Squid. *I'd be the one swooping in to save hapless serving girls from their own ineptitude. Instead, I'm the hapless serving girl.*

Squid's knuckles practically dragged along the floor as she hobbled to the service elevator, tapping her staff pass against the scanner. The elevator chugged its way to the fiftieth floor, opening onto a bustling maze of hectic kitchens, industrial cold rooms, and giant aquariums of unhappy-looking lobsters and nervous blowfish.

The floor manager directed Squid to a cold-room that seemed implausibly far away. Fortunately, the inventory assistant didn't give Squid a hard time, seeming quite eager to be rid of her. He practically football-lobbed the carton to Squid, sending her staggering into a wall several feet away.

"Thanks!" called Squid.

The inventory assistant kept his hand over his nose, waving her away vigorously. Squid desperately wanted to loiter on the kitchen level, away from the jabbing, snarling patrons below. But the customers would start screaming for blood if they didn't have their vodka raspberries, and Squid didn't want to let York down.

She was heaving the carton down a polished corridor when she caught a faint noise coming from a side passage, like someone trying not to cry. She followed the sound to a tinned-goods closet, the quiet sobbing muffled through the door.

Squid hesitated. She really should get the raspberries to the bar before they melted into soggy blobs, and the closed door clearly suggested that whoever was inside wanted to be left alone. Squid started to walk away, the sound of sobbing growing fainter behind her.

Sometimes, you hid because you wanted to be left alone. But sometimes, you wanted to be alone because you thought no one cared, no one understood and no one could help.

Squid knocked softly on the door before pushing it open a crack. The sobbing stopped abruptly and then burst into a fresh wave of stifled whimpering.

"Are you okay?" said Squid, peering into the storage room.

Racks of tin cans lined the walls, and a skinny young man with curly hair sat on the floor, crying into a pile of wet napkins. He appeared to be covered in an entire buffet and half the wine menu.

"I can't take it anymore," he choked, hiding his face in his hands.

"I know how you feel," said Squid. "And this is my first day."

She sat down beside the shuddering man and, steeling herself, plucked several pieces of scrambled egg from his hair. At least, she hoped it was scrambled egg. The man wore the black dress-shirt and trousers of a senior staffer, red epaulettes on his shoulders.

"And I thought the dance crowd were rough," said Squid.

"I just… I just really need the work…"

"You should get a proper job," said Squid. "You seem normal. I'm sure you could find something better."

"I'm covered in salmon paste!" he wailed. "I'm not even human anymore!"

Squid wasn't sure how to respond to this except to pat the man awkwardly on the shoulder. She found a tissue in his pocket and dabbed at the cranberry sauce on his face. It was then that she realised it wasn't cranberry sauce.

"What happened?" said Squid, her chest tightening.

"They didn't… They didn't like the platter. They just…"

He curled up on the floor, making sad little gasping noises.

"You should get that looked at," said Squid gently. "Pick up some bandages from the pharmacy."

She pulled three dollars from her waistband and tucked it into the man's pocket.

"They have to get their replacement platter," he whimpered. "Please don't make me go back…"

"It's okay," said Squid. "I'll take it up."

He blinked wetly at her. "You'd do that?"

"Sure," gulped Squid. "I'm already covered in gunk, anyway."

The man's mouth turned into a wobbly "W". He staggered away eagerly with the carton of raspberries, leaving Squid with a crumpled delivery docket and his staff pass. Squid turned the card over delicately in her fingers. It wasn't a flimsy yellow plastic pass like the Daily staff had. This was silver-blue alloy with holographic streaks, filigree circuitry glittering along the razor thin edge. You had to last six months to get a card like this.

As Squid headed for the elevator with a fresh dinner platter, she had a vision of a skinny tree-snake trying to swallow a hippopotamus. All she had to do was deliver the platter.

And not retaliate.

The platter actually smelled pretty good, and Squid couldn't imagine what anyone would have to complain about. She was tempted to swipe one of the fried camembert cubes, but decided to be mature about it. Plus, there were undoubtedly surveillance cameras in the elevator.

She stepped out onto level eighty-three, embarrassed by her own gawping reaction. The plush carpet was woven from midnight-blue silk, with translucent stars drifting across the floor. Rivers of muted light poured slowly from the ceiling, like rain streaming down a glasshouse. The corridors curved in winding deltas, so that the guests were rarely in sightline of one another. Squid padded past the lines of golden oak doors, feeling as though she'd stumbled into a fantasy world.

A shadow flickered down a side corridor, and Squid instinctively ducked out of sight. Her heart skipped a beat, not convinced of what she'd seen. After a brief pause, she followed the figure, hugging the bends in breathless silence. As she approached a corner, she dashed forward, peering carefully around the pale blue wall.

There was no mistaking the figure now. It was Grief, striding down the corridor, still in his Daily uniform. Squid crept along the hallway after him, her footsteps silent on the luxurious carpet. Grief seemed to know exactly where he was going, striding with cool purpose.

Voices suddenly approached from farther down the corridor, and Squid slid into a side passage, trying not to lose her dinner platter. She waited for the chatter to fade before sneaking back into the main corridor. Grief was gone, but Squid had seen enough.

She would have time for questions later, but now, she had a delivery to make. She found her way to room eight-three-five-nine and rapped on the door.

*As long as it's not Mal, I'll be okay*, thought Squid.

"About time!" hollered a woman's voice from inside.

Two men and two women occupied the semicircular room, the curving window boasting a spectacular vista of the city skyline. Squid hadn't even realised it was already night, but she felt incredibly grateful that it was.

The occupants of the room were gangster chic, straight from the catalogue. Sleek designer gear in shades of black and blacker, their expensive jackets tossed over the red leather chairs, their guns openly holstered. They wore their attitude like a fifty-foot billboard up in lights, and Squid recognised the type. Someone like Ferret didn't need attitude. He had a pair of pliers and no flinch reflex.

"Oh, God," said the dark-haired woman, covering her nose. "What is that?"

"Your dinner platter," said Squid.

"You've got to be kidding," said the bruiser with sunglasses.

"Enjoy your meal," chirped Squid, turning to leave.

A tall man with white-blond hair leaned against the door, his arms crossed. Squid noticed a spatter of red on his sleeve.

"You expect us to eat that?" said the blond man.

"I don't care what you do with it," said Squid evenly.

"You're going to be sorry you said that," said the bruiser, getting to his feet.

They all seemed slightly surprised when Squid laughed. The blond man slapped Squid hard across the face.

"You think that's funny?"

Squid looked steadily at him.

"You think you're scary because you could break my neck or shoot me in the head? That's not scary, that's clumsy. I know people who could cut out your tongue and gouge out your eyes and make it look like a shaving accident. Who could make you confess to crimes that don't even exist, without leaving a mark. Who could do all that and make you feel like you deserved it. And you think that bashing a skinny kid who won't defend himself makes you some kind of big shot. Well, newsflash, little fish: you're just a bunch of gutless thugs with a bit of cash. And you wouldn't last a day in my shoes."

Squid heard the click of the trigger and ducked as splinters sprayed off the door. She normally couldn't dodge a bullet, but when the gun was being fired by someone who'd had a few drinks, her odds improved remarkably. Three more guns left their holsters and Squid swung the contents of the serving tray across the room. The tattooed woman ducked a flying tureen, and the bruiser with the sunnies caught a milk jug to the skull. A bullet miraculously ricocheted off the tray, and Squid rammed her shoulder into the blond man, sending him crashing onto the floor. Squid flung the tray at the dark-haired woman and bolted out the door.

She commandeered an elevator all the way to the ground floor, hitting a full sprint almost before the doors completely opened. Iluvian security already swarmed the floor, and Squid wove through the confused partygoers as holographic lights dipped in and out of the walls. Voices yelled over the crashing music, and Squid felt a hand grab her shirt. She twisted in a tight figure-eight and burst through the main doors, minus her reflective straps.

She raced across the pavement, charging through the late-night drunks and nuzzling couples.

"Squid!"

She ignored the voice as she slid into an alleyway, following her familiar rat-run home. After several blocks, her footsteps slowed to a flagging halt. Prosperity Mansions wasn't home anymore. There was no "home". And she still didn't have a job.

"Squid." Grief rounded the corner breathlessly. "Thanks for waiting."

"I was kind of in a rush."

Grief leaned forward, trying to see Squid's face.

"What happened?"

"I happened."

There was a sullen silence. Next time, she'd eat the bloody camembert.

"You have something in your hair," said Grief, reaching over.

"Stop it," said Squid, pushing his hands away roughly. "Just stop it. Please."

She leaned against a wall, putting her face in her hands. She wanted to be a million miles away, a million years ago, in a completely different universe. And a completely different person. It hurt so much to be her, when the distance between who she was and who she wanted to be remained such an irreconcilable gulf.

Squid finally took a deep breath, letting her arms fall to her sides.

"You should keep the job," she said. "I bet you and York would make a killing."

"Yeah," said Grief. "I'd end up killing someone."

"I'm serious. If you can't hold down a job, you'll end up like me."

Grief shrugged, his hands in his pockets.

"You're not so bad."

"I eat out of Dumpsters."

"We're working on that."

Squid knew she risked sinking into another puddle of self-pity, but it was hard to stay positive when you'd just been chased from your job by security. Again. She could only keep trying, but right now, all she wanted to do was eat cream buns and listen to angst-fuelled ballads played at full blast.

"You like York, don't you?" said Squid.

"Sure, she's nice."

Squid thought of York's easy smile and genuine kindness. She reminded Squid a little of Grief: confident, sociable, destined for success, as long as there was nothing holding them back. She could never be like York, but perhaps there was still a way for her to be a better Squid.

Grief took her hand gently, and Squid felt warm rumpled notes being pressed into her palm. She looked up at him in surprise.

"Grief—"

He closed her fingers over the money.

"You should go get your watch," he said.

Squid stared at the handful of small notes and change. That was twelve hours of abuse and grabbing and drinking water upside down.

"I can't—"

"It's just money," said Grief. "I want you to have your watch back.

Maybe it'll stop you from looking so disoriented all the time."

"I don't—" began Squid, then stopped herself. "Thank you."

Grief stretched his back, pulling off the reflective yellow straps. "But first, how about you shout me to dinner?"

*

Namiel watched the footage, his expression inscrutable. Minor incidents at the Iluvian were common—drunken scuffles, fistfights, the occasional poisoning in the private suites. These were to be expected in the hospitality industry.

There were those who thought badly of the Iluvian and considered it a den of vice, albeit an expensive one. But the Iluvian had standards, and discretion was god. Namiel stood by that principle without compromise. Unlike the Kabukuri Club, where everything had a price. Especially the things that shouldn't.

The footage of Squid taking on four armed mercenaries with a buffet tray brought a faint smile to Namiel's lips. She was one of Ferret's strays, and Namiel had an unspoken understanding with Ferret. The man was a quiet worker and a respectful businessman. Namiel didn't have a problem with Ferret.

Of course, Squid wouldn't be welcome back at the Iluvian. However, it was a kinder fate than the one awaiting the four mercenaries who'd opened fire inside Namiel's establishment. Each of the doors on level eighty-three was hand-carved from a single slab of three-centuries-old golden oak, shipped in from a wild grove on the private island of Malisands. Namiel was very attached to those doors.

However, that wasn't Namiel's biggest problem tonight. He switched off the surveillance cameras in the viewing hub, and replayed the *other* footage.

The man had moved like a shark shadowing a trail of blood, his Daily uniform shining a bright yellow *X* on the screen. At one point, the man glanced up at the camera, a disturbingly familiar face staring directly at him. Namiel blanked the screen with a slight shiver, his finger hesitating over the delete command.

He felt that he should call Ducabre, or perhaps Verona, but it wasn't Namiel's war. His neutrality had been hard won, and he had more money than anyone needed. Neutrality and discretion were the foundations of the Iluvian and the life Namiel now led. But still, this was a disturbing development.

Namiel's finger slid across the screen and tapped a glowing icon.

*Save.*

# TWELVE

Casey didn't live in a particularly bad part of town. She'd lived in bedsits and apartments all over the city before deciding it wasn't worth having a spare bedroom if you had to dodge bullets while doing the laundry.

She had ended up on Venice Canal, a neighbourhood of run-down art deco apartments that wore their glory days like a retiree in a faded prom dress. The Manhattan-style studios were luxurious compared to Squid's coffin box, but the price you paid was unreliable hot water and more rats than a busted granary.

Most of the people here were families on the way down, artists on the way up, and seniors who'd refused to budge when the sky had rained with napalm in the last war, and they sure as hell weren't leaving now. It smelled pretty bad because of the canal, but you could walk down the street without ducking for cover, and there was a pretty good bakery on the corner.

Unfortunately, Casey's part of town had just gotten a whole lot worse.

It was close to four in the morning when Casey headed home, and she saw the glow from seven blocks away. At four blocks, she was coughing from the smoke, and at two blocks, she could see the leaping flames.

The entire building—her building—was on fire. It looked like a towering jack-o'-lantern, grimacing as orange light spilled through the exploding windows. Casey pushed to the front of the disoriented crowd, many of the residents still in their pyjamas.

"Is anyone still inside?" yelled Casey.

The residents looked at each other in a daze, some of them sobbing, others staring blankly at the bonfire of their lives. Casey mustered the crowd into groups: ground floor, first floor, second floor and onwards. Apartment one, apartment two, apartment three. Nobody knew their neighbours, but they knew which room they lived in. It was difficult to account for everyone—Tucker Hobson was staying with his daughter that night, and Daisy Lo was probably still at cabaret rehearsals—but no one was obviously missing. There weren't entire families unaccounted for.

As the firefighters brought the blaze under control, the crowd gradually melted back into a confused, traumatised blob.

"It's a miracle no one was killed," said a slim man in a dark jacket. "It'd be a shame if someone was tied up in number six-two-four when it went up."

Casey's blood turned to ice, everything around her darkening except a spotlight on the smiling man who was already vanishing into the crowd. She flattened several unshaven poets as she ploughed frantically through the throng, trying not to shoulder-charge a knot of elderly women who looked like they could probably withstand it.

"Stop!" yelled Casey, knowing it was no use.

She lost him down an alleyway, chasing the sound of a motorbike roaring away.

Six-two-four.

Her apartment.

And someone— Oh, God…

Casey punched the familiar icon on her phone, praying for him to answer. The phone rang for an eternity before the receiver picked up.

"Riego!" said Casey.

*"This is Riego; leave a message."*

Casey stared at the screen, her heart beating painfully in her chest. She flagged down a car, or rather, she stood in front it and slammed her hands on the bonnet, her badge gleaming like a shotgun.

She didn't have a portable siren, but she screamed threats of arrest at every car in her way, which had a similar effect. She wasn't going ballistic. She was just—

There was no reason to think Riego had been in the building. It was just some punk having a go. Just another cowardly message from Pearce. But she'd been ignoring Pearce's messages, and maybe he'd decided to go for something a little closer to home.

Casey burst through the doors of the station like a bull charging into a dance recital.

"Has anyone seen Riego?" she gasped.

No one had seen him since that morning, when he'd declared he was going to have an early, long lunch. Casey searched the cafeteria, the research library, the main office, constantly ringing his phone to the same recorded message.

*He's probably home*, thought Casey. *I'm not even thinking straight. That's how badly they've shaken me, and I can't afford to fly off my brain now.*

It was almost dawn when she arrived at Riego's place, sprinting up the curving staircase and battering on his door. If Riego wasn't inside, if he'd been in her apartment, if he was—

Casey had almost bashed down the door when it finally swung open, and Riego stood blearily in the doorway.

"Casey?"

"Why the hell aren't you answering your phone?" she yelled.

Curious faces peered out from neighbouring doors, and Riego waved Casey into his cosy apartment.

"I think some wiseguy lifted it this morning," said Riego. "I tried to tell you, but you've been doing that thing where you're trying to be somewhere I'm not."

A cascade of relief and guilt washed through Casey. Riego was okay, and everything else could wait until morning. The gutting of her apartment, the implications for the Werner case—those would sink in later. Right now, the adrenaline had run out. She could stay at the station bunks until she found a new place, and luckily, she was too much of a minimalist to have had much personal stuff. Things didn't matter. People mattered.

Riego was still wearing his "I didn't come all the way to this country to be treated like this" face, waiting for Casey to respond. She knew it had been unfair to avoid him, but a part of her had thought he wouldn't notice. And part of her thought he'd be grateful.

"I've been busy," said Casey weakly. "Sorry."

Riego took in Casey's ragged appearance, and his expression turned a fraction more forgiving.

"So, why do you smell like burnt tortilla?" said Riego.

"My apartment burned down."

"Whoa." Riego rolled back as though buffeted by a large wave. "Like someone left waffles on the stove?"

Casey rubbed her eyes, the exhaustion creeping in. She'd saved for seven months to buy that second-hand couch. And she'd had a birthday letter from her nephew in the dresser drawer.

"I don't know," said Casey. "I should get started on the paperwork."

"I saw Salamina Bombay today," said Riego.

Casey stopped at the door. Doctor Bombay had been one of Werner's university professors, and Werner's notes had been peppered with references to her guidance. Casey's own attempts to speak with Doctor Bombay had been met with stony, monosyllabic denials.

"What do you mean by 'saw'?"

"I sat in on one of her lectures," said Riego. "And it turns out my second cousin's niece's husband goes to the same book club as her best friend's wife's secretary."

Casey was fairly sure Riego didn't have a second cousin, but this was probably beside the point.

"According to Mina—"

"Mina?" Casey raised an eyebrow.

"She's actually very friendly—"

"When you get past the legal threats?"

Riego crossed his arms like a parent refusing to continue a bedtime story due to interruptions.

"Sorry, go ahead," said Casey. "What did *Mina* say?"

"According to *Doctor Bombay*, Werner went to her for advice on a lot of his projects. Kid had a special interest in autonomous surveillance—dreamed of intelligent probes in volcanic ocean vents, rovers drifting through Jupiter, satellites sailing to distant galaxies. He'd been working for years on some kind of compressed encryption—putting years of high-resolution surveillance data on a wafer the size of a fingernail. A few months ago, Werner said he'd gotten the final piece of equipment he needed, just had to test it. Then everything went silent."

Autonomous surveillance devices capable of storing massive amounts of data. It was certainly lucrative, with applications in just about every piece of technology you could dream up. But Casey still couldn't figure out how this made Werner a marked man. Unless he was threatening to defect.

Or had recorded something he wasn't supposed to.

"What are you thinking?" said Riego.

"I think… it can wait 'til morning," said Casey.

Her mind was already crawling over the new information, but she couldn't shift the cold lump in the pit of her stomach. She couldn't shake the chilling image of Riego tied up in a burning apartment, the door swinging closed.

"Want to crash here tonight?" said Riego.

"No!" Casey paused. "I mean, I should go."

Riego looked at her doubtfully, then shrugged.

"Okay. Just remember, I'm your partner. I'm supposed to watch your back, not eat your dust."

Casey turned up the collar of her jacket as she headed for the door.

"I don't think it was coincidence that you lost your phone today," she said. "Be careful."

"Get some sleep, Casey," said Riego. "I'll be fine."

*

Ferret didn't live at the Chival, despite the fact that he could have occupied one of the extravagant penthouse suites. He preferred to keep a low profile, and penthouses at the Chival were the underworld equivalent of a large, feathered headdress complete with flashing target.

Ferret lived in a modest two-bedroom house in the quiet suburb of Apple Grove. The lawns were always clipped, and children occasionally played in the street. The children did, however, stay off his lawn with terrified vigilance.

It looked like any other house, although closer inspection would reveal an electrified grid just under the grass, automated sniper barrels around the windows, and strategically placed piano wire in the hallways.

Coming home was always a little like executing a prison break in reverse, but it was routine to Ferret. Survival was more important than comfort, more important than happiness, more important than conscience. What you wanted would change. What you thought was right or wrong would change. But everything depended on your being alive.

Ferret had started his criminal career as a messenger. He could find people who didn't want to be found, and deliver messages they didn't want to receive. He had risen through the ranks at a steady pace and become someone who issued messages. But there was always the overhanging threat that if you didn't pay any heed, Ferret would deliver the message himself.

It had been some time since he had actually received a message, particularly in his own home. However, by the time he switched on the living-room light, his gun was already drawn, aimed and on the verge of being fired.

The woman sitting on his plush caramel lounge smiled faintly, her fingers drumming once on the armrest. Ferret swallowed, and after a moment of suicidal temptation, forced himself to casually holster his gun.

"Verona," said Ferret. "To what do I owe this pleasure?"

Verona continued to smile, her eyes and mouth so neat, they seemed painted on. Two elegant sandalwood sticks held her dark hair in a tidy twist, and her immaculate sapphire-blue suit made his lounge look as though it had fallen from a tip truck.

The fact that Verona was in his living room, alone and apparently unarmed, made Ferret more nervous than if she'd turned up with a dozen armed guards and a hydrogen bomb. Guards and guns, he could handle. The three dozen sniper rifles undoubtedly aimed at his head through the walls—much more complicated.

"I expect you know why I'm here," said Verona.

Ferret could practically hear the sand draining from his timer, the loud hiss of life drawing to a close. The bionic eye assignment had crossed a line, but everyone knew a war was brewing. You could wait for it to crash over you, or you could take the first shot and dig in for the fight. Unfortunately, the fight had come to him a lot sooner than anticipated. He had to admit it would send a dramatic signal to Pearce's camp.

Ferret allowed himself a quick glance around the room. As far as he could tell, nothing had been disturbed. Either Verona was jamming the bugs, or she wanted Pearce to hear this. And "this" would probably be Ferret dying horribly.

"I wouldn't presume to guess," said Ferret, the back of his neck prickling from a dozen invisible cross hairs.

Verona's smile remained fixed, and Ferret was fairly certain she still hadn't blinked.

"The gauntlet's been thrown," she said. "The torching of my shipment was a declaration of war, and in doing this, Pearce has engineered his own downfall. He's a crumbling anachronism, unprepared for the onslaught he's unleashed."

"Then you underestimate Pearce."

"But I don't underestimate you," said Verona, her smile widening slightly. "Loyalty isn't your strong point, Ferret. One of the many reasons for your longevity in an unpredictable industry. No point in following a falling leader, is there?"

Ferret knew better than to answer a question like that.

"The outcome is far from decided," he said.

"Why don't you help Pearce to decide it?" said Verona, rising gracefully to her feet. "Oh, but no one's seen or heard from Pearce in weeks, have they?"

She knew. Somehow, she'd gotten wind of the rumours, and she was making her move. It could still be a ploy by Pearce to make Verona overconfident, leaving her open for a massacre. But Verona clearly wanted Ferret to give the tree a shake so she could see what fell out.

Verona ducked beneath the invisible wire in the doorway.

"Consider this a friendly warning," she said. "Unlike Pearce, I can be forgiving. But cross me again, and your next visitor might not be so cordial."

And then she was gone.

Ferret quickly scanned the house for foreign bugs, already planning his next few moves. Verona was right: no one had seen Pearce in weeks, and people were getting suspicious. It wasn't uncommon for Pearce to vanish for extended periods, but this time, it was different.

Ducabre had taken over jurisdictions previously controlled by departmental heads, and Pearce wasn't the only one lying low. His faithful Rottweiler, Raphael, had also been more invisible than usual, which usually meant something very unpleasant was about to happen to someone very powerful. Then again, perhaps someone had finally put him down. On top of that, more and more of their headquarters had been declared off-limits, and the internal surveillance loop had spread a little wider despite Technology's protests.

Ducabre was hiding something, and Ferret didn't like it. If something had happened to Pearce, the syndicate faced a meltdown at the worst possible moment. However, Ferret prided himself on having a plan for almost every contingency, and he certainly had one for this.

Perhaps it was time to make his move.

*

Squid left the house just before dawn. Grief was still asleep, sprawled across the floor like a happy starfish in the grey light.

The air was still damp when she arrived at Trey's pawn shop, and Squid rubbed her arms as she waited by the door. She could see movement in the back room, and Trey eventually caught sight of her through the smeared glass.

He made her wait another ten minutes before opening the door, a mug of steaming coffee in one hand.

"What do you want, Squid?"

"I'm here for the watch," she said, following Trey inside.

"You know that requires money."

Squid pushed a scrunched wad of cash and a smattering of coins onto the counter.

"Two hundred dollars, right?" said Squid.

Trey picked through the pile sceptically, pocketing all the notes.

"Well, that's the two hundred you owe me."

"Hey!" Squid slapped her hands over the pitiful pile of coins. "You can't do that!"

Trey leaned his elbows on the counter, almost nose to nose with Squid. His expression was a great big "So sue me". Squid wanted so badly to wrap her hands around his neck and start throttling, but Trey was twice her size, and he had a shotgun.

And he was right.

"There's still… four dollars fifty," said Squid. "The watch isn't worth anything to you. Please."

Trey leaned back in his chair, putting his feet on the counter.

"Honestly, I'd give it to you," he said. "But it's already gone."

Squid's brain whited out with incandescent anger.

"What do you mean, 'It's gone'?" she said, her voice oddly calm.

"It got snapped up. But for fifty bucks, I'll tell you who bought it."

Things snapped inside Squid, like violin strings in the middle of a solo.

"I don't have fifty bucks," she said, every word like a body dropping into the bay.

"Then I guess I don't know who bought it."

Squid's hands curled into white-knuckled fists, her whole body shaking. Trey suddenly seemed to realise how many breakables there were in his store and quickly scooped the remaining coins from the counter.

"Okay, special discount," said Trey. "Mal's got it."

Squid felt as though all the blood had drained from her body, soaking into the ground beneath her feet. Fate couldn't possibly hate her that much.

"You told him it was mine," said Squid flatly.

"It's just business."

Squid wanted to etch those words on Trey's headstone, preferably after burying him alive with a loudly ticking clock.

After wrangling a primitive phone from Trey, she left the pawn shop like a zombie, stumbling mindlessly down the narrow streets. Pieces of her could have fallen off and she wouldn't have noticed. Her watch was as good as gone. Knowing Mal, it was probably in tiny pieces, embedded in the tread of his Hummer. But worse than that, all of Grief's money was gone.

Squid felt her eyes prickling, and she wanted to bang her head against a wall until all the pain went away. She felt as though some kind of chute was supposed to open up and send her tumbling into a cosmic bin labelled FAILED HUMAN BEINGS, next to the basket of duff chicks and broken birthday presents.

She couldn't go home. She couldn't bear to tell Grief that she'd wasted all his money, watching his face as he tried to tell her it was okay. Because it wasn't okay. She wasn't okay.

Squid leaned against a wall, the despair and frustration sloshing around inside her. She was sick of being bullied, being scared, being useless. And she was the only one who could change that.

She started walking again. She would earn two hundred dollars today, somehow. The Iluvian had always been her emergency plan—if all else failed, there was always the Iluvian. But even they wouldn't take her back now. She would have to be creative. She would have to be persistent.

She would have to compromise.

*

Squid's first stop was easy money, if you didn't mind braving blood-borne diseases. It was just something to get that first bit of cash, to pep her up for what lay ahead.

The back room of Fletch's pawn shop resembled a poorly kept lab, with shelves of glistening red vials, and storage coolers bearing innocuous labels. Fletch didn't deal in the hardcore stuff, but Squid had a feeling that this had more to do with equipment than ethics.

Squid rolled up her sleeve, forcing herself to watch as the thick red liquid slid up the tube. It made her giddy, but you'd be stupid to leave Fletch unsupervised with a syringe.

"Just three-by-fifty," said Squid, eyeing the stand of empty vials.

"Where's your cute friend today?" said Fletch.

"He's not my friend," said Squid automatically.

She'd never gotten the hang of making friends. The only reason Casey hovered around was because she thought she'd get karmic kudos for rehabilitating Squid. And Squid had found Grief in a car trunk after he'd suffered some kind of brain damage. If he'd met her before, in his other life, he wouldn't have looked at her twice except maybe to veer away in case poverty was contagious.

Squid winced as Fletch switched vials.

"If you need cash, I've got a delivery across town," said Fletch. "A hundred at the destination, no questions."

Fletch nodded towards a red and white cooler labelled BEER. Squid had no doubt that anyone opening the cooler expecting to find beer would be grossly disappointed. The two paths branched in front of Squid, stark as day. She could take the cooler, grab a car and have the cash in less than an hour. She didn't know for certain that the cooler contained illegal goods. She could easily return the car. And she'd be halfway home.

And a step closer to Ferret.

The right choice was obvious, but it still felt like a punch in the guts.

"Sorry," said Squid. "I've got some stuff to do."

Fletch shrugged, capping the last vial.

"Sure you do, Squid." She slid fifteen dollars across the table. "See you around."

Squid rubbed her arm as she wobbled into the sunlight, her head feeling like a runaway balloon. She could have used that fun-sized juice right about now.

She hated going to Fletch's, but it had gotten her through some pretty lean times. Squid always had a hell of a time trying to explain the needle marks to Casey, and usually ended up having to supply a urine sample anyway. But this would be the last time, because things were going to change.

It was late morning when Squid arrived at the grey government building at the dog-eared end of town. The Metropolitan Job Centre was a featureless block full of cubicles and touchscreens, with scruffy queues trailing from neutral grey counters. Fresh-faced high-schoolers clutched skeletal resumes, middle-aged empty-nesters shifted uncomfortably in their outdated suits, and the chronically unemployed sagged along the line like beanbags being rolled across the floor.

Squid fell into this last category, although she tried to look more like a fresh-faced high-schooler who'd fallen on a bit of hard luck these past six years. You didn't come to the MJC if you were a professional looking to change careers—you had the Monte Cristo Agency for high-end corporates, or the Blue Duck House for funky young prodigies, and a hundred other online placement agencies for everyone else.

But if all else failed, there was always the good old MJC, where it wasn't uncommon to stroll into your interview with a half-empty bottle of whisky and an imaginary friend. There were so many tired faces and blank eyes, hollow people who'd heard "no" so many times, they'd forgotten there was any other answer. It was a terrible thing, to feel that no one believed in you. To never have had that chance to show people what you're worth.

"Next!" called the granite-faced woman at the counter.

Squid stepped forward and waited under the woman's spotlight glare.

"Four-three-seven, two-nine-five, or eight-six-one?" said the woman robotically.

"Huh?" said Squid, as politely as possible.

"Are you looking for training, looking for a program, or looking for work?"

"Looking for work."

"Two-eleven or two-thirteen?"

"Uh..." Squid wondered if she'd missed the instructional video on the way in.

"Are you a returning applicant or a new file?" said the woman, her voice like a garbage disposal grinding up a steel pipe.

"New?"

The woman made a few rapid ticks on a sheet of paper and stamped it hard enough to leave an embossing. She thrust the page at Squid.

"Follow fifty-four," said the woman.

Squid tried desperately to decode this before following the woman's gaze to the floor. A cluster of thin, numbered lines streamed across the scuffed linoleum, leading into the maze of cubicles beyond.

Feeling a little like Theseus striding into the labyrinth, Squid followed line fifty-four into the grey city. The smell of cheap coffee permeated the air, and the sound of ancient printers buzzed around her. Identical black lines swam in her vision, and just as she started to get a facial tic from trying to disentangle them, she arrived at a cubicle labelled 54.

A friendly-looking man with a loose tie sat at the desk, and he waved Squid inside.

"Hi, my name's Brian," he said. "Could I have your sixty-eight, please?"

This time, Squid caught sight of the number on her stamped form, and handed it over.

"Take a seat," said Brian, skimming the form.

Squid had tried to make sense of it, but the page was covered in columns of random numbers, with angry-looking crosses drawn next to some of them. Brian's expression became faintly worried as he looked over Squid's form.

"Oh," said Brian. "Oh…"

The descending pitch of Brian's *oh*s suggested to Squid that she hadn't made a very good first impression on the gatekeeper.

"I really want a job," said Squid. "I like offices, and people, and cats."

She smiled hopefully.

"Oh…" said Brian, his gaze reaching the end of the form.

"I'll take *anything*," said Squid.

*I just need a hundred and eighty-five dollars by the end of the day.*

"Okay," said Brian, with a slightly uncertain smile. "I guess we'll start with the profile."

Brian's fingers tapped across a sticky keyboard, and the monitor made an unhappy beeping noise.

"So, what's your highest level of education?" said Brian.

"Twelfth grade."

"Do you have any formal training?"

"No."

"Informal training?"

"No."

"Professional qualifications?"

"No."

"What was your longest period of employment?"

Squid paused, deciding not to ask for a definition of "employment".

"A day."

Brian stared at the dull orange screen, as though searching for a compliment in response to an awful meal.

"Oh… well," said Brian. "Maybe I can set you up with some training. The military are looking for more Frontline Barrier Personnel—"

"I need a job today," said Squid firmly.

"Okay…" Brian continued tapping codes into the keyboard. "Oh, I have just the thing. No experience. Instant cash—"

"Uh, I'm not on good terms with the Iluvian," said Squid hurriedly.

Brian paused. She could almost hear herself clanking into the Way Too Hard Basket. Brian recovered and continued scrolling across his screen.

"There's a position at the Kabukuri Club, waiting tables," said Brian hopefully.

Squid's stomach twisted itself into a complicated balloon animal. She knew the Kabukuri Club, and she knew what "waiting tables" meant. You might not survive the Iluvian with your dignity intact, but you might not survive the Kabukuri Club. Full stop.

But it was a job. And they would take her.

Squid stared at her choices, trying to figure out which was the more adult decision. Which was the more responsible decision. Life was full of sacrifice and compromise, but sometimes, you needed a line in the sand, or you lost yourself completely.

"Anything but that," said Squid quietly.

Brian let out a troubled sigh, his fingers typing various combinations of criteria. For some time, the only sound was the clicking of the keyboard.

"If you don't mind me asking, what exactly have you been doing for the past few years?" said Brian.

Squid stared at her hands in her lap.

"Screwing up, mostly."

"Yeah, I get a lot of that," said Brian, not unkindly.

"What happens to them usually? The hard cases?"

She saw the look in Brian's eyes, and his gaze flicked back to the screen.

"Oh, you're in luck," he said. "A casual's pulled out for the afternoon. If you can get to Arum Valley Mall, you can have the shift. No experience needed."

"What's the job?" said Squid warily.

Brian handed Squid the job docket.

"Take it from someone who's seen the hard cases get harder," he said. "Just take the job."

# THIRTEEN

Arum Valley Mall was an open-air shopping village designed to resemble a quaint heritage district, without the sewage and stray dogs. Large glass shopfronts gleamed, and faux-handcrafted signs hung from wrought-iron brackets. Islands of dwarf lemon trees and basil bushes dotted the wide cobbled streets. It was the kind of place visited by fashionable shoppers who wanted the cachet of appearing down to earth.

On the one hand, Squid was enormously grateful she hadn't ended up somewhere seedy. On the other hand, she had never seen a cupcake suit before, let alone worn one. She wasn't entirely convinced they should even exist.

Mr Tamini, the manager of Cutie Cupcakes, was a nervous-looking man with a small handlebar moustache and thinning hair. He had the generic look of a helpful uncle who was always afraid of upsetting somebody. Mr Tamini pointed from the cupcake suit to a lacquered tray of bite-sized chocolate cupcakes.

"It's a big cupcake, handing out little cupcakes!" said Mr Tamini.

He looked at Squid with eager expectation, as though desperate for her to see the brilliance.

"Yay," said Squid with a weak smile.

It took her almost half an hour to struggle into the suit, with Mr Tamini's enthusiastic assistance. Despite being moulded from foam, the suit must have weighed twenty kilos, including all the icing and sprinkles. Squid peered out from a face hole in the front, her arms and legs poking out at awkward angles.

Mr Tamini handed Squid the tray, and she gripped it with some difficulty, barely able to see around the rotund cupcake suit.

"Smile!" said Mr Tamini.

"I am," said Squid.

"Big smile!" he said, giving a demonstration of a panicked grin.

Squid forced her face into a demonic grimace and trundled out into the basil-scented sunshine.

She had been hoping that the shoppers at Arum Valley Mall would be upmarket hippies and snooty women in twinsets. Unfortunately, the demographic skewed more towards hulking private-school boys who tried to tip her over, bratty children wanting to tear her sprinkles off, and hip young professionals who didn't bother stifling their laughter as they grabbed cupcakes from her tray.

Squid was tempted to slap away anyone who didn't look like they deserved a cupcake, but instead, she forced a smile and chirped, "Cutie Cupcakes, the cutest cakes in the city!"

By late afternoon, her feet were in agony, and the inside of the suit was soaked with sweat. Her legs started to tremble, and Squid wondered if it had been such a good idea to give blood that morning. The world suddenly tilted dangerously, and she lay down quickly beneath a lemon tree, waiting for things to stop spinning. A wail started up by her feet, and Squid rolled over to see two small children bawling.

"The cupcake's dead!" screamed the little girl.

"Uh, no, I'm not," said Squid, trying to right herself.

A flustered couple rushed over, shooting disapproving glares towards Squid.

"It's okay, sweetie," said the perfectly coiffed father, ushering the children away. "It's just a lazy cupcake."

Squid stared after the family, her face burning with the injustice. She'd been on her feet for hours, and she'd been nice to almost everyone. She was quite sure that heat stroke was setting in, and she was ready to collapse.

And this was still day one.

She stared at the horizon, and it seemed that her working life stretched before her in an endless haze of days like this. Work. Survive.

Exist. Smile. This was what she wanted, and yet, she felt as though the day could hardly get worse.

"Heya, cupcake."

Squid wondered if it'd be an offence to assault someone while wearing a cupcake suit, or whether she could call it interactive art. Casey had once said that anything involving the word "assault" was an offence—

Squid stopped when she saw the man, hating the fact that her face turned even redder.

He was gorgeous.

Squid normally didn't pay much attention to these things, since she was usually trying to avoid being run over, stabbed, or crushed by falling barrels. But the man standing before her had a smile like hot chocolate in winter, and a face like a magazine cover. His clothes were San Cruza Drive meets Tibetan markets, and arm in arm with him was a very familiar figure.

"Squid?" said the woman, her hand intertwined with the man's.

Squid wanted the ground to open up, promises be damned.

"Alabama," said Squid, feeling that nothing more needed to be said.

Alabama Stahl had been the girl-most-likely. Cheerleader, school dux, with a new car every birthday. She'd gone on to study international empire management at Harvard or something, and that was the last Squid had heard of her. Mostly because she blocked her ears whenever the name came up.

"What have you been up to?" said Alabama with a smile that cost more than a small hospital.

"You know, just stuff," said Squid, willing the day to fast-forward to when she'd be sitting on the couch, crying into a tub of ice cream.

"That's so great," said Alabama brightly. "I've just been promoted to vice president of the European arm of Dorset Blaise Recruitment, and Bastian and I just got engaged!"

Alabama held up a blinding rock, squeezing her fiancé's arm affectionately.

"We're going to Nepal for our honeymoon," continued Alabama. "But then Bastian has to run off for another shoot in Tuscany."

"Oh… You're a model?" said Squid faintly.

Bastian gave a flattered laugh.

"Oh, you," said Alabama. "Bastian's a photographer. His cover for *Aqua Vie Journal* won this year's International Marine Photography Award."

"Alabama," said Bastian modestly. "I'm sure your friend isn't interested."

Actually, her "friend" was hoping for a convenient bonfire to hurl herself onto.

"I really shouldn't keep you," said Squid stiffly. "It was lovely seeing you again, Alabama. Nice to meet you, Bastian. Please, have a cupcake. They're… the cutest cupcakes in the city."

"That is such an adorable outfit," called Alabama, giving Squid a dagger of a wink as she and Bastian walked off into the glorious sunset.

In another life, Squid would have sat on the cold cobbles and sobbed herself into a mess of mucous. But today, she scrubbed down the empty tray and struggled out of her humid cupcake suit.

"Very good," said Mr Tamini, handing Squid an envelope. "Good cupcake."

"Thank you," said Squid tiredly.

She stuffed the four rumpled tens into her pocket and began the trek out of Arum Valley. She knew she should count herself lucky—she was young, alive and finally free of a complicated past. But still, seeing Alabama and Bastian, it was enough to drive her into the arms of—

Squid found herself outside the Fess, a cool westerly sweeping the trash across the broken lot. It looked like a bikers' bar, with blacked-out windows and flickering neon signs. But you didn't come here for the booze.

The bartender didn't look up as Squid wedged herself against the counter, keeping her head down in the crowded bar.

"Hey, Wesson," said Squid.

"Heard you'd gone straight," said the bartender. "Guess I was wrong."

"Need some clean cash. Got a hook-up?"

"You don't come here for clean, Squid." Wesson stacked another empty glass.

"What've you got?"

Wesson's smile blended into the scar that stretched across his cheek. "Question is, have you still got it?"

A black box that needed its homing chip deactivated netted Squid a quick thirty. Diagnosing a fried security cable in a car belonging to a "friend" of a "friend" of a "mate" scored her twenty. She cut a fast deal with a sweating man who needed a couple of bullets removed, like, now. Squid was far from qualified, but for forty-five bucks, he wasn't going to get a surgeon.

Squid quickly counted the cash, wiping the blood from her hands. She'd made more in an hour at the Fess than she had all day at Arum Valley. And she wasn't doing anything illegal, per se. It was tempting to think she could coast along the edge, doing what she was good at, where people didn't look at her like some kind of freak. It was so much easier here. Almost like coming home—

A figure loomed out of nowhere, and a large hand grabbed each wrist before she could pull away into the crowd.

"Hello, Squid."

The voice was like a trail of sulphur rising from the depths of Hades. The floor seemed to fall away, taking Squid's stomach with it.

"Mal…" gasped Squid.

Mal twisted Squid's arms behind her, lifting her clear off the ground as she kicked helplessly at the air.

"Nice of you to show your face again," he said.

Squid knew from experience that starting any sentence with "I can explain" usually ended in a concussion on the railway tracks.

"I'm sorry about the car," she said. "I'll make it up to you!"

"You *wish* this was about the car," growled Mal.

"I swear I didn't know you were involved with the shipment," squeaked Squid.

Mal's arms tightened around her ribs, and she could feel her organs squeezing into unusual places.

"Verona's very unhappy," said Mal. "And when Verona's unhappy, people lose bits."

The bar had gone rather quiet, like party guests trying not to notice someone gurgling to death beside the tiramisu. A loose circle of Mal's buddies stood meaningfully around the pair.

"I can explain!" wheezed Squid, tiny stars exploding across her vision.

"Why don't we start with the Auger, six years ago, and we'll take it from there?" said Mal, his voice dangerously soft.

Squid felt like an egg about to turn into an omelette, her vision blacking out as her ribs made faint cracking noises.

"I think you should let her go," said a low voice.

The Fess suddenly got a whole lot quieter.

Squid swivelled her gaze to the suicidal figure and saw Grief standing alone in the crowd, like Spartacus before the Romans.

Squid made desperate noises, shaking her head urgently and rolling her eyes towards the door. Grief was crazy, but Mal was *crazy*. With a gun.

"What are you going to do about it?" said Mal.

"I don't know," said Grief. "But I'm *dying* to find out."

Grief's eyes lit up with sinister anticipation, and Mal studied the newcomer coolly. A strange unease rolled through the bar, with all eyes trying not to watch the showdown.

"Don't I know you from somewhere?" said Mal.

Grief's gaze turned subzero.

"I said… let her go."

Squid made futile gasping noises.

Mal's eyes suddenly sharpened with recognition, like a harpoon sailing through a sheet of glass.

"Well, isn't this interesting?" said Mal with an unpleasant grin. "Now, why would the—"

Grief moved like a rogue bullet, landing a single punch before anyone could react. It wasn't like a barroom punch or a boxing jab. It was the kind of punch invented by the military to bring down rabid elephants. Mal was out cold before he hit the floor, and Grief was already racing from the Fess with Squid in tow.

A few shots followed through the doors, but Mal's buddies seemed more concerned with getting Mal back to base than giving chase. Even so, Squid and Grief didn't stop running until they were halfway home.

"That was Mal!" gasped Squid, when she finally slowed enough to catch her breath.

"I'll remember that," said Grief grimly.

"You can't just... I mean, he's... Verona's going to..."

She swayed slightly, feeling nauseous.

"I don't think I had a choice," said Grief softly. "Why was he..."

"He's been holding this crazy grudge for years," shivered Squid. "I was like eighteen, and he was just some hoodlum—"

"You've been running from this guy for six years?"

"I know!" said Squid. "Isn't he insane?"

Grief shook his head, and they trudged along the empty street in silence.

"What were you doing there, anyway?" said Squid.

"You were gone when I woke up," said Grief. "When you didn't come back, I thought maybe you'd driven a burning truck into the bay."

"I don't do that anymore."

"Don't you?"

Squid felt a surge of irritation. She was exhausted and hungry, and some of her ribs were in the wrong place. The last thing she needed was someone prodding her with questions and metaphors when all she wanted to do was crawl into a hole.

She pulled the cash from her pockets, shoving it into Grief's hands.

"I couldn't get the watch," said Squid. "I'll pay you the rest later."

Grief looked at the stained notes in his hands.

"Is that what you—" began Grief.

"And you don't have to follow me around all the time. You're not my—"

"Friend?"

"We're not friends!" snapped Squid. "You're just some guy I found in a trunk."

There was a silence.

"You don't look so good," said Grief.

"I'm fine. I—"

Squid didn't know how she ended up on the ground, and for a moment, she thought Grief had hit her. The last thing she heard before everything faded to black was Grief's worried voice, calling her name.

*

The skirmishes had erupted into full-blown attacks, with three warehouses, an armoury and two casinos going up that morning. Both sides were still pecking at the edges, but it was only a matter of time before someone went for a serious bite.

Ducabre didn't glance up as Rojin entered the office.

"There's been a sighting at the Fess," said Rojin.

"Motive?"

"Unclear."

Ducabre kept his eyes on the screen, watching the shifting dots on the map, each streaming a constant line of statistics.

"How many witnesses?" said Ducabre.

"Over fifty."

"How fast is word spreading?"

"I can slow it down," said Rojin evenly.

Ducabre gave an imperceptible nod.

"Move the schedule forward," said Ducabre. "Intensify the

elimination of enemy strongholds."

The target had surfaced, which meant time was running out.

*

She was burning up.

Squid seemed frighteningly insubstantial in Grief's arms, and he felt a stab of irrational fear that she might just evaporate, leaving him grasping at vapour. His grip tightened a little as he sprinted home, hoping he'd know what to do once he got there. He wanted desperately to take her to the hospital, but Squid had made it clear that people like her went to the hospital to involuntarily donate organs.

She'd turned a sickening white just before she collapsed, but she was flushed with fever now. Even through her damp clothes, he could feel her skin burning. Grief wasn't sure if she just forgot to look after herself sometimes or felt she didn't deserve looking after. He'd seen her go for days without eating unless prompted, as though it were something that just slipped her mind.

Squid's face looked a little sunburned, and her lips were starting to crack. Maybe it was dehydration, maybe heat stroke. Maybe some exotic, liquefying fever; he couldn't tell. He couldn't remember what he was supposed to do.

Grief reached into his mind, but it was like clawing at the dark. What he needed wasn't there—only shadowy legions, waiting for him to venture too far from the light.

He filled a bath with lukewarm water and lowered Squid into it. He wasn't sure if he was confusing this treatment with something else or getting it mixed up with a horror movie he'd seen once. He had a feeling he was supposed to remove her clothes, but he suspected she'd rather have her brain melt than be undressed while unconscious.

He settled for placing wet towels around her forehead and neck, and trying to feed her small sips of cool water. She seemed to drift in and out of restless fits, bursting into bouts of mumbling and mild flailing. When her temperature finally started coming down, Grief dried her off with a hair dryer, wrapped her in a towel and tried to settle her on the couch, where she continued to mutter incoherently.

He only caught a few phrases, including "Not a lazy cupcake" and "Alabama". At one point, she wailed, "And he's gorgeous!" before breaking into quiet sobs, but she quickly drifted back into an agitated slumber.

Grief could only begin to guess what had happened today. Squid had obviously lost the money somehow and made herself sick trying to get it back. The needle marks worried him almost as much as the strange bruising on her arms and shoulders, as though heavy straps had been wrapped around them. And then there was the baffling scent of chocolate frosting, all of which together conjured up disturbing images in his mind.

He didn't know what else to do and finally went to sleep propped up against the couch, his chin resting on a cushion. He dreamt of silent screams and shoes full of blood. Of warm bodies and empty hearts, and a crushing loneliness that stripped the sanity from his bones.

He'd been a breath away from a name tonight, and his body had reacted while his mind had still been cowering. The gates were rattling now, hungry arms reaching for him through the bars. He didn't know who he was, but he knew what he wanted.

A cosy house, his sleepy Squid, bright mornings full of pancakes and cream. This was his safe place, and the howling world could tear itself to pieces outside, if only he could stay.

He awoke some time during the night, a faint voice by his ear.

"Grief?" murmured Squid.

"Mmm?"

"About what I said before…"

"Mmm."

"I had a bad day."

"Mmm…"

Grief felt something pressing against his face, and he realised it was a cushion.

"You shouldn't sleep like that," said Squid. "You'll ruin your back."

He wrapped his arms around the cushion and nestled on the floor, chased into sleep by visions of cupcakes and swooping demons.

# FOURTEEN

Casey woke to the sound of a locker swinging open, and she rolled over to look at her alarm clock. Except her alarm clock had burnt to a crisp yesterday, and she found herself staring at Deus undressing instead.

"Rise and shine," he said, pulling his suit from the station locker.

He was changing out of uniform, which meant he must have had a meeting with the higher-ups that morning. Casey swung her legs stiffly from the bunk, grimacing at her watch.

She'd overslept, and she was still wearing yesterday's clothes. At least she didn't have any meetings today.

"Gale was looking for you," said Deus, buttoning up his shirt. "You know these bunks are for officers reviving before the drive home, not permanent accommodation."

Casey wanted to sling something back, like a smack in the mouth. But only because she was tired and felt like she had a hangover. And she was starting to feel pissed off about losing all her clothes. She should have listened to that bloody insurance salesman.

"I'll sort something out," she said, pulling on her jacket and heading for the door.

"I'm sorry about your apartment," said Deus. "You should be careful."

Casey tried to find a hint of a menace in his words, but his expression was one of perfunctory concern.

"I'll find the guy," she said.

Casey ran a hand through her hair, without much effect, and went hunting for Gale. She followed the trail of frantic officers to the epicentre of yelling in the ops room. Case data flashed on multiple wall screens, and almost every officer had radio earpieces going. The room was a chaotic stream of police coming and going, with Gale at the heart of the storm.

Chief Superintendent Gale was a sharp-eyed woman in her forties who had the unenviable task of being police middle-management. Her job involved balancing the demands of politicians with professional rule of law while managing a desperately under-resourced station, keeping the hysterical media at bay and dealing with the personal problems and egos of all the police under her command. Not to mention the small matter of preventing and solving crime in the city.

Gale often had the look of someone stalking a kindergarten with a cattle prod, just daring some snotty toddler to give her the finger.

"Plover and Vinh on the Palace Royale explosion," barked Gale. "Sanchez and Tyce on the Old Mason Factory gunfight. Wong and Jakande, the Salvete Club bombing. Diaz, sort out those two bodies in the bay. Casey, in my office."

By the time Casey realised she'd been summoned, Gale was already tapping her foot by the glass door. Gale didn't bother closing the blinds, and you didn't need to lip-read to see the show.

"You've got twenty-four hours to solve the Werner case, or it's closed," said Gale. "I've already pulled Riego from the case."

Casey had seen it coming, but the timing was a kick in the guts.

"Chief, I—"

"I'm sorry, Casey, but we've got far bigger problems," said Gale. "I'm sorry about the fire. I'm sure Deus can fix you up with something."

Casey was still in mid-sentence when the door closed behind her, and everyone was suddenly engrossed in their files. She'd had a dozen arguments prepared—not good ones, but she'd still wanted to give them a swing.

Twenty-four hours.

You could get a lot done in twenty-four hours if you were desperate enough. If you were willing to make some tough decisions and sacrifice just a little of your soul.

She found Deus at the processing office, flicking briskly through the inmate case files. On the periphery of awareness, Casey wondered where the duty officer was, but mostly she was focused on blurting out the words before her throat seized up.

"I need to get into the Iluvian," said Casey.

It was like yanking out stitches or diving into icy water. She didn't have time to angst about integrity. Pride wouldn't solve the Werner case.

Deus crossed his arms, leaning against the cabinet.

"I'm guessing you don't mean VIP entry to the Phoenix Lounge?"

"You want me to spell it out?" said Casey.

She wasn't in the mood for games, but she had no leverage, and Deus knew it. If this were a poker game, all Casey had were Scrabble pieces. And mostly Zs.

"Humour me," he said.

Deus watched Casey with careful detachment, as though curious to see if she'd finally snap and try to stuff him into a filing cabinet. Casey took a calm breath.

"Werner was a regular," she said. "I need access to his room."

"That's quite a request."

"Then I overestimated you."

Deus smiled faintly, like a bare-knuckle boxer warming up before a fight.

"Namiel's just increased security, but I can ask around," said Deus. "Now, what I want in return…"

Casey felt as though she were sliding towards a pit of lava and all she could do was grit her teeth and hope it didn't sting.

"There've been… rumours… that things are unstable in Pearce's command," said Deus. "I want to know if there's trouble in Hades."

Deus clearly overestimated Casey's criminal connections, but right now, she'd take it.

"I'll see what I can dig up," she said coolly.

Deus's smile showed just a hint of teeth.

"I'll be in touch."

*

Squid woke with a headache and the sensation of being slightly damp all over. Yesterday was a blur of grey faces and colourful taunts, and the kind of blast from the past that shredded palm trees into atoms. However, the most important event had been a moment, a line, a look.

Mal had *recognised* Grief.

A ball of excitement fizzed inside her, mingled with a heavy dose of apprehension. Grief clearly hadn't wanted Mal to finish his sentence, and Grief's pattern of behaviour had rapidly gone from harmlessly eccentric to dangerously sinister.

She couldn't ask Mal—Squid's chest still hurt when she breathed, and her ribs made a worrying clicking noise when she sneezed. However, she had other resources.

Grief still lay half-curled on the floor, and Squid's inclination was to slip quietly from the house. However, he'd gone looking for her last time, and she didn't want him to worry. She knelt beside him on the carpet, watching his closed eyes twitch in restless dreams. His breathing was rapid, and his eyebrows knotted fretfully, sweat beading on his brow. Allegedly, waking people during REM sleep made them tired and cranky, but Squid felt that she might actually be doing him a favour.

She poked at him gently, and when that had no effect, she shook him lightly.

"Grie—"

She thought he'd moved fast at the Fess, but that had nothing on what happened now. It was like being hit by an invisible truck. Squid found herself staring at the ceiling, a clenched hand crushing her throat, and a man she didn't recognise staring coldly down at her.

Squid tried to yelp, but no sound escaped—nothing in, nothing out. She dug her fingernails into his hand, fighting desperately for air, but it was like scratching at the side of a bus. The pressure on her throat increased, Grief's eyes still hard and dead, and Squid felt a surreal pop in her neck.

Her eyes were rolling back when she heard the sudden intake of breath and saw the recognition washing through his eyes. The pressure on her throat abruptly vanished, and Grief's expression filled with confused horror.

Squid twisted out from under him and bolted behind the couch, edging towards the window. It took a few feeble coughs before air started flowing again, and every breath made a terrible wheezing noise.

"Squid?"

Grief got to his feet, trying to smooth away the shaking in his voice. He quickly shrugged off his disorientation, and Squid wedged herself farther behind the couch.

"I guess I'm not a morning person," said Grief lightly.

He tried to smile, but it frayed awfully at the edges. For a moment, the only sound was a soft high-pitched wheezing as Squid tried not to breathe.

"Are you okay?" said Grief.

Squid tensed, watching Grief's reflection in the window.

"Excuse me," he said finally, his voice strained.

He walked stiffly into the bathroom, and the bolt slid across. The sound of running water burbled noisily, and after a long pause, Squid crept cautiously to the door.

"Grief?" she said softly.

There was no reply, but she thought she heard a muffled sob. Squid waited by the door a little longer, but the awkwardness of knowing he didn't want to be heard finally ushered her away.

She zipped up her collar as she left the house. It would undoubtedly come up in bruises later, which would make getting a job even more fun. But that hardly mattered now. Grief was fast losing the plot, and she'd be forced to take serious measures if things continued to slide.

Squid made her move at the Just Desserts Bakery. With its

raspberry jam donuts, powdered cinnamon buns and crystallised Venetian hearts, it was a reliable honeypot. She pounced on her target as he left the shop, a large tray of sticky delights balanced in his arms.

"Riego!" said Squid.

"Oh, no…" said Riego, trying to jog away.

Squid trotted easily alongside him, and Riego eventually slowed to a resigned walk.

"Just take a jam one and go away."

"I need to see Casey," said Squid.

"Do I look like Casey?"

"I'm out of credit."

"I'm not a phone. But you could try feeding me coins and see what happens."

"Are you soliciting bribes?" said Squid archly.

"Are you obstructing an officer on duty?"

"You're not on duty," said Squid, looking meaningfully at the tray of donuts.

"I'm on donut duty."

"There's no such thing," said Squid, a little uncertainly.

"You need to widen your horizons," said Riego. "Get a boyfriend, or girlfriend. Go to law school. Join a guerrilla gardening club."

"I'm working on it."

"Sure you are. I'll tell her, but I can't promise she'll come. Just take a donut and get out of here."

"I'll be waiting at the coffee shop!" said Squid, waving a jelly donut as she loped away.

"Only because you want her to buy you breakfast," called Riego, shaking his head.

Riego had been Casey's partner for as long as Squid could remember. He was always a little exasperated, a little resigned, but he seemed a good guy. For some reason, he reminded her of one of those employees who put on a happy face every morning while some wistful melancholy clung to their hearts.

Squid hunkered down outside the coffee shop, preparing for a long wait. She was surprised when Casey turned up within the hour, looking harried.

"Two black coffees and a raisin toast," said Casey, hijacking a passing waiter.

"I don't drink coffee," said Squid.

"They're both for me."

"You don't drink coffee."

"I do today," said Casey, sliding into a window seat. "What happened to your voice?"

"I swallowed a bug."

"Must have been some bug," said Casey. "So, what's exploded now?"

"Nothing," said Squid defensively. "I got a job. Well, I did a job. A legitimate job. I was a Novelty Nourishment Guidance Infotainer."

Casey looked at Squid sceptically, taking a sip of her steaming coffee. She pushed the plate of raisin toast towards Squid.

"You haven't seen Ferret?"

"Nope. All straight now."

Squid beamed angelically.

"And how's your photophobic squatter?" said Casey.

Squid paused, subtly pulling her collar a little higher.

"Actually, I was wondering if you could do me a favour." She jotted a series of letters and numbers on a napkin. "Can you trace this number plate?"

"Only if you tell me why."

Squid glanced around the sunny cafe, every face as forgettable as hers. And probably with just as many secrets.

"It's the car I found Grief in."

Casey stared wordlessly at the seeping sequence, then tucked the napkin into her jacket.

"There's something wrong with him, isn't there?" said Casey.

"No. He's just— Just let me know as soon as you get a hit, okay?"

"Okay. But be careful. You can't tell me there isn't something fishy about his story."

Casey finished her second cup of coffee and gestured to the waiter for a third.

"Is everything okay?" ventured Squid.

"Peachy," said Casey. "My apartment burned down, and they're closing my case. If you want to help, I need to know if there's a power struggle going down at Pearce HQ."

For a surreal moment, Squid felt as though she and Casey had traded places, with Squid finally on her way up, and Casey headed down the slope in a billycart with no brakes.

"Ferret never talked about—"

Squid paused, Ferret's last few words echoing back to her. She hadn't just messed up a smash-and-grab that night; she'd blown a major operation in a pretty epic way.

And no one had come after her.

The fact that Ferret hadn't ended her at the pier suggested he had bigger problems to deal with. And something big enough to worry Ferret was something Squid didn't want to meet. She'd been so grateful to be alive, so delirious with her new life, that she hadn't thought about that night again.

Ferret said he couldn't promise no one would come after her. But Ferret was her section head—it was his call whether or not to squish her out of existence. There were only three people who could go over Ferret's head, and one person who might go through it.

"I'm just guessing, but I think Pearce is letting the small fry slide," said Squid. "Senior staff are pulling rank and stepping on toes, and the section heads aren't happy about it."

"Why the sudden shuffle?"

"I don't know. I'm out of the loop now."

Casey smiled ruefully into her coffee.

"Hey, I brought you something," said Squid, pulling a silver-blue card from her pocket. "It's a Monthly staff pass for the Iluvian. Even disconnected, it's worth a packet on the black market. But I'm sure you'll find some lawful use for it."

Casey took the elegant silver card, the pale circuitry glimmering in the light.

"Thanks, Squid. You know, I wasn't sure if you could do it. Straighten yourself out. I'm proud of you."

"Yeah, well…"

Squid couldn't help feeling a twinge of guilt as Casey strode away. If only she knew what a mess Squid still was. Somehow, she had thought going straight would change her life, and she'd wake up every morning beside a vase of fresh daisies, with a sunny personality to match her shiny new life.

Instead, she was still the same social defective, leading a marginally more hygienic life. But it was progress. And every step took her further from Ferret, from Pearce, from her old chain reaction of catastrophes. She'd done things in the last few days—normal people things—that she'd never imagined she could do. She could make this work.

But a small niggling thought continued to hover in the back of her mind that there remained one rather important thing that needed taking care of.

*

The house was empty when she returned, the windows breezily open, the blankets neatly folded at the foot of the couch.

Squid wasn't sure what she'd been expecting—a sobbing mess, a dangerous stranger, a nonchalant Grief cleaning his nails. When it came down to it, she didn't know a hell of a lot about Grief. Who he was. What he wanted. Why he was still here.

He cooked half-decent pancakes, and he could strangle someone in perfect silence. All things considered, Squid was leaning towards making a discreet exit. Yet she'd come back to this house, expecting to find him.

Part of her wanted to leave, to just vanish into the city. There was such relief in being alone, without anyone hovering over her, without anyone judging her. But despite his actions, there was still something so lost about Grief, like a duckling tossed overboard on open seas.

Squid moped around the house until she discovered that the computer was still hooked up to the nimbus. She resisted the urge to run a search on Alabama and Bastian, certain that their glittering awards and cute holiday snaps would send her spiralling into despair. Instead, she waded through the employment sites, which made her feel even worse.

She jotted down a few of the more promising ads, determined to at least work her way up from giant cupcake to giant cleaver. Even if she only managed to hold down each job for a day, she was still technically working.

Grief still hadn't come back after sunset, and Squid started to wonder if he'd finally gone. She wasn't sure whether to feel relieved or disappointed, and found herself wishing she'd paid more attention when Grief was making pancakes.

She started browsing the news sites, headline after headline of violence and chaos. Pearce and Verona were like Titans locked in battle, their ringing blows smashing up the city. Squid suddenly stopped at an article, goose bumps prickling across her skin.

Two grainy photos sat beneath the headline, each picture showing a man in his thirties, the image clearly cropped from a family barbeque or a camping trip.

TWO MORE GANGLAND EXECUTIONS SURFACE.

She'd only seen their faces for a moment, through the fogged-up glass as they tried to roll her into the bay. And now they were smiling out from the screen, their decomposing bodies in the city morgue.

A shot to the head, a long drop, and a small headline in a sea of newsprint. According to the article, they'd been quiet, normal men who'd kept to themselves and worked for Verona Enterprises. Except that quiet, normal men who worked for Verona Enterprises tended to pack guns and always wore gloves.

Squid stared at the screen, feeling as though the answer lay right in front of her—she just didn't know how to put it together. The two men who'd tried to kill Grief were dead—

The screen suddenly blacked out, and the lights followed half a second later, plunging the house into darkness. Squid dropped to the ground, her heart pounding as she listened to the silence. Crickets chirped outside, and the occasional car hummed past. When no creeping shadows slid through the windows and no sinister scratching started at the door, Squid decided the electricity company had finally cut off the supply.

She groped her way to the linen cupboard and helped herself to a torch, the feeble halo doing little to dispel the suffocating dark. There were no spare batteries in the cupboard, but Squid was certain a house like this would have lamps and candles stashed somewhere. A cursory search turned up a few more tins of tuna, a wad of faded love letters, and a pile of adult magazines that looked as though they'd been leafed through recently.

Squid couldn't help missing her wind-up lamp, and she tried not to think about all the things she'd lost through her own incompetence. Pieces of herself, adrift in an uncaring city. She forced the thoughts from her mind. What mattered was now. What mattered was here. But it didn't stop her from aching.

She finally hauled down the attic ladder, surprised at how noiselessly it unrolled. She climbed gingerly up the cold rungs, imagining how ironic it would be if the squatters had squatters. However, the cramped, dark space remained silent as she stood on the exposed beams—not even the obligatory scuttle of roaches or rats. Squid shone the torch around the attic, and froze.

Guns.

Lots. And. Lots. Of. Guns.

Pistols, revolvers, semi-automatics. Even a Reaver .22. All in various states of careful disassembly, like rodents being conscientiously dissected. Assorted rounds of ammunition and curious little metal rods were lined up according to size. Rumpled pages torn from biology texts lay neatly on the floor, most of them featuring clearly labelled diagrams of the human brain.

Squid's first, desperate thought was that Mrs Charlton must have had an unhealthy hobby. However, the towel on the floor was neatly folded. And it was still damp.

Muffled through the floorboards, Squid heard the front door click open, and she had the horrible sensation of having stumbled into a B-grade slasher flick. If this were a comedy, there'd be some humorous explanation for all of this. But as Squid glanced at the stained pages on the floor, she decided it'd take a hell of a writer to turn this into laughs.

She slid urgently down the ladder, shoving it back into the ceiling as footsteps approached. She spun around in panicked indecision before bolting into a bedroom, her torch finally fizzling out of power. At that moment, her phone beeped loudly with a message.

*Plates came thru. Registered to Pearce Syndicate.*

Squid heard a soft snick behind her, and all her regrets flashed through her mind. Surprisingly, there weren't as many as there used to be.

A soft glow infused the room, and Grief stood in the doorway with a plastic lighter in his hand.

"Hey," said Grief quietly.

He stood perfectly still, as though afraid Squid might dive out the window if he moved. In this fragile moment, Grief radiated such vulnerability, such fearful hope, as though all the bravado had been stripped away, and all Squid had to do to demolish him was step away.

"Hey," said Squid softly.

Grief's entire being seemed to relax, his spirits seeping back.

"I got you something," he said, trying to smile.

Squid followed him into the living room, and on the polished coffee table stood her red silk lantern, the gold-embroidered bamboo shoots shimmering in the firelight. Dreamlike, she traced a finger down the cool silk, a strange throbbing in her chest. It still had the stub of red candle in the bracket, unlit since that birthday so many lifetimes ago.

"How did you find it?" said Squid.

"Went to a couple of pawn shops. Visited a few people."

"You didn't—"

"I just talked to them," said Grief, a little reproachfully. "I'm very likeable, you know."

"So you keep telling me."

Squid ran her fingers slowly down the wire frame, gazing at the lantern like it was the face of a forgotten friend. A fragment of music, a familiar scent, the touch of a well-loved memento—they were such powerful triggers, for memories good and bad. And these were the dreams, the nightmares, and the lessons that made you who you were.

"I wasn't sure if you were coming back," said Grief quietly.

"Well, I'll probably look for new digs once they cut off the water."

Grief stared silently at the floor and then finally lifted his gaze to meet Squid's.

"Squid, I'm so sorry—"

She closed her hand around his, and Grief stopped in surprise. She gently tilted the lighter flame towards the molten candle.

"Let's do something about this dark," said Squid.

*

Dinner was fresh mushroom tortellini with a side of Greek salad and two portions of flawless coconut pudding. Grief swore he'd found them in a Dumpster, but Squid was pretty sure that by "found" he meant "swiped", and by "Dumpster" he meant "restaurant".

"Looks like you had a fun evening," said Grief, nodding at the pile of tins and adult magazines.

"I figure once we run out of candle, we can burn the mags in a bin."

"A touch of the slums in the comfort of your own living room."

"It's not our living room."

There was an awkward silence, and Grief concentrated on his salad, trying not to look at Squid.

"Is there anything you want to tell me?" said Squid.

Grief went for a flippant smile, but it was strained.

"Why don't you tell me which of my dark secrets you've uncovered, and we'll go from there?"

Squid stared at the last bite of pudding sitting sadly on the plate. Things had gone from messy to complicated to downright psychotic, and all because she'd let people into her life. People belonged outside: employers, landlords, the guy who sold second-hand pies. You didn't let them in, where they ruined the furniture and trampled over you with lies.

"Never mind," said Squid, rising to her feet.

Grief stood up.

"You found the guns."

Squid wanted so badly to walk out the door, to just keep walking until the landscape changed to snow and deserts and fields of towering sunflowers.

"It's none of my business," said Squid flatly.

"I didn't want to scare you. I'm sorry."

Squid kept her gaze on the window, a humourless smile twisting her mouth.

"You're like that parrot who bites people and then says, 'Sorry'," said Squid. "And then it bites them again. For all we know, the parrot thinks 'Sorry' means 'Gotcha'."

She saw the stab of hurt in his eyes, but she couldn't bring herself to say anything more. She wasn't a nice person. She wasn't a good person. She was just…

Squid, the girl who hid in corners and dark places. Who shied from people and their brightly coloured lives. Who always said the wrong thing, at the wrong time, and left everyone she touched a little less happy for having met her.

A girl who served no purpose in the world, unless she chose one.

"Do you want me to go?" said Grief.

The silence seemed to stretch forever, getting thinner and thinner until it surely had to snap.

"I want to help," said Squid. "But the arsenal in the attic is hard to ignore."

"They're not… They're just…" Grief searched for words. "I just see things in my head sometimes, and I had to know if they were real, the things I knew. I kept a few of the guns from that night, picked up some odds and ends from the Emporium, but I'll get rid of them. Right now. I'll never—"

"You can't keep pretending that the past doesn't exist. Those things in your head won't just go away."

"It's not me anymore," said Grief. "This is my second chance. Like how you started over."

"But I know what I left behind. You have to know where you came from, in order to understand what you are now."

Grief was silent, and his eyes took on a strange, hollow look, as though reflecting the haze from a distant city burning to the ground.

"I want to show you something," he said.

He reached for his collar, and Squid tensed, her heart beating hard against her ribs. Grief slowly unbuttoned his shirt and, after a moment's hesitation, shrugged it to the floor. Squid's breath caught in her throat.

His body was a battleground of scars. A bullet wound beneath his ribs. A puckered gash across his side. A curve of punctures down his hip. And around his chest, something that looked disconcertingly like the start of an autopsy. Some of the injuries spoke of vicious fights and near misses, but some of them looked self-inflicted, particularly around the wrists.

Squid's gaze traced the patchwork of scars, the lantern casting soft shadows across his skin.

"I just remember fragments, flashes," said Grief. "I wasn't just some guy in the wrong place at the wrong time. Someone wanted me dead, and maybe I deserved it. I can't go back to that."

"It's still your life, Grief. You can't just disown it because you don't like it. You don't get to press reset and start over. If you were a bad person, you have to make up for it. If you were a good person, you have to find out who did this to you. You have to take responsibility for your life, and all its consequences."

"I almost killed you…"

"So, don't do it again."

Squid scooped up Grief's shirt and pushed it gently against his chest. "This still isn't a shirt-optional household," she said.

Grief's smile was like a faded bow pinned to the side of a rotting mammoth.

"Sleep on it," said Squid. "We'll work it out tomorrow."

Squid curled up on the couch, listening as Grief cleared the table and made up his bed on the floor. He wouldn't stop running; she knew that much. But the demons weren't chasing him; they were already here. The man who'd tried to strangle Squid would keep trying to break out, and she couldn't afford to wait for that to happen. That'd be like cuddling a time bomb, telling it everything was going to be okay, right up until it turned you into gristly putty.

It was time for drastic action.

# FIFTEEN

She was charged up with sugar and caffeine, and the world buzzed around the edges like a broken television. Casey waited impatiently outside the courthouse, making a beeline for Deus as soon as he strode down the sandstone steps.

"Casey…" said Deus, glancing at her pupils with mild concern.

"Instability in the top tiers," said Casey. "Demarcation issues, and the branch heads aren't happy. Maybe a power struggle. Maybe a power vacuum. But Pearce is letting the lower levels slide."

"How serious is—"

"Enough to say he's taken his eye off the ball to watch the incoming meteorite. Pearce has his hands full, and someone's taking advantage of that." Casey flicked a silver card from her pocket. "I'll sweeten the deal. Monthly. Iluvian. You can hack it, sell it, or use it to shave. Just get me in."

Deus slid the card into his jacket.

"Eleven thirty. Cardiac Chaos. Have fun."

*

Casey had never been much of a clubber. She'd spent most of her high-school years wandering the back alleys looking for trouble, and reading the political news. Clubs were places for dancing away your troubles, and drinking until your brain stopped working. You went there to forget about the horrors unfolding outside, and Casey didn't want to forget.

Cardiac Chaos was a mosh pit on steroids. The entire hall pulsed with a solid mass of people, all jumping to booming electronic beats on fast forward. Laser lights flashed in a hundred retina-searing colours, slicing through the crowd at dizzying speeds.

Casey half-expected security to descend as soon as the optical scanners picked her up, but perhaps the lasers interfered with their accuracy. Or perhaps Deus had come through for her.

A hand suddenly grabbed hers, and Casey instinctively pulled away. The hand maintained its grip, and through the strobing lights she saw a perky waitress smiling up at her.

"I'm York," said the woman. "Don't let go, or you'll spend the next five hours moshing your way to the door."

York led her through the thundering halls, down oddly empty corridors, and up a convoluted selection of elevators. She moved through the Iluvian like an eel through a maze of coral, familiar with every crevice and hollow.

"Thanks, by the way," said Casey as they ascended in a softly lit elevator.

"Golden Boy makes it worth my while," said York. "Two get-out-of-jail chits and a record-wipe. I definitely prefer to be owed favours when it comes to Deus."

York gave Casey a wink as the doors opened onto level eighty-three.

"Follow me. Look casual. Don't make eye contact," said York, stepping into the plush hallway.

Casey's skin prickled as they passed through pale archways of cascading light. Hundreds of cameras had to be picking up their progress, but York's ability to turn favours into more favours had probably dealt with that. Casey couldn't help wondering how many get-out-of-jail passes Deus had handed out over the years, and how many criminal records had been wiped after a handshake under the table. Sure, Casey's motives were honourable, but that was how most unforgivable things began.

York paused outside a door, the digits 8382 inlaid in gleaming silver. She glanced at her watch, tense for the first time.

"When I say 'go', you have one hundred and twenty seconds

exactly," said York. "You have to be out by then or not at all."

Two minutes. Casey had spent all day going over the case notes, cramming for this two-minute exam. Everything depended on her finding what she needed in less time than it took her to floss.

The door gave a barely audible *click*.

"Go!" whispered York.

Casey slipped into the room, sweeping her gaze around the silk-papered walls. Elegant wooden drawers, a sleek bureau, a modern lounge in lipstick red. The room would have been purged after Werner's death, but there had to be something. A clue. A hint.

The surveillance scanner came up clean. All the drawers were empty. No secret compartments in the desk. No uneven surfaces on the walls. The seconds sped past, and Casey was running out of ideas.

If there was a message, a key, a note, he would have put it somewhere he could get to in a hurry, but secure enough to avoid the Iluvian clean-up crew. But there was nothing here—everything in the room had been scoured and searched.

Everything in the room—

Casey stopped, her eyes drawn to the panoramic window. Most of the windows in the Iluvian didn't open, but some of the private suites had glass panels that could slide open about the width of a palm. Enough for a burst of fresh air.

Or a scrawny arm.

Casey yanked open the window, pushing her arm outside as far as it could reach. She ran her hand down the gritty glass, her fingers catching on something—a faint ridge, like a piece of sticky tape. She strained against the window, her fingernails hooking at the raised edge. As the seconds ticked down to zero, Casey managed to peel the tape from the glass, bursting out of the room in time to see York sprinting away down the corridor.

"What happened to 'Don't run'?" said Casey, racing after her.

"The loop cascade just ended," said York. "We have to be inside the elevator in seven seconds."

Casey waited for York to finish the sentence, but the alternative was obviously beyond contemplation. They slammed into the elevator doors with seconds to spare, and York stabbed frantically at the button. Casey could almost hear the cameras switching on down the corridor, like a wall of rushing water in a flooding submarine.

York's watch gave a soft beep as the doors slid open, and both women lunged into the elevator.

"Do you do this often?" gasped Casey, as the elevator began its smooth descent.

"This is the Iluvian," said York with a wink.

The elevator doors opened onto the thumping beats of Cardiac Chaos, and York slipped easily into the crowd.

"Give my love to Golden Boy," grinned York. "And good luck."

Casey waved a thank-you as she pushed into the steaming crowd, grateful for those extra cups of coffee. By the time she emerged on the sidewalk, she felt strongly inclined to mutter things about "young people these days". Even the polluted air of Baltus City smelled good after the stinking humidity of the club.

Casey waited until she was several blocks away before taking her hand carefully from her jacket. She unclenched her grimy fist to reveal the smooth piece of transparent tape still stuck to her fingers.

She had her clue. Now all she had to do was crack it.

*

Squid crept from the house like a guilty shadow, stepping lightly around Grief's slumbering figure. She had seen denial before—she'd lived it for long enough. But she didn't have Casey's patience, and she already knew what happened when you allowed a life to run its merry course towards implosion.

Squid didn't bother with the Fess. If Mal was lurking her haunts, he wouldn't bother with "hello" this time. Tempting as it was to just ask him who Grief was, Mal's answer would probably be a knuckleduster through the skull.

There weren't a lot of people who'd be happy to see Squid—that was just the way it was. Trouble dragged behind her like a string of tin cans, but she got by. And there was still one person who could help.

At a cost.

She picked up a car in West Downtown that was double-parked outside the Kabukuri Club. It was a hotted-up Alpha Tybalt, midlife-crisis red, with blinding gold rims and zirconia grills. Unfeasibly pneumatic silhouettes decorated the leather interior, and an industrial subwoofer filled the trunk.

It wasn't technically criminal, but it should have been.

Squid coasted over to Drop-Off Eight, parking in the laneway behind Pearce's mechanical chop shop. She didn't have credit for a heads-up to Ferret, but this was a busy drop-off—it wouldn't take long for someone to slot this into the disassembly line.

She found a stained lottery ticket in the glove box and scrawled a note. She slapped it onto the dashboard before sliding from the car and disappearing into the night.

*Ferret. Need 2 C U. Squid.*

*

The knock came at two in the morning. It didn't remotely resemble the secret knock, and it didn't sound like it was trying to. Kirsk was already squeezing through a gap in the back when a shadow loomed over her, and she didn't need passable night vision to recognise the holster at its side.

Kirsk inhaled to scream and a hand clamped over her mouth.

"It's me, Casey," said the shadow. "I need you to come with me."

Kirsk had seen this happen before—other cops, other homeless people who knew too much, and then just empty cardboard boxes waiting for a new squatter. The hand gently released, and Kirsk inhaled to scream.

The hand clamped down again.

"It's me, Casey," repeated the figure patiently, although it sounded like it was trying not to punch a hole in something. "I think I've found something Werner was trying to hide, but I don't know why it's important. I have until sunrise to solve the case or it goes to filing purgatory. Please, Kirsk, I need your help."

The hand pulled away carefully, and Kirsk inhaled.

"What did you find?"

Casey handed her a grubby plastic strip, caked in soot and bent around the edges. Kirsk turned her camp light to maximum, holding the strip against the glowing LEDs.

"I found it stuck to the window at Werner's Iluvian suite," said Casey. "Is it some kind of code, or is it just sticky tape?"

Kirsk stared at the strip, particularly at the gigantic whorl of a thumbprint on the sticky side, which incidentally, would have matched Casey's. To most people, the strip would have looked just like sticky tape—maybe a fraction thicker, a touch more pliable, and no perforated tear at either end. But Kirsk had seen sketches of this a very long time ago.

"It's a processor," said Kirsk. "The freak actually did it."

"But it didn't show up on the scanners. How can it be a processor if there are no metallic components or transmission signatures?"

"I don't know. Those weren't a part of the original concept. Do you handle all your forensics like this?" Kirsk brushed gently at the grime.

"What kind of a processor?"

"I think it's a data-slick processor and drive," said Kirsk. "For high-capacity storage. But I'll need an optical pico-sine microscanner to know if I'm right, and that's assuming he's using a recognisable form of encoding. Got that kind of equipment handy?"

Casey's eyes flickered through a mental inventory, and she seemed to make the kind of decision that shouldn't be made at two in the morning while on caffeine withdrawal.

"Sure," said Casey. "But we only have until sunrise."

*

Squid waited by the Olde Ice Creamery, around the corner from Drop-Off Eight. The shop wouldn't open for another six hours, but she couldn't buy anything anyway. Some people had breakfast at Tiffany's; Squid had breakfast at the Olde Ice Creamery.

She'd hear Ferret's car from here, and in the meantime, she could distract herself from what she was about to do by dreaming of scoops of Tuscan Fig and Cognac Toffee Marmalade.

It wasn't backsliding. It was more of a sidestep and maybe a line-dance shuffle. But she was doing it for all the right reasons. There was a soul on the line, and for once, it wasn't hers.

"This is a surprise."

Squid almost crashed through the shopfront as she spun around, wondering how she hadn't seen his reflection in the glass.

"Ferret," croaked Squid.

He looked exactly the same, with his neatly brushed hair and slim grey overcoat. Then again, he hadn't changed much since she'd first met him. If Squid didn't know about the medical technology Pearce's henchmen had access to, she'd be tempted to find it suspicious.

"Thanks for the gift," said Ferret. "Not quite to my tastes, but I appreciate the thought."

Squid swallowed the instinctive fear rising in her chest. She'd tried so hard to get away, and now she was back in the woods, trying to bargain with the wolves.

"I want to know about the car I dropped off," said Squid. "Registration TLX84772."

"You expect me to remember one car out of the millions I've processed?"

"Yes."

Ferret managed to snuff out the smile before it appeared. A cool breeze fluttered down the laneway, and Ferret put his hands in his pockets.

"It's not what you expected, is it?" he said. "No money. No home. Still scratching up food where you can find it. Not a lot's changed, has it?"

Squid straightened her shoulders.

"I'm doing fine. I got a job."

This time, a small smile did break through.

"The cutest cupcakes in the city," said Ferret.

Squid felt her face flushing an incendiary red, and she resisted the impulse to hurl herself into a convenient abyss.

"Things are shaking up, and talent will rise," said Ferret. "You're a gifted young woman, Squid. And now is the time when you can make it work for you."

It seemed as though the world were pulling away, leaving Squid and Ferret standing on a hanging patch of starlight.

"I—"

Squid knew she was supposed to refuse. This was the classic test of every hero: to resist the temptations of evil and continue their rugged road towards the light. The very rugged, hungry, humiliating road.

"What do you mean?" said Squid.

"It's called a promotion. It's called power, access, information. Do you want to spend the rest of your life afraid of people like Mal, or do you want people like Mal to be afraid of you?"

Squid had spent her entire life being afraid, always trying to be something she wasn't. Always chasing things that would never be real, always running from who she was. But she wanted to believe it was her choice—that chasing a fantasy was still somehow better than embracing a nightmare.

"So I can be like that thug you sent after me that night? The one with the eyes?"

Ferret's gaze cooled slightly.

"His name's Spencer," he said. "He got the broken nose from a seizure he had when he was fifteen. The bulging eye is from the brain tumour they found. His parents sold their kidneys to pay for his operation, and he works for me to pay for their dialysis. Everyone has a story, Squid. You should know that."

Squid looked away, feeling her uncertainty grow.

"Right and wrong," continued Ferret. "Good and bad. You know how subjective, how capricious the world is. There's nothing wrong with getting what you want for a change."

"I think you gave me that speech six years ago. It didn't work out so well."

"They're called the hard yards, Squid. You don't cruise into this career on a wave of money and luxury unless you cruise straight out in a body bag. You show me you can survive it. You show me that you deserve it. And then you start moving up. You're alive. And you're here. I'm holding the door open, Squid, but it doesn't stay open."

It should have been an easy choice. She wanted to believe that honest hard work and persistence and smiling more would get her what she wanted. But in reality, only people like Alabama got what they wanted. People like Squid just watched.

"The car," said Squid firmly.

"I have a job coming up," said Ferret. "Complete it without annihilating the payload, and I'll tell you everything I know about the car."

Squid felt herself stepping over a line, into a ghost world of good intentions and questionable acts. But sometimes a sacrifice had to be made to bring someone else into the light.

"Agreed," she said.

Ferret suddenly withdrew his hand from his pocket, tossing something small and translucent towards Squid. She instinctively ducked, and the object hovered for a moment before executing a gentle landing on the ground by her feet. Ferret's expression suggested that Squid wasn't the biggest idiot he'd ever met, but she was moving in that direction.

Squid reached tentatively for the ethereal object. It was a phone, or what a phone might look like if you had an artist's soul and more money than the military. It was a slender pane of fogged ice, about the size of a lighter, floating with pinprick icons that flared into holographic screens at her touch. The Diffraction Zeisser lens could resolve to microscopic detail, the acuity speakers could rival a battalion of sopranos, and she couldn't even guess at the bypass codes this thing could dream up.

The weight of it was like the perfect skipping stone or the hand of a newborn child. She wanted to just stand there and stroke it, turning it slowly in her palm.

Even though the internal GPS would report her exact whereabouts to Ferret, even though every word would undoubtedly be monitored, if temptation could fit into her pocket, this would be it.

"Expect my call," said Ferret.

As he disappeared into the maze of run-down factories, Squid couldn't help wondering if this was going to feature in her next flashback of terrible mistakes.

*

The Data Analysis Lab at the station was deserted. Partly because you needed several layers of permission to access the equipment, but Casey saw this as another case of obstructive bureaucracy.

Kirsk had picked her way fussily through the massive screens, inspecting equipment that resembled half-constructed doomsday devices. She had finally settled on something that looked like a large inside-out telescope, with adjustable lenses perched on rotating stalks, like a mechanical dandelion.

Kirsk smoothed the data-slick onto a glass plate, and the machine hummed as her fingers sped over the input screen. A beam of light bounced from one lens to another, forming an intricate web that grew finer and finer until it seemed to disappear completely on the strip of tape.

Casey paced impatiently as Kirsk fiddled with the console, adjusting the lenses and muttering to herself.

"He's using frickin' amino acids and graphene," mumbled Kirsk, her fingers dancing over the screen like shadow puppets on fast forward. "It's a biomimetic substratum—that's why it's not showing up on your scanners."

Like plastic bags made of taro starch. Or guns made of plastic and bone. So, Werner had found a way to smuggle data from Pearce HQ, and obviously, someone had found out.

"What's on the slick?" said Casey.

"Mostly fingerprints," said Kirsk. "No offence, but the data's pretty badly corrupted. And what's left is… I don't know if *encrypted* is the right word."

Kirsk's hands slid carefully over the screen, and Casey had the slightly dizzying sensation that she was falling through a galaxy of binary.

"The compression is incredible," said Kirsk. "It'll take me weeks to pry this sucker apart."

"You've got three hours."

"Now I know how Scotty felt," muttered Kirsk.

Casey wore a track in the carpet, darting nervously to the door at every noise. She felt like she was checking her watch every minute, but each time she looked, another half hour had gone by. The dawn shift would start flooding in soon, and Casey's twenty-four hours had turned into one.

"Time's up," said Casey. "What have you got?"

"I'm not sure," said Kirsk, plugging several cables into the interface. "But I think it's a fragment of audio."

Kirsk tapped the screen, and a hiss of static crackled from the speakers.

*"I don't know… serious… don't want to end up…"*

Casey recognised the voice, and from Kirsk's pallor, so did she. Werner sounded older than he did in his home videos, and a lot more frightened.

*"…You know what your choices are… What will happen if you don't…"*

The second voice was deeper, more confident. Slightly menacing.

*"...Want some insurance..."* Werner again. *"...If this goes bad... If Pearce finds out..."*

*"...Let me deal with Pearce... Just get them ready..."*

Casey suddenly realised she'd stopped breathing. The deeper voice flashed through her brain like a bolt of blinding light. She knew that voice.

It was Grief.

*

Casualty reports were always so depressing.

Verona scrolled down the list, assessing the gaps that needed to be filled, the rapid promotions that would need to be made. Attacks had steadily escalated on both sides, and people had begun to mutter about mutually assured destruction. However, the outcome was far from assured and, as far as Verona was concerned, definitely not mutual.

Pearce had experience, resources and infrastructure, but Verona had one critical advantage: a hierarchy free from competent, ambitious lieutenants. While it did inspire the occasional "I'm surrounded by fools!" tantrum, it also meant that power struggles were generally limited to the occasional black eye between Clef and Mal.

It wasn't a productive long-term strategy, but it was a key difference at a crucial time. Pearce had allowed his hierarchy to stagnate, growing top-heavy and restless in an environment clouded by rumour and secrecy. All it took was the scent of blood, a spark of imagination, and the sledge driver would be a patch of red on the snow.

At least, Verona hoped so.

"Heavy losses at the Bullpit Rail Yard," said Clef from across the room, both hands darting across an array of hovering screens.

"Tell Targus to withdraw," said Verona. "Torch the warehouse on the way out. Status on Sebel's target?"

"Munitions depot destroyed," said Clef. "Thirty-nine casualties."

The list on Verona's screen automatically updated, thirty-nine names turning red. The Galloway Munitions Depot was Pearce's key weapons interchange in the south of Baltus City. Without it, fresh supplies would have to come by road, which meant his allies were on a drip feed that Verona could easily snip.

Strategically, it was a victory with acceptable losses. But Verona couldn't suppress a bitter twinge. Mal was supposed to have headed that mission, and if he had, there'd be far fewer names on her casualty list right now.

Unfortunately, Mal was still unconscious after getting into some barroom brawl. He had a knack for organising military operations with hundreds of heavily armed participants and a convoy of armoured trucks, yet he still found time to get flattened in seedy bars.

There were times when Verona couldn't wait for the war to be over, so she could start sorting out this henchman situation.

The office doors slammed open, and both of Clef's hands were suddenly toting loaded pistols aimed at the door. Mal strode in like a blast of sleet, half his face still swollen and the colour of blackberries.

"I've been waiting to hear the story behind—" Clef stopped at Mal's expression.

He looked like a messenger hurled from Heaven with a tablet full of bad news.

"The Rottweiler's gone rogue," said Mal.

*

Silence and static. And a politely recorded message.

Squid's number was disconnected. Not just out of credit. Disconnected. Casey punched the icon about a dozen times before the recorded message started sounding snippy.

The voice on the data-slick had definitely been Grief's—a little harder, a little more threatening, but definitely his. Casey remembered his voice by her ear, one hand gripping her wrist.

*I'm happy with the progress of my own investigations.*

She'd always known something was screwy with his story, but things had just gotten a whole lot nastier.

"What happened?" said Kirsk, her voice shaking. "What were they talking about?"

Werner had made a breakthrough: data-slicks he could smuggle in and out of Pearce HQ. Someone had found out and wanted Werner to do something behind Pearce's back.

And that someone was Grief.

Casey pulled out the other data-slick—the one with the numbers. It had to be the second clue, the key to what Werner had discovered, what he'd recorded, what someone wanted so badly, they were willing to kill for it. Without Werner's remote drive, these fragments were all she had. It was like trying to reconstruct a mosaic from two broken tiles. Archaeologists did it all the time, which was probably how they ended up with eight-armed goddesses.

A door creaked open down the hall, and distant voices broke the morning silence.

"Shut it down!" whispered Casey, peeling the data-slick from the machine.

Kirsk was still tapping icons when Casey dragged her from the lab, footsteps now approaching from several directions. They raced into the evacuation stairwell just as figures rounded the corner, and Casey didn't hang around for the "Hey, what was that?"

Fatigue was kicking in hard when Casey finally pulled into the slums, dawn breaking over the castles of punctured tyres.

"The man on the recordings," said Kirsk, "he's responsible for what happened to Werner, isn't he?"

It was a lot to assume from a few seconds of scratchy audio. The previous year, Metropolitan North Command had gotten stung pretty badly when their damning wiretap of a terrorist plot turned out to have been selectively edited to the point where it resembled a mashup dance track. No matter how incriminating the sound bite, context was crucial.

Then again, Squid wasn't answering her phone.

"I promise I'll keep working on it," said Casey.

Sunlight climbed the concrete pylons as Casey hit the freeway. Everything was supposed to be coming together now, the clues converging as the case slammed into its deadline. Instead, everything remained disconnected and uncertain, like a school of silver fish scattering in her path.

She couldn't help feeling that while she'd been chasing the darting slivers, she'd somehow missed the looming shadow passing overhead. She had an eerie vision of a ten-foot shark gliding noiselessly through the water, and the terrible feeling she knew why the squid was missing.

Casey punched on the siren, streaking across the city towards Marley Drive.

*

It wasn't poker night, but Ferret's screen had been illuminated for several hours. The image this time was a lusciously rendered English garden, and Technology was the only one present. Her avatar strolled across the screen in a medieval dress of amethyst and silver, plucking at climbing tendrils of blood roses.

*TECHNOLOGY: You know it's practically suicide.*

Ferret smiled faintly.

*REBIRTH: Ye of little faith.*

*TECHNOLOGY: I'm Technology, not Faith.*

Faith was a corrupt archbishop who kept Pearce onside with the religious right and sold confessions on the side. None of the poker circle had much to do with him.

*REBIRTH: And I'm Rebirth, not Suicide.*

There wasn't actually a Suicide. For obvious reasons.

*TECHNOLOGY: When your entire street went dark last week, I thought you'd finally had it. Ducabre finally realised you were up to no good.*

Ferret grinned.

*REBIRTH: I'm always up to no good. Which brings us to*

*TECHNOLOGY: Suicide.*

*REBIRTH: Opportunity.*

The rumour mill had gone into overdrive, and sneaking suspicions had exploded into rampant speculation. Some said Pearce had been quietly overthrown. Others said he'd been killed by a horde of Verona's nano-drones. Still more said he'd gone to ground in anticipation of an apocalypse no one else knew about. But the general consensus was: Pearce was gone.

*REBIRTH: You can gain power through violence or leverage. Through raw strength or nerve points. You know my preference. Corruption has the list. You can say no.*

Technology's avatar turned a thorned rose slowly between her fingers, the castle behind her fading into twilight stars.

*TECHNOLOGY: It's off the nimbus. I'd need the physical drive.*

*REBIRTH: Consider it yours.*

Ferret slid his finger to the log-off icon, and Technology's avatar suddenly raised her hand, the log-off icon greying out abruptly.

*TECHNOLOGY: The rumours. Do you think Pearce is dead?*

Ferret paused, ignoring the slight chill creeping over him.

*REBIRTH: No. I think he's afraid.*

*

The reports were a constant stream of bad news getting worse.

Ducabre's temples throbbed, and he needed very badly to throw someone off a bridge. He hadn't fought this hard and climbed so ruthlessly just so he could stare at screens all day. But then again, things hadn't exactly gone to plan.

Everything had been under control, or at least fixable, until Rojin's lapse of self-restraint had turned their hierarchy pyramid into a burning merry-go-round.

A report slid onscreen as Rojin entered the office.

"Phase-five targets have been eliminated," she said.

Ducabre skimmed the list, the status of the target and the number of civilian casualties printed beside each item. Rojin generally kept collateral low, when she could be bothered, and most of the casualty figures were in the realm of single digits—

He paused at a line: *426*.

Ducabre wondered whether this had been a typographical error, but knowing Rojin, this was the less likely explanation.

"I didn't know the Kabukuri Club was Verona's," said Ducabre.

"It isn't."

There was a tense silence. It was rumoured that the Kabukuri Club paid Pearce, Verona, and various officials quite handsomely in exchange for being left alone to conduct its "business". Ducabre had no patience for power plays or personal vendettas, which was how he'd gotten his reputation. It was also why he carried six guns at any time so he wouldn't have to bother reloading if he had a particularly irritating day.

However, disposing of Rojin now would mean losing the war, and he had no intention of ruling over a pile of ashes.

"Any progress on the drives?" said Ducabre.

"Some of them are heavily encrypted with evolving code, and others have no apparent initialisation process."

"You don't know how to turn them on?"

Rojin bristled slightly. "I repeat my recommendation that we destroy them. They say the man he took down at the Fess was Verona's lieutenant. They're saying Raphael is rising."

"He's the only one who knows what's on those drives," said Ducabre. "And he knows where the copies are. If we destroy ours, we're waiting for a bullet in the dark."

Ducabre usually explained himself with a loaded gun, but he didn't want a repeat of that night on the bridge and the start of this whole goddamned mess.

"Priorities?" said Rojin.

was connected to Pearce. He was connected to Werner. He was bloody guilty of something, and if she waited until she had evidence, exhibit "C" could be Squid's corpse.

It was a hell of a time for Casey's phone to ring, and she would have let it go to voicemail, except it was Riego.

"Not a good time," said Casey, keeping Grief in her sights as he wandered into the kitchen and started organising cutlery.

"You're telling me," said Riego, the chatter of the station raucous in the background. "You'd better get down here, pronto."

"I'm in the middle of something."

"I'm not going to say this is more important, but if I had to rank it one to ten, where one is the coffee machine breaking down, and ten is nuclear annihilation, I'd say this is a seven."

Casey wanted to wait until things hit eight, but if something was going down at the station, Riego shouldn't have to deal with it alone.

"I'll be right there," said Casey.

Squid would have to wait.

"You should come over for dinner sometime," said Grief. "I think Squid would like that."

Something about this whole set-up was creepy as hell, and Casey desperately hoped that Squid's body wasn't propped up in a rocking chair somewhere, with wistful Connie Francis tunes playing on the gramophone.

As Casey made her way back to the car, she hoped she was making the right call. Hopefully, Squid was fine, and Casey was overreacting. But she now knew three things about Grief.

He was connected to Pearce.

He was connected to Werner.

And he was a liar.

*

The station had gone from frenetic to frantic, sitting just a few notches short of abandon-ship panic. Riego made several urgent gestures to Casey as she entered the ops room, mostly suggesting that she should keep her mouth shut.

This time, Gale didn't bother with closed doors.

"I am this close to taking your badge and your gun," said Gale.

Casey glanced at Riego, who mimed someone taking cover from a hail of missiles.

"Unauthorised use of lab equipment," continued Gale. "Unauthorised visitor access to secure station facilities. I'm already dealing with a city blowing itself to pieces. I don't need officers adding fuel to the rumours of vigilantes and rogue cops. Procedures are not suggestions. If you believe that rules are there to be broken, you don't deserve that badge."

Casey saw the surveillance footage playing on the screen beside Gale, the mop-headed figure of Kirsk tagging along behind Casey. She knew "sorry" wouldn't cut it. Plus, she wasn't, really.

"Do you have anything to say for yourself?" said Gale.

Casey ignored Riego's pendulous head-shaking.

"I'm following a fresh lead, with strong evidence—" began Casey.

"Werner's been designated a cold case," said Gale. "The paperwork went through this morning. The file's gone to storage."

Casey could feel it slipping away from her.

"Chief, I just—"

"Let it go, Casey," said Gale, her voice like a nail gun in a room full of coffins. "The oddball crusader thing's getting old."

The room dipped to awkward silence.

"Report to Archives," said Gale. "Dismissed."

Casey didn't remember leaving the room or making her way through the murmuring crowd. This case was supposed to be different—it was supposed to be a strike against Pearce, against the untouchability he flaunted through the city with blood and empty shells.

It was supposed to be an elderly couple at the grave of their son, knowing justice had been served. It was supposed to be a homeless woman sleeping better at night, the memory of her friend a little less bitter. It was supposed to be the law coming good, showing people that the system worked, once in a while.

"Casey…" Riego gently guided Casey from the path of an approaching trolley.

The trolley rattled past like a freight train through the desolate night.

*Snap out of it*, thought Casey. *You're not some trenchcoat tragic with a bottle of scotch in one pocket and a picture of his dead wife in the other.*

"I'm sorry, Riego," said Casey. "You shouldn't have had to deal with that."

"I'm used to it. But I guess I've got to work on the miming thing."

"I'm serious, Riego. You should switch partners—"

"I'm where I can do the most good," said Riego. "So, this gesture means 'stop talking'. And this gesture means 'really, stop talking'."

Casey shook her head as they tramped down the stairs to the sub-basement levels.

"Casey…" Riego hesitated. "The charges against Olsen were dropped this morning."

Casey stopped on the staircase. Sam Olsen. The guy who'd firebombed Riley. They had damning evidence. They had a confession. The only thing they didn't have was a smoking detonator, and only just. It was a sparkling, textbook case by Deus, and if there were holes in the case, you could sieve plankton with it.

Things like this happened all the time—an alibi here, a piece of lost evidence there, but this was beyond flagrant. It was as though Pearce had the judiciary sewn up so tight, he didn't even bother with the pretence.

"Leave it, Casey," said Riego. "I mean it."

"What do you think I'm going to do?" said Casey, already thinking of a hundred possibilities.

Riego unfolded a printout, glancing over his shoulder.

"I got this from a friend in Processing," he said.

It was a mugshot of a slim man with sharp eyes and blotchy stubble.

He looked like any other pickup on a Saturday night, but put him in a leather jacket and a malicious smile, and he was watching Casey's building burn.

"That's the guy who torched— That's the guy from the fire," said Casey. "The arson suspect."

Technically, *her* arson suspect, but she was damned sure the culprit hadn't been an unattended waffle iron.

"The same guy who lifted my phone that day," said Riego. "What's left of him was found at the base of Upton Towers last night, ten foot wide and one inch thick. Cops are calling it suicide. Everyone else is calling it black-eye justice."

"They think cops did this?" Casey paused, Riego's expression sinking in. "They think *I* did this?"

"I'm just saying maybe pull back on the ranting, lay low, file some cases."

"Do *you* think I did this?"

"Of course not," said Riego, as though she'd asked him if her cap made her head look big. "But don't give them a pattern where there isn't one."

Casey stared at the grainy printout, the cocky eyes glaring out over the mugshot board: *Ben Maluka.* It could have been Pearce's cleanup crew, but Squid said he wasn't bothering with the small fry.

Clearly, someone was.

# SIXTEEN

The sun set slowly into wisps of pink and orange.

Grief closed his eyes, a few lines of a song coming back to him. Something about a man waiting by the window every night, waiting for his... friend to come home. He couldn't remember the lyrics, just fragments of a tune and a wash of familiar melancholy.

Squid had left without waking him, creeping out like a child from a monster's lair. He knew what he was becoming, despite all his efforts, and he couldn't blame her. One of these days, she wouldn't come back.

And maybe it was today.

It seemed almost like one of those game shows where the image was slowly revealed, square by square. The night with the burning truck: square one. Remembering his steps through the Iluvian: square two. Most of the tiles had been turned now, and Casey's visit had almost completed the picture.

The boy's face had been like a hand rising from the grave, reaching out with hollow-eyed vengeance. Grief remembered the face, but not like this, not sunny and smiling. He knew it horrified, terrified, staring at him, pale and bloody.

Blood on his hands. Blood on his soul.

Grief gripped his head, as though he could wring out all the memories and start afresh. Tabula rasa. The sun rises, and it's a new day. And if you kept running, your shadow would never catch up.

A shape flickered across the lawn, and Grief slid behind the door. Hinges creaked softly, and a pair of eyes peered warily inside.

"Why are you standing in the dark with a fork?" said Squid.

"I didn't want to waste the candles without you," said Grief.

He held out the fork.

"And there's French toast if you're hungry."

Squid padded over to the bench, inspecting the plate of cold toast. Even in the dark, he could see the line of tension running through her body. Her movements were a little sharper, her steps a little quicker, as though something were making her nervous. Maybe it was him. Maybe it was something else.

Grief moved over to the kitchen bench, and Squid's eyes darted up.

"Anything you'd like to tell me?" said Grief.

Squid paused, like a gecko on the wall, trying to figure out if it had been spotted.

"All you have to say is 'no'," said Grief softly.

Squid looked away, and he could almost see her entire day playing back across her face.

"I saw Ferret today," said Squid.

Grief's fists clenched slightly.

"The car I found you in was part of Pearce's fleet," she continued. "Ferret can tell us who it belonged to. We're a name away from—"

"Why's it so important to you? Why can't we just be like this?"

"Because it's not real. The house, the flowers, the French toast: they don't make you normal. They don't make you someone else. You can wear nice clothes and shower 'til your skin bleeds, but it doesn't change what you are."

*What you are.*

Grief took a step back, as though she'd physically shoved him.

That's how she saw him. Something hiding in the shell of another man. Like a parasite, like a demon, like a horrific front page story waiting to happen.

"Grief, you don't become someone else by changing the things around you. You do it by changing who you are inside. And to do that, you have to know what's inside."

"I know who I am, I just—"

"What's your happiest memory?" said Squid.

"I don't—"

"Your saddest memory?"

Grief was silent.

"There are so many things I wish I could unsee or undo," said Squid. "But not if it means losing all the wonderful, brilliant, meaningful things as well. Good memories tide you through the bad times. Bad memories temper reckless actions. Without my memories, I'd still be a whimpering mess in the gutter. Without your memories, you're living a fake life, in a fake house, with fake feeli—"

"They're not fake!" snarled Grief.

He suddenly realised he was holding Squid by the wrists, and she was staring at him with those eyes. Wide and fearful. Like the way she looked at Mal.

This was definitely getting filed under "bad memories".

"Squid, I…"

He let go, and to his surprise, she didn't dive behind the couch. Instead, she continued to stare at him, looking as though she wanted to shake him, or slap him, or lecture him some more.

He realised then how much this mattered to her. He'd been pottering away in his living dollhouse, while Squid had been out there facing the avalanche with a toy spade and a worried expression.

"What did Ferret have to say?" said Grief.

"I, uh, he's going to get back to me."

He continued to stare at her expectantly.

"I just have to help him with something," said Squid.

The way she said it suggested she'd be moving furniture or picking up groceries. Instead, it'd probably involve stolen cars, burning choppers, and enough bullets to ballast the Queen Mary. If he tried to talk her out of it, she'd just slip away again.

"Why's it so important to you?" said Grief.

Squid paused, as though trying to articulate something she didn't completely understand.

"I feel as though, to become the person I'm supposed to be, I need to help you become the person you're supposed to be."

"What about your promise to Casey?"

"I still have until my birthday," said Squid, giving Grief a faint smile.

The candles cast a soft glow across the living room, and in the distance, a string quartet began to play Pachelbel's Canon in D. Grief's gaze travelled down Squid's body, stopping at her hip.

"I think you have an orchestra in your pocket," said Grief.

"Oh." Squid patted her clothes and pulled out a phone with better fidelity than the opera house.

Grief couldn't help admiring the sleek piece of technological desire, barely hearing Squid's end of the conversation before the phone slid back into her pocket.

"Where are we going?" he said.

Squid looked as though she were about to protest the whole "we" situation, then stopped herself.

"Feel like a walk?"

*

Drop-Off Thirty-Nine was behind the boardwalk of Anna Maria Beach. During the day, the place screamed with kids and flustered parents, gangly teens gawking at the beach, and smooching couples sharing ice cream cones.

But this was how Squid saw the world—locked-up stalls and darkened rides. The Ferris wheel hanging against a cloudy sky. She and Grief were the only people on the deserted walk, like the solitary survivors of some silent calamity.

It was kind of soothing.

"Hey, if this stall were open, I bet I could win a prize," said Grief, studying the lock on the SHOOT A RACCOON shutter.

"I'm not sure people should be shooting raccoons," said Squid distractedly, walking onto the gravel lot behind the boardwalk.

A nondescript blue sedan was parked behind the popcorn stands, and Squid circled the vehicle carefully. Apparently, the mission package was in the glove box, and according to Ferret, it was self-explanatory.

Squid slid into the driver's seat, hoping for the umpteenth time that she hadn't made a huge mistake. Agreeing to a mission sight unseen was always a bad idea—like blind dates and meals with the word "surprise" in them. But her choices were clear: accept the mission or let Grief's alter ego emerge on his own.

She definitely preferred the mission.

The package was larger than expected, wrapped in brown paper and string, like an antiquated care parcel. Grief landed in the front passenger seat, watching curiously as Squid unravelled the layers.

"What if it tells you to do something really awful?" said Grief.

"Ferret said I'd be fine."

"Were those his exact words?"

Squid tried to remember his exact words and decided they were probably more along the lines of "Good luck".

"Hey, where'd you get that raccoon?" said Squid.

Grief held up the plush animal, its big black eyes staring mournfully at her.

"I thought it could keep your octopus company."

Squid's mouth turned into a small, upside down *U*.

"I'll return it," sighed Grief.

It was technically stealing, but Squid couldn't help feeling a twinge of empathy. Grief didn't actually have anything of his own—just clothes from a former life and a toothbrush from the Twenty-Four-Whatever.

"Keep it," said Squid. "And pay them tomorrow in cutlery or some—"

Squid yelped as something slithered from the package and down her legs. In a blur, Grief's arm was around her waist, hoisting her from the seat. They pressed against the passenger-side door, breathlessly still and listening for movement.

"Um, I think it's okay," said Squid. "I think it's a dress."

Grief considered this for a moment.

"A dress."

"You can let go now."

Grief prodded the pile of fabric with his foot, not entirely convinced it wasn't deadly. Squid carefully lifted the supple, shimmering garment, and tried not to let her mouth fall open.

It was a stunning Lumina Xiao.

An elegant number with shoestring straps, in a delicate apricot cream. The asymmetrically embroidered bodice swept down into layered waves which seemed to change the shape of the dress as it moved.

"Are you feeling creeped out?" said Squid.

"I think I'm feeling jealous," said Grief. "Slick phone, pretty dress. I think they call this 'grooming'."

Squid pulled an envelope from the crinkled paper, and a gilded invitation slid out. It was even more impressive than the dress, with a stained-glass design of crimson and silver. A holographic retinal ID was tastefully incorporated into the water lily motif, admitting one "Vienna Couralie" to "Thandie Holbourne's Monster Graduation Party!"

"Is that Holbourne as in Governor Holbourne?" said Grief.

However, Squid was preoccupied with the architectural blueprints accompanying the invitation. She presumed this wasn't standard issue for the guests. A red cross was marked on level three of the mansion, along with a photograph of a GX-issue encrypted hard drive.

Making an educated guess, Squid supposed she had to go to the party, snatch the drive and deliver it to Ferret. Squid looked at the blueprint again, her heart already going into premature seizures.

*Go to the party, snatch the drive—*

Squid felt a sudden swell of nausea, the first in weeks. She forced herself to take a deep breath.

*Go to the party—*

"Squid? You look really— Squid?"

"I'm fine. I just don't see how this is going to work. Thandie's in high school. There's no way I could pass for eighteen."

"It's Governor Holbourne's party," said Grief. "So, there'll be plenty of older guests."

"I mean, Vienna Couralie. I look nothing like a Vienna, let alone a Couralie."

"Squid? Is something wrong?"

"No, it's just— What if someone asks me how Ambassador Couralie is doing? Or how I'm enjoying university?"

"How about I go with you?"

"As what? My chaperone?"

Grief flicked back his hair.

"I can be the dangerous, older boyfriend."

Squid blinked slowly, and Grief shrugged.

"You can go on your own if you want."

Squid stared at the invitation, her sweaty palm prints seeping across the silver ink. She'd worked long and hard to repress her teen years. Her fondest memory of high school was learning to pick the locks on the storage cupboards so she could hide inside.

"It doesn't say 'plus one'," said Squid.

"Let me handle that," said Grief with a grin.

*

They called this place Deep Freeze. Where officers went into exile. Where case files went to sleep and never woke up. The walls were unbroken rows of filing drawers, dull grey and neatly labelled, stretching from floor to ceiling.

A steady stream of files slid out from a chute in the wall, filling a massive in-tray that looked suspiciously like a shark tank. It gave new meaning to the phrase "drowning in paperwork".

Casey scooped up another bucket of heavy, yellow envelopes, hauling it to the sorting desk.

"This system is really inefficient," said Casey. "I'm sure there are files at the bottom that are older than I am."

Riego shrugged and pointed to a large red sign hanging above the tank.

WORK FASTER.

"I think this is supposed to be like the martial arts kid washing windows, or the Japanese boy planting pebbles," said Riego.

"Authoritarian bullying through pointless tasks?" said Casey.

"Learning patience."

"All I'm learning is that I should switch off the cameras next time."

Riego put down his stack of files.

"Sometimes, I think the reason you don't follow the rules is because you don't think there should be any. Just you."

Riego joked about these things all the time, but this time, he sounded like he meant it.

"Of course I believe in rule of law and procedural justice—"

"Then why are we in Siberia?"

Casey decided now wasn't the best time for a frank diatribe against bureaucracy.

"I'm getting a refill," said Riego. "Want anything?"

*Pearce's head on a stick*, thought Casey.

"No, thanks."

It was a rotten time for a guilt trip. Sitting under the fluorescent lights in a windowless basement, surrounded by mountains of unsolved cases. At least on highway patrol you got to pull a few hoons off the road. On desk duty, you got all the breaking news. Down here, cities could rise and fall, and unsolved cases would keep sliding down the chute.

Casey paused on a wrinkled envelope, the label yellowed at the edges.

HOMICIDE

VICTIM: DAMIAN ORLIASSO

STATUS: COLD CASE

Casey remembered this one. She'd spent sleepless nights over it, punching the sandbag at the gym until someone put up a notice complaining about the bloodstains. Orliasso had been a financial controller on the city council—nice house, fat salary, trips to Switzerland every summer. Everyone suspected there were irregularities in the accounts, but it was just another untouchable problem until Orliasso walked into the Commissioner's office one morning with a briefcase full of files and a request for witness protection.

Cases like this went down in accountant folkore—the rare instances when a timid number-cruncher got to be the hero. Unfortunately, Orliasso's story ended with seven bullets to the head and a missing briefcase. The newspapers had had a field day. The word "debacle" appeared two hundred and seventy-three times over the next two weeks, usually following the word "police".

Casey leafed through the file. She'd always wondered how they'd never caught the assassin despite the street cameras, CCTV in the hotel, dozens of interviews and a forensic report as thick as your—

She flicked quickly back through the file. There were entire sections of the forensic report missing, and the digital evidence sleeve was empty. The case summary referred to forty-nine interviews, but there were only forty-two transcripts in the envelope.

Casey stared at the file, trying not to jump to career-ending conclusions. It didn't have to mean anything. Maybe someone had a sloppy day. Maybe they deserved the word "debacle" on this one.

Four and a half hours later, Casey was ready to embark on a career-ending bender. When Riego finally strolled in with a tray of biscuits, cabinet drawers hung open all over the place, and Casey sat cross-legged on the floor amidst a spreading pile of case files.

"We're supposed to be putting the files *into* the cabinets," said Riego.

"That was a long coffee break," said Casey, not looking up from the envelope she was slicing open.

"Just catching up on the news," said Riego. "Didn't think you'd miss me."

Casey pulled a folder from the envelope, leafing quickly through the contents and scribbling in her notepad.

"Did you know we had DNA evidence in the Keong case?" said Casey.

"The marine?"

"Lance Corporal Cynthia Keong, mysteriously murdered right before Major Fraser defected to Kazmenistan. The DNA evidence was never made public, maybe because we don't have it anymore."

Casey held up an empty media sleeve.

"Or the speed camera photograph in the Garcia hit-and-run," continued Casey, holding up another slim file.

"The rock star who was dating the Governor's daughter?"

"Only according to the gossip pages, but I guess we'll never know."

"Casey, what are you trying to—"

"The Winchester fraud case. The Benini weapons haul. The Arcana drug bust."

Casey held up one more file, and her expression was like an axe swinging home.

HOMICIDE

VICTIM: TOL WERNER

STATUS: COLD CASE

"The ballistics report is missing," said Casey. "And I'm guessing it's gone from the server and the nimbus, and if I went to my computer right now, the backup wouldn't be on my drive anymore."

The room filled with the sound of biscuits getting stale.

"Why can't you just leave it alone?" said Riego quietly.

Casey felt as though she'd been shot, the breath draining from her lungs.

"You think nobody knows?" continued Riego. "You're not a superhero, Casey. You can't fix the city. You can't save the world."

"I can try," said Casey. "Why did you even join the police? The free coffee?"

Riego's gaze turned cold.

"I wanted to help people," he said. "Then I realised there is no justice, just people. And I can't save everyone, but maybe one day, I'll be in the right place at the right time. And that'll have to be enough."

Casey looked down at the yellow spread of lies and broken promises.

"It's not," she said. "Not for me."

She hadn't seen the fork in the road, hadn't seen their paths diverge, but now she realised that she and Riego had chosen different sides.

"Sam Olsen's dead," said Riego.

And the killer punches just kept coming.

"They found him hanged in his motel room about three hours ago," he continued. "It's being filed a suicide."

Casey's thoughts fell quickly into line, a line that formed a great big flashing arrow.

"I'll be right back," she said, racing for the door.

"Casey, where—"

She didn't wait for the rest of the sentence. Everyone knew that the city was rotten. That corruption and crime infiltrated every level of business and politics. But people just shrugged and kept their heads down. You had to be a certain kind of crazy to stand up, knowing you'd get mown down.

And another kind of crazy to stand up and survive.

*

Austen Park wasn't a suburb. It was a social status. Like having the right kind of cufflinks or the appropriate country club membership. It was where serious, middle-class professionals became respected pillars of the community. A nursery for future CEOs and senators, before they moved on to places like Sapphire Waters.

Casey pulled up outside Valencia Gardens, a tiered apartment complex overlooking a lush central courtyard. The Spanish-villa pretensions were favoured by those wanting to project a subtle European earthiness without sacrificing their wrap-around TVs.

Deus didn't look surprised to see her, although he made polite comments to the contrary.

"I'm surprised you don't sleep at the station," said Casey, barely waiting for an invitation before stepping into the unlit apartment.

"I don't think the bunk's big enough for the both of us," said Deus mildly.

*I don't think the station's big enough for the both of us*, thought Casey.

Casey had never really thought about Deus's apartment, although she'd half-expected something brutally minimalist, perhaps with a room of antique bisque dolls. Instead, it was comfortably furnished with a vintage lamp here, a sleek modern cabinet there. A wobbly painting of the seaside by "Alicia, age 9" from the Police Charity Auction, hung beside a canvas print of Garry Shead's *Free*.

"Can I get you a drink?" said Deus.

"You could put on a shirt."

Deus crossed his arms and continued standing in front of the charming Provincial sideboard.

"Why are you here, Casey?"

Casey had run out of road and she was just charging through the undergrowth now.

"Orliasso. Keong. Winchester. Benini," said Casey. "Notice a pattern?"

Deus didn't take his eyes off Casey as his hand slid into the drawer behind him. Casey kept a grip on her gun as he pulled out a scanner wand.

"I trust you don't mind," said Deus.

Casey stood stiffly as he passed the wand slowly over her and finally put it aside.

"Don't tell me you're surprised," said Deus.

"How long have you known?" said Casey. "The systematic destruction of evidence. The link between Pearce and bloody everyone."

"Long enough to know what works and what doesn't. You can get angry, go rogue, do some damage and end up in a padded cell. Or you can work with the system but outside of it. I like to think of it as working in an alternative system."

There was something about the way he said "alternative" that conjured up images of chalk outlines involving lots of pieces.

"Olsen," said Casey. "Was that the alternative system?"

"Riley got a new job in Community Services, by the way," said Deus. "She's taken up parkour cycling and she's doing great."

Deus looked so steady, so composed, like he was chatting about a new art exhibition, or discussing his favourite restaurant. Casey shivered slightly.

"And Maluka?"

"Most of the residents in your block have been rehoused with relatives or in temporary accommodation. They were all uninsured, but they're alive. This time."

Casey's head swam with conflicting impulses. Deus and his buddies, his connections, his resources, and all the time, they should have had serious quotation marks around them. He was talking about using his position in the force to run a vigilante operation. He was talking about execution without a trial. Cold-blooded murder under the guise of justice.

"I know what you're thinking, Casey. And I know if you didn't feel the same way, you wouldn't be here."

Deus took a step forward, silhouetted against the balcony archway. Outside, climbing roses wound their way over the railing, hanging from an ornate iron trellis.

"You can't fight Pearce with books and procedure," said Deus. "He's the kind of bad you can't reform. The kind of evil you can't put away. You could spend the next fifty years dredging bodies from the river, watching good people die in a city so rotten that people are born in a state of decay. Or you could do something about it."

Casey could see why Deus gave people the creeps, but she had to admit, he was damned persuasive if you were a certain kind of angry.

"Like killing people without a trial?" said Casey.

"Big picture, Casey. Big picture."

Deus leaned back, his eyes hard with a strange kind of fire.

"I'm being promoted to superintendent at the end of the year," he said. "In six years, I'll be the youngest Chief in Met West history. In twelve, I'll be playing golf with the Governor while my wife and two kids are having brunch with the Mayor. And long before then, Pearce will be a bad memory, and criminals will really have something to fear in Baltus City."

Casey felt as though she were standing in the aftermath of a tornado, surrounded by upside-down houses and inside-out cows. Deus had his whole life mapped out, probably including where he'd meet his future wife and what school their theoretical kids would go to.

"You're not alone, Casey," said Deus. "There are people fighting the good fight. You can take the moral high road, or you can make a difference."

Casey wanted to believe that you could do both, but when the system was so corrupt, when the forces allied against you were so great…

She could feel the genesis of a hundred questionable action movies right here.

"How the hell did you make superintendent?" said Casey.

It wasn't the most relevant question, but her thoughts were still catching up. Deus cocked an eyebrow.

"Think about what we've discussed," he said. "Goodnight, Casey."

She was left standing on a jasmine-wreathed walkway, her thoughts churning in an unhealthy direction. There were things you couldn't undo, acts that couldn't be forgiven. But when lives were at stake and monstrous deeds went unpunished, there were those who were willing to take on that burden.

The only question was: could she pull the trigger in cold blood and call herself justice? Casey shivered again, her head throbbing. Everything would look different after a good night's sleep. By morning, it probably wouldn't even be a question.

*

Rojin woke sharply, aware of a presence in the room. Beneath the covers, her hand wrapped around her Reaver, her lidded eyes scanning the dark.

There were fifteen layers of security in the Chival before you arrived at her door, and another twenty-eight by the time you reached the bedroom. Most intruders would be sliding in pieces down the disposal chute well before Rojin laid eyes on them.

"Rojin..."

She swivelled her gun to the dresser, where her phone sat silent and dark. She edged closer—no missed calls or blinking messages, nothing incoming, but the onscreen ID displayed a name she hadn't seen in a long time.

*Pearce.*

"Rojin." The voice was definitely coming from her phone, but it sounded strangely garbled, as though it had passed through a distortion filter. "You look well."

"Pearce?" said Rojin, warily lowering her gun.

"I was disappointed to hear about Jace. Olsen. Maluka..."

The number of criminals inexplicably "committing suicide" had been steadily rising for months. Ducabre wouldn't risk another war, but Rojin was running out of patience. And people.

"The Stain have stepped up their attacks, but Ducabre's instructions are—"

"Ducabre's been out of his depth since the Raphael incident," said Pearce.

*And no one's heard from you since that night*, thought Rojin.

"May I ask for identification before proceeding further?" said Rojin.

A garbled voice over the phone was just a garbled voice, even with Pearce's carrier ID.

"Congratulations on Kabukuri," said Pearce. "I trust the dish was cold enough."

Rojin's expression remained unchanged. Revenge had ceased being cathartic a long time ago. It was just another action, another breath, another step.

Rojin knew there was no justice in the same way she knew there was no God. Because bad things happened. Horrific things happened. Acts of grotesque and monstrous inhumanity happened to innocent people, and they kept on happening and would never stop. You had to take care of yourself, because no one else would.

And there was no pleasure in revenge, because there was no meaningful victory against a tide that had no end.

"Your instructions?" said Rojin.

"It's time we removed the Stain."

# SEVENTEEN

Squid felt like a freak.

The sun climbed steadily towards noon, and her dress was going to be all sweaty and crinkled before she even got through the gates. Her hair was already falling out of its updo after forty-five minutes of her clinging to the back of a truck, and her shoes were scuffed from the long walk. Grief had insisted on pinning a fragrant white gardenia to her dress, and it had started to wilt.

*Great entrance, Squid.*

"You look fine," said Grief. "You scrub up all right."

"I look like a lemur in a dress."

"Well, if you'd let me do your makeup as well as the hair—"

"Using a dead woman's hair accessories is bad enough," said Squid. "I draw the line at using a dead woman's makeup. It's practically a horror movie—*The Lipstick*. Where the dead woman starts saying things with the main character's mouth."

"You're panicking."

"I'm not— Oh, God—"

Squid froze outside the sweeping silver gates of the Governor's Lodge. Energetic pop music boomed across the manicured lawns, and exuberant guests danced all over the colourful floats or mingled in elegant white gazebos. Grief had been right about the age mix—there seemed to be as many dignitaries and celebrities as there were overexcited teenagers.

Squid felt her stomach lurching, like a zombie climbing out of the Dizzzynator ride.

*This isn't a party; this is a job*, Squid repeated to herself. *Remember why you're here.*

"If they don't let you in, go home and wait for me," said Squid. "I won't be long."

"Why wouldn't they let me in?" said Grief, leaning back with a "What's not to love?" expression.

"You look like you stole those clothes off some rich guy after you beat him up with a garbage can."

"It's called fashionably distressed," said Grief. "Styles have changed since you were in high school."

"Clearly," said Squid, striding over to the security checkpoint.

The retinal scan went without a hitch. Ferret might send you to hell, but he'd send you to hell with impeccably forged ID.

"Your invitation, sir," said the guard to Grief.

"He's my plus one," said Squid.

"The Governor's Lodge doesn't have a plus-one policy," said the guard.

"Oh... but... he..." said Squid.

She glanced at Grief and noticed he wasn't even looking at the guard. He seemed to be grinning at a group of girls in tiaras and miming something.

"Sir, I have to ask you to—" began the guard.

"Lyndon," said Grief, glancing at the guard's name tag. "I think Miss Holbourne wants your attention."

The guard glanced towards the Executive Penthouse float, where a leggy blonde and her posse of girls were enjoying colourful mocktails. The queen bee pointed to the guard with a perfectly filed talon and waved Grief in with a wink.

"Uh, enjoy the party," said the guard as Grief glided past.

"That's disgusting," muttered Squid.

"I think a wink is pretty chaste, considering some of the gestures the other girls were making," said Grief.

"I mean, letting someone in just because they're pretty. If you happen to be attractive, people are suddenly nicer to you. They're more likely to give you a job. Paramedics try harder to resuscitate you. If you're ugly or antisocial, good luck."

Grief stared at Squid.

"Oh, my God, you've let your awkward high-school experiences scar you for life and send you into a life of crime."

"It wasn't just high school," said Squid. "We're talking kindergarten, preschool. No one wants to play with the funny-looking kid with bad teeth. And I haven't been scarred; I'm just realistic—"

"There's nothing wrong with crooked teeth."

"Says the guy with veneers."

"I don't have veneers," said Grief, running his tongue analytically over his teeth.

"How would you know? You don't even know your own—"

Squid gasped as Grief suddenly grabbed her around the waist, pulling her beside him.

"Miss Holbourne," said Grief politely to the approaching girl.

Even without her stilettos, Thandie Holbourne stood a good head taller than Squid. Her hair was sunkissed blond, and her micro dress was stunning slashes of turquoise silk.

"I'm sorry you didn't get an invitation," said Thandie with a blinding smile. "I stopped seeing you around for a while. Should I tell my mother you're here?"

"I'm sure the Governor knows," said Grief, returning the smile.

Squid looked from Grief to Thandie, her heart pounding its way up her throat. This wasn't being recognised by a thug in a bar. This was being recognised by the Governor's daughter, in the Governor's high-security compound, in the middle of a covert mission.

"Enjoy the party," said Thandie, giving Squid a lazy smile. "Cute dress."

Thandie sashayed back to her adoring clique, and they disappeared towards the sound of graduation karaoke. Squid stared at Grief.

"I have never seen her before in my life," said Grief. "And I'm sure if I had, it was purely platonic."

"Because you know what happened to the rock star, right?" said

Squid. "Anyway, we just lost the luxury of time. We have to be done and gone before someone else recognises—"

She stopped in her tracks.

"Squid?" Grief glanced around in alarm.

Squid stared across the crowded lawn, the sea of glittering dresses and winged boys a blur in the foreground.

*Flash. Click. Smile.*

Bastian meandered through the shrieking high-schoolers, taking photos as they posed in ebullient groups. Squid decided that the universe just hated her.

"You know him?" said Grief.

"He's the fiancé of a girl I used to know," said Squid, steering Grief away quickly.

Grief glanced over his shoulder, eyes narrowing.

"I suppose he's all right, if you're into… good-looking types."

"Don't look! Don't look!" said Squid urgently, picking up speed.

"Squid?" a voice called after them.

She clenched her eyes shut. She could already feel her face turning a blistering red, sweat prickling her upper lip.

*Just kill me now.*

"Bastian," said Squid, forcing a mangled smile. "What a surprise."

"Hey," said Bastian with a warm smile. "Alabama's chatting to Senator Marcello, so I thought I'd make myself useful."

"I'm sure everyone really appreciates having such professional photos taken at their graduation party," said Squid.

"That's sweet of you to say," said Bastian. "Actually, how about…"

Bastian raised his camera, and Squid's heart stopped as she prepared to throw herself between Grief and the ten-thousand-dollar piece of equipment.

"Sure," said Grief with an easy smile, putting his arm around Squid.

*Flash. Click.*

Squid blinked like a googly-eyed tree frog scooped from the leaf litter.

"So, are you two…?" said Bastian.

"No!" said Squid. "I mean, uh, he… I… We… really have to go! But great seeing you, and I'm sure Alabama has my tag for the photo. Cheers!"

Squid dragged Grief past the tables of artistic hors d'oeuvres, through a line of flowering arbours and into a crowd of bouncing teenagers screaming along to the chorus of a graduation dance mix.

"Weren't you supposed to use me to make him jealous?" said Grief.

"None of what you just said made sense," said Squid, unfolding a scrap of instructions from Ferret.

*ES: 1100-1300 = 0*

*HC = 1*

*X = 1!*

Somehow, Ferret had neutralised the electronic surveillance system for a two hour window. The hard copy—security guards—she'd have to deal with on her own. The target had to be recovered, not destroyed. Squid bristled a little at the exclamation mark.

She glanced up at Grief.

"What are you doing?"

"I'm dancing," said Grief. "We're hiding in a herd of dancers, and the people who aren't dancing get picked off by the lions."

"I'm not sure you should be dancing like that at a high school party."

"Did you see the girl with the cat ears?"

"Did you see the guy squirting milk from his eyes? Equally attractive."

Grief eyed Squid thoughtfully.

"Have you ever actually been asked to dance?"

"Of course. Maybe. No. I don't remember. I'm busy."

Squid squeezed her way out of the crowd, making a discreet beeline for the pergola adjoining the mansion. The party itself was on the sprawling lawns, and the grounds nearest to the main building were devoid of guests.

"This whole high-school thing really gets to you, doesn't it?" said Grief, catching up. "Did you even go to your prom?"

"Yes," said Squid flatly. "But I've moved on. I'm not in high school anymore."

"But you still see yourself as that girl," said Grief. "Standing awkward and friendless in the corner the entire night—"

She'd moved on, but it still felt like a javelin through the chest.

"How did you—"

"Hey!" said a security guard, emerging from a side door. "You're not supposed to be here."

That turned out to be an unfortunate choice of words.

Grief's arm wrapped around the guard's throat, and his other hand was a blur as it twisted a spot near the base of the neck. Squid gaped as the guard hit the ground without a noise.

"Did you just Vulcan Nerve Pinch that guy?" said Squid.

"I don't know," said Grief, stripping the guard of his radio and gun. "But I'm pretty sure he'll wake up again."

Squid was uneasy about the "pretty sure" part, but she was even more worried about the guard's patrol buddies.

Their window of time had just gotten a whole lot smaller.

*

Clef sounded worried, which wasn't unusual, but even over the radio, Verona could sense the ripple of uncertainty.

"We've just intercepted a call from the Governor's Lodge," said Clef. "There's been a sighting of the Rott—of Raphael."

"He's there? Now?" said Verona.

"It sounds like he's at the party. Uninvited."

*How very Raphael*, thought Verona.

However, even she couldn't suppress a slight shudder of… something. There were over five hundred guests at that party, most of them just kids.

"Pearce's response?" said Verona.

"Encrypted. But our satellite feed shows that twenty-four trucks just mobilised from Pearce HQ, and Sebel reports an assault chopper lifting off from their air base five minutes ago."

An assault chopper. Heading for the Governor's house.

"Send Mal's team," said Verona. "Capture the target alive if you can. If you can't, take him out."

"Engagement with Pearce?"

"Avoid collateral. We're not making this a battleground."

She ended the transmission.

If Raphael had entered the fray, God help them all.

*

Squid had no idea how he'd managed it, but Ferret had outdone himself.

Every security door beeped open upon her approach, the electronic locks switching to green. It was eerie, knowing that someone was watching her over the surveillance cameras, but it saved her a hell of a lot of time trying to bypass an unfamiliar system.

"I wouldn't mind living somewhere like this," said Grief. "You could have a room for everything. A music room. A fossil room. A trophy room."

"What kind of trophies?" frowned Squid.

"My raccoon," said Grief. "I'd have more by then."

Squid suddenly scrambled behind a line of Roman busts, dragging Grief to the floor. A pair of guards rushed past, talking urgently into their radios before disappearing down a marble staircase.

Grief fiddled with the controls on his appropriated radio, catching a few words through the static.

*"... stations... secure perimeter... code red..."*

"That doesn't sound good," said Grief.

What it sounded like was their window slamming shut and taking several fingers with it. As long as the mark was an easy grab-and-run, they might still make a clean exit. Squid stopped at the last door on the right, and the security lock blinked green.

The richly furnished study resembled something from a vintage children's book, with a standing globe of polished brass, shelves of opalised ammonites, ornate wicker cages full of stuffed finches, and walls covered with moody paintings. Huge windows in the far wall overlooked the boisterous garden party, flooding the room with afternoon light.

It was probably too much to ask for the room to be empty except for the hard drive sitting in a carry bag.

"Found it," said Grief.

He stood holding an oversized portrait of an intense-looking clown, the bare wall revealing an electronic safe.

"How did you—"

"Can you open it?" said Grief.

Squid began stripping the wires from the lining of her bra. She hadn't brought nearly enough equipment, but there was only so much you could pass off as underwear infrastructure, especially when it was obvious you didn't need a lot of it.

"Could you turn that thing around?" said Squid.

Grief shuffled the painting aside, politely averting his eyes. Squid pulled the last of the lockpicks from her hair, neutralised the external sensors with a poisoned kiss of code from her phone, and pried the fascia from the control panel. It was a privately installed safe, retina and password locked. An Erlein Engineering core. Once the fascia was removed, you had sixty seconds to bypass the circuit before the alarm went off.

The lock used compressed-frequency wiring, and what she needed was half an hour, a safe-cracking kit and a refresher course. What she had was sixty seconds and a piece of underwire.

Her fingers moved like a spider in its death throes. Even at the height of her training, she'd rarely cracked the minute mark. She could feel herself trembling, a tense pressure building inside her head.

"Squid—" said Grief.

Something in his tone strongly suggested she should look up, but if the safe went into lockdown, the drive was as good as gone.

Ten seconds.

"Uh, Squid…"

Five seconds.

Squid's whole body shook now, her ears ringing with her heartbeat.

Zero.

*Click.*

Squid swung open the safe, grabbing the drive from its bed of papers. She finally followed Grief's gaze to the rattling chandelier and realised that she wasn't the only one shaking.

The whole mansion vibrated, the air filling with a deafening hum.

"Did we trigger something?" said Grief.

"Like a self-destruct?" said Squid. "This is the Governor's Lodge, not some mystical temple."

"Well, unless this is one seriously rocking party, I don't think the lodge is—"

The study suddenly darkened, and a hulking shape of black steel and glass rose across the windows. The rotors were a screaming blur, the guns of the assault chopper already swinging towards them.

*My God,* thought Squid. *They're not going to—*

The windows shattered into fountains of glass as the chopper opened fire. Squid and Grief dove back through the door, a storm of feathers and upholstery following them down the corridor.

"Talk about overzealous security," gasped Grief.

"I don't think that's the Governor," said Squid.

Windows shattered behind them as they sprinted down the hall, the shadow of the chopper gliding across the walls. A pack of guards charged up the stairs ahead, and Squid detoured down a side passage. Gunshots followed them all the way to the ground floor, marble chips pinging off the walls.

Squid was halfway out the back door when her corsage abruptly plumed into a shower of wilted petals. Grief yanked her back inside, gunfire quickly carving a Squid-shaped hole in the wall. Outside, screams mingled with the grunt of armoured trucks and machine gun fire.

"What the hell…?" Squid tried to catch her breath.

People in dark suits strode through the panicked crowd, armed with automatic weapons and dodging fire from the armoured trucks. Security guards scrambled in confusion, trying to herd the guests towards cover.

"Squid, there's a door out the side," said Grief. "Take cover behind the line of tables, lose yourself in the crowd, get out of here."

"Grief, what—"

"They're after me."

Squid stopped at Grief's expression.

"Grief, the whole point of—"

He suddenly cupped her face in his hands, his eyes burning with words he couldn't bear to say.

"Just remember," said Grief, "you're not that girl anymore. I look at you and I see…"

Grief swallowed.

"Take care, Squid."

And with that, he launched himself through the door and into the waiting gunfire.

*

One gun. Eight rounds. No regrets.

Well, maybe a few, but Grief wasn't going to reminisce. He made it to the gazebo and sprinted away right before it got pulverised by the chopper, exploding into tornados of splintering wood. Cars turned into sieves, and tables into mulch, as he darted between the burning floats, gunfire strafing across the lawn after him.

All of Squid's warnings were made flesh here, amidst the screaming children and the smoke-filled sky. The longer Grief ran from who he was, the more he endangered those around him. He'd been selfishly clinging to a life that didn't belong to him. A life he didn't deserve.

He considered surrendering, but he wasn't sure which side was least likely to riddle him with holes. While he was willing to take responsibility for his past, he wasn't convinced that death was a prerequisite. Unfortunately, the chopper seemed hell-bent on turning him into gritty pâté, although a couple of tranquiliser darts had also clinked against the walls.

Grief was still two hundred yards from the nearest gate when gunfire pinned him inside the boat sheds. Bullets tore through the tin roof, and Grief threw himself beneath a forty-foot yacht, splinters of fibreglass raining down. The hull shuddered as ammunition ripped up the deck, the ground quaking as an army of hostile trucks approached.

He could wait for them to drag him out, or he could go out in a very brief blaze of stupidity. Neither option seemed particularly appealing, but life was full of decisions like that. Grief checked his magazine, quickly snapping it back into place.

His only hope was that Squid had made it out. That she wouldn't be too angry with him. That somehow, she'd—

The wall of the boat shed collapsed into rubble, demolished by the bull bar of a hulking five-tonne Hummer. It was daffodil yellow, with an incongruous spoiler, and it was the closest thing Grief had ever seen to a sports tank.

The passenger door kicked open, and the vision inside was like a rose unfurling. Elegant waves of peach silk rippled in the exhaust, and Squid held out her hand.

"Get in!" she yelled.

Grief dove into the Hummer, slamming the door as bullets bounced off the reinforced windows. Squid stomped on the accelerator, cables spilling over her legs like the intestines of the beast.

"I'm really glad to see you," said Grief.

Squid made a distracted grunting noise, struggling to control a steering wheel larger than she was. She pulled on a forest of gear sticks as the Hummer extracted itself from the boat shed, roaring across the lawn. Bullets rattled off the exterior, and Grief's head knocked against the roof as they drove—a little unnecessarily—over a smouldering fairy-princess float.

Squid aimed for a side gate, and a squad of armoured trucks rushed to cut them off. Suddenly, a shadow descended in front of them, huge curving windows like predatory eyes, a slicing rotor slashing overhead. For a horrifying moment, Grief thought Squid was going to play chicken with the chopper. However, this thought was displaced by the even more disturbing realisation that the chopper was aiming a different barrel.

"Is that a missile launcher?" croaked Grief.

He gripped his seat as the Hummer charged, and he glimpsed a flare of orange. Squid suddenly spun the wheel, sending the vehicle skidding sideways around the hovering chopper. Behind them, an armoured truck exploded into flames.

Grief found himself flung against the window, then sprawled across Squid's lap, then pinned back in his seat.

"There's a wall! There's a wall!" yelled Grief.

She gave no sign of having heard him.

"Huber Valdesdt, Series One-Nine-Five," muttered Squid. "I always wondered if the ads were true."

She pushed the accelerator to the floor, and there was a sound like a thousand Furies tearing their claws through girders and rock. The impact sent Grief slamming into the penguin-leather dashboard, then almost backwards through his seat. If he hadn't already had amnesia, he'd certainly have concussive issues now.

Squid's expression remained one of steely concentration as she drifted across four lanes and onto the freeway. The Governor's Lodge fell further behind them, along with a growing chorus of sirens.

"That was actually less traumatic than my high school prom," said Squid.

Grief nodded weakly, suspecting that his own prom had probably been quite nice.

"Next stop: Ferret?" said Grief.

"Quick detour," said Squid. "I'm in the mood for answers."

*

Rojin strode from the chopper, tossing her helmet hard enough to knock out a nearby soldier. People veered urgently from her path, like ants fleeing a gigantic magnifying glass.

Rojin had half a mind to shoot every team leader here, and because the other half of her mind had been lost some time before, there was no little voice coughing in polite protest. True, Verona's people had gotten in the way, as had the shrieking civilians, but none of that should have been an obstacle to a hundred guns and several tanks. There was no good reason for Raphael to have escaped, aside from the fact that he was Raphael.

An unfortunate messenger stepped into the line of fire, visibly wilting under the heat of Rojin's stare. He held out a radio, his arm shaking violently.

"We intercepted a message on the police scanner," said the messenger, trying to simultaneously whisper the Lord's Prayer.

Rojin's fingers closed over the radio, pressing the playback key.

*"...complaints from neighbours... Squatters in the Charlton house... One man, one woman... Twenty-six Marley Drive..."*

A burst of static, then a second voice.

*"...Roger that... Plover and Vinh here... We'll check it out..."*

Rojin flicked off the radio, the information already triangulating. The bridge, the Fess, the Governor's Lodge.

Marley Drive.

Perhaps it'd be a good day after all.

*

They ditched the Hummer at the edge of the slums, in the shadow of a broken crane. Squid had actually ditched the crane here some years before, after a fruitcake of a job culminating in a slow-motion chase down the freeway. She couldn't even remember how she'd managed to snap the end off.

The Hummer would have made a sweet delivery, but in the slums it'd house a neighbourhood. And Ferret would get what he wanted, as long as Squid did.

The area was busier than usual, with displaced people flowing in from all over the city. Apartment complexes were burning down; entire office blocks had been blown off the map. It wasn't a good time for visitors, but Squid only had two hours before Ferret started looking for her.

She found Kirsk in her usual hideout, holed up in a nest of empty crates. She seemed even more skittish than usual and almost bolted at the sight of Grief.

"He's a friend," said Squid. "He just, uh, had an accident."

Grief casually ruffled the broken glass from his hair.

"You're still working for Ferret?" said Kirsk nervously.

"Not exactly," said Squid. "But I need a favour."

She placed the GX drive on an upturned crate.

"I need to know what's on it."

Kirsk carefully picked up the dull metal oblong, the casing half the length of a finger.

"This is military-grade," said Kirsk. "Government-encrypted, I'll bet."

Kirsk selected a few wires and connectors from the clutter, quickly hooking up a computer that appeared to have been built from tinfoil and cutlery. After a few rapid keystrokes and a series of flashing screens that seemed subliminal in speed, Kirsk's brow furrowed.

"It's a customised encryption," said Kirsk. "Almost like Syndicate algorithms."

"Can you decipher it?" said Squid.

"No offence, but this sounds like the kind of thing that'll get me killed," said Kirsk.

Only a few months earlier, Squid wouldn't have come here. She would have gone straight to Ferret, no questions asked. But life had taken a few funny turns since then, and now, she saw choices where she used to see blank rock.

She'd seen the shadow of a massacre today. Terrified high-schoolers running for their lives, their clothes shredded by the shrapnel. Pearce was out of control, and you could bet tomorrow's papers would read "Military Training Mishap" or "Movie Stunt Goes Wrong".

"The drive belongs to Governor Holbourne," said Squid. "And I think it has something to do with Pearce. It's probably dangerous to get involved, but I've already made my choice. The rest is up to you."

"Could it damage Pearce?" said Kirsk.

"I hope so."

Kirsk stared at the screen, encrypted characters reflected in her glasses.

"I'll need some time," she said, rolling up her matted sleeves.

One and a half hours later, Squid sat on an empty paint tin, trying to repair her dress with spit. It gave her hands something to do while her mind bellyflopped around like an intoxicated lorikeet.

"It's fine," said Grief, gently pulling Squid's hands from the torn silk. "I'm sure he wouldn't have given it to you if he wanted it back intact."

Squid scowled, trying to brush the soot from her skirt.

"How about I come with you to see Ferret?" said Grief.

"No. Go home. I'll make the drop-off—"

The computer suddenly gave a series of rapid, high-pitched chirps, like a surging waterfall of crickets.

"Hey," said Kirsk. "I think we've got something."

File headings filled the screen, and Kirsk clicked several at random. Spreadsheets, databases, names, dates, transaction numbers. It seemed to be a record of monetary amounts transferred into the Governor's account and then back out again.

"Corruption," murmured Grief.

"Clearly," said Squid.

Grief didn't seem to hear her, his eyes narrowing as he skimmed the dense streams of data.

"She was double-dipping," he said with a humourless smile. "Distributing bribes for Verona as well as Pearce."

There had to be millions of transactions, implicating senior officials, politicians and obviously the Governor herself. It painted a massive web of corruption that compromised almost every government department in Baltus City.

"I don't get it," said Squid. "You couldn't really use this information unless you took everyone down: Pearce, Verona, half the bloody city."

"A changing of the guard," said Grief, his eyes glowing from the light of the screen.

Kirsk looked uneasy, and Squid cleared her throat.

"Grief, how about you head home? Kirsk, can you make a copy of this?"

Kirsk tapped quickly at the keys.

"I'm making the drop-off with you," said Grief.

"No," said Squid firmly. "Ferret doesn't know you exist, and believe me, you want to keep it that way."

"How about you let me deal with Ferret?" said Grief, a hint of a growl in his voice.

The tapping stopped abruptly, and Kirsk's eyes swivelled towards Grief, filling with dawning horror. The rest was a blur—the start of a scream, and Grief's arm was around Kirsk's neck, his hand over her mouth.

"Grief!" yelled Squid. "Let her go!"

Squid pried frantically at Grief's arms, and he abruptly released the gasping woman. Kirsk staggered into Squid's arms, quickly cowering as

Squid rounded on Grief.

"What the hell is wrong with you?!" said Squid.

"He's the one," gasped Kirsk. "The one who killed Werner."

There was a shock of silence, and Grief turned pale.

"No, I…" he began.

"Kirsk, what are you talking about?" said Squid, keeping her voice calm.

"Casey made me decode a data-slick," said Kirsk. "Werner hid it before he died, and it's his voice. He's threatening Werner."

"Take a breath," said Squid. "Are you sure it was Grief?"

Kirsk closed her eyes for a moment, and when they opened, her gaze was unshakeable.

"Yes."

Squid knew that voices were notoriously difficult to ID, particularly covert recordings. But it was a truly terrible thing when no one believed you, when people condescendingly clucked that you must be mistaken.

"Grief, did you know Werner?" said Squid.

"No," said Grief. "I mean, I don't know. I don't remember…"

She could see the despair in his eyes, the hint of fear.

"Kirsk," said Squid gently. "We're going to leave now. I'm going to find out what's going on, but I promise that Grief won't hurt you. Whoever is on that recording, it's not who Grief is now. It's hard to explain, but please trust me."

Kirsk stared at Squid as though she were insane. Squid didn't exactly have a reputation for psychological stability, but from Kirsk's expression, she was careering into completely new territory.

"Take care," said Squid.

She strode through the jagged silhouettes, twilight turning into sombre night.

"Squid…"

"You're coming with me," said Squid. "But if you ever do that to her again—I don't care who you are, I don't care who you were, I will kick your goddamn head in."

Grief nodded, eyes down. He trailed a few paces behind Squid as she marched from the slums.

It was time to end this.

# EIGHTEEN

Drop-Off Fifty-Two was an abandoned lot behind the remains of Saint Merici's church. Broken windows marred the mouldering walls of the building, and even potential squatters didn't attempt to breach the boarded-up doors. The church was occupied mostly by bats and lizards these days, and the sight of dark flocks streaming in through the windows was enough to deter most God-fearing visitors.

"Let me do the talking," said Squid. "Just stand there and look harmless."

Grief nodded, although he seemed to interpret "there" as right next to Squid and "harmless" as gruffly intimidating. A shadow detached from the trees and paused at the edge of the lamplight.

"Enjoy your side trip?" said Ferret.

"We had to ditch the escape vehicle," said Squid.

Ferret's gaze combed over Grief.

"Who's your—" he began.

Anyone who didn't know Ferret would have seen his expression change from impassive to inscrutable. However, what Squid saw was Ferret's expression change from mild impatience to gut-wrenching, bone-shattering terror.

He stared at Grief, the stricken moment hanging with a million permutations, and Squid saw it flash across Ferret's eyes—he was deciding whether or not to *run*.

A beat passed.

"Hello, Raphael," said Ferret amiably.

"Hello, Rebirth," said Grief with a cold smile.

Squid suddenly found herself contemplating whether or not *she* should run. Ferret turned his gaze to Squid like a dark spotlight, and she glanced at Grief, who stared back at her. It was then that she realised Grief had run out of material.

"Okay…" said Squid. "I guess we, uh…"

Ferret's eyes suddenly narrowed, and his gaze tore through their bluff like a comet through a spider's web.

"Squid, care to explain?" said Ferret, still maintaining a careful distance.

When it came to dealing with criminals, honesty wasn't always the best policy. However, when it came to Ferret, he'd probably piece things together faster than she could lie. Squid tossed Ferret the drive.

"So, tell me about the car," said Squid.

Ferret caught the drive, quickly scanning the signal code on the back. Satisfied, he glanced shrewdly at Grief.

"You already know about the car," said Ferret.

"Humour me," said Grief.

Ferret snatched another clue.

"You don't remember…" said Ferret, his eyes lighting up with intrigue.

They could dance around this all night, but after weeks of curiosity mixed with blobs of insanity, Squid was in favour of asking the obvious question.

"Ferret," said Squid. "Who's Raphael?"

An unpleasant smile crept across Ferret's mouth, like a child receiving a particularly unexpected and dangerous toy.

"He's the only person alive who can take down Pearce. Raphael, a.k.a. the Rottweiler, Pearce's Shadow, the fastest-rising officer in Syndicate history and the apparent successor, until the night he betrayed Pearce. Or so the rumour goes."

Squid tried to feel surprised, but a part of her had seen the signs. The bursts of violence, the obsession with guns, the expensive tastes. It had *high-level henchman* written all over it. But still, there had been moments when Grief seemed so gentle, so vulnerable, so honest, it was hard to reconcile the two sides of the man.

"What do the rumours say now?" said Grief.

"That you were planning a coup," said Ferret. "A plot to overthrow Pearce and seize control of the Syndicate. Somehow, Pearce got wind of the secret project you and Werner were working on. The next thing we know, you're missing, presumed dead. And Werner's just dead."

"But there's nothing about Raphael killing anyone, right?" said Squid.

"Raphael killed people before breakfast, after bed, and everything in between," said Ferret. "He was Pearce's second, and he didn't get there by having a conscience. Some people say he killed Werner, suspecting the boy had betrayed him."

Grief didn't appear shocked by any of this, although he'd grown very pale. His eyes seemed to swim in and out of focus, as though struggling between two sets of very different memories, unable to hold on to either one.

"Grief," said Squid. "They're just rumours. If you don't remember any of this..."

False memories were ridiculously easy to implant, and if Grief were going to latch onto something, Squid didn't want it to be "kill, kill kill".

"The car," said Grief. "How did I end up in the car?"

Ferret shrugged, although his eyes remained needle sharp.

"The car is Security's fleet," said Ferret. "From what I gather, Security intercepted you just before you managed to complete the project. You were neutralised and being taken back to HQ for interrogation when Verona ambushed the retrieval team. Things got... messy. And it would appear you got away."

Squid decided that any of Grief's whimsical scenarios would have been better than the one unfolding, including the escaped-supermutant one. She had imagined the uncovering of his identity to be a celebratory revelation, with karmic points *ka-ching*ing off the scale.

But Grief wasn't some self-absorbed playboy learning about life on the streets, or a depressed financial consultant rediscovering joy. He was a ruthless criminal on the run from just about everyone, and Squid wasn't sure where you went from there. But one thing was clear—people knew he was alive, and they were determined to fix that.

"If we get out of the city, we could lay low, go to Lantau Island—" said Squid.

"Time to stop running, isn't it?" said Grief. "I seem to recall someone telling me that not so long ago."

"Very touching," said Ferret. "But there's a war going on, and Raphael's the only one who can stop it."

Squid and Grief both stared at Ferret.

"You can wait for them to hunt you down," said Ferret, "or you can finish what you started and take control of the Syndicate."

One of the things Squid found both frightening and reassuring about Ferret was the fact that he always seemed to have a plan. Only minutes earlier, he'd probably believed that Raphael was dead. Now he was orchestrating a coup on his behalf.

"Even if I could, I don't want it," said Grief.

"It's not about what you want," said Ferret. "If things continue to escalate, there won't be a city left. I'm not the only one in the Syndicate who believes that Pearce is out of touch. You can fool most people most of the time, but it doesn't matter if everybody's dead. Say yes, and I can put things in motion. Say no, and you're on your own. I need an answer in three hours."

Ferret didn't wait for a reaction before vanishing in a swoop of passing shadows.

"Grief?" said Squid, hoping that the man who answered was someone she recognised.

"Three hours," said Grief. "That's enough time for a shower and a jam roll, right?"

*

Damage control was in overdrive, with PR's crew churning out headlines and footage as fast as they could deposit the bribes. The disaster at the Governor's Lodge was nothing short of insanity, and Ducabre had reached the limits of his patience.

"Should I begin with the fact that you destroyed the Governor's Lodge, or the fact that you didn't recover Raphael?" said Ducabre.

"Your instructions were to bring him in," said Rojin. "I was attempting to do so."

"Your attempts are getting costly."

"As was your decision not to kill him."

Any other Security chief, at any other time, would have found themselves with a brand new orifice. However, with Raphael gone rogue, Pearce in virtual communications silence, and Verona rattling at the gates, someone had to show a little restraint, and it clearly wasn't going to be Rojin.

"I'm reclassifying your assignment," said Ducabre. "Your Raphael contingent is now under my jurisdiction. Your priority is Verona."

Rojin's gaze darkened a shade.

"The word is out that Raphael's back, and no one knows which side he's on," said Rojin. "As long as he's alive, people will doubt Pearce's hold on the city."

"Then erase that doubt," said Ducabre. "Commence the final burn."

*

Grief chattered blithely most of the way back, commenting on the snaking traffic, the cloudy constellations, about anything except the fact that he was a cold-blooded killer who shot people at "hello".

"I wonder how long it takes a coral reef to recover from a plague of starfish," said Grief. "I'm thinking of getting a new shirt, maybe blue. You can shower first, since you always complain about the hot water. Although we could always—"

"Grief…"

"We could probably repair that dress. Do you feel like sashimi?"

As they neared the house, Squid drew slowly to a halt, her hair tumbling down as she pulled out the last of the pins.

"Grief."

Talking wasn't one of Squid's strong points. She actually didn't have a lot of strong points, aside from stealing cars. But she knew a thing or two about evasion and where it led.

A fine drizzle misted down from the skies, haloing them in the glow of a dying street lamp.

"What do you remember?" said Squid.

Grief was silent, a writhing anguish in his eyes.

"Only fragments, only flashes," he said softly. "But it's not me. I couldn't… What you see, what I feel…"

He took Squid's hand, pressing her palm gently to his face.

"This is me," he said. "This is real."

Grief's skin felt warm against her fingers, his pulse beating against her wrist. She wanted to believe him—that somehow he had an evil twin, or an alien parasite, or suffered the occasional demonic possession. But the truth was, most people were just people, no matter how desperately they tried to escape the fact.

Squid suddenly froze, a shadow passing, black on black.

"There's someone in the house," she said.

Dark shapes moved across the windows, a flash of torchlight outlining a figure. An unmarked squad car was parked out the front, and it wasn't Casey's.

"Stay here," said Grief, slipping quietly across a neighbouring lawn.

Squid crash-tackled him into a bed of tiger lilies.

"What the hell are you doing?" she hissed.

"Our stuff is in there," said Grief. "Your lantern—"

"Leave it. It's just stuff."

Squid felt a chill of strange silence, and the house seemed to take a breath. Suddenly, the windows shattered, followed by the walls—the entire building exploding across the landscape. Grief curled around her as flying debris shredded the lilies into pulp. Orange light filled the sky, flames billowing from the shell of twenty-six Marley Drive.

Squid staggered towards the collapsing pyre, and Grief dragged her back across the lawn.

"There are people in there!" choked Squid.

"Not anymore," said Grief.

Squid barely noticed the figures closing in, the laser sights sliding over her clothes. Something rose inside her, burning like the ruins of a dream as Grief pulled her down a laneway, plunging them into the corkscrew veins of the city.

Pearce ruled the city with fear and money, greed and violence. And Squid had been a part of it, complicit in a system where the currency was blood. She thought she could just walk away from it, like an oddball teenage phase or a bad haircut. Do a few good deeds and call it even.

But now she realised it wasn't enough.

Not even close.

*

The station was in flat-out catastrophe mode. Even Casey had been dredged from Deep Freeze to man the front desk, taking reports from an endless stream of hysterical civilians.

"Casey," said Riego, looking uncharacteristically pale. "Gale wants to see you."

As it turned out, Gale didn't want to see Casey. From the thunder on her face, Gale wanted Casey's heart on a platter with a dozen knives in it.

"Your gun and your badge," said Gale.

"Chief? What—"

"You've been suspended, Detective Sergeant Casey," said Gale. "There was an explosion at twenty-six Marley Drive tonight. Two officers dead."

Casey's stomach wrenched. An explosion. Squid and Grief. Two officers dead.

"Constable Plover and Constable Vinh were investigating rumours of squatters in the Charlton house," said Gale. "Tell me you had nothing to do with that."

Casey struggled with a dozen responses, but all she managed was a stunned silence.

"Your gun. And your badge," said Gale, her eyes permafrost cold.

Dreamlike, Casey unclipped her holster, feeling oddly disembodied as she set her badge on the desk, as though she'd just excised her soul and left it on the table. She wasn't sure if she was imagining the ringing phone until Gale answered it, her voice sounding muffled and distant, as though Casey had already passed into a different realm. When the phone finally clicked back into its cradle, Gale looked as though she'd aged twenty years in the space of the call.

"Get out," said Gale, her voice hollow.

Casey stepped from the office into an eerie stillness. The usually frantic ops room was deathly silent except for the soft crackle of the police radios, every single one tuned to the same ambulance callout report.

"Casey," said Riego. "Deputy Commissioner Drake's dead."

*

It was like watching the spread of a plague.

Pearce's assault teams hopped from target to target without any interest in consolidating ground, just scorching it. Clearly, Pearce was betting that Verona would break first, leaving him to pick up the pieces at his leisure.

Verona's hands slid over the map, drawing teams from locations already hit to those in the path of destruction. Pearce had more minions, more weapons, and more money, but he also had Ferret, which would hopefully even the odds a little.

Ferret was one of the oldest heads alive, and an opportunistic survivor. Hopefully, he'd recognise an organisation grown stagnant and unstable, and make his move. You'd never find Ferret at the centre of a ripple, but the odds were he'd thrown the stone.

On the other side of the nerve centre, Clef's hands pattered to a sudden stop.

"We've lost Saint Aloise," said Clef.

"What do you mean, *lost*?" said Verona.

She'd had words with him before about using ambiguous phrases like "take care of the witnesses".

Clef tapped on his screen, and an image appeared on Verona's display. She stared at the satellite photo: a crater the size of a city block, littered with mangled hospital beds and burnt-out ambulances.

Pearce was shutting down the organs of the city, cutting its arteries and letting it bleed. The time for war games was over.

"Clef," said Verona. "Initiate contingency 'War's End'."

*

Casey willed it to be natural causes. She willed time to stand still, to reverse. For the next moment never to come.

It had been a drive-by. In the parking lot beneath Drake's apartment complex. Five bullets, all critical, and no one heard a thing. Casey didn't need a forensic report to know that the casings would be Reaver .22s. She already knew there'd be no surveillance footage, no witnesses, no leads.

Riego tried to follow Casey from the station, and she may have cuffed him to a desk. Everything was a dull, red haze around her, the streets silently waiting for judgement to descend. All that time, she'd dismissed Riego's flippant patter as fanciful exaggeration. But she felt it now, a tiny, silent spot about to explode into a mushroom cloud the size and shape of the city.

Casey's fingers dialled an unfamiliar number.

"Deus," said Casey. "I'm in. I need an optical pico-sine microscanner, a place to use it, a pair of automatics, and a truckload of ammo. No conditions. No favours. Just get me the goddamn stuff."

# NINETEEN

The dusty back room was piled high with analogue relics: VHS tapes, vinyl records, audio cassettes. As far as criminal fronts went, the store's psychedelic décor and faded lime curtains did a good job of deterring genuine shoppers.

This wasn't a known drop-off point, and to the best of Squid's knowledge, it wasn't even affiliated. However, the sleepy-eyed teen behind the counter nodded them through without so much as a secret signal.

"I trust you've reached the same conclusion I have," said Ferret.

"I want him gone," said Grief.

"That is," said Squid, "we want Pearce arrested, tried and put behind bars for a really long time."

She and Grief had debated this point on their way here. Or rather, she had debated this point loudly while Grief marched grimly towards a personal French Revolution.

"Werner had a secret storage drive," said Ferret, "with enough incriminating evidence to put Pearce away. It's being kept in a secure section of Headquarters that even I can't access. But Raphael can."

"Hold on," said Squid, feeling that certain details were being conveniently glossed over. "Why hasn't Pearce destroyed it?"

"Because it has Raphael's project on it," said Grief, only half in question. "And they're having trouble figuring it out."

Ferret's expression gave nothing away this time.

"And what, exactly, would happen to the project information if we retrieve the drive?" said Squid.

"I see it as a win-win situation," said Ferret pleasantly.

"How do I get in?" said Grief.

Squid had enough reservations to fill a five-star restaurant, but she knew better than to hit the brakes in front of Ferret. He'd been a decent employer to her, but it didn't mean he wouldn't arrange an "accident" if she got in his way.

"How do *we* get in," said Squid.

"You'll need allies, favours," said Ferret. "I can arrange a few meetings, but it's up to Raphael to seal the deal."

*

The docks were a chaotic rush of activity. With half the ports reduced to charcoal, Alamo Pier spilled at the seams. Squid briskly sidestepped a runaway trolley of fascinators, a trail of sparkling feathers drifting over the sweaty dockhands.

"Do you believe him?" said Squid. "The secret drive. The mysterious project."

"I believe Pearce won't stop looking for me," said Grief. "I believe people will continue to die unless I do something about it."

"It doesn't strike you as slightly suicidal?" Squid stopped outside a secure loading bay. "Pearce's idea of a warm welcome is a flamethrower, kindled with the favourite toys of a hundred orphans. And that's assuming you can convince anyone that you're Ra—"

A circle of guns materialised around them, and the half-dozen loading hands suddenly looked a lot less like loading hands. Squid's arms went straight into the air, and Grief paused, struggling with several conflicting impulses.

"We're expected," said Grief firmly.

The cargo bay was stacked with towers of wooden pallets, dull yellow forklifts chugging down the busy aisles. Their armed escort deposited them in front of a tanned man in his late thirties, dressed in a cowboy hat, a white singlet, and jeans. He looked up from his wafer-thin pad with a broad smile.

"Heya, pirate," said the man.

The moment hung for an agonising second, and Squid tried not to choke on the silence. She could see the uncertainty in the man's eyes, mingled with a hint of fear. A dozen guns waited for a sign.

"Smuggling," said Grief. "Looking good."

The man relaxed slightly, his smile turning into a friendly scowl.

"Where've you been?" said Smuggling. "Boss monster's been going through the D-Man, and you know how I grate with the number three."

Squid boggled quietly, trying to determine how much of that was English.

"Things are getting a little rough at the top of the tree," said Grief. "Someone's going to fall out of the nest."

Grief shot Squid a facial shrug, and she tried not to pass out from hyperventilation.

"I hear ya," said Smuggling. "So, Rebirth says you're the man with the plan."

"The ships are burning while the old man hides," said Grief, his voice deepening, like a darkly rolling tide. "Where do you see yourself in a year, Elias?"

Something in his words evoked images of a city in ruins, a wasteland of graves, a crumbling empire clinging to a smouldering flag.

"Standing," said Smuggling.

"HQ's calling," said Grief. "But I need a key under the mat."

Smuggling's gaze sharpened, and Squid could almost see the coin spinning in the air. Heads or tails. Red or black. A handshake or a bullet to the head.

"I've got a shipment headed inside tomorrow night," said Smuggling. "But once you're in, you're on your own."

*

It took a bit of hunting to dig up Kirsk. Literally.

A tray of donuts bought her a direction, and Casey finally hit pay-

geek in a ditch beneath a rusted car.

"Did you get evicted from the other hovel?" said Casey, peering into the makeshift nest of wires.

Kirsk shrank further into the ditch, only the glint of her glasses giving her away.

"I thought I'd save everyone the trouble and dig my own grave," said Kirsk.

"No point in keeping it warm," said Casey. "I need your help."

"Am I the only hacker in the city?"

"No. Just the best."

"You mean the cheapest," said Kirsk. "Look, if I wanted to commit suicide, I'd play *Ziggurat Resurrection Wars* for five days straight."

Casey could have played the Werner card. Stoking the guilt, the anguish, the rising fear. But she wasn't that far gone. Not yet.

"I'm taking back the city," said Casey. "I think a part of you wants me to go away. But a part of you is waiting for me to say 'Join me'. So, Kirsk, what's it going to be?"

The glasses were motionless, hanging in the darkness like twin moons.

"What do you need?" said Kirsk.

*

The gutted theatre occupied a lonesome strip in the failed suburb of Marmalade Circuit. Every second shop was a burnt-out wreck, littered with broken bottles and waterlogged plastic bags.

"This looks like somewhere you'd go to be assassinated," said Squid, stepping into the musty foyer.

"Or to watch a really interpretive amateur play," said Grief.

Mildewed red curtains hung from sagging rafters, framing a stage that was barely more than a few raised boards. Squid might have guessed they had the wrong address, if not for the eight-foot, nearly invisible display screen standing incongruously on the platform. It could have been an artistic statement about the death of live performance, and Squid wasn't sure if she was supposed to clap.

The rotting floorboards moaned beneath their feet, and the shadows dripped with unseen surveillance devices. Grief gave her a reassuring smile, but it wasn't nearly enough to dispel the tension.

"Technology," said Grief. "Always a pleasure."

The screen rippled, like a giant eye blinking, and text began to scroll across the glossy surface.

*Hello, angel. Rebirth says you have a proposal. Convince me.*

A giant countdown appeared onscreen, digits flashing down from sixty seconds. Squid resisted the instinct to hack the screen and stop the countdown. This wasn't her test.

"Werner was yours," said Grief. "The drive was mine. Pearce took both, and I think we have a problem with that. I can deliver a future; Pearce can't. And when I'm done, the world will be divided into those who helped and those who didn't."

Squid expected Grief's pitch to be longer and more dramatic, possibly involving free steak knives. However, each word was steeped in subtext, as though referring to a vivid library of events that only he and Technology were privy to. The counter drained to zero, and the screen sat blank for a while.

*I can give you clear passage through the lower floors. Drive is in the Safe. Don't know how to access it, but Laundering has been there. If you succeed, Werner's work is mine.*

"Aside from my project," said Grief.

*Agreed.*

"Um," said Squid. "I just wanted to say I'm sorry about Werner. I heard he was a nice guy."

The screen remained blank, and Squid wondered if she was talking to a piece of unattended equipment.

*Thank you. Good luck, angel.*

With a loud crackle, the screen burst into a sheet of green flame.

"Are we supposed to put that out?" said Squid.

"I'm sure it's just an effect," said Grief doubtfully.

Squid emptied an expired fire extinguisher onto the blackened glass, deciding that Marmalade Circuit didn't need another incendiary emergency.

Outside, the dusty air tasted of cinders and burning rubber, but it wasn't just this suburb. Every day, the coiling smoke covered more of the city. Even the gated communities couldn't escape the snowfall of ash. Since the bombing of the hospitals, the entire city stood tiptoe on the edge of anarchy.

Squid hoped that Casey was all right, but it was beyond the ability of the police to fix this. They were a paper umbrella in a tropical cyclone, and it was up to people like Squid, people like… Raphael, to end the storm.

"You're really getting into this whole Raphael thing," said Squid.

"If it gets us what we want," said Grief.

*Be careful what you wish for*, thought Squid.

She had wanted so desperately to uncover Grief's identity, to return him to his own life so she could return to hers. But now that Grief was finally fading into Raphael, Squid couldn't help feeling a sense of aching loss.

"You okay?" said Grief, and it was still him—the cheerful, dancing, pancake-making guy looking back at her.

"Sure," said Squid. "I guess next stop, Laundering."

*

Casey was impressed. Even through her grim rage and rogue-cop mentality, she had to admit that Deus had it together.

He'd set up headquarters in a private warehouse: bare concrete rooms and blacked-out windows. Through half-open doors, Casey glimpsed cutting-edge lab equipment, fully kitted hospital pods, banks of humming servers, and experimental hydroponic lamps. It looked as though the whole outfit could be cleared from the building in less than ninety minutes.

"One optical pico-sine microscanner," said Deus, standing beside an open door.

The multi-limbed scanner hung over the control panel like a mantis over a beetle. Casey had no idea how they'd gotten the machine into the room, but Kirsk was already crawling over it with fussy scrutiny.

"I think I deserve a few answers," said Deus, watching Kirsk with casual interest.

"I think we all do," said Casey. She turned to Kirsk. "I found this in Werner's apartment. It's another data-slick, isn't it?"

Kirsk took the transparent strip, delicately peeling off the piece of paper with its sequence of numbers.

"*Another* slick?" said Deus.

"Werner found a way to make data storage devices that don't show up on our scanners," said Casey. "I think he was smuggling information out of Pearce HQ."

Deus's eyes took on a discomfortingly predatory look, his gaze following the flimsy slick into the scanner.

"A pico-sine scanner isn't exactly discreet," said Deus.

"Werner could turn a toaster into a helicopter," said Kirsk. "All he'd need is a polycrystalline, thermal-shock resistant lens, and he could convert a standard microscanner."

An odd memory tugged at Casey. "A lens? Like a really big diamond?"

"If you could afford a diamond that size, you may as well get the pico-sine scanner," snorted Kirsk. "The cut would have to be really specific—I'm talking microns. You wouldn't want to screw up a rock like that."

"Casey, is there something you—" began Deus.

A mobile phone beeped, and Casey ducked into the hallway with an apologetic shrug. She took a deep breath before swiping the flashing icon.

"Hey, Riego," said Casey, forcing a cheerful tone. "Sorry about before."

"Casey, where are you?"

She could hear traffic in the background, so Riego wasn't at the station, but it didn't mean the call wasn't being monitored.

"I'm just gathering my thoughts, taking some time out," said Casey. "Are you okay?"

"Casey, we both know you're not gathering your thoughts. You're gathering your arsenal. I'm not going to be okay until I see you're not getting seriously badass on the city. How about you come over? We can talk, or eat, or whatever."

Casey closed her eyes for a moment. Part of her wanted so badly to go over and rant and bawl and commiserate over trays of cherry chocolates.

Good old Riego. Always there for her, and all she brought him was heartache and trouble. When this was all over, she'd have to make it up to him somehow. At least they'd assign him a new partner now.

"Take care, Riego," said Casey, and ended the call.

*

Argyle Classique was an upmarket department store overlooking the Bella Rosa shopping district. Every floor glittered with ornate silverware and fountaining chandeliers, and each customer was personally guided, or perhaps supervised, by immaculately uniformed staff.

Laundering's usual base was the Palace Royale Casino, where black money came out sparkling. However, since Verona had levelled the casino, she'd been forced to relocate to Argyle Classique, where untraceable gift vouchers came in seven-digit denominations. Judging from Laundering's foul mood, she wasn't happy with the move.

"Thought you were rotting in the muck somewhere," said Laundering without any trace of sympathy.

Laundering was in her early fifties, impeccably dressed in a tailored white suit. Her hair was close-cropped and bleached silver, and small silver hoops threaded the length of one ear.

"I'm not that easy to bury," said Grief.

"You've moved down in the henchman department," said Laundering, throwing a disparaging glance towards Squid.

"I'm not a hench—" began Squid.

"I don't care," said Laundering. "I'm busy reconstructing a fifty-billion-dollar operation that's had its guts blown to pieces, so this had better be good."

Grief took a measured step forward, ignoring the circle of minions reaching into their crisply tailored jackets.

"I guarantee that by the end of the week, you won't recognise the landscape," said Grief, his voice a low purr. "And if you're on the wrong side when the dust settles, the unfortunate state of your operations will be the least of your worries."

The silence was like a three-tonne slab of ice swinging towards an unsuspecting head.

"I could take you out right now," said Laundering calmly.

Squid's gaze darted around urgently, trying to determine whether the silver platters were bulletproof, and how many staffers she could take down with a ruby candelabra.

Grief smiled faintly, his eyes lazily tracing the six feet between him and Laundering.

"Please try," said Grief, his voice dripping with consequences.

Squid could see this ending a variety of ways, mostly involving her and Grief riddled with bullets. It was an insanely cocky bluff, and she was already mentally smacking Grief's head against the pavement outside. However, a voice in her subconscious, the part of her that recoiled from swarms of spiders and feared the rustling dark, told her that he wasn't bluffing.

Fortunately, Laundering seemed to hear the same voice.

"So, you can't even remember how to get into the Safe?" said Laundering.

"You're going to remind me," said Grief.

"I've only been there once. It's the penthouse floor, Pearce's sanctuary. You can only access it via the central elevator, and aside from Pearce, you and Ducabre are the only ones with access. You need a physical key, a retinal scan, and a sequence of three passwords. So, unless you have a revelation, you'll need Ducabre's cooperation."

"I think I can arrange that," said Grief.

"I'd like to see—"

Laundering's comment was interrupted by an explosive rumble, and the marble floor suddenly tilted about ten degrees. Crystal glasses shattered into expensive splinters, and rare wooden carvings slammed into the walls.

"Perimeter!" barked Laundering. "What the hell is going on?"

Her radio burst into a jangle of yelling.

*"…they're going for the communications hub… second generator down… returning missile fire…"*

"That's our cue," said Squid, grabbing Grief and bolting for the stairs.

"I think that went well," said Grief, ducking a flying chair.

"Yeah, we're going to have a chat about that—" Squid dodged a falling chandelier. "So, who's Ducabre?"

"An old friend."

"A friend like he'll help us, or a 'friend' like he'll blow your head off and use it as a candy jar?"

"Maybe the second one."

Squid slid into a wall. "What do you mean, *maybe*?"

Grief grinned, and there was the ghost of someone else in his face.

"One last stop, Squid."

*

Kirsk was onto her second slab of Crash Cola, skydiving through several thousand layers of compressed multimedia code. As much as

Casey felt responsible for Kirsk, if she had to watch another hour of geek decoding, she was going to start smashing things.

Deus hadn't warned her against wandering through the complex. He hadn't even made any sinister comments about staying away from particular locked rooms. The building seemed to be a quiet hub of conscientious activity—a subdued vigilante central for Deus's secret organisation. Casey even noticed a few familiar faces, including Visha from Forensics and Matt from Ballistics.

It was hard to predict how she'd feel about this when her fury died down. If it ever did. The vigilante road was a dangerous one, full of fear and hatred and escalating violence. Last year, a mob of "concerned citizens" had set fire to the house of a suspected paedophile. Except they had the wrong house, and an innocent family of five had had to be collected in dust pans.

It wasn't that Casey didn't feel the same urge sometimes, but there was a big difference between thinking something and pulling the trigger. The danger was getting it wrong. The danger was losing perspective. There were no lines to cross, just shades of light and dark that often seemed indistinguishable.

If there'd been a room marked DO NOT ENTER, it would have been the silent office in the northeast corner of the warehouse. A tidy desk sat beside the one-way window, beneath a cityscape of stars tangled up in smoke.

Deus stood motionless in the dark, staring at the empty desk.

"Deus?" said Casey.

He kept his face in the shadows, a trace of a rasp in his voice.

"Has she finished decoding?"

"She should have something soon."

The silence seemed an invitation to leave, but Casey had never been good at keeping her head down. Deus had always been the model officer: cool, composed and competent, albeit with emotional walls that made Alcatraz look like a pile of bath foam. But in this private moment, in the darkness stained with grief, Casey realised that the distance between them was a lot smaller than she'd believed.

"She spoke at my graduation," said Deus softly. "She gave a speech like something from the old days, all passion and poetry and words to set your heart on fire. When I lost my parents in the Old Central Riots, she came to their funeral, with cars still burning on the roads. And now…"

Casey followed his gaze to the desk, neatly arranged and waiting. Several thoughts suddenly clicked together—a glance across the hall, a fragment of a phone call, the clack of boot heels down a deserted corridor.

"Drake," said Casey. "She was a part of this."

"She *created* this," said Deus. "She saw evil every day, and some days she won, and some days it got away. And when it got away, she hunted it down. She always said, 'Justice works. Justice first.' And only when the system fails, through corruption and apathy, do you take action."

Casey felt as though her world should be turning upside down, but all she felt was the same hollow loss. Drake, her hero. Drake, the vigilante. But now, Drake was gone. And whatever Casey felt as an idolising bystander was probably a mere sketch of what Deus was going through now.

"I'm sorry," said Casey gently. "I didn't know about your parents."

Everyone knew that Deus had a law enforcement pedigree. They joked that he was born with a badge in his fist. His mother was in Riot Squad, his dad in Homicide. But that's where knowledge turned to rumour, and when it came to Deus, rumour turned quickly to silence. Casey had always assumed his parents had left town after the Old Central Riots, maybe moved to Vancouver like her own folks.

"You move on," said Deus. "No one is indispensable. No one is irreplaceable. And the fight goes on."

And the walls went up. There was something deeply discomforting about it, like watching a polar bear searching for land, swimming through an iceless sea.

"You really are a piece of work," said Casey.

"Excuse me?"

"The wife and kids, the house and hobbies, the connections and the power. Living this persona you've created. You have to give yourself space to grieve, to laugh, to be a person as well as a cause. Otherwise, Riego's right: one day, you're going to wonder how you ended up waist-deep in someone else's blood."

Deus's expression remained unreadable.

"I'm not the one demanding a truckload of guns," he said.

"Yeah, well, I'm not going to use them all. And in between insubordinate rampages, I know how to relax."

"Really. And how—"

There was a quiet knock at the door, and a man with electric-blue hair peered in.

"Joshua," said Deus. "What do you need?"

"Um, there's a cranky woman in the scanner room, says she's out of cola," said Joshua. "She also mentioned that she's cracked the encryption, but she says the first point is more important."

*

Narcotics occupied a discreet compound at the edge of Willow Plains. At first glance, it resembled a drowsy ranch inhabited by elderly sheep and extremely chilled-out geese. From a distance, you couldn't see the bars on the windows, and unless you were particularly unfortunate, you'd never realise just how electrified the fences were.

It was a carefully painted picture of idyllic isolation, but even out here, the acrid smell of incinerating homes rolled in from the city.

"I don't like how those windmills are positioned like sniper towers," said Squid.

"Don't sweat it," said Grief. "Let me deal with this."

The sniper towers weren't the only things making Squid nervous. She could feel Grief slipping away—even the way he spoke was changing. She wasn't really sure what to do, or whether she should do anything at all.

The instant Grief's foot touched the porch, a dozen ranch hands materialised around them, forming a semicircle of shotguns and pistols. Before Squid could reach for the sky, there was a blur and a distinctly unpleasant click. The head rancher suddenly found his head in a chokehold, a gun pushed so far up his chin he could smell the bullet.

"I'll just invite myself in, shall I?" said Grief.

Inside the rustic homestead, a massive antique armoire retracted into the wall and became a rather charming elevator. Half a mile down, bunkered in the limestone, Squid and Grief emerged inside Narcotics' gleaming research facility. Staff in spotless lab coats moved through sterile white corridors, carrying softly bubbling vials and canisters marked with graphic warnings.

"I've been looking forward to your visit, Raphael," said Narcotics.

Narcotics was a slim, dark-haired man with a demeanour somewhere between incisively shrewd and dreamily absent. His expression was evocative of a determined scientist trying to perform experimental brain surgery on himself.

"I understand you've been having some memory troubles, and I might have just the thing…" said Narcotics.

His gloved hands picked delicately across a tray of pills and gel capsules, brightly coloured and gleaming like tiny polished gemstones. Narcotics was a firm believer in presentation. The trade was partly about addiction, partly about keeping your clients alive, but mostly, it was about PR.

The nasty stuff with hoodlum cred came in roughly pressed pills with barely legible symbols. The exclusive delicacies, for your celebrities and CEOs, came in shimmering translucent capsules, like globes of golden caviar or iridescent sapphire beads.

"I actually need something for Ducabre," said Grief.

Narcotics' hand paused over a sea-green capsule shaped like a split pea.

"Something that won't kill him," said Squid.

Narcotics' hand continued across the tray.

"Not straight away, at least," said Grief. "We need him coherent and compliant for at least fifteen minutes."

Squid wasn't particularly comfortable with this part of the plan. It was one thing to bribe or coerce someone; it was another to remove their ability to choose altogether. But every time she tried to discuss the point with Grief, he quickly shut down the conversation, as though the decision had already been made.

Narcotics tilted his head slightly, as though sloshing a soup of information around his skull.

"A delicate challenge," he said. He quickly tapped a message on his wrist comms. "Well, while we're waiting, perhaps I can interest the lady in something."

"Waiting for what?" said Squid, her gaze darting around anxiously.

"A touch more confidence, perhaps," continued Narcotics. He held out a clear blue pill, perfectly round, and intense as the eye of a god.

"It's called beer," said Squid.

"You're talking about false confidence," said Narcotics. "I'm talking about the real thing. A quicker mind, an easier smile, a smoother voice, a stronger grace. A carriage that doesn't leave you cringing, regretting things spoken or unsaid."

Squid looked warily at the pill, tempted to snatch it just for shininess value. Popularity in a pill. It sounded like a delusional fantasy she'd had more than once while curled up on a concrete floor, listening to her stomach digesting itself.

But she'd come to realise there were no quick fixes. Courage in a bottle, or sex appeal in a deodorant, didn't make you less pathetic. Personality wasn't something that came in a capsule, or with a job, or in a name. Personality was formed through your experiences, your actions, your friendships.

It was something that evolved through the choices you made. Anything else was just a mask for what lay beneath.

"I'm good, thanks," said Squid.

Narcotics' next offer was interrupted by a pristine attendant passing him a slim walnut case—the kind of box you might keep an expensive pen in.

"Ah..." said Narcotics. "I must warn you that this is still experimental."

Squid was pretty sure almost everything in the lab was experimental, as well as most of what it put on the street. Narcotics lifted a slender hypo from the case, its anodised body ending in a pressure-triggered needle spray.

"There's only one dose," said Narcotics. "It should render the subject cooperative for at least three minutes, after which there may be... side effects."

"What kind of side effects?" said Squid.

Knowing Narcotics, it could well involve exploding, imploding, or a complicated combination of both.

"Let's just say... don't use it on anyone you care about," said Narcotics.

"No," said Squid firmly. "Let's be specific—"

"It sounds fine," said Grief.

He reached for the hypo, but in a blur of apricot silk, it was already tucked into Squid's underwear waistband with only a minimum of indecent exposure. Lumina Xiao wasn't known for her pockets.

"Thanks," said Squid. "We'll keep that in mind."

*

Kirsk seemed remarkably lucid for someone whose blood caffeine was nearing toxic levels, aside from the fact that she was talking like a racetrack announcer on fast forward.

"I've decoded the first thirty-seven layers," said Kirsk. "It's the schematics for the remote drive. Hardware, software, settings, access. It's got an inbuilt passive tracker RAFID with a range of two clicks, and you can't even switch the thing on without a binary light key. The guy is absolutely awesome."

Kirsk paused.

"Was…" she corrected herself.

She hiccupped sadly.

Casey glanced at Deus, unsure if she'd somehow missed a whole generation of technology.

"Kirsk," said Casey. She pointed to herself and Deus. "Coppers."

"Oh," said Kirsk. "For those who prefer blowing things up to putting them together, we've got the frequency and passcodes to access the drive, but the unit has to be switched on."

"So, we still have to go in and get it," said Casey.

"You mean Pearce HQ?" said Deus flatly.

"Kirsk, what did you say about a tracking device?" said Casey.

"Werner's remote drive has a locator chip," said Kirsk. "Which means, if you can get within two miles of it with a randomised-frequency identification scanner, you can track it down."

"This binary light key—to switch it on—do we have one?" said Casey.

"A binary light key uses specific wavelengths of light in a particular combination to activate a mechanism." Kirsk held up the strip of paper, with its sequence of numbers. "And I think these describe the wavelengths."

"Casey, could I have a word?" said Deus.

Tact and timing were Riego's strengths, while Casey liked to think of hers as the ability to crash and burn and get up again.

"I need to get into Pearce HQ," said Casey.

"I can do a lot of things, but I can't do that," said Deus.

"Can't or won't?"

"The last time we tried to take down Pearce on his own ground, half the city burned."

"Half the city's already burning."

Her mobile buzzed and Casey reached automatically for the *Reject* button, then stopped. She didn't recognise the number, but the caller had entered their ID as *Squid.* Her finger slid to the answer button.

"Hello?" she said cautiously.

"Hey Casey, it's Squid," came a familiar voice. "Can we meet up?"

# TWENTY

Squid wished she had something a little less conspicuous to wear. But if she had to die in something, she could have done worse than Lumina Xiao.

She rubbed her bare arms as she waited on the corner, trying to look like she was headed to an exclusive soirée. Ferret had asked to meet Grief alone at the record store, and Squid assumed it was some henchman-to-henchman thing. She thought it'd be a good opportunity to check in with Casey, and she tried not to think of it as a last goodbye.

"Hey, nice dress," said Casey, jogging across the pavement. "Are those bloodstains?"

"Uh… You know what a klutz I am," said Squid. "So, how've you been?"

Casey's eyes narrowed slightly as she followed Squid into the coffee shop.

"Good," said Casey. "You?"

"Good."

There was a slightly awkward silence, and Squid glanced at Casey's hip.

"You're off duty?"

"You're working for Ferret again."

"No! Not really— I—"

Casey shook her head, a humourless smile twisting her mouth.

"I guess I shouldn't be surprised."

"No, Casey, it's—"

Squid was tempted to say "It's complicated", but that was just an invitation for Casey to slap her.

"Things are going down in a serious way," said Squid. "You should lay low for a few days, visit your sister in Vancouver. The Syndicate's about to be ripped wide open, and I'm trying to light the fuse."

Casey's eyes remained hard.

"Is that what your 'amnesiac' friend is telling you? The one who seems to remember an awful lot when he wants to? Has it occurred to you that you're being played? That you're being set up for something?"

It had crossed Squid's mind, but so had the theory that this was all a dream. And that she was actually a pineapple.

"I'm not a neurologist," said Squid. "For all I know, people do wake up from ten-year comas, or have weirdly inconsistent amnesia. He's going through some personal stuff, and maybe he just needs someone to believe in him. Like I did."

"You're not the best judge of character, Squid. It's how you ended up in this mess."

Squid tried not to show how much that stung.

"It's not a mess. It's my life. And I'm working on it."

Casey's eyes suddenly narrowed again. At this rate, she was going to have serious crow's feet before her second iced tea.

"Are those bruises?"

Squid tried to pull up her nonexistent collar. The makeup must have washed off days ago.

"No, I just— I kind of walked into—"

"An anaconda?"

Squid knew she'd just hit a new low in Casey's disappointment.

"I gave you a chance to start over," said Casey. "Most people never get that, and I'm starting to think you didn't deserve it."

Nothing about Casey's words should have been a surprise, but it still hurt like hell to hear her say it.

"I *am* leaving it behind," said Squid. "Just give me a week."

"I already gave you a deadline."

"It's an arbitrary date. You can change it."

"No, I can't," said Casey. "Because that's the difference between a good person doing bad things, and a bad person making excuses.

August eighteenth, Squid, and we're talking hours now, not weeks. The next time I see you, I'm putting you away."

Squid was left sitting at the table, with Casey's rumpled change and a glass of cold tea. She felt a strange kind of symmetry, a queer circularity.

A rock and a hard place.

But this time, things were different. Because this time, Squid was going to blow the rock to smoking pieces.

*

It was panic on all fronts at the station. Riego hadn't seen chaos like this since the Old Central Riots, but this time, they weren't taking the fight to Pearce. Pearce was demolishing the city of his own accord, with more than a little help from Verona.

They'd converted the Met West training halls into triage camps to soak up the overflow from the remaining hospitals. Officers crashed in the bunks for an hour before heading back into the fray. Everyone pretended not to look at the casualty reports, but morale was lower than a breakup via nimbus-tag.

The city was in meltdown. Casey was about to go ballistic. And Riego wasn't sure which would be worse, but he knew that both had to be stopped.

"Chief!" called Riego, falling into step beside Gale.

"Not now, Riego."

"I know it's not SOP, but the fastest way to take the steam out of this dogfight is to knock over one of the kingpins," said Riego. "Both sides are in disarray, resources are stretched. We bring in Pearce, the damage stops. We deal with the fallout."

"Great. We'll just 'bring in Pearce'. Get back to work, Riego."

"Listen, Chief, there's enough dirt in the archives to make an arrest. The charges won't stick, but that's not the point. We can muster a squad to march him out of HQ—"

"No one's ever made it to the top floor, and we don't even know what the bastard looks like. For all we know, he's orchestrating everything from the Maldives."

"He's here. This is *his* city, and he'll never let anyone else have it. His weakness is he thinks he's untouchable, and if we—"

"Look, Riego, I'm sorry about Casey. But we've been down that road before. We need more than rumours and circumstantial evidence. We need a smoking gun."

Gale pulled away through the heaving churn of officers, leaving Riego stranded in her wake. Part of him was already drifting back to work, responding to the cacophony of urgent callouts. It was easy to go through the motions—listen, talk, save people. Do what you can, but don't get involved. The colourful stories kept people at arm's length. Give everyone a smile and no one your heart. You couldn't change the world, but you could make it a little better.

The problem with Casey was that she cared too much. She let it get under her skin. She took everything personally, and her heart was a knot of scars for it. There was something so raw, so earnest about the way she responded to the world, it was hard not to feel a strange fire stirring in response. She was a constant, vivid reminder of why it was important to care, why it was important to act, especially when no one else would.

With every passing minute, Casey raced closer to doing something irreversible, and Riego didn't want to find out about it on the news.

They needed a smoking gun. So, maybe it'd have to be his.

*

Casey tried not to imagine fire raining from the heavens. Or apocalyptic music flooding through the streets. She couldn't afford the luxury of melodrama now, but the meeting with Squid had been a shot between the eyes.

She'd spent years believing in that kid. Believing in redemption.

Believing in new leaves and second chances. It was a hell of a heartbreak at a godawful time, but as Deus said, you moved on.

"How is it outside?" said Kirsk. "I can hear sirens all the time."

"You're better off in here," said Casey. "How's the data coming along?"

Kirsk rubbed her eyes.

"I've been trying to figure out the middle layers. The coding is similar to the first slick, but some of the layers look like they're changing, but I don't know why or how."

Kirsk adjusted the lenses, fiddling with the output levels.

"Changing like someone's accessing them?" said Casey.

"You can't remotely access a data-slick—"

"*...like someone's accessing them?*"

Kirsk and Casey both jumped at the disembodied voice.

"*You can't remotely access a data-slick—*"

Casey stared at the speakers, chills crawling up her back.

"Is that thing... repeating us?"

There was a beat of silence.

"*Is that thing... repeating us?*"

"Oh, my God," said Kirsk. "The bloody thing's *live.*"

She yanked the cable from the speakers, as though pulling the life support from a malevolent ghost in the machine.

"In a few minutes, I'm going to think that's extremely cool," said Kirsk. "But right now, that is just way too... wow..."

So, not only had Werner found a way to make undetectable data storage devices, he'd found a way to make undetectable surveillance bugs that recorded directly onto an undetectable data-slick. It was the kind of technological jump that changed the landscape. In a few years, they'd find ways to detect it, ways to jam it, but in the meantime, whoever had this technology had an edge you could decapitate empires with.

The door scraped open, and both Kirsk and Casey jolted at the noise.

"Casey," said Deus with a faint smile. "I have a surprise for you."

Casey strongly suspected that at this stage of the story, it couldn't possibly be anything good. If she was lucky, it'd be a shiny new gun. If she was unlucky—

Two tall, lean figures followed Deus into the room. Casey's hand whipped for her gun, forgetting that it was still on Gale's desk. She only recognised the figure on the left, but it was all she needed.

"Hello, Officer," said Mal.

*

Grief felt peculiar.

He felt queasy and dizzy and incredibly lucid all at the same time. His body wanted to lift cars and shatter walls, while his mind hung in an oddly still place. Thinking about the cluttered floor of Squid's apartment, the plate of pancakes on the kitchen bench—it was like looking at neatly framed postcards from a holiday you could barely remember. But then, thinking about the fire and the blood and the unbearable cold, it was like walking through a movie screen and finding yourself at the OK Corral.

Grief told himself it was just the amnesia sorting itself out—it didn't change anything. He was still that helpful guy scrolling through the job ads, cooking up breakfast, looking out for his friends. Well, friend.

That's who he was. Grief pretending to be Raphael. Not the other way around.

"Sounds like you have everything you need," said Ferret.

"Except the truth," said Grief.

A brooding saxophone solo drifted through the beaded curtains. Grief couldn't be sure that Ferret had selected the track, but he was pretty sure nothing inappropriately cheery was going to break the mood.

"A man like you doesn't put himself on the line for a mysterious hard drive unless he knows exactly what's on it," said Grief.

Ferret didn't smile.

"There is no drive."

Grief managed to look coolly unsurprised, although he was actually watching the curve ball whiz past.

"We both know that men like Pearce don't go to jail," said Ferret. "There's only one way to remove someone like Pearce, and you're the only one who can do it. Squid will help you get in, but ultimately, she's a good kid. She'll help you 'get the drive', but she won't help you do what you have to do."

Ferret's words sank in. He was talking about murder in cold blood. An execution. Grief could convince himself it was self-defence, a case of survival rather than retaliation. But there were some things that couldn't be undone, couldn't be forgiven. He didn't know if he was capable of looking a man in the eyes and pulling the trigger.

"Don't doubt yourself," said Ferret. "Don't doubt who you are and what you're capable of. I've watched you rise through the Syndicate for eight years, and I know what kind of a man you are better than you do. We've lined them up, Raphael. All you have to do is knock them down."

Grief couldn't help imagining Ferret sitting on one shoulder, with devil horns and a pitchfork, while Squid sat on the other shoulder, with angel wings and possibly also a pitchfork.

"You know better than to treat me like a puppet, Rebirth," said Grief. "You want a return on your investment, and I want Pearce. I'll do what needs to be done."

Ferret smiled this time and gave a slightly mocking nod.

"I would ask a favour, though," said Ferret.

He drew a plain steel letter opener from his coat. It was constructed from a single piece of metal, battered and scratched but hand-sharpened to a wicked edge.

"Give this to Squid and ask her, 'What is it?'" said Ferret.

Grief assumed this was some kind of master/disciple koan, although he suspected it wasn't the kind that led to inner peace and karmic harmony.

"I don't suppose you've managed to line up a change of clothes for me and Squid?" said Grief.

Ferret flicked out a piece of paper, scrawled with an address.

"In case you had any doubts about who you are."

Footsteps approached from the shopfront, and Grief ducked quickly behind a stack of eight-millimetre reels. Ferret had already vanished by the time a hunched figure lurched through the swinging beads.

"Ergh…" said Squid in what probably passed for "Hello".

She looked like a mop of grubby silk, slumped so low her knuckles were practically brushing the floorboards.

"Are you okay?" said Grief.

"I'm fine," sighed Squid.

"How's Casey?"

"Errgghh…" Squid slumped lower.

Grief tried not to be alarmed by her rapid downward progression. At this rate, she'd be horizontal within the next two questions.

"Hey, Ferret gave us a place to check out," said Grief. "Do you know what the codes mean?"

Squid straightened up enough to peer at the scribbled address.

"We're not getting in there," she said. "Alaviere isn't a gated suburb; it's a gated dimension. You know those amazing apartments you see in the middle of the city, but no matter where you walk, they never get any closer? That's Alaviere."

Grief suspected that Squid was exaggerating a little. He squinted at the handwritten codes.

*ES = :)*

*HC = :)*

*X = U*

"Ferret says all the security's onside," said Squid sceptically. "I'm not sure what the target means, though… Did he say what we had to do there?"

"I think we're supposed to wait until the action starts. You know, have a shower, grab a bite."

"Chill out before our epic heist…" Squid sagged further.

"Did Casey say something to you?"

"No…"

Squid had gotten a lot better at hiding her feelings, but she was still a terrible liar.

"You're following your conscience," said Grief. "Not everyone's going to understand that."

Grief wasn't sure if he was following his own conscience or Raphael's. Part of him railed against the idea of deceiving Squid into helping him, but part of him calmly argued that it was the only way to protect her. The only way to rid the world of Pearce.

Squid gave him a lopsided smile.

"Come on," she said. "We've got an evil empire to destroy."

*

This was not a happy surprise.

It was worse than the time Casey's parents got her a Skankz Glamour Bride Doll for her birthday instead of the electrified truncheon she'd asked for. It was worse than when management had promised the department new pistols and delivered shonky sweatshop guns that fired at random forty-five degree angles. It was almost as bad as the time someone had left a gift box on the hood of her car, blood already seeping through the ribbon.

Mal and his colleague had been restricted to the scanner room, where they seemed content to lounge around, making Kirsk spill her cola every time they smiled. It was actually Mal doing most of the smiling. His colleague, Clef, looked as though this was the worst day of his life.

"You can't possibly be serious," said Casey, trying to keep her voice low.

"You're the one who wouldn't drop the Werner case," said Deus. "The one who wanted to get into Pearce HQ. They're the lesser of two evils."

"Are you sure about that?"

Everyone knew Mal, although you'd never find him on the system for anything more than a parking fine. Casey had never faced him down herself, but she'd visited plenty of officers in hospital who had. The other man, Clef, was apparently the brains. The guy who could get them into Pearce's stronghold.

"We're not the bad guys," said Mal. "Well, not the *really* bad guys. Pearce's people call your group the Stain. We call you guys the Ghost Line. Better, right? Practically friendly."

Clef closed his eyes.

"Friendly." Casey's voice was cold. "You people cheat, lie, steal and murder. You ruin lives on a daily basis, leaving trails of devastation wherever you go. We could never be *friendly*."

"Pearce organised the hit on Drake," said Clef. "His top gun, Rojin, pulled the trigger. Verona has no vendetta against the police. You're right, we'll never be friendly, but there are lines we don't cross. It's up to you to decide what's more important—your pride or the city."

There was a tense silence. No one in the room would have known it, but Clef actually didn't care much about the mission either way. He was still mulling miserably over his parting encounter with Verona, during which he'd tactfully argued against her sending both her most senior staffers on what looked like a suicide mission.

Verona had placed her hand gently on Clef's arm, sending all kinds of shivers through his body. She'd gazed deeply at him with those bright, luminous eyes, and said, "It's a risk I'm willing to take."

While Clef replayed this mental loop for the seventy-fifth time, Casey was coming to some conclusions of her own. Verona was offering them a chance to take down the most powerful crime lord in the city. Whether one unchallenged dictator was better than two warring factions was a matter of conjecture, but Casey knew this: if this was her only chance to bring Pearce to justice, she'd take it.

"Let me make this perfectly clear," said Casey, her words etched in stone. "There will be no random killing. There will be no collateral damage. This is an unofficial police operation, not a Verona mission. We get in, we get the drive, we get out. Nothing explodes, and nobody dies. If you stray from those directions, I will shoot you. Is that understood?"

"Who died and made her Drake?" muttered Mal.

"Drake," said Casey.

You could have suffocated an elephant with that silence.

"Ahem," said Kirsk. "I've configured a binary light key with the coded wavelengths. All you have to do is insert the key, and we can do the rest from here."

Casey took the slender cylinder. It was the length of a finger and perfectly clear.

"Okay," she said. "Time to pay Pearce a visit."

# TWENTY-ONE

Alaviere was like an island within the city. Lush, misty gardens encircled a central swirl of towers, each one a unique piece of architectural art. On particularly foggy days, the tips of the apartments poked above the milky white, like a lonely world floating in the ether.

Squid felt like an intruder in some fantastic world, with silent guards nodding them through fortress-like gates, and security checkpoints clicking open on approach.

"I keep expecting a unicorn to run between the trees in slow motion," whispered Squid.

Grief didn't respond. He'd grown oddly quiet as they made their way through the stately grounds, towards a tower of blue glass and marble—Coeur Esuria. The ivory-cream doors were carved with scenes from Greek mythology: a minotaur, a winged god, a man being eviscerated. Squid wasn't sure how welcoming that was supposed to be.

A blip of light flashed from the lintel, tracking onto Grief's right eye. Squid had no idea how Ferret had gotten them this far—Alaviere was foreign-owned and exclusive as hell. Any minute now, she expected a squad of security to pounce, or perhaps just incinerate them via satellite.

The tall doors swung open noiselessly, revealing a vaulted foyer of amber glass. The floor was a spectacular mosaic of Caravaggio's *The Beheading of Saint John the Baptist* rendered in breathtaking detail.

"Pretentious? No…" said Squid, glancing around suspiciously for Roman columns.

Grief headed for the elevator, his expression one of vague concentration, as though listening to a distant voice.

"Grief? Are you okay?" said Squid.

"Mm… Fine… Are you hungry?"

Squid had a feeling she was getting the autopilot response.

"I think I have the plague."

"Mm… Maybe scones…" said Grief.

Squid followed him into the elevator, curlicues of rose gold forming the internal cage. Another blip of light homed in on Grief's eye, and Squid's gaze darted to a panel of buttons beside the door, cryptically marked with symbols that bore a vague resemblance to insects playing charades.

"Looks like you need a passcode, but I bet I could—" she began.

Without hesitation, Grief punched a sequence of symbols and swiped his index finger on a blank section of the panel. The doors closed silently, and the elevator began to rise.

"Grief?"

His expression was intense now, like a man walking boldly to the guillotine. He stood unblinking, barely breathing, falling into a personal event horizon.

"I think I used to live here," said Grief softly.

The elevator doors slid open.

Squid's jaw fell a hundred and fifty floors. There were penthouses, and then there were *penthouses.* And then there was *this.* It was as though the souls of a hundred penthouses on their last karmic cycle had been reincarnated into one sinfully luxurious apartment.

Sunlight flooded in through walls of flawless glass, and underfoot, the spotless white carpet felt like the downy fur of some genetically engineered baby animal. Elegant silk lamps hung over sumptuous green chaise longues, and the kitchen resembled a minimalist marble curve. The bathroom was the size of a suburban house, tiled in Venetian glass, with a sunken tub you could do laps in.

Grief trod grimly through the silent rooms, unfamiliar shadows finding hollows in his face.

"You remember living here…" said Squid.

"It wasn't living."

Squid reined in her response. This place was hedonism on a stick. It was exactly the kind of pad you'd show someone if you were trying to recruit them into a life of crime. However, Grief's expression resembled that of a man watching the concrete block around his ankles sink into the lightless deep.

"Um, how about some clean clothes?" said Squid, making her way to the closet.

The walk-in wardrobe had more labels than an international boutique, with silk shirts in everything from peacock blue to red jade, dinner suits so sharp you could cut yourself, and indulgent robes embroidered with Chinese dragons and cherry blossoms. Squid didn't dare to ask about the racks of exquisite dresses, ranging in size from girl-next-door to supermodel.

Grief eventually found Squid in aisle five, sitting on the floor and petting a fuzzy slipper as though it were a baby bunny.

"I think it's alive," said Squid, holding it up to him.

"Did you find anything you like?" said Grief, trying not to sound like a clinically depressed corpse.

Actually, Squid would have liked to give Ferret a good kick in the shins. He would have known this would happen. She could see entire soliloquies on the ramparts gusting through Grief's gaze, spiralling into bleak questions about who he was, what he was.

Squid butted her shoulder gently against his.

"It's just stuff," she said. "It's not you."

The haunted edge in his eyes softened a little.

"I don't seem to have anything in the jeans-and-a-T-shirt range," said Grief.

Squid tensed at his use of the word "I". She couldn't ignore the feeling that Raphael was coming home. Some tides couldn't be stopped—all you could do was cling to a tree and prepare yourself for the new landscape.

"I think… this one for you," said Squid, holding up a dark blue shirt.

"You can shower first," said Grief. "Although technically, you could shower while I have a bath, and we'd probably still be in different postcodes."

"I'll go first. You can mope around some more."

She finally settled for a pair of flattering black pants and a sleeveless top with an asymmetrical oyster hem. After a hot shower and a change of clothes, the apartment started to feel like just another place to lie down. Even Grief seemed to relax a little, emerging from the designer kitchen with an armload of protein bars.

"I guess I mostly ate out," he said.

Squid settled on a chaise longue, while Grief curled up on a blanket nearby. They napped through the afternoon, while the sun slowly set over the rim of the world.

"Why do people call you Squid?" said Grief.

"I supposed because I'm spineless…" said Squid, rolling over sleepily.

She was silent for a while, watching the foggy moonlight drift across the carpet.

"It was a nickname my parents gave me," she said quietly. "Because I was always…" She mimed being pressed against a window. "…On the outside, looking in."

"There's more freedom outside," said Grief.

"There are also more wolves and bears and hailstones the size of watermelons."

Grief looked doubtful about this last point.

"I suppose your understanding of the landscape is different if you've never felt the weather," he said.

Squid couldn't tell if this was a profound observation about the importance of experiencing misfortune in order to understand it, or whether the protein bars had started to ferment.

"Oh." Grief rifled through his pockets and held out a slender metal blade. "Ferret asked me to give this to you and say, 'What is it?'"

Squid turned the scuffed blade in her hands, the edge a razor thread of light.

Tool. Weapon. Gift.

Ferret never gave up. Every point had a counterpoint. Everyone had a story. And everything was subjective. An amnesiac could have two souls, and a petty thief could be a hero.

"I guess it's kind of funny," mused Squid, "that someone like me found someone like you. Although it also would have been funny if a group of nuns had found you. Or an uptight accountant. Or a neurotic bridezilla."

"I'm glad you found me…" said Grief.

Squid shifted, curling up against the back of the lounge. If she hadn't been the one to find him, Grief would probably be somewhere else right now, being someone else. Maybe meditating with the nuns, or hauling the accountant to flash-mob dance parties, or helping the bridezilla realise she was marrying the wrong guy. Then again, if she hadn't found Grief…

Squid pressed her eyes shut.

"I think I should go in alone," said Grief.

"And maybe you should take off your shirt and put on a bandana—it'll make you bulletproof."

"I just mean, this is kind of my fight—"

Squid sat up abruptly.

"You mean this is Raphael's fight," she said sharply. "*Our* fight is getting the drive and putting Pearce away. I don't know how many times I have to say this, but you're not Raphael. I don't think I like Raphael, and I'm not even going to ask why he's got two beds. I know you. I like you. And you're not that man."

Squid could almost see the struggle swimming through his eyes. She found it hard to understand how two such different people could occupy the same body, share the same past. Grief blinked, and a familiar grin found its way to his mouth.

"So, you like me, huh?" said Grief.

He dodged the cushion.

"You know what I mean," said Squid.

Grief flopped onto his back, staring at a vaulted ceiling smudged with starlight.

"What are you going to do after all this?" said Grief.

"Assuming there is an 'after all this'."

"You could travel. See the world. Learn to be prickly in a dozen different languages."

"You could move somewhere full of olive groves and vineyards. Run a quaint little bistro, be the easygoing guy with the tragic past."

"Or we could run a criminal empire together…" said Grief.

He wasn't smiling, and Squid didn't dare ask if he was joking. It occurred to her, in a faintly surreal way, that if she partnered up with Raphael, she'd be vaulting up the food chain so fast, she'd be orbiting Saturn.

"I don't think we should even—"

Squid jumped at the sudden chime, a message flashing on her phone.

*Showtime.*

# TWENTY-TWO

Their ride was a heck of a departure from their glamorous stopover, and Squid wondered if there'd been any point in having a shower.

The crate was just tall enough to sit in, and there must have been fifty crates stacked in each truck. Squid sat near the breathing holes, a polar bear cub snoozing in her lap. She'd asked Smuggling what the polar bears were for, and he'd just muttered something about taking all the trouble to bring them in only to have them end up in the sewers.

"What exactly did Smuggling mean by 'cover yourself in bears during the scan'?" said Squid.

"I think it's pretty self-explanatory," said Grief, plonking a drowsy cub on his shoulder.

The delivery convoy rattled its way through Old Central, past ornate sandstone buildings and cracked laneways. This had been the hub of Baltus City once upon a time. It was still a hub, but of a different kind of business now.

The truck slowed, and clipped voices exchanged code phrases. Squid shifted to a horizontal position, letting the curious cubs clamber over her. A high-pitched hum steadily intensified, and through the slats, Squid saw a grid of orange light crawling over the crate. Grief lay perfectly still in a slightly contorted position, his hip aligned with the bolting mechanism on the door.

Squid didn't have to pat him down to know he'd kept a few souvenirs from the house. When Grief's old shirt had reached a Cinderella state of tatters, it hadn't been hard to spot the two pistols tucked into his waistband. He'd never really explained what he'd been doing with those dismembered guns in the attic, and she hadn't pressed the point. But now, passing through the gates into the fortress of

Pearce HQ, she couldn't help wondering if Grief's agenda ended with recovering the drive.

The trucks rolled into Pearce's underground warehouses—a subterranean city of illicit goods and restricted technology. Thanks to a blind eye from Smuggling's crew, Squid and Grief quickly lost themselves in rows of antique coral carvings and military-grade weapons. Freight halls turned into transit corridors, concrete gave way to marble.

Grief wound his way up through the building, his footsteps growing surer. Security doors whispered open for them like a mechanical tide, and although they had to dive for cover at every passing minion, Squid could almost imagine it was Raphael stalking his domain.

She could see Grief's whole demeanour changing in this place. A more calculated tread, a harder spark in his gaze, a tension running through him like a pistol cocked to go.

"Do you remember where the central elevator is?" said Squid.

"We have to find Ducabre first," said Grief.

"We should at least take a look at the panel first. If the elevator uses a Syndicate control circuit, I might be able—"

"This isn't a double-parked van, Squid. We find Ducabre. Then we find Pearce."

There was a hint of a snarl in his voice, and the way he said "find" suggested the word was interchangeable with "kill". It was as though a mask had come up, and Squid was finding it increasingly difficult to see Grief behind those eyes.

"Ducabre could be anywhere," said Squid. "The elevator's a stationary target."

"But if you screw up the elevator, it's all over."

There was a deeply unpleasant silence, and Squid had the sensation of staring down a bear about to charge.

She was losing him.

She wanted to grab hold of Grief, as though she could somehow keep him here with nothing more than her bare hands. But this place was burning through him, reshaping him before her eyes. Knowing when to let go and when to hold on—understanding the difference was probably half the road to happiness.

"Grief, I think we—"

The corridor abruptly plunged into darkness, an urgent klaxon screeching from all directions. Almost immediately, red emergency lighting flickered on, and Squid and Grief darted into a side passage as a frantic patrol rushed past.

"I think we need to define 'all over'," whispered Squid.

Another deployment of security guards marched past, headed by a fierce woman with a thin, dark braid. Her radio crackled with reports in overlapping staccato.

*"…security breach in the eastern sector… Initiating lockdown…"*

In the dull red glow, Squid exchanged a look with Grief.

"I guess we have company," said Grief.

*

Casey was not happy about the klaxons. She wasn't happy about a lot of things, but the klaxons were right up there.

"When you said you could get us in, I assumed you meant undetected," said Casey.

Clef continued to fiddle with the innards of the security panel, oblivious to the screaming klaxons.

"For crying out loud," growled Mal, aiming his gun at the control panel.

Clef sparked two final cables together, and the panel blinked green.

"A bullet isn't a universal key," said Clef dourly.

"And you're a lapdog," said Mal.

"And you're an overcompensat—"

"Leave it at home," snapped Deus, forcing open the door.

Casey followed him down the twisting corridors, veering away from the rush of voices and trampling boots. It reminded her of those hardcore training sims—the ones she'd detested at the academy. She used to complain about the unlikelihood of being trapped in a submarine with fifteen infectious mutant cannibals, or having to rescue hostages from a cult of circus-themed assassins.

Or being deep in the core of Pearce HQ with nothing more than a motley crew of criminals and an unjust suspension.

"Got anything?" said Casey.

"Still screening out the interference," said Clef, delicately adjusting the settings on the RAFID scanner.

They crept further into the heart of the complex, and Casey could almost feel the walls throbbing.

"So, you're one of those lovable rogue cops they keep making movies about," said Mal, jogging easily alongside Casey.

"And you're one of those granny-trampling psychos who never make it to the end," said Casey.

"Damn! That was once, and she came out of nowhere," said Mal.

"So, want to tell me why Verona really sent you?"

Mal's gaze slid into a sidelong glance. He was the kind of person who didn't worry about lying, because there was little incentive in using guile when you had a fist like a flying tractor.

"The window's closing," said Mal. "The Rottweiler's resurfaced, and if he rejoins the old man's side, we'll never take Pearce down."

"Once more, without the tough-guy lingo," said Casey.

"Raphael's back," said Mal. "Pearce's second. It took us weeks to confirm he was even missing. He's the guy who keeps them all in line. The bullet you don't see coming. They say he rose so fast 'cos he doesn't have a conscience weighing him down."

"How scientific."

"Let's just say he makes me look like the good cop," said Mal.

Casey was trying to picture the comparison when a flash of silver caught her eye.

"Where'd you get that watch?"

Clef suddenly interrupted with a raised hand, the scanner lighting up with concentric ripples.

"I've got something," he said. "That's odd—"

Clef suddenly jolted, his leg giving way in a spatter of red. He hit the ground like a prizefight knockout as a patrol charged around the corner, the corridor erupting in gunfire. Deus and Mal returned fire while Casey dragged Clef towards a nearby doorway.

"Take the scanner!" gasped Clef, shoving it into her hands. He pushed her out of the way and a gun appeared in each hand. "Go!"

Deus slid something into her pocket, yelling over the buzz of ricocheting bullets.

"It's good for one door!" said Deus. "Get it done, Casey!"

He shouldered her aside, grunting as his vest took a bullet. Casey's last glimpse of them was a blur of red and black, the trio bunkered down against a storm bearing down. Her steps pounded to the beat of the shots, the noise growing fainter as she drew farther from the battle.

She had to focus on the task ahead. Get the job done. You dealt with the psychological fallout on your own time. Casey swiped her finger over the scanner screen, orienting herself with the view of the complex. She wasn't overly impressed with Clef's efforts in getting them inside, and she was even less confident about his programming skills. The readings were clear, but rather than taking her farther into Pearce HQ, the signals sent her farther and farther towards the outskirts. On the upside, there was less security here, but on the downside, Casey wasn't interested in crates of beef jerky and spare tank-treads.

Logic started to poke vicious holes in her heroic plan. What if they'd removed the locator chip, if they'd set up a decoy, if the drive was already long gone? Her entire plan hinged on reckless gambits and questionable hunches. And she had a feeling the consequences were waiting around the corner with a set of brass knuckles.

Casey slowed and then took a few steps back. The scanner screen pulsed softly, a bright point of light holding steady to her left. The sliding storage door seemed no different to the others she'd passed, but the security terminal beside it looked newly upgraded. According to the scanner, the drive was about sixty feet through there.

Now would have been a good time for Clef or Kirsk to make an appearance, but she was on her own. Casey reached into her pocket, sliding out Deus's parting gift. Holographic blue streaks danced across its surface—the Iluvian pass.

Good for one door. Deus must have had it hacked with a nasty kamikaze virus. She'd seen a couple of these before, and it'd probably crack the security as well as melt the card, wreck the terminal and, in some cases, take out an eye.

Casey could have stood there for hours, second-guessing her judgement. But every moment brimmed with decisions, and if you didn't want them to sweep through your hands unshaped, you had to know in your heart where you stood.

She swiped the card, and a brilliant blue flash engulfed the corridor. Casey hit the wall behind her, fingers crackling with threads of live current. She hunched on the ground until the scenery stopped spinning, her skin tingling like a swarm of hornets. She'd have to have words with Deus later.

Wisps of smoke rose from the terminal, but the security door had jolted open about half a foot. The scanner lay several feet away, the screen cracked and blank. Whatever lay on the other side of the door, she'd have to face it with a pair of eyes and a borrowed gun.

Casey took a deep breath, sweeping the singed hair from her eyes.

*Here goes everything.*

*

Gunfire and yelling.

Two of Squid's least favourite things. Her overwhelming instinct was to run as far as she could. Grief seemed to have the same compulsion, just in the opposite direction.

"He'll be on his way down," said Grief. "Ducabre always hated offices."

"I saw an elevator back there," said Squid. "Do you think there'll be a sign?"

"Even though he should stay in the Safe. Where Pearce weathers the storms of dictatorship."

Squid had a feeling they were travelling down separate paths now, their arms stretched across the gap, fingers barely touching. She wanted to hold on. She wanted it more than almost anything else.

"Do you know if the central elevator is gearless traction or regenerative roomless? Oh, look, another elevator!"

Squid ran ahead, and everything went into slow motion. The elevator doors slid open, a dozen smoky faceplates staring out like a compound eye. She skidded across the marble, a battery of guns rising to meet her. Grief's arms crossed over and down to his hips, and came up with pistols firing.

Five troopers were on the ground before they even left the elevator, and Grief was on his second magazine by the time he reached cover.

"You still think we should go opening elevators?" said Grief.

"How much ammo do you have?" said Squid.

"Enough to get to Pearce."

"Then you have enough to get out."

Grief jerked back as a bullet claimed a chunk of the wall.

"What do you—"

Squid tucked her letter opener into Grief's belt.

"I want that back," said Squid. "Now get out of here."

She didn't look back, racing away down the scarlet-washed passage. She heard her name lancing through the gunfire, but Grief would get over it. He couldn't reach Pearce without the serum from Narcotics, and he wasn't quite crazy enough to go down in a pointless blaze. He'd have to leave—cursing her scamperiness, but alive.

In her head, it had been so much simpler. Avoid the patrols, get the drive, cue victory music. She'd never really gotten the hang of consequences—never had the patience to really listen, understand, persist. She'd always run away when things got too tough. From people, from work, from rejection.

It was so much easier to close your eyes and hide. It was so much easier to run. But it was only when you stopped running that you found a place to stand.

A lanky shadow pulled out in front of her, and Squid found herself staring down the barrel of a gun.

"Squid," said Mal.

His expression could have cracked a coconut.

"Mal," said Squid.

There was a silence, which could have been full of bitter memories rising but was more likely Mal thinking of something to say. Squid's gaze travelled down his arm.

"That's my watch," said Squid.

"Come and get it."

There was another silence, full of slightly distracted hostility.

"I don't suppose you know where the central elevator is?" said Squid.

She was tempted to ask Mal what he was doing at Pearce HQ, but from the belt of ammunition draped over his shoulder, it wasn't a social call.

"Give me one good reason I shouldn't shoot you right now," said Mal.

God, she didn't have time for this.

"No," said Squid. "You've had this obsessive grudge for six years, Mal. I was eighteen. I didn't know it was your getaway car. And Verona bailed you out after five weeks. Let it go."

"I was three feet away! In the middle of a ram-raid—"

"And I was too busy wishing I was dead, so how about we call it even?"

She hadn't meant to be that honest, but she was done with saying the wrong thing at the wrong time. There was only what you said, when you said it, and how you dealt with the fallout. Mal's expression remained resentful, but he finally shrugged.

"There was a big-ass elevator six corridors down, two turns right," said Mal. "It had lots of lasers around it."

"Lasers?" said Squid weakly.

"Had," said Mal, blowing the smoke from one of his guns.

Everyone had a story. Some were just more messed-up than others.

"Thanks…" said Squid, moving cautiously past Mal.

"Hey," called Mal. "If you're still alive in twenty-four hours, the watch is yours."

Squid smiled faintly.

"It's mine anyway."

She strode away into the red. Twenty-four hours could be a lifetime. And by the end of the night, it was anyone's guess who'd be left standing.

*

He followed her footsteps but lost her in the turns and echoes. It was like a nightmare, all blood and shadows and hellish light. Thunder and fire and screams, and Grief couldn't tell if it was the fighting or all in his head.

All he knew was that Squid intended to self-immolate in some way. She seemed to understand the basic concept of communication, but the execution left worlds to be desired. She probably planned to survive—hence the letter opener. The gesture would have had more impact if she'd given him her grandmother's wedding ring rather than a random bit of kit her boss had given her that morning. Then again, Squid didn't really *have* anything else.

Undoubtedly, Squid thought she could sneak into the Safe and steal the drive. No blood shed, no souls lost, no experimental hypos turning people into mush. Except it wouldn't be the drive waiting in the Safe.

There was no drive, according to Ferret. The problem was, Grief *remembered* it. But why it was important, or where it was now, remained as elusive as the location of the central elevator. He ran in desperate circles, a maze of wrong turns, and still he couldn't remember.

The only memories were the ones he didn't want. Laughter. Screams. The laughter coming from a hollow man, and all the screaming was on the inside. It was a terrible cliché: the wealthy, powerful man who wanted only to be loved. But stepping inside that apartment had been like a knife through the heart. Every step a blade, plunged again and again. And all the while, a face, pale and bloody, haunting him with promises unkept.

The spectre of loathing and isolation in that place had been overwhelming, like a swamp closing over his head. It had been a world away from his life with Squid—a life of sunshine and rain, bad food and precious warmth. Everything about her was so unfiltered, so real. Around her, Grief felt as though he could finally breathe.

He saw the shadow at the same time as it saw him, and it moved almost as fast. Arms grappled, dodged and counter-struck. They slammed into one wall, and then back against another, arms locked, guns twisted outwards.

The man's face was gaunt in the dull glow, a smudge of blood on his lip, a graze on his cheek.

"I was hoping I'd find you," said the man, his grin like a vest of dynamite. "My name is Arios Deus. You wouldn't know me, but I remember you."

"I have a generic face," said Grief.

"Remember the blockade on Albion and Rutledge?" said Deus. "Eight years, four months and twenty-seven days ago. Remember squadron four-two-five."

A chill raced through Grief, sharp and electric. The Old Central Riots. The blockade. His first major command. The landmines—

*Oh, God.*

Suddenly, he could remember it like a bad dream—the ones you woke from, sobbing with gratitude that you still had your teeth, your limbs, and your loved ones. He could remember the horror welling inside him, but he hadn't stopped, hadn't held back. Grief couldn't tell if the horror was Raphael's or his own, painting imaginary feelings onto a monster of a man.

"It took me two years to get a name," said Deus. "Another three for a glimpse of that face. You've worked hard to stay off the system, Raphael."

*It's not me*, thought Grief. As though it were that easy.

All those things he'd done were still inside him. All that violence and inhumanity, soaking through him like cheap rum in a Christmas cake. It wasn't enough to change. You had to make amends.

"Whether or not you believe me, I'm sorry for what I did," said Grief. "I can't take it back, but I can end it. And tonight, one way or the other, I will."

"Why should—"

Grief only hit the man hard enough to daze him, laying him carefully in a storage closet. He'd have time for apologies later. Now he had demons to exorcise and suicidal squids to rescue.

Grief took a breath and headed for the central elevator.

*

The central elevator looked like a door to another dimension.

It would have been fairly unassuming, had it not been the size of a castle drawbridge. The elevator could have transported entire villas, and knowing Pearce, it probably had.

Squid picked her way carefully around the smoking laser stations, scraps of torn metal littering the ground. The bloody drag marks across the marble suggested the corridor hadn't been deserted when Mal had come this way.

The elevator access panel was firmly affixed to the wall, and Squid briefly wished she'd kept the letter opener. But hopefully, it was reminding Grief that she'd be back, and she'd be angry if he'd killed anybody. At the very least, it'd come in handy if he ran out of bullets.

Squid grabbed a wedge of metal, and after a few nasty cuts and a mental note to get her tetanus booster, she managed to pry the control casing from the wall. She probably had an ice cream cake's chance in hell of cracking the Safe, but if she could summon the elevator, it'd be a start.

She'd assumed all the training was standard back when she first met Ferret. Cars, safes, security doors. She'd never wondered why she was learning to hack, crack and hotwire Syndicate security. Or how many other operatives Ferret had seeded through the organisation, waiting for his signal.

It took a mid-level bypass to send the elevator chugging down. Squid was still trying to get the doors to open when a chunk of wall disintegrated beside her. Two security troopers appeared down a side corridor, bearing down like a pair of cannonballs. Squid pressed herself into the alcove, her hands working blind in the recesses of the panel.

Detach the access control cable, cut the integrated neural node, invert the holographic sensor. She had a hard time telling the blue wire from the black wire at the best of times, and when her eyes were closed due to spraying debris, all she could hope for was that nothing burst into flames.

Another blast, and she crossed one final wire. As security personnel flooded in from other corridors, mechanisms whirred deep within the walls, and the elevator doors began to open. Squid squeezed inside, tearing off the interior access panel as bullets rapidly dimpled the back wall. All she could hear were the seconds of her life ticking down while her hands fumbled desperately with the mesh of wires.

A wave of startled shouts rolled down the hall, and Squid risked a furtive glance. The guards were falling out of formation, trying to get a clear shot at something in their midst. A trooper sailed overhead and crashed into a nearby wall, while another three skidded across the floor like hockey pucks. A trickle of gasps followed the blurry figure.

Grief emerged from the scrum, charging down the hallway and scattering anyone in his way. He swung into the elevator beside Squid, returning fire through the doors.

"How're you going?" said Grief. "Because I've got four rounds left."

"I thought—"

"Three."

"—I told you—"

"Two."

"—to get—"

"One."

"—out of here!"

Grief boomeranged his gun through the doorway, hitting one trooper squarely in the throat.

"Did you?" said Grief mildly.

"Argh!" growled Squid, yanking the override cable free.

Sparks flew, and a line of blue fire raced up the wires and over her hands. She ignored the popping noise in her shoulder as she hauled on the cable, her tendons stretched taut. Slowly, the doors began to close, and Squid slammed her fist on an unmarked button at the top of the panel.

Grief landed a solid kick on the chest of an advancing trooper just before the doors clanged shut, and the elevator lurched into a steady ascent. The furious yelling faded beneath them, and Squid sagged to the floor, cradling her blistered fingers and wishing she had a bucket of snow. Grief took her hands gently, examining the burnt pads.

"I knew you were going to do something that involved setting yourself on fire," he muttered.

"I didn't exactly douse myself in petrol and dive into a fireworks factory."

Grief's expression suggested she'd come pretty close. He looked at her hands again.

"I'm sorry," he said softly.

"Grief..."

"Will you still call me that when this is all over?"

Squid doubted she'd be around when this was all over, but still, the answer mattered.

"It depends on who you are," she said. "Now that you know who you were, you can choose who you'll be. History isn't destiny if you learn from your mistakes."

"You're starting to sound like Casey," said Grief with a wan smile.

He suddenly tilted his head.

"Do you feel that?" he said.

Squid nodded, heart pounding.

The elevator had stopped.

*

It resembled something from a Gothic science fiction movie.

Casey trod carefully through the vast storage room. Contorted metal racks towered overhead, spilling with an evolutionary broth of mechanical devices. Ancient Omatatron drives with rusted cartridge slots, chunky Ziptanks with anodised shells, piles of desperately beige magnetic cassettes. She could even see newly released Ruebee drives, thin as credit cards, glinting in the dull red glow.

It reminded Casey of a movie she'd watched as a child, in which the hero's friends were all turned into objects, lost in a castle cluttered with curios. Casey had the eerie thought that maybe Pearce had turned all his failed minions into sad little data drives locked away in the darkness.

Casey eyed the endless rows of forgotten machinery. It'd take her days to sift through this, assuming she'd even recognise the drive. She could probably narrow it down to a ten-by-ten area, judging from the scanner's last coordinates, and she was looking for something with a keyhole.

It was a long shot, but her whole life had been one stubborn long shot waiting for a place to land.

She'd only searched half an aisle when something raised the hairs on the back of her neck. It wasn't a sound—it was more like something trying not to make a sound. Casey crouched behind a shelf, peering through the steel grid. A shadow vanished into another shadow, like a demon flitting through the blood-red light.

Casey slid the safety off her gun, listening for a sound that wasn't there. She held her breath, ignoring the painful thumping in her chest. It was all down to her. Clef, Mal, Deus, Kirsk, Werner—they all needed her to finish this.

She heard the faintest footfall on the other side of the grill, saw the shadow parting from the darkness.

"Hello, Casey," said Rojin.

*

Squid was elbow-deep in the entrails of the elevator panel, occasionally giving the sealed doors an ineffectual kick. Grief wasn't sure if applying abrupt force to the doors was supposed to stimulate the release mechanism, but he suspected it was just Squid reaching critical levels of crankiness.

She looked as though she'd been hit by a nail bomb, but Grief didn't dare ask if she was all right. He wasn't sure if it was the blood loss or the burn shock, but Squid seemed to have decided that her suicidal plan would have worked just fine if Grief had followed her instructions to leave. She'd even suggested that perhaps the elevator had frozen due to them exceeding the weight limit, at which point she'd shot him an accusing look.

Grief busied himself searching the pocked steel walls for hatches or panels. What he really wanted to do was lie down with a cold compress on his forehead. Or perhaps extract his brain altogether and hurl it into the path of a speeding train. Memories swirled through his head, mingling with dreams and delusions and half-forgotten nightmares.

Deus's words had been like a truck crashing through a set of cardboard doors. The haunting fragments spun together, rising up in a monstrous mosaic. This identity he'd created—this happy, blameless man—felt more and more like a childish charade. Like a papier mâché doll coming apart in rough water. Grief could feel his skin prickling, as though Raphael were growing in a chrysalis, ready to split him open like a discarded shell.

The memories weren't just flashes of someone else's life anymore. He could remember *being* Raphael. He could remember the things he'd done—

The world seemed to spin in a burst of nauseating light, and he could feel the water rising over his head. Grief stared down at his hands, expecting to see blood staining his fingers.

"Grief…" said Squid. "How about you sit down for a bit?"

"I'm fine."

"'Fine' is high tea at Victoria Gardens. You're high tea at Victoria Gardens when it's being attacked by rabid baboons carrying flamethrowers. I've got this one."

She gave him a weak smile and turned back to the panel. Grief felt himself swaying, terrifying impulses surging through him. She was so small, so fragile—he could break her into pieces like a breadstick, and he could remember—

Squid's arm clanked inside the gutted panel.

"Seriously," she said. "Sit down, because I'm not going to catch you if you fall."

But she already had. From the first sandwich to the last smile, she'd been keeping his head above water, keeping his soul afloat. He didn't know if he could fight it anymore, but if he became Raphael, he wouldn't just lose his soul—he'd lose Squid.

There was a soft hiss, and the elevator doors began to open onto impenetrable darkness.

"Impressive," said Grief, rising to his feet.

"I didn't do anything," said Squid, puzzled.

A pair of arms suddenly reached through the doorway, dragging Squid into the pitch black, her cry of surprise abruptly cut off.

"Squid!" yelled Grief, aiming his gun into the void.

The doors began to close, and without hesitation, Grief slid through, almost expecting the floor to vanish beneath him. His feet met with soft carpet, his eyes still straining in the dark. The silence was suffocating as he edged his way carefully around the unseen furniture. He listened for breathing, for movement, for anything, but he suspected the last noise he'd hear would be the click of a trigger.

*Click.*

Grief spun around, his gun arcing to aim. A lamp flared into life, and his vision fuzzed in the sudden glare.

"Welcome back, Raphael," came a dry voice.

Ducabre stood only yards away, his arm locked around Squid's neck, his gun pressed hard into her temple.

"Put down the gun," said Ducabre.

"What makes you think I give a damn about her?" said Grief.

"If you didn't, I'd already be dead."

*Damn.*

Grief wouldn't get out of this alive. He'd get Squid killed, just like he got Werner—

*A cluttered workshop, rolling hills of half-constructed mechanical dreams. Someone else's voice coming out of his mouth.*

*"Interesting work—this substratum."*

*"That's not the good bit." Werner, bright-eyed and shining with enthusiasm. "I've increased the compression by almost half a million permutations. I just need the right lens to speed things up."*

*"Have you shown this report to anyone else?"*

*"That's kind of an ominous question, Raphael… No, my report to Technology isn't due 'til tomorrow…"*

*Cogs ticking. Doors opening. A blur of light to a drowning man.*

*"Omit this. I might have a proposition for you."*

"You have three seconds," said Ducabre. "Then it's just you and me, old friend."

Grief could tell from his voice that Squid was already dead.

"One," said Ducabre.

If he put down the gun, there'd be no one left to stop Pearce.

"Two."

The greater good, the tough decision, the sacrifices we made—

"Thr—"

Grief dropped the gun, his mind roaring with a million conflicting voices.

"You might want to think about your next move very carefully," said Grief. "At some point, I'm going to stop humouring you. And you know what I'm like when I'm… unhappy."

Ducabre's expression was impassive.

"That would have worked, once," he said. "I looked up to you. I believed in you. Eight years, Raphael. We fought our way to the top, and you betrayed me."

"Then I guess we're even," said Grief.

*Dim lights, tense voices. Iluvian windows overlooking a city drunk with lights.*

*"They searched my workshop." Werner's face, pale and worried. "I don't know if I can go through with this."*

*"Keep it together, Werner. I can protect you. And when it's all over, it'll be worth it."*

*Werner's eyes, full of fear and doubt. A small nod, a solemn smile.*

*"What's next?"*

*The shadows closing in. Ducabre suspects, if he doesn't already know. A fog of eyes and ears turning into knives.*

*"We make our move. Tonight."*

Grief tried to focus on the solid ground beneath his feet, the flush of light against the panelled walls. Maybe ten feet between himself and Ducabre. Grief could stop the second shot, but not the first.

"You have to the count of three to tell me where the copies are," said Ducabre.

"What copies?"

"One."

*The data. The slicks. Thin and glistening.*

"I don't know! I don't remember!"

He looked desperately at Squid, and her eyes were fixed on him—

maybe pleading, maybe accusing. For once, he couldn't read them. As though she were already gone.

"Two."

Grief couldn't remember. Even with Squid's life in the balance, he couldn't remember.

But Raphael could.

*Home stretch on a starless night, crossing the Baltus Bay Bridge. Werner had the hard drive on his lap, fretting over the tail they'd lost five blocks back. Suddenly, up ahead, a bank of headlights rippled across the bridge, like a stage coming to life for the final act.*

*Too late to turn. An engine roared, and he saw her standing on the roof of a car, taking aim, coat flapping in the bayside draft.*

*He heard the crack. Saw the hole in the glass. And Werner's shirt turning red. A second shot, a scream of metal, and then—*

*Squid.*

It was like a galaxy of stars unfurling, hurtling through the sky in dying flames. He could feel himself dying, awakening, becoming.

"Three," said Ducabre.

Squid closed her eyes.

"It's here," said Grief.

He drew the letter opener from his belt, a thin wedge of silver light. Slowly, he dragged the blade across his wrist, brilliant crimson running down his fingers. He could feel it now, the cold conviction burning through his veins, pouring out into a world that cowered in his grasp.

He reached into his flesh and pulled out a single data-slick, smooth and wet with blood.

"Now let her go," snarled Grief. "Or so help me, God, you'll wish you'd saved that bullet for yourself."

Squid gave an odd little sigh, relaxing suddenly.

"Ducabre," she said. "You can let go now."

Ducabre lowered his gun, and Squid pushed his arm aside gently. She stepped towards Grief, her gaze locked on the flimsy strip between his fingers.

"Squid…?" Grief reeled, everything changing shape, changing place.

It couldn't be— Pearce, Ducabre, Ferret, Squid—weaving an elaborate hoax to find the data-slicks. The last few weeks with Squid—a setup, a long con, a cruel lie—

Squid let the empty hypo drop from her fingers, her eyes watering.

"You couldn't use an airport locker like everyone else?" blurted Squid.

"I—"

And suddenly his face was pressed against the carpet, the world pitching and buzzing. He heard a rip of fabric, and small hands were bandaging the slash across his wrist.

"I don't know how long Ducabre's going to be like that," said Squid. "If he explodes, just turn your face away."

Grief tried to move, tried to stand, but the world slid out from under him. Everything seemed to be tumbling, disintegrating, falling into the sky. He felt Squid's arms wrapping around him, holding him still.

"Grief, it's really important that you don't move," said Squid. "I'm going to get the drive, and then I'll be right back."

"No," breathed Grief. "Pearce—"

"Grief," said Squid. "Let *me* deal with Pearce."

She abruptly kissed him on the forehead and then slipped into the darkness.

*

Part of Casey had wanted a showdown.

Part of her wanted to go down, guns blazing, setting the sky on fire with judgement and damnation. However, that kind of thing always looked more fun than it actually was. And you left a bastard of a mess for your coworkers.

Casey was already down six shots, playing cat and mouse between the looming shelves. The derelict drives cut mangled silhouettes, and she could hear Rojin stalking the aisles like a junkyard panther.

"Stand down, and you can walk out of here," said Rojin, her voice snaking through the darkness. "I have no quarrel with you."

Casey wondered if that ever worked. She didn't have a speck of doubt that one of them would leave here horizontally, and her bet was on the homeless cop with only four rounds left. Then again, Rojin had already fired three from her Reaver, and if Casey could get her to empty a magazine, she'd have to reload.

"Well, I have a hell of a quarrel with you—" began Casey.

She ducked as a bullet scored the wall behind her, and she darted across another aisle.

"You're on the wrong side, Detective," said Rojin. "The law is a shield, but not for the victims. The law protects the powerful, the wealthy, the corrupt. It turns a blind eye to their depravities, letting monsters roam unpunished, heaping scorn on the abused."

It was an easy line, but something in Rojin's voice suggested it was more than just ideology. It was *history*. Somewhere behind the murderous psychosis was a badly broken mind, kicked into pieces and rolled awkwardly back together.

Casey crept across two aisles, trying to circle in closer to the scanner's last coordinates.

"You can't give up on something just because it isn't perfect," she said. "Things take time to evolve, to learn from their mistakes—"

Casey bit back a curse as a bullet grazed her thigh, another sparking off the shelf behind her. She hobbled quickly down another row, skimming the crowded racks.

"Lies don't evolve," said Rojin coldly. "They just grow more elaborate. Courts and jails, laws and loopholes. The law is a lie to make people feel safe. But they're not safe, are they, Casey?"

Actually, Casey was starting to think that Rojin and Deus would make a seriously disturbing power couple. It was tempting to take the vigilante path, to become your own vision of justice. But justice was only a step away from vengeance, and vengeance only a breath from monstrosity.

"People are never safe in the company of self-created monsters—"

Casey jerked back as a bullet buzzed past her cheek. Rojin had one bullet left, but at this rate, it was all she needed. Casey crouched at the base of a shelf, sweat soaking through her shirt, her vision straining in the dim light.

She risked a quick visual scan of the far shelf, and a shape caught her eye, about twelve feet up, wedged beneath a hulking Black Star PA drive. A slim green case with deconstructed seams. It looked like something built from lovingly collected parts, with a small hole in the fascia—about the right size for a binary light key.

Casey let out a slow, silent breath. If she played things out with Rojin, there was a chance she could take her out. She could eliminate Pearce's top assassin, avenge Drake and probably Werner. But every passing moment was a choice, and Casey only had time for one.

"There is no justice," said Rojin, her voice hollow. "Only what you create with your own hands. Give up, Casey. You'll never make it out of here with the drive."

Casey pressed her eyes shut. She should have paid more attention in the training sims. She should have called her family more often.

She should have said goodbye to Riego.

"I don't have to," said Casey.

She fired at the same time as Rojin, their bullets crossing in the dark. Casey sprinted down the aisle, pacing her shots.

Three.

Two.

One.

Casey leapt for the shelf, grappling her way up the overloaded racks. Drives spilled beneath her hands, smashing onto the concrete like plates at a wedding. The wire shelving sliced her fingers, but none of that would matter in about two seconds. Rojin's magazine slapped into place, the drive still just out of reach.

What Rojin didn't understand was that justice wasn't about your own safety, your own life, your own future. Justice was about doing what you could and trusting that others would carry on the battle. Keeping the light on for a humanity worth protecting.

Casey launched herself upwards, one hand gripping the rack, the other aiming for the drive. She plunged the binary key into the slot, and a throb of pale yellow light rippled out.

She didn't hear the shot. Hell, she didn't even feel it until she smacked onto the concrete. An excruciating sense of wrongness burst through her right shoulder, tearing across her chest and down to her fingertips. Casey tried to move her arm and bit back a scream as a boot landed on her shoulder. She heard a second shot, and a small shower of green carbon fibre clattered onto the floor, a shattered binary key clinking beside her head.

"How many of you made it in here?" said Rojin.

Casey looked up at the smoking barrel, trying to breathe through the wall of pain.

"Seventeen."

She saw the bullet this time, and her left shoulder joined the screaming in her right. Her entire torso sent hysterical nerve signals to her brain.

"One more chance," said Rojin. "How many?"

Casey's last words welled up in her throat.

"I'm sorry no one protected you. But we'll keep fighting. To protect people like who you were, from people like who you've become."

Rojin's gun locked onto Casey's forehead.

"First, you have to survive."

Rojin suddenly jolted, a splash of crimson spreading from her chest. Her eyes turned towards a ceiling lost in shadow, and as she hit the floor, the gun slid from her grasp.

Riego stood at the end of the aisle, a wisp of smoke drifting from his gun. He slapped the comms patch on his vest as he raced towards Casey.

"Officer down!" barked Riego. "We need a medic *now*."

Casey's vision sank into lightless clouds, the ground tumbling away beneath her. She wanted to say something, maybe "hello", maybe "what the hell took you so long", but she felt as though an anvil had crashed through her chest. Her ears filled with muffled ringing, drowning out the wail of distant sirens.

Then Riego was there, his hands pressing firmly against the sticky mess of her shoulders. Through the falling darkness, Casey could see him trying to smile.

"Hold on, crazy," said Riego. "I brought the cavalry."

*

*Six years earlier*

Squid crouched on the floor of the truck, the cargo area illuminated by the feeble light of her phone. Surrounded by towering pallets, she concentrated on keeping her hands steady as she wrote an address across a sheet of rough brown paper. She tried to make all the letters the same size, but they still looked like a drunk-tank lineup.

From the darkness at the rear of the truck, she heard the *click* of a safety sliding off.

"Hands where I can see them," came a woman's voice. "Slowly."

Squid froze. Crammed between the heavy cartons, there was nowhere to run. She raised her hands, turning to see a woman in a leather jacket, black jeans and scuffed boots. But it was her green newsboy cap that Squid recognised.

The woman tapped a radiolink on her collar.

"Riego, it's Casey. I found the stolen truck."

A muffled voice replied over the radio. "Is it still full of chocolate?"

"Cargo looks intact."

"Are there any cherry liqueur ones?" came Riego's voice. "Do you think they'll give us a—"

"Casey out," snapped the woman, looking faintly embarrassed.

Squid stared, vaguely aware that her mouth hung open. The last time she'd seen the woman in the green cap, she'd appeared to be single-handedly trying to take down the Kabukuri Club. Squid had skidded all over the road, trying to dodge the firefight, perhaps running over a few of the Kabukuri enforcers for good measure. There'd been talk in the slums about a woman in a green cap charging around Baltus City, raining merry hell down on the thugs and dealers.

Casey stepped forward, kicking open the rumpled sheet of brown paper. A lone giftbox of milk chocolate macadamias slid out, along with a folded note.

"No, don't—" began Squid.

Casey scooped up the letter, keeping her gun trained on Squid, her gaze skimming the smudged handwriting.

*Dear Mum,*

*Happy Birthday! I hope you like your new job. I have a job too. I work for an orthodontist. I'm doing fine. Don't worry about me. I miss you.*

*Love, Squid.*

Squid pressed her trembling lips together as Casey glanced quickly around the truck and then back at Squid.

"You stole a chocolate-delivery truck in order to steal a box of chocolates so you could send it to your mum?"

Squid nodded weakly, wondering if—based on Casey's expression—she was about to get shot in the face. After a pause, Casey's eyes narrowed slightly.

"You work for an orthodontist?"

"He removes teeth," said Squid shakily.

And then, without quite knowing why, she burst into shameless, uncontrollable tears. Somehow, the thought of dying here, surrounded by piles of chocolate macadamias, seemed unbearably tragic. And yet, if she had to be shot or arrested by anyone, it was a little less terrible to be undone by the woman in the green cap.

Casey nudged the box of chocolates with her foot, her expression shifting reluctantly from mean-cop to somewhat-annoyed-cop.

"Did you take anything else? Damage the truck?"

Squid shook her head, trying to bring her snuffling under control.

"I jswan… Yre hro…"

After some more shuddering sobs from Squid, Casey lowered her gun with a bottomless sigh.

"Look, I'll buy you a box of chocolates for your mum."

Squid blinked blurrily at her, wondering if maybe, just maybe, she wasn't as hopelessly alone as she'd imagined. Casey holstered her gun and pushed open the doors of the stifling truck.

"Come on," she said. "Let's get you a cup of tea or something."

*

Squid moved silently down the corridor, trying not to think about Casey's parting words. She owed Casey so much more than a cup of tea and a box of chocolates, but she would never fit into Casey's ordered world, not completely. Surprisingly, this didn't bother her as much as it used to. Squid still wasn't sure where she belonged, if anywhere, but she knew with absolute conviction that, right now, she was exactly where she needed to be.

The Safe wasn't a level so much as a realm.

She'd left Grief and Ducabre in the antechamber, although neither of them was all there at this point. Ducabre stood absently by the lamp, his mind locked away or unravelled. Grief lay twisted on the floor, clutching at the carpet as though trying to crawl out of his own skin. Squid hoped there'd be enough of them left to fix when she returned.

A pair of black oak doors marked the entrance to Pearce's private world, two milky jade death masks staring out like sentinels. She detected no obvious locks or traps, and she crept into a wide hallway carpeted in blue silk, the walls panelled in vintage mahogany. Softly glowing brass sconces lined the adjoining corridors, and silver chandeliers glittered from vaulted marble ceilings.

Archways opened onto galleries of glorious Renaissance paintings and winding libraries that smelled of temperature-sensitive parchment. Squid glimpsed a spotless surgical theatre through sealed glass doors, and the scent of fresh water wafted from another room lost in draping tropical foliage. If Raphael's apartment were a rubber dinghy, this was the mothership.

Perhaps it had been naïve to expect the hard drive to be sitting in the middle of an empty vault, caught in a shaft of celestial light. Perhaps Squid should have cut her losses, regrouped, gone to ground. But she was out of time.

Squid hadn't understood much of the exchange between Grief and Ducabre, aside from the usual alpha-male growling. The transparent strip Grief had pulled from his wrist was clearly important, but no one seemed coherent enough to explain the details. All she knew was that Grief was fading, consumed by the creeping shadow of Pearce. And according to Ferret, whoever had Werner's drive had the power to topple Pearce. So, here she was.

It felt like a private, deserted city, cocooned from the cold realities of the world outside. A restful silence spilled through every room, like a soothing tide lapping over bare feet. Squid could see why Pearce never left this place—it was an untouchable kingdom, floating over the city and its problems.

A splash of red drew her eye, and Squid moved carefully across the corridor. A door stood slightly ajar, revealing a room fringed in curving boughs and muted starlight. Somehow, slender saplings grew out of the floor, pale branches arching towards the ceiling. In the centre of the room, resting on a bench of smooth eucalyptus, sat a slightly battered silk lantern. Squid didn't need to check to know that it was hers. She didn't need to ask to know why it was here. She didn't need to turn around to know she wasn't alone.

"Enjoying the view?" said a voice mildly.

A man stood in the doorway, dressed in a pale blue shirt and black tailored trousers. He looked to be in his late sixties, with Arctic blue eyes and the kind of face that might have been rakish a few decades and several operations ago.

"Are you the decoy Pearce?" said Squid.

"What makes you think there's a Pearce at all?" he replied. "It's just a name and a reputation."

"And a man who gives orders. I have to say I was expecting more of a twist."

"That's always been your weakness, Squid. Seeing complicated problems instead of simple solutions."

Squid kept her mouth shut. She could get into a verbal slapfight with Pearce, or she could… well, probably die, but perhaps take a criminal empire with her. She just needed a moment to think.

"What do you want?" she said.

His gaze was brilliant and unbreakable, his voice softly electric.

"I want you to unshackle yourself, Squid, and realise what you're capable of. You've spent your life following all the wrong rules, being ashamed of who you are, scraping for the approval of people who will never understand. But in my world, on the other side of the glass, you can be exactly who you are meant to be. And you have the potential to be extraordinary. When this conflict ends, and it will soon, there'll be positions to fill, work to be done. You could have your choice of havens at the Chival, or Halo Towers, or Rosetta Gardens. You'll have a job you want, surrounded by people who respect you. And this time, you won't be doing small-time jobs to pay the rent. You'll be working because you want to. Because you're good at it. Because deep down, you enjoy what you do. You know I'm right, Squid. You don't belong in a world that sees you as useless."

Squid swallowed, her gut twisting. She tried not the think of the stench and the sweat of the Iluvian, the humid filth of the Dumpsters, her silver watch sliding across the felt—

On her bare wrist, she could almost feel it, smooth and cool against her skin. She still remembered snapping open the suede box, and Casey's gruff shrug as she grumbled about the commercialisation of birthdays.

The choices you made, the people you met, all subtly changed the course of your life. Every bump and bend, every fork and obstacle shaped its direction, leading you to where you stood right now.

And right now, Squid finally understood what she was capable of. She would choose her fate rather than slide towards it. Because it wasn't what she *had* that mattered, or even what she *did*. It was the choice she made, between a rock and a hard place.

"I'm not that girl anymore," said Squid.

Pearce was a quick draw, but not as fast as Squid. Her hand was a blur—a flash of laser crosshairs, a searing light—the photo was taken and dispersed across the nimbus by the time the bullet smashed through the screen. A hot trickle stung her right temple, and her fractured phone lay smoking on the ground.

"Now they know what you look like," said Squid.

*Down to the retina. Booyah.*

Pearce adjusted his grip, aiming squarely at Squid's forehead.

"You realise all unauthorised signals are jammed," he said calmly.

"You realise Technology's moved on."

Pearce's expression didn't change, but Squid had some experience with expressions that didn't change. *Time to die, Squid.*

"Think. Carefully," snarled a voice.

Pearce didn't turn around. "Hello, Grief."

"Hostage again, Squid?" said Grief, edging into the room, his gun locked on Pearce.

Sweat matted his hair, his pallor giving him the semblance of a waxen figure animated by vengeful purpose.

Pearce tucked his gun slowly into his jacket.

"You know I'm not that kind of man, Grief," he said, opening his empty hands peaceably.

"I know exactly what kind of man you are," said Grief.

His eyes blazed, a crucible of guilt and blame and dying light.

"Grief, let's just get the drive and go," said Squid.

He didn't seem to hear her, his gun still aimed at Pearce. Blood seeped through Grief's bandage, a droplet sliding down the nose of the gun.

"Kingdom's crumbling, Pearce," said Grief.

"Calamities swell and subside, but nothing really changes," said Pearce. "They arrest a few people, make a few noises, but they're knocking blossoms off a tree without knowing how deep the roots run. People forget the Bauer Mine Trials, the Hammerford Six, the Old Central Riots. No one's ever held your job for more than five years. I've held mine for fifty. I'll still be here when you're a few pithy words on a slab of granite."

"Wanna bet?" said Grief, his voice dangerously soft.

"Grief—" said Squid.

Through the panoramic window, a river of flashing red and blue flowed around the complex. Squid looked from Grief to Pearce, unsure who she should be more afraid for.

"You're not that man anymore," said Pearce. "Walk away, Grief, and you get to keep your blameless new life. I have no interest in you."

"I've had a lot of time to think these past few weeks," said Grief. "About what kind of a man I am. Could I slaughter my way to the top of my career? Could I incinerate a street full of men and women? Could I execute an old man in cold blood?"

Grief stared down the barrel of the gun at Pearce.

"So, I ask myself: am I that kind of man?" he said.

"Grief, please don't," said Squid softly.

The last of Grief seemed to flicker, swallowed by the mask of another man's face. And then Squid realised it wasn't a mask.

"I'm sorry, Squid," said Raphael.

There was almost no sound as he pulled the trigger, just a sickening *crack* as Pearce jolted, seeming to hang for a moment in the aftershock. A trail of red slid down his face, and slowly, like a desiccated leviathan, he sank to the floor.

Squid caught Pearce before he hit the ground, and she lowered him gently to the carpet. A thousand panicked urges screamed through her head, but of the three brains in the room, hers was the most intact.

There was nothing she could do for Pearce, but in his final moments, he deserved her pity. At least, Squid assumed he was dying. The small dark hole in Pearce's forehead pulsed with ruby liquid, but oddly, the back of his head hadn't blown open like a smashed melon. The exit wound was just as neat and round, matting his white hair with blood and clear fluid.

Squid's gaze crawled up the wall, stopping at a short metal rod the width of a pencil, rimmed in seeping red. Like all those rods in the attic at Marley Drive.

Pearce blinked.

His eyes stared blankly upwards, his mouth open in a slightly surprised *O*.

"Grief," said Squid. "What did you do?"

Raphael sagged, as though his bones had dissolved, his eyes staring at things she couldn't see. The modified gun dropped from his hand, a choking noise rising from his throat. Everything seemed to fall away from him—Grief, Raphael, who he was, what he was—leaving him raw and alone. He sank to the ground, his whole body heaving with silent sobs.

Squid wasn't sure if they'd won or lost, or both. Grief had gone the moment he'd pulled the trigger, but Raphael seemed even more lost and alone than the bright-eyed man she'd found in the trunk a lifetime ago.

Squid wrapped her arms gently around Raphael, holding him as the room flooded with rising lights of red and blue.

# TWENTY-THREE

Six hours of surgery later, Casey didn't feel a hell of a lot better. Despite the morphine, she still felt as though there were an elephant sitting on her chest, periodically stomping on her neck. She shared a twin room with a dozen other haphazardly placed patients, but through the blurry light, she could make out a familiar face.

"You call this taking time out?" said Riego.

"Nice to see you, too," croaked Casey. "What happened?"

"Aside from you? Gale decided to make a swoop. Figured we had enough evidence to make a few arrests."

Casey squinted at Riego, who calmly took a sip of hot chocolate.

"How the hell d'you manage that?" said Casey.

"You left me some interesting reading in Deep Freeze. I talked to some people who knew people, I pulled ranks I didn't technically have, and I guess maybe I went a little…"

"Ballistic?"

Riego gave a crooked smile. He stared into his drink for a moment, wisps of steam rising from the mug.

"Did you know Squid and her buddy were in there tonight?"

Casey tried to sit up, and nearly passed out.

"Is she—"

"They're okay, kind of," said Riego. "But Pearce isn't."

His words hung like a strange, breathless dawn. As though the city were about to sail into uncharted waters on whatever Riego said next.

"They're still putting together the pieces," he continued. "But from what I hear, we've got some interesting times ahead."

*

Raphael hadn't taken off the handcuff. There hardly seemed any point. He was alone in the hospital room, one wrist shackled to the battered bed frame. Through the door, he heard trolleys squeaking and urgent voices rushing past, but everything felt oddly still. Oddly flat.

He remembered a fog of white coats, the sting of stitches. He remembered Squid holding his hand, but he was starting to think he'd imagined that part. What he'd done this time hadn't been instinctive self-defence. It hadn't been a burst of anger or confusion. It had been him. And it had been unforgivable.

This time, she wasn't coming back.

Raphael stared at the ceiling, listening to the slow drip of the IV. He wondered how long he should lie there feeling morose before he went outside to see what was going on. He deserved to stand trial, accept his sentence, serve his time. But if this was his last night of freedom, he didn't want to spend it in here.

He'd only just unlocked his cuff when the door swung open, and Raphael quickly slid his hand behind his back, tucking the IV needle under the covers. An authoritative woman in a navy suit stepped inside, a faintly exhausted aura trailing from her. She waited for the door to close quietly behind her.

"I'm Chief Superintendent Gale," said the woman. "You're the one they call Raphael."

"When they're in a good mood," said Raphael.

Gale said nothing for a moment, her expression one of scrutiny tinged with pity.

"Your associate tells me you recently suffered a head injury," said Gale. "Temporarily affecting your memory and possibly your judgement."

"I'll buy that if the jury does."

Oddly, Gale's expression of pity deepened. She straightened up slightly.

"Our teams have started recovering the intel on your data-slick," said Gale. "I think there's something you should hear."

*

Glass had never seemed so thick. Or the other side so far away.

Squid pressed her palms to the vending machine, staring sadly at the hanging bars of chocolate. She'd left all her tools at HQ, and it'd look awkward if she got her arm stuck in the dispensing slot. After all, she was supposed to be going straight now. No more excuses.

The hospital corridor buzzed with doctors and trolleys racing in every direction. Grief—no, Raphael—would wake up soon, and Squid hadn't decided where she should be. She'd watched him shoot an unarmed man in the head, seen the body fall, the blood crawling past pale, blank eyes. She wasn't sure how you moved past that, how you saw past that.

But Casey had. Every time she'd held out her hand to Squid. Every time she'd given her a second chance, hoping that one day she'd balance the books. There was a world of difference between stealing a car and gunning someone down, but no one was beyond redemption if they were willing to change.

"Squid!"

She turned to see Mal charging down the hallway, handcuffed to an officer who looked as though he'd been unwillingly attached.

"Mal…" said Squid warily. "What happened?"

"Got nicked in the leg," said Mal, waving carelessly at a gaping gunshot wound in the thigh. "Not as bad as Clef. Being a hacker's cool until you get shot in both your knees."

There was a hint of satisfaction in his voice.

"What were you even doing there?" said Squid.

"Bringing down the house!" boomed Mal, grinning as several dozen patients dove for cover. The attached officer blanched.

"Um, you can keep the watch," said Squid, "if you like it that much."

"There's no point then, is there?"

He tossed her the silver watch and headed for the emergency ward.

"Hey," he called over his shoulder. "Tell your cop friend to put in a good word for me."

Squid nodded, wondering if Casey had been secretly taking other criminals under her wing—although trying to reform Mal was pretty darned ambitious. But probably no more than having faith in fallen angels.

Squid knocked gently on the door, and when no response came, she slipped quietly inside. She found Raphael sitting up in bed, his head tilted back against the wall, eyes staring at the splotchy ceiling. An audio player rested on the table, on top of a yellowed manila file.

"Raphael?" said Squid.

A faint, sad smile formed on his lips, but his gaze remained on the ceiling.

"I'm glad you came back," said Raphael softly.

"I don't have anywhere better to be. And I think I deserve a little exposition, starting with that thing you pulled from your wrist."

"Recordings," he said, closing his eyes. "Six months' worth. Pearce. Ducabre. Everyone I spoke to. There's a snippet on the player."

Squid tapped the screen gently, listening as the muffled crackle gave way to voices. Raphael's was the first, tense and low.

*"…in place. I'm ready, but the question is, are you?"*

With a slight tingle of shock, Squid recognised the second voice.

*"Don't play that attitude with me. Bring it in, and I'll handle the rest."*

Deputy Commissioner Drake. The voice of shining law and order from a hundred radio announcements and newscasts.

*"I need more than that. There are people willing to testify, but before I blow this open, I need to know I can protect them. You're the only one left who knows my cover."*

*"Don't be so melodramatic. All the procedural paperwork is there—"*

*"We both know that things disappear."*

A pause. Then Drake's voice.

*"Do it."*

The snippet crackled to a stop.

Squid glanced at Raphael, his eyes still closed. She picked up the faded file, an unfamiliar name on the cover. She half-knew what she'd find inside, but it still snatched her breath when she lifted the cover.

He looked so much younger, smiling out from a brittle photograph. His uniform was neatly pressed, the bars on his shoulder already showing the rank of detective. Squid's gaze skimmed the neatly printed pages, a terrible lump forming in her throat.

He'd been undercover for nine years.

Squid's fingers tightened on the flimsy cardboard, trying not to think of the scars traced over his body, not to mention his mind. She sat on the edge of the bed and gave Raphael a gentle nudge.

"At least you were almost right about your age," she said. "What should I call you now?"

Raphael opened his eyes weakly.

"I don't know. Maybe I should go someplace where they don't have names. They just point at you." His gaze stopped on her wrist. "You got your watch back?"

"Yes!" Squid held it up proudly. "And I didn't have to give anyone money or blood."

Raphael suddenly grabbed her wrist, staring at the watch.

"Is that the time?"

"What? You have someplace to be?"

"Actually, yes," he said, lunging out of bed. He grabbed Squid's hand and gave her a tentative grin. "Do you trust me?"

*

They borrowed a squad car from behind the hospital—*one last time*, said Squid. Raphael drove, weaving across the pocked highways, leaving behind the ragged silhouette of the city. The fields were midnight seas, the moon a slender crescent when they reached the tree—Squid's tree—atop the gently sloping hill.

Raphael groped around the base, digging a metal box out from the roots.

"I don't suppose you have a chocolate bar in there?" said Squid.

Then she noticed the plunger protruding from the top. Without warning, Raphael pushed down the handle, and a sound like tiny firecrackers filled the sky. A hundred paper lanterns plumed into light, strung through the branches like luminous Christmas baubles. Squid gaped at the gently swaying lanterns—the tree transformed into a colourful, ethereal dandelion puff.

"Happy birthday," said Raphael.

Possessions, places, people—they came and went, grew old, fell apart, and changed. But experiences formed the fabric of your life, woven into memories that helped you understand who you were, and why you were. Memories were a gift you could hold on to, when everything else had been taken away. They were a scrapbook of emotions, triumphs and setbacks, that line of ink that told your story, stopping at the point where you stood right now.

Squid gave Raphael a sidelong hug.

"Thank you," she said.

Raphael wrapped an arm around her, sighing with satisfaction at his handiwork.

"I was a little worried that the tree might explode," he said. "And then you'd cry."

"That sounds like my other birthdays."

They stood in silence for a while, gazing up through branches threaded with stars.

"It's kind of funny… that my name turns out to be Adam," said Raphael.

"I've heard funnier names."

"It's just… your name, on your license…"

"I prefer Squid," she said firmly. "So, what should I call you?"

Raphael grinned, looking out across the starlit fields.

"Anything you like."

Side by side beneath the tree, they lay and watched the lights go out. And when dawn melted over the horizon, that elusive day finally arrived.

Tomorrow.

# TWENTY-FOUR

It took a lot of cleaning up, in every sense.

For the first time in almost fifty years, there was no one sliding words onto the editor's desk, nodding to the judge in the crowded courthouse, slipping thick envelopes into strategic hands. Headlines punched, charges stuck, and pillars of the community found the thin blue line knocking at their door.

Casey's suspension without pay turned quietly into medical leave, which she suspected the newly promoted Superintendent had something to do with. Deus's warehouse had changed address, but the interior remained remarkably unchanged.

"The media says you're doing a star-spangled job of cleaning up the city," said Casey. "Still need this place?"

"Pearce is gone, but others will rise," said Deus. "Enjoy the sunshine while you can."

A waiting question bubbled to the surface.

"Will Rojin make it to trial?" said Casey. "It's just they're saying…"

Deus paused at a door.

"It's easy, most of the time, keeping the sides distinct," he said. "Enemy, ally, hero, villain. The lines blurred more than I expected, but I guess the ideal that I trust is Drake's. Justice works…"

"Justice first," said Casey.

Deus pushed open the door, and Kirsk swung around in her chair.

"You're alive!" said Kirsk.

"I told you Casey was fine," said Deus flatly.

"I thought he was being euphemistic," said Kirsk, trotting over to Casey. Her tone turned mildly accusing. "You didn't keep the drive on for long."

"Sorry, I was busy being shot to pieces," said Casey.

"We only managed to download three percent of what was on the drive," said Kirsk. "But the stuff is incredible. Holographic matter projectors, implantable VR lenses, flying cybernetic mecha!"

"I've offered Kirsk our indefinite hospitality," said Deus. "If she'd like to continue working on the data."

"I'm not staying," said Kirsk. "I'm just… helping out a bit."

"I'm sure Werner would have been happy to know that you're looking after his work," said Casey.

Kirsk nodded sombrely. "Deus told me about the posthumous medal for Werner. That he was working with an undercover agent to bring down Pearce."

"And he succeeded," said Casey.

In a way.

*

The air had cleared around the ranch, but Narcotics hadn't noticed. His staff was busy preparing for the move—an inconvenient consequence of the Syndicate collapsing, and Narcotics was preoccupied with his newest patient.

As far as he was concerned, Ducabre's temperament had improved dramatically as a result of the experimental hypo. Instead of menacing people and spattering their brains all day, Ducabre's favourite pastimes now included watering the herb gardens and reading quietly to the less-responsive patients.

The compliance aspect of the drug had lasted all of five minutes, but the chemical afterburn had changed his neural networks in ways Narcotics struggled to decipher. The girl who'd administered the dose—Squid—had come by a few days ago to check on Ducabre. Wringing her hands quietly, she'd followed him around the garden, as though hoping for some kind of forgiveness. At one point, Ducabre had gently tried to braid her hair, which seemed to upset her more.

Personally, Narcotics felt it was an improvement for all parties concerned. After all, if you could change someone's personality with a pill, you could transform entire populations. You could rewrite the whole criminal rehabilitation system. You could reshape the world, one dose at a time.

*

They said he'd lost his mind. The metal rod had punched clean through his brain, taking important bits of his frontal lobe with it. Allegedly, he was still coherent; he just couldn't remember much. That explained why Pearce was here, or, rather, down the hall, but Rojin was rather irate at the padded walls.

They'd given her a new heart, and she could feel it ticking in her chest like a grandfather clock. They said it had been an absolute miracle that she'd survived, but Rojin knew miracles had nothing to do with it. She'd survived worse.

Her attorney had assumed she'd plead insanity, but Rojin had been even more insulted when the prosecution recommended the same thing. It said more about them than it did about her.

Insanity was putting up with evil. Letting the bloody trail of victims grow ever longer, ever more horrific. Insanity was shrugging and sighing and praying for change instead of picking up a gun and making it. *She* wasn't the problem.

Rojin stared at the cloudy moonlight drifting across the hospital ceiling.

*There was nothing wrong with her.*

Then again, it had been a busy year, and perhaps a short rest would do her good. Rojin slowly closed her eyes and fell asleep to the ticking of her new heart.

*

A criminal overlord had to know how to make an entrance. However, it was knowing how to make an exit that distinguished a stylish overlord from one with longevity.

By the time the paramedics had wheeled Pearce into the waiting ambulance, Verona was already on a private jet, headed for an undisclosed island in the Mediterranean. While Pearce was being questioned by frustrated investigators, Verona was sipping pomegranate juice on a beach, under brilliant blue skies.

Ultimately, that was the difference between Pearce and Verona.

You had to recognise when to cut your losses and make a gracious departure. There were too many loose cannons in Baltus City now, too many voices waking in the shock of fresh air. Stay and they'd tear you apart. Wait a while and they'd whittle themselves down. Verona had patience.

Baltus City had reclaimed itself. For now.

*

At times like this, it felt as though everything and nothing had changed.

Drop-Off Twenty-Six.

It looked exactly the same as it had that night, when she'd opened a trunk and discovered that fate had a twisted sense of humour. Now, Pearce's syndicate had collapsed, Verona's organisation had become decidedly disorganised and the city was sailing into uncertain new seas.

And Squid was waiting for Ferret.

"I suppose I should stop giving you assignments," said Ferret, stopping at the cusp of the lamplight.

"You got what you wanted, though, didn't you?" said Squid.

Ferret smiled faintly.

"You never really get what you want. You just change the direction of the story a little."

Everyone had a story. Ferret had been the first to teach her that, to listen to hers. Which was probably why she hadn't called Casey here.

"What'll you do now?" said Squid.

"Organised crime, disorganised crime. It doesn't really make a difference," shrugged Ferret. "There's no place in your shiny new world for me."

There was no regret in his voice, just experience.

"You probably won't see me again," he said.

"You know how to find me," said Squid. It was more observation than invitation.

Ferret's smile, as usual, was less than comforting.

"Always."

And for the last time, he disappeared into the shadows.

*

Casey hadn't regained the full use of her arms, but Met West had approved the use of an exoskeletal support that Werner had been working on. Aside from the occasional cyborg joke, it was fairly unobtrusive when she had her jacket on, and it freaked out the thugs no end.

She hadn't seen much of Riego lately, and Casey figured he just needed some space. She'd been trying to think of a grand gesture of sorts—a way to say "thanks" and "sorry" and maybe a few other unsaid things. A hamper of chutney just wasn't going to cut it. In the end, she'd slid a blank IOU into his locker, which she felt pretty much summed it up.

The station was still a flurry of activity in the post-Pearce clean-up, and Casey almost didn't see Riego until he stopped at her desk.

"So, pulped any hearts with that robot claw yet?" he said.

Casey flexed her fingers, the metal brackets flowing over her knuckles.

"No, they made me sign this 'appropriate usage' thing. You've been keeping busy."

"Tying up some loose ends. I handed in my resignation this

morning."

Something inside Casey fell through an unexpected trapdoor. She forced a neutral smile.

"Oh," said Casey. "Time to move on, huh?"

"It's never really been my scene. All the shooting and the yelling. Reminds me too much of family reunions."

Casey was pretty sure Riego's last family reunion had involved sedate old women, tea cakes and chai.

"I'm taking a position in Disadvantaged Services," continued Riego. "Community Liaison. I'd like to try fixing people before they get to you guys."

They'd worked alongside each other for years, but suddenly, Casey felt as though she'd never really known Riego. Never really listened to him. He hadn't been an enigma; she'd just never bothered getting to know him beyond the wild stories and the easygoing smile.

"I'm sure you'll do great," said Casey. "I mean, we'll still catch up and all that, right?"

"Actually, I was thinking maybe we could... see more of each other."

Riego gently slid Casey's IOU across the desk—a single handwritten line along the bottom.

*Return to sender: All I gave was given freely.*

Some great partnerships ended in a hail of bullets. Some ended in a stroll into the sunset. And some partnerships didn't end at all. They just... changed.

"I'd like that," said Casey.

*

She didn't have a job, exactly.

But with Riego gone, Met West Command needed someone to pick up their coffee and biscuits, and Squid was happy to be in their good graces. Casey said it was so she could keep tabs on her. Super Deus just eyed her like a great sea eagle studying a small, beached guppie.

But it wasn't the intermittent income that kept Squid here.

After an intensive debriefing, mountains of counselling, and reams of psychological profiling, Detective Inspector Adam Grief was back on active duty. The name change had raised some eyebrows at the Registry—it sounded like the moniker for a superhero, or a supervillain. Detective Grief. He said it gave him motivation to make Captain.

Baltus City Police had kept things quiet, but there was no mistaking the glares Grief still received. The death threats had subsided, but Squid felt he might appreciate a friendly face.

"Sanchez and Tyce, we have a warrant for Rutherford Bank, vault thirty-seven," said Grief. "Kosticou and Diaz, tell the archbishop if he won't come in for questioning, I'll be making the request in person. Wong and Jakande, greenlight for Governor Holbourne. Bring her in."

The officers scattered briskly to their duties, and Grief flashed a smile at Squid.

"How're you doing?" said Squid.

"I'm not sure," said Grief. "I feel like I've been wearing so many different faces, I'm not sure which one's mine anymore."

"The one you have isn't so bad."

"Well, you've seen them all. I guess you're my constant, hey, Squid? Keep me on the right track?"

"Back at'cha."

A fresh round of officers made a beeline for Grief, brandishing hefty reports and half-completed forms.

"You know," said Squid, "there's an unattended car out front. If we just kept driving, who knows, we could end up in Spain, or Egypt…"

Grief grinned.

"One day, I'll take you up on that."

Squid easily sidestepped the gaggle of officers, balancing a plate of gingerbread stars on one hand. Casey had casually mentioned earlier that if Squid behaved herself and didn't steal any biscuits, maybe they'd consider making her a cybercrime consultant. And for the first time in, well, ever, she thought there might be a Squid-shaped niche in the universe after all.

The world changed, life changed, but the driving force behind it all was people changing. Allowing themselves to be shaped by their circumstances, or fighting to change themselves and those around them. There were no quick fixes, no magic pills, no waking up and becoming someone else. But there was hope, and determination, and sometimes, a little faith from someone who could see the person you were trying to become.

Because it wasn't just cars that could be rebirthed. Sometimes, it was people.

* * *

# ALSO BY DK MOK

The Other Tree
Hunt for Valamon

# ACKNOWLEDGEMENTS

Three is a magical number. It's a number of transitions and revelations, beginnings and endings and perfect bowls of porridge. *Squid's Grief* is my third novel, and it's with immense gratitude that I reflect on the support of those who've believed in me from the very beginning, as well as the encouragement of the wonderful people I've met along the way.

My deepest thanks go to my family for their unswerving love and support. My sisters, Anne and Cecilia, are a constant source of inspiration, motivation, wisdom and delight.

I've been fortunate enough to have worked with editor Vikki Ciaffone on all three of my novels, and her commitment, insight and enthusiasm have made each experience a wonderful one.

My thanks also go to copyeditor Richard Shealy for his keen eye and grammatical acumen; and to cover designer Errick A. Nunnally for his gorgeous artwork.

I'd also like to thank Kelly Hager, Darby Karchut, and my friends at Thorbys and Room 332 for their encouragement, support and general geekery.

A special thank-you goes to fellow author Mitchell Hogan, whose generous advice on self-publishing was invaluable in helping me to navigate through uncharted waters.

Finally, my thanks go to all the readers who've joined me on these strange and wondrous journeys. Let's see what tomorrow brings.

# ABOUT THE AUTHOR

DK Mok is a fantasy and science fiction author whose novels include *Hunt for Valamon* and *The Other Tree*. DK's work has been shortlisted for an Aurealis Award and a Washington Science Fiction Association Small Press Award. DK graduated from UNSW with a degree in Psychology, pursuing her interest in both social justice and scientist humour. She lives in Sydney, Australia, and her favourite fossil deposit is the Burgess Shale.

If you'd like to be notified whenever DK has a new novel out, you can sign up to the New Release Mailing List: dkmok.com/Contact.html.

You can find more information at www.dkmok.com.